Praise for

'A tense, taut and totally au[thentic...] first page and doesn't let go. *Death in Kabul* immerses you in 2003 Kabul, riven by corruption where danger lurks in every alley. Be careful whom you trust in this city without mercy'

D. V. Bishop, author of *City of Vengeance*

'A vividly portrayed murder mystery in a fresh and fascinating setting. With wonderful characters and a great plot, I hope this is the first of many from this duo'

Susi Holliday, author of *The Last Resort*

'Authentic, thrilling and brilliantly plotted, *Death in Kabul* is a cracking action thriller that brings the city vividly to life'

Marion Todd, author of *See Them Run*

'Rich and atmospheric, *Death in Kabul* plunges us directly into the grubby, noisy streets of the capital and to a murder investigation that kept me in its thrall to the end. I loved being a part of Mac's world and only hope I get to see him again'

Louisa Scarr, author of *Under a Dark Cloud*

'A rip-roaring, page-turner of a novel with a truly clever and original plot. *Death in Kabul* is a stunning exploration of life in 2003 Kabul, and a fantastic start to an exciting new series!'

Sheila Bugler, author of *The Lucky Eight*

'One of the most authentic thrillers I've read for ages. Drags you headfirst into the colourful Kabul underworld, and sends you barrelling down its backstreets at a frenetic pace that just doesn't let up'

Robert Scragg, author of *End of the Line*

'It's a first class police thriller with a big difference. The investigation whips through shady characters and locales at breakneck pace but the setting removes all the familiar procedural techniques, keeping you on the edge of your seat right to the stunning finale. Explosive stuff!'

D. L. Marshall, author of *Black Run*

'A fast-paced and gripping thriller that conjures up vivid images of deserts and alleyways, stolen artefacts and bloodied sands, where knowledge is currency and murder is committed behind a mirage of lies'

Ian Skewis, author of *A Murder of Crows*

'Superbly plotted – if you like your thrillers brimming with authentic detail and non-stop action, this is for you!'

Margaret Kirk, author of *In the Blood*

'A bumpy ride through mystery, lawlessness and betrayal in mountainous Afghanistan that leaves you constantly looking over your shoulder. *Death in Kabul* throws together an eclectic cast of characters, driven into an unlikely alliance by a shared quest for justice – even if justice means something different for each'

Heleen Kist, author of *In Servitude*

'This exciting and compelling crime thriller is like nothing I've ever read before. A colourful, visual depiction of life in Kabul coupled with a fast-paced investigation, this book truly transports you to somewhere else entirely. *Death in Kabul* is 100% one of my books of the year!'

Roxie Key

Death in Helmand

Alison Belsham is the author of the internationally acclaimed Tattoo Thief trilogy, which has been translated into 15 languages and was a No.1 bestseller in Italy. As well as writing crime, she is collaborating with her brother Nick Higgins on an action thriller series set in Afghanistan. She is a co-founder of the Edinburgh Writers' Forum, providing professional development and networking for writers.

From 2003 to 2007, Nick Higgins worked in Afghanistan as a security advisor on a variety of projects encompassing the UN, private military companies, the US Embassy and others. He has lived in or visited all the locations mentioned, including Lashkar Gah City in Helmand Province, nearly three months in a guest house in downtown Kandahar City, Herat City and Kabul.

Also by Alison Belsham and Nick Higgins

The MacKenzie and Khan series

Death in Kabul
Death in Helmand

A.BELSHAM & N.HIGGINS

DEATH
IN
HELMAND

CANELO

First published in the United Kingdom in 2022 by

Canelo
Unit 9, 5th Floor
Cargo Works, 1-2 Hatfields
London, SE1 9PG
United Kingdom

A CIP catalogue record for this book is available from the British Library.

Print ISBN 978 1 80032 746 7
Ebook ISBN 978 1 80032 745 0

Cover design by Tom Sanderson

Look for more great books at www.canelo.co

Printed and bound in Great Britain by Clays Ltd, Elcograf S.p.A.

For the murdered Afghan staff from Alternative Incomes
Programme/South – Helmand, 2005

Abdul Qader Khan Zaki

Nader Khan

Mia Khair Muhammad Khan

Feda Muhammad Khan

Noor Ahmad Khan

Helmand Province, 2004

Afghanistan's southernmost province — a barren waste-land of sand, rock, narco warlords and terrorist insurgents. The Helmand River carves a verdant path from north to south, irrigating two-thirds of the world's poppy cultivation.

A 300-kilometre drive through the Desert of Death from the capital, Lashkar Gah, brings you to the Pakistan border, and to the teeming opium-and-arms bazaars of Bahram Chah. Here, nothing is traded as cheaply as a man's life.

This is Afghanistan's most dangerous territory. Any westerner brave — or stupid — enough to set foot here risks being extorted or kidnapped. And the outcome is rarely good…

Prologue

March 2004

Marja District, Helmand Province

Kasper Hendricks blinked furiously and cleared his throat at the same time. His eyes were watering. The Land Rover Discovery 110 directly ahead of them was churning up a cloud of dust and he was eating it.

'Hey, Zaki, shut your bloody window, *ja*?' He spoke English with a heavy Dutch accent, but the driver seemed to understand him, and did what he was told with a scowl. Hendricks breathed a sigh of relief. God, he hated this damn country. They were on the main road from Lashkar Gah to Marja District and it was nothing more than a dirt track. Less than a third of Afghanistan's roads were paved, and that percentage took a nosedive in Helmand Province. The Land Rover's tyres crunched on the stony surface and Hendricks made a mental note to make sure his was the lead vehicle on the return journey.

Of course, there should have been a couple of Hilux SUVs ahead and behind the Well Diggers Land Rovers, but their ten-man police escort had failed to materialise in Bolan, where they usually picked them up. According to the local police chief, most of his men had gone down the road to a colleague's wedding in Khushhar Kalay. All he could spare was a spotty, eighteen-year-old trainee with an ancient AK47 and a single magazine. How much use would that be? Hendricks wondered if it even fired. Not that it mattered – they'd been driving up and down this road on a weekly basis for months and, so far, the police escort had never had to earn its extortionate dollar payments. Far more likely, the kid would let off his weapon at the wrong moment, which was why Hendricks had chosen to put him in the other vehicle.

He let his eyes wander over the wide swathes of green fields on either side of the road. Green now, but in a couple of months they'd be splashed with purple, pink and white poppies as the summer's first opium crop came into bloom. He despised it. He'd seen the havoc wreaked by this nefarious trade on the streets of Amsterdam, his home city – skinny kids with hollow eyes, turning up dead with a needle hanging out of their arm or jabbed between their toes. Such misery had no right to such a pretty genesis.

Meanwhile, he couldn't deny that the work Well Diggers did – mending and maintaining Helmand's irrigation systems – contributed to the problem it was supposed to be helping to obliterate. He closed his eyes. Maybe it was time for a change of job. His glory days in the Dutch Royal Marines were long gone, but there had to be something better than being the security manager for an NGO that, in his opinion, was doing as much harm as good. And which, with its left-leaning politics, actively discouraged him from carrying the tools of his trade. He'd have felt much better if he'd had his trusty Glock tucked under his armpit and an M4 stashed in the footwell.

'*Niet mijn schuld*,' he muttered under his breath to no one in particular. Don't blame me.

The two Afghan engineers sitting in the back of the Land Rover were in frenzied conversation and ignored him, while Zaki hardly gave him a glance.

An abrupt change in the background noise of the road surface made Hendricks open his eyes. Their own engine noise was suddenly accompanied by a higher-pitched whine coming from behind. He whipped round in his seat and peered back down the road. Four motorbikes were drawing up on them. Fast.

There were two men on each bike. The pillion riders held short-barrelled Krinkov AKs. Although generally regarded as crap, the rifles would do what was required in a situation like this. Two up was always suspicious, but this time it looked terminal. They were getting closer, weapons coming up on target. On him.

'Zaki, accelerate,' he screamed at his driver, grabbing for the handheld VHF radio so he could warn the car ahead. 'Faster, go, go, go.'

Zaki's grip on the wheel tightened as he rammed his foot to the floor, but Hendricks realised in a nanosecond it wasn't going to make any difference. Well Diggers' begged-and-borrowed vehicles had no power compared to the speeding motorcycles.

The first two bikes sped past him and came level with the leading Land Rover. The other two bikes drew level with his window.

As the pillion rider took aim, their eyes met. The man smiled at Hendricks as his finger applied pressure to the trigger. Hendricks ducked down into the footwell as a hail of automatic fire shattered the window glass and rained in on him. Zaki's scream was cut short as a bullet tore through his throat. In the back, the two engineers panicked for an instant before death claimed them.

The Land Rover veered sharply to one side as Zaki's body slumped forward against the wheel. It swerved them out of the line of fire and Hendricks took advantage of it to throw himself out of the passenger door and down towards the gully that ran alongside the road. He heard the gravel shriek as one of the bikes skidded to get out of the way of the careering vehicle, but he couldn't afford to stop and watch their fate. Glancing ahead, he saw that the lead vehicle had ground to a halt at the side of the road. He ran up to it in a low squat and wrenched the handle of the front passenger door. The weight of the police cadet's body pushed it open and fell heavily on top of him. Bullets were slicing through the car's body panels like hot knives through butter, and one drilled into the boy's skull, spattering Hendricks with blood, bone and brain matter as it acted as a shield for him. He pushed the dead weight to one side and reached into the cab for the kid's AK. Its stock was slippery with blood. He flipped the change lever from safe to full auto, praying there was a round in the chamber – no time to check. The boy hadn't managed to get a single round off before being shot. Heart in mouth, Hendricks moved towards the rear end of the vehicle.

As the vehicle behind him lurched down into the gully, he was suddenly exposed. The pillion riders, not much more than kids themselves, saw him and swung their weapons towards him. Hendricks wrenched the cocking lever back, feeding a round into the empty chamber. Pulling the trigger, he swung his body in an arc to spray-and-pray the bikes and their riders. But…

Fuck! No!

Nothing happened. *The bloody firing mechanism.*

As soon as this thought had formed in Hendricks's mind, a bullet deleted it, and every other thought, tearing through his grey matter, pulverising his synapses, replacing his consciousness with an explosion of red, then black.

Then nothing.

Fifty metres up the road, a teenager on his way to the local market heard the gunfire and dropped down into the ditch. He watched as the lead Land Rover, its windscreen shattered and bloody, simply stopped in the middle of the road. He watched, unblinking, as the second vehicle tipped onto its side in the small canal, ending up on its roof. He watched, unmoved, as the four motorbikes accelerated away, the shooters shouting gleefully to one another. A moment later, the Land Rover in the ditch burst into flames.

When the bikes had disappeared, the youth clambered out of his hiding place and jogged down to the stricken Land

Rovers. Of course, all the occupants were dead, but that wasn't his concern. He stopped by the intact vehicle and peered in through the passenger window until he saw something worth taking. No weapons, but a battered leather bag caught his eye. He stretched an arm inside to grab the bag's shoulder strap, carelessly trailing a sleeve in the dead driver's blood. Snatching the bag to his chest, he unbuckled the tab and looked inside.

It was as he'd hoped.

Dollars. Lots of dollars.

Now he needed to make himself scarce. He jogged off in the opposite direction to the bikes.

The Land Rovers' engines were silent, the whine of the motorbikes had receded into the distance, and there was no longer the sound of the tyres crunching over the stony road surface. Just the soft murmur of the flames and the irregular plinking sound of cooling metal.

Chapter 1

Alasdair 'Mac' MacKenzie wiped the sweat from his forehead as he walked into the Global bar, even though it didn't seem any cooler in here than it was outside. It was mid-afternoon and the place was quiet. He nodded at a couple of Global stalwarts murmuring over half-drunk lagers – permanent fixtures in here – and made his way over to the bar, where Ram, the Gurkha barman, was tearing the label off an empty beer bottle to stave off the boredom.

Ram grinned when he saw it was Mac. 'Hey, Mr Mac, how are you doing today?'

'I'll be doing a hell of a lot better when you've poured me a cold lager.'

'Coming up.'

The door opened again and Basima Khan appeared, scanning the bar until her eyes lit on Mac. She came across the room and slipped into an easy embrace.

'What do you want, Baz?'

'White wine would hit the spot.'

Within a couple of minutes they were sat at their usual table, drinks untouched in front of them as they caught up on each other's day so far.

'Ah, here's Ginger,' said Mac, as a tall bruiser with a shock of red hair strode in and looked round. His boyish face broke into a grin when he saw the pair in the corner.

6

'Good to see you, mate.' He slapped Mac's back as the Scot stood up to greet him, then kissed Baz on both cheeks.

'What can I get you?' said Mac. 'We're celebrating my new contract, so don't hold back.'

'Then make mine a Lagavulin.' He sat down as Mac nodded to Ram. 'Is Jananga coming?'

Major Jananga was the Kabul City Police detective they'd both worked with the previous year – and a man who Mac considered his first real Afghan friend. But he wasn't around tonight. 'He's away on some training course somewhere.'

Ginger laughed as Ram placed a tumbler on the table in front of him. 'How to make friends and torture people?'

'Harsh,' said Baz, giving him a reprimanding look.

Ginger winked at her and gave a shrug. 'So, tell me about the new job. When do you start?'

'I've got a few weeks left on this contract, followed by a two-week break – Dubai with Baz – then I start the new job.'

'With that New Zealand outfit, right?'

Mac nodded. 'They seem pretty cool. What about you?'

Ginger's cheerful demeanour evaporated. 'Nothing yet. Maybe you could put in a good word for me with the Kiwis?'

'Of course, but it's a pretty small outfit.' Mac felt embarrassed. Ginger had been looking for a position for weeks, while Mac had waltzed straight into a new job before his current contract was even up.

Baz gave Ginger a sympathetic look. 'What will you do if you can't find anything?'

'Head back to Blighty, I suppose.' Ginger frowned. 'But I don't believe my prospects will be any better there. Just a security guard job in an office building…'

'Wait,' said Mac. 'I heard something about a possible job down in Helmand.' He got out his phone and started scrolling through his messages. 'Yes, this is it. A small NGO called Well Diggers. Might be in the market for a new head of security. A mate gave me the heads-up.'

'When was that?' said Ginger. There was a note of urgency in his voice.

'Couple of days back. It's an outfit based in Lashkar Gah. Providing local employment by fixing the irrigation channels and the *karez* tunnel system.'

'Let me have the details.'

As Mac forwarded the message to Ginger's number, a shadow fell across the table.

'Man, you don't want to go anywhere near that job. Believe me.' The words were spoken in a lazy Midwestern drawl.

'Logan!' Baz was on her feet and throwing her arms around the tall man now standing behind Ginger's chair.

'When did you get back?' said Mac. 'And how's Xiaoli?'

Logan had – for want of a better word – 'assisted' Mac and Jahanga in bringing a notorious smuggler, trafficker and murderer to justice the previous year, and while other ex-soldiers might style themselves as mercenaries while working security jobs in Afghanistan, he was the real deal. Xiaoli was his adopted Chinese daughter.

'She's good. Settling in with Mom and Dad back home, attending high school. All going well.'

Ginger turned to him. 'So, tell me, why don't I want that job?'

Logan grimaced. 'You haven't heard what happened down there?'

Mac and Ginger shook their heads.

'It was bad. The guy they had doing security was murdered, along with several of their local engineers. An overenthusiastic robbery, apparently.'

Ginger raised an eyebrow. 'So shit happens to other people. This is Afghanistan, remember.'

'Yeah, and that's Helmand, and it's a whole different ball game down there.'

Ginger shrugged. 'Still gonna apply for it. I've reached a point where I don't have much choice. Unless you've got a job for me, Logan?'

Logan waved at Ram. He didn't need to order – Ram knew exactly what Logan would want. 'Look, the place is a hot mess of warring drug factions. You gotta make sure you get on the right side of certain people, and if you're on their right side, you're on someone else's wrong side. You can't win.'

'Yeah, but Ginger will fail to get onto anyone's right side, so he won't be on anyone's wrong side either,' said Mac, trying to lighten the mood a little.

Ginger laughed, but Logan seemed unconvinced. 'Don't say I didn't warn you.'

Chapter 2

May 2004

Kabul, Afghanistan

Ginger generally liked a man who could admit he'd made a mistake, but he didn't like Lars Vinke. He knew it the moment he walked into the empty office which Vinke had borrowed for the purpose of interviewing a new chief of security for Well Diggers' Helmand operations. Of course, he hadn't expected a pat on the back for turning up, but Lars Vinke hadn't stood up to greet him, or even looked up from the notes he was making on the CV of the previous candidate.

When he finally finished, he passed a comment which Ginger thought uncalled for.

'That guy...' He shook his head. 'He's not going to last out here.'

Ginger didn't rise to the bait. He didn't give a shit about the other blokes he was up against. All he cared about was whether he firstly wanted the job and secondly got it. And given he had few irons in the fire and a dwindling bank account, wanting it was a given. The prospect of dragging his sorry arse into the job centre back home in Gravesend was not appealing. Ten years in the Paras and two years in Afghanistan didn't seem to carry the same currency in north Kent as it carried here in Kabul, but he was fast running out of options.

Vinke ran a hand through his white blond hair and stared up at Ginger with slate grey eyes. 'And you are?'

'Chris Jameson.' He waited to be invited to sit.

Vinke rifled through the pile of CVs at his elbow, finally extracting one that Ginger recognised as his own. The Well Diggers project manager scanned the couple of sheets and then smoothed them on the desk in front of him with a bony hand.

Ginger sat down uninvited, assessing his potential new boss. Scrawny and skeletal, his Well Diggers polo shirt hung off his spare frame, and his arms were sinewy and corded, rather than muscular. He looked like a man with no appetite for life, someone who took no pleasure in what the world afforded. Ginger couldn't picture his face with a smile on it.

At last, Vinke looked up. 'Let me tell you a little about Well Diggers.' His English was good, his Dutch accent hardly perceptible. 'We are a small, Anglo-Dutch NGO and we have projects throughout Afghanistan, and also in several other countries in the region. I'm the team leader for our work in Helmand Province – we're based in Lashkar Gah, where I employ a mixture of Dutch, English and local engineers to oversee a local workforce on the ground.'

'What is it exactly that you do?' said Ginger. Of course, he knew the answer to this – he'd done his homework – but he needed to appear interested.

'We are financed by the generosity of private donors to create local jobs that will therefore relieve agrarian workers of the need to facilitate the cultivating and harvesting of opium poppies. Around Lashkar Gah, the fields are irrigated by a system of canals and *karez*. The *karez* system is a network of ancient underground aqueducts, channels constructed to bring water from the lakes and rivers to irrigate huge areas of arable land. We provide work for several thousand men engaged in clearing and repairing the *karez* tunnels to carry water to areas that have been afflicted by drought.'

Enabling the farmers in those districts to plant more fields of poppies. Ginger kept the thought to himself and let Vinke continue to paint a rosy picture of the organisation's beneficent presence in Helmand.

'You will know, of course, what happened to our last head of security?'

Ginger nodded. Everyone in Kabul knew by now. This was surely why he was in with a chance of securing the job. There weren't a lot of men, even out here, who would relish the thought of stepping into a dead man's shoes, and the last guy had been shot dead in inexplicable circumstances on the road between Lashkar Gah and Marja. At least according to what Logan had said.

'I... We...' – Ginger noted Vinke's change of emphasis – 'made some mistakes in our security policies.' He sighed. 'Our activities in Helmand help the local population, and we'd never experienced any animosity. I'd discouraged the routine carrying of weapons – I wanted us to set an example for the good. There was no reason for our team to be attacked. They were helping the farmers.'

What a naive idiot. There was always a reason for some faction or other to attack westerners meddling in Afghan affairs. But at least Vinke stopped short of blaming the guy who'd died.

'So you have no idea who was responsible for it?'

'Not the names of the perpetrators. But they stole a bag of cash. They were probably just opportunists, common thieves. We'll never find them.'

'And what about now? Have you changed your view about carrying weapons?' said Ginger. He'd be damned if he'd venture out into the Helmand countryside without a full security detail, appropriately armed and fully under his control.

'I'm looking for someone who'll beef up our security and give my teams one hundred per cent protection.' He glanced down at Ginger's CV. 'You look like you could be a suitable candidate. Talk me through what you've been doing for the last couple of years out here.'

This told Ginger enough. He'd got the job. He could relax. He recapped his CV for Vinke, and then again for the Well Diggers country manager, who joined them. The head honcho, a sweating, barrel-chested man called Stijn Anholts, seemed almost as clueless as Vinke, which explained why Vinke was still in his job after what had happened.

Well Diggers, do-gooders, whatever. Ginger had their measure. A high level of self-regard for the important work they were engaged in, with no understanding of the social and political complexities of a busted country that didn't really want their help. It was exactly why they needed to hire someone like him to keep them safe in the big, bad world out there. Or at least in Helmand Province.

'How soon can you start?' said Vinke, straightening up the pile of CVs on the desk.

'As soon as you can get me on a plane down to Lash.'

Chapter 3

Lashkar Gah might have been the provincial capital of Helmand, but it couldn't be more different from the thriving metropolis of Kabul. With less than a tenth the population of the Afghan capital, Ginger wasn't even sure that it qualified as a city. As he'd looked down on it from the plane, it had looked like nothing more than a handful of dirty pebbles nestling on the green ribbon of arable land created by the Helmand River.

A garden city once, perhaps, with parkland along the riverbank and wide, open streets that had been laid out, grid-like, by the Americans in the 1950s when they arrived to instigate their magnificent Helmand irrigation project. Half a century later, after Soviet occupation, civil war, Taliban rule and a decade-long drought, it was tired and shabby. Progress had stalled and, according to the guys Ginger had asked who'd been there, the general consensus was that it was moving backwards.

Lashkar Gah airport was certainly nothing to write home about. Ginger hated flying, but he hated landing even more and touching down on the short gravel runway in the small twin-prop Louis Berger plane was noisy, bumpy and hardly reassuring. Ginger only dared breathe again once they'd come to a final standstill on a small area of hardstanding at the very end of the strip. Still, he knew he'd been lucky to get a spot on the flight. Louis Berger was a construction company working on the road link to Lash, and they were the only people, apart from the military, that flew in and out of the city regularly. And unlike the UNHAS flights that served the rest of the country, you were allowed to carry your weapon on board the plane.

The heat hit him like a sledgehammer when he disembarked, beating down on his head and reflecting up from the tarmac relentlessly. The cold sweat brought on by the landing that had his shirt clinging to his chest dried instantaneously, but his armpits felt clammy as he hefted his bergan onto his shoulder. There was no bus waiting to take them to an air-conditioned terminal, just a hundred-metre walk to where a collection of vehicles was parked, and where a solitary Louis Berger mechanic leaned on the bonnet of his Land Cruiser, chatting with the pilot on his ground-to-air radio.

Parked up next to him was a Land Rover with a faded Well Diggers decal on the side. As he got closer, he could identify Lars Vinke's taut profile through the side window. Vinke didn't bother getting out of the vehicle as Ginger approached, but said something to his driver, who got out and took Ginger's bag.

'Good flight?' he asked, as Ginger climbed into the back seat, relieved to be out of the heat.

'Contradiction in terms,' said Ginger. 'Always happy to be back on the ground.'

Vinke turned round in his seat to look at him. 'I thought you spent years in the Parachute Regiment?'

Ginger grinned. His fear of flying had been legendary in B Company. 'That's right, I was. And I was always the first one to jump!'

Vinke didn't seem to find it funny. Something told Ginger that working with the Dutchman was going to be hard graft. He just had to hope that not all of the Well Diggers team had a broomstick up their arse. As they drove off the airfield, the twin-prop was already manoeuvring itself into position to go back down the runway – clearly nothing worth hanging around for here.

From the ground, Lash was even less prepossessing than it had been from the air. As they drove through the edge of town, Ginger's eyes darted from one side of the road to the other, drinking in every detail. To succeed at his mission, he would need to know this ground like the back of his hand, and this was where it started. The buildings were run-down and patches of land that might once have been gardens were now just bare earth. Hungry-eyed kids played amid filthy litter, sticking out a hand for *baksheesh* whenever an adult passed by. Teenage boys ignored the rest of the traffic on whiny-engined scooters, while older men in even older cars made liberal use of their horns. The market stalls they passed were reasonably stocked with seasonal produce, but Ginger guessed that for half the year at least the goods on offer would be sparse. The glances he got when they were stopped in traffic were dark and hostile – the area's long history with foreign interlopers meant that even those purporting to do good were viewed with suspicion, and Ginger sensed a mood that was anything but friendly.

However, he was here now.

He hoped it hadn't been a mistake.

–

'Man, that's one hell of a list. Lars isn't going to agree to half of it,' said Tomas Bakker, Well Diggers' softly spoken chief engineer. His hair was as red as Ginger's own, but in contrast to Ginger's short back and sides, Bakker's hair curled long over his collar and he sported an impressive beard. Ginger also had a beard, but it had been something of a struggle and still looked a little wispy in places.

'Half? You should be that lucky!' The logistics manager, Jagvir Nagpal, was an Afghan Sikh and Lashkar Gah local. It was his job to recruit men and source equipment for each of their projects. He was a short man with a bulging paunch and engaging, intelligent eyes. He gave a low-pitched laugh as he tossed Ginger's list back onto the table. 'What do you Brits say – he's going to have kittens?'

Ginger nodded, his lips pursed. Their responses were not entirely unexpected. Vinke had been uncommunicative on the ride in from the airport and had handed him over to Bakker and Nagpal as fast as possible. Nagpal, however, had spent the last week schooling him in what Well Diggers did and how they went about it, so Ginger could come up with new security protocols to ensure all personnel were kept as safe as humanly possible, whether out in the field, at the organisation's office in the Helmand and Arghendab Valley Authority building downtown, and in the two houses they rented for the western staff to live in.

Currently, in Ginger's opinion, none of these places were secure from attack, and in a province with the highest levels of insurgency, kidnap and organised narco crime, he would have his work cut out. He started by making a plan for each of the buildings, including the establishment of safe rooms, which none of them currently had. The next job was to draw up operational protocols for transit within Lashkar Gah and for field trips out to the various sites at which Well Diggers was working. Now, he was sharing his shopping list with Bakker and Nagpal to see if they had anything to add. Removing things from the list wasn't an option as far as he was concerned – it was the bare minimum that he would need to do the job.

'Lars is running this division on a shoestring,' said Bakker. 'If he wants any of this stuff, he'll have to go to Anholts in Kabul and ask for extra money.'

Nagpal shook his head. 'The chief won't like that.'

Bakker nodded in agreement. 'For a start, I reckon kidnap and ransom insurance is simply out of Well Diggers' league. We're a small operation, tiny budget. There's huge pressure for as much of that as possible to go into the work, rather than our expenses. Listen to me, Chris...'

'Ginger,' said Ginger, unconsciously putting a hand up to his hair.

'Okay, Ginger,' continued Bakker. 'Lars is a peacenik. He won't like having to spend on weapons and men. So, my advice is to put twice as much on the list as you want. He'll haggle with you, throw half the stuff off. Then you've got what you need.'

Ginger smiled ruefully. 'You might have a point.' Even saving lives required playing politics.

'Also,' said Nagpal, 'Lars will have an opinion on everything and will never take your advice on anything.'

'Seriously?' said Ginger.

Bakker shot the Sikh what Ginger interpreted as a warning glance, but he didn't comment.

Nagpal, looking admonished, picked up the list again. 'Let's start with the men you're asking for.'

'We need twenty-four-hour protection on the two houses. Three rotating shifts of two men is the bare minimum. Then, this building' – they were sitting in the Well Diggers office on the third floor of the HAVA building – 'has no security to speak of. I propose putting a three-man team on the main door throughout office hours. When it comes to moving around town, an armed guard in every vehicle, and out of town, full escorts – two extra vehicles with a minimum of four armed men in each.'

'Right,' said Nagpal. 'I can arrange a meeting with the head of the governor's militia – we'll be able to hire any number of guards from him, for the buildings and for our transportation. And we can use the police for field trips. That way we'll be keeping the two main narco factions on side.' He jabbed a finger at the next item on the list. 'But I don't think Vinke will pay for you to have a number two.'

Ginger's proposal was to hire an ex British Gurkha sergeant to act as his assistant for training and running the guard details.

'And weapons for all these bodies?' said Bakker. 'They'll cost plenty.'

'The militiamen and police have their own,' said Nagpal, 'but we'll need to provide ammo for training and operations.'

'You can source that?' said Ginger.

'Sure,' said Nagpal, rubbing his thumb against his index and middle finger, 'as long as Vinke comes up with the *baksheesh*.'

Ginger frowned. 'He's going to have to – or he'll end up with more blood on his hands.'

Chapter 4

Lashkar Gah, Helmand Province

Ginger stared at the report on his desk and wondered what sort of man Kasper Hendricks had been. What path through life had brought him to his final ignominious end on the deserted road to Marja? He only had the bare bones of the police report to go on. A report that, in the absence of eyewitness testimony, was three parts guesswork and the rest supposition. Strangely enough, the one thing the report wasn't making any guesses about was who had been responsible for the attack. All that was clear was that the Well Diggers convoy had been ambushed, and that they had been travelling without an acceptable level of protection – no escort vehicles and just one armed police guard, who seemed to have been taken out without firing a single shot in return. In the absence of any ballistics reports, examination of the abundant empty cases scattered at the scene led them to believe that all the shots fired had come from Krinkov AKs – but these were ubiquitous throughout the province, and gave no clue as to the identity or affiliation of the shooters.

The translation of the medical examiner's report on the bodies was similarly scant, but not much detail was needed here, as far as Ginger was concerned. The project's head of security, three Afghan engineers, two drivers and the young policeman with them had died in a hail of gunfire. All of them had multiple bullet wounds and all but one had been killed instantly. The other, one of the engineers, was still alive when the first Land Rover rolled over into the canal – as evidenced by the mixture of blood and canal water found in his lungs. He'd drowned as he bled out, trapped in the back seat of the stricken vehicle.

Ginger put the reports back into their folder and leaned back in his chair. It was the third time he'd read them and there was nothing new to learn. The office he'd inherited from Hendricks in the HAVA building looked out over a patch of brown grass, straggly bushes and, across the road, at the turquoise dome and intricately tiled minaret of the Lashkar Gah Mosque. Living in Kabul, he was used to hearing the *salat*, or call to prayer, five times a day – it punctuated the waking hours as regularly as clockwork, even if he didn't heed its call.

There was a knock on his open door and Nagpal's head appeared around the edge of it.

'Have you seen Lars or Tomas yet today?'

Ginger shook his head. It was early and he'd already noted that Lars Vinke seldom arrived in the office before ten. 'I've got a meeting with Vinke at eleven to discuss the shopping list.' He wasn't particularly looking forward to it. He needed to do some straight talking with the Dutchman about real and present dangers, and the need for armed accompaniment for all of his staff, wherever they were going.

Nagpal stepped into the room. 'I was supposed to see Tomas first thing, but he's not in his office yet.'

'Nagpal, got a moment, mate?'

'Sure. Maybe let me get us a cup of tea first?'

'A brew would be great.' Ginger liked Nagpal – he was easy-going and seemed to have a good sense of humour. And he made a proper mug of tea, not the glasses of stewed green water that most Afghans offered.

'So, what did you want to talk about?' said Nagpal, after he'd set down two steaming mugs on Ginger's desk.

'The attack,' said Ginger. 'I've got a couple of questions.'

Nagpal shook his head. 'A bad business. We lost valuable men – there aren't many engineers here in Lashkar Gah, and now who wants to come and work with us?'

'It shouldn't have gone down the way it did,' said Ginger, 'and I'm not going to let something like that happen again.'

'Mistakes were made, that is for sure.'

Mistakes didn't begin to cover the clusterfuck that had happened. The more Ginger had learned about the incident, the more infuriated he'd become. Hendricks was unarmed. No proper police escort, just a kid with a weapon he probably didn't know how to handle. They had been driving a route that they used week in, week out, to visit the work sites – same time, same place: totally predictable. They'd handed themselves to the attackers on a plate as far as Ginger was concerned.

He frowned. 'What I don't understand is why they went without a proper police escort.'

'I spoke with the police commander afterwards,' said Nagpal. 'Many of his men were attending a colleague's wedding. He didn't have enough to spare for Hendricks.'

'You're shitting me. But Hendricks went ahead anyway?' First massive mistake.

'He argued with Lars, but the boss said not to worry, nothing would happen.'

'You heard him say that?'

Nagpal nodded. 'My desk is just outside Lars's office and the door was open. I could hear him talking to Hendricks on the phone.' He glanced round to check Ginger's door was shut. 'Before the attack, Lars never took security that seriously. He would say, "We're helping the people of Helmand, we're their friends, they won't hurt us."'

'But he was wrong.' It was hard to believe how naive some of these NGO managers were, but Ginger had heard of similar things happening in Kabul. 'Who do you think was responsible for the attack?'

The Sikh thought for a moment, fingering the solid steel kara bracelet on his right wrist that attested to his faith. Then he shrugged. 'I could write you a list, but there isn't enough paper. Outside the city, Helmand is carved up between numerous factions.'

'Of the Taliban?'

'Sure, they add to the mix. But the countryside is divided between different narco gangs – opium is really the only crop that makes money in Helmand. The Taliban frown on drug-taking by Afghans, but they're quite happy to see their followers making a profit from the west's craving for heroin. The biggest opium producer in the area is Akhtar Jamali. He's a Baloch tumander – a tribal leader – based on the border with Pakistan. Closer to Lash, the opium crop is controlled by Feda Khaliq, a brother of Wadaan Khaliq, the governor. And there are others, with links to gangs in Sangin and Ghazni. The money sloshes through Helmand and some people get rich. Different warlords are paying the police, the National Security Department and the governor for protection or to turn a blind eye. Some of the drug money finances the Taliban, some of it finances the Taliban's enemies. Everyone has an agenda, an alliance to serve or a vendetta to fulfil.'

'But how could Well Diggers be involved in any of this?'

'Our work is to provide irrigation to the farmers – the legit farmers. We fix the canals and waterways, only to see the land we've irrigated being used to grow poppies. Lars has been vocal in his... disappointment at this. He's made the governor angry on more than one occasion.'

'But you don't think...'

'You're right. The governor wouldn't order an attack on one of our convoys. But, like everybody else, he has connections, and they do what they think fit. And Khaliq isn't the only person Lars has offended. He has a poor understanding of the way things work here and when he opens his mouth, too often he puts his foot in it.'

'It sounds bloody complicated, if you ask me.'

Nagpal smiled and shrugged. 'The Afghan way.'

'But you get it?'

'I was born here in Lashkar Gah. So was my father and my grandfather. I'm one hundred per cent Afghan, but as a Sikh

23

still I'm treated like an outsider.' His fingers went to his steel bracelet again. 'Sometimes, this has advantages. Mostly not.'

'So who else might have done it?'

'I would look at the motives for such an attack. Political or robbery? The engineers often had sums of money for paying for materials the workers needed. This would have been known.'

'Would it also have been known that the convoy was without its usual police escort?'

'Someone in the police could have tipped off a contact – that's always a possibility.' Nagpal looked at his watch. 'I must go for my meeting with Tomas.'

Once he'd left, Ginger considered what he'd said about the motives for the attack, and the implications for the security protocols he needed to set up. If the police couldn't be trusted...

'Ginger?' There was another knock on the door and Nagpal reappeared. 'Tomas still isn't in his office and he's not answering his phone. Neither is Lars.'

'They share a house, don't they?'

'On Herat Street.'

Ginger tried Vinke's phone as he and Nagpal went down to the HAVA building parking lot. Something wasn't stacking up right, and as Nagpal drove the five minutes from the office to Herat Street, Ginger checked his weapon – an ancient but reliable Stechkin he'd brought with him from Kabul.

They drew to a halt outside the Well Diggers compound and Ginger put a hand on Nagpal's forearm to stop him getting out of the Land Rover.

'A moment,' he said. 'Let's just look around first to see if anything's askew.'

He flicked off the Stechkin's safety and studied the street. It was in a residential area, and all was quiet at this time of day. A few of the compounds had guardians standing at the gates, but they were mostly old men, earning a handful of afghanis for keeping an eye on the women of the house.

'Everything looks normal,' said Nagpal, and they got out of the car. But then, as they came closer to the gate of the Well

Diggers compound, he slowed down. The heavy wooden door in the wall surrounding the compound stood ajar.

'What is it?' said Ginger, practically whispering.

'Mahmoud?' said Nagpal out loud. There was no answer.

He turned to Ginger. 'Usually, Mahmoud sits just inside the gate, but he stands up if he hears a car stopping outside, just in case he needs to help carry in shopping or equipment.'

There was no sign of the guard. But there was a scruffy bit of paper pinned onto the wooden door with a tack. It was crudely printed with a scrawl of Pashto script.

Ginger snatched it down and held it out to Nagpal, who took it from him and studied it for a few seconds. Then he crumpled it up and shoved it into his pocket.

'It's just a nightletter,' he said.

'A nightletter?'

'The Taliban use them to threaten and cajole the local population into doing what they want. This one says anyone giving assistance to westerners will be punished. By which they mean killed.'

'And they do that?'

Nagpal gave an apologetic shrug. 'Sometimes. It's a never-ending struggle for power. The nightletters are just one of the tools they use to gain the upper hand.'

Ginger had been holding his weapon pointed at the ground, but he stepped ahead of Nagpal and raised it as he pushed the gate further open with his boot. 'Mahmoud?' he called.

The only answer was the barking of a dog, further up the street.

Ginger scanned the bare earth in front of the house with eyes narrowed against the sun. Then he saw it, lying in the black shadow of the building. It was unmistakably a body, but looking into the shade from the bright sunlight, he couldn't see more than that. Lowering his weapon, he ran forward, calling out as he ran.

'Tomas? Lars? Are you here?'

Ginger knew from the clothing that it wasn't Mahmoud and as he reached the body, he realised that it was Lars Vinke, lying on his side with his face mashed up against the base of the house wall. Ginger tucked the Stechkin into the back of his jeans and felt Vinke's neck for a pulse. Nothing. And his flesh was cool to the touch – not completely cold, but certainly lower than body temperature.

'I think he's dead.' Ginger reached out to roll Vinke towards him.

'*Paam kawa!*' Nagpal came up behind him, staring down. 'Look out – it might be booby-trapped.'

They both stepped back. Ginger could see heavy bruising on the side of Vinke's throat.

'What about Tomas?' said Nagpal.

Ginger drew his weapon again. 'Come on, let's check inside.'

They went through the house, room by room. There was very little to see. In the kitchen, a solitary broken plate suggested there might have been a struggle, but there was no blood, no broken furniture, no footprints. In a small alcove off the kitchen, Ginger came across a stack of folded bedding.

'What's this?' he said, as Nagpal stood in the doorway.

'Ah, that would be for Nazanina – the housekeeper. She sleeps in the house two or three nights a week, rather than walking back to her home.'

'Would she have been here last night?'

'No, I think yesterday was a day when she wasn't working here. But we can check her roster back at the office.'

Upstairs, things looked completely normal – two bedrooms, one tidy, one less so, but nothing that raised suspicions. Nagpal tried both their mobiles. They could hear Vinke's phone ringing outside, but not Bakker's. Ginger went back out and scoured the stony ground in front of the house – no footprints here either.

And absolutely no sign of Tomas Bakker.

Chapter 5

Lashkar Gah, Helmand Province

Ginger stared at the body of his dead boss and wondered where the missing engineer was now. One thing was clear – he needed to go up the chain of command and that meant speaking to Stijn Anholts in Kabul.

But before reporting, he wanted a fuller picture.

'Nagpal?' he called back through the open front door of the house.

The Sikh arrived a moment later, wiping his mouth on his sleeve. His black beard glistened with water and there were splashes down the front of his shirt. Ginger wondered if he'd been sick or had merely needed a drink of water to head it off. Whichever, it didn't matter. He knew from experience that the level of crime-scene protocol followed in the UK simply didn't exist out here, and that the police barely had the capability to take fingerprints, let alone more detailed forensics.

'Would you agree that the most likely scenario is that Tomas Bakker has been kidnapped?'

'It is likely, Ginger,' said Nagpal. 'Unless the intruders, whoever they were, killed him too.'

'But there's no body, and nothing in the house or out here to suggest another murder. Can we get a search of the surrounding area organised?'

Nagpal nodded. 'Sure. We need to call the police – they'll organise a search if we pay them.'

'Seriously? Isn't that their job?'

27

'You might think so, but they often demand payment from the victim's family to investigate a crime.' He sounded suddenly exhausted, and Ginger realised that shock was setting in.

'We have to assume the gate guard is missing, possibly taken too. What is his name?'

'Mahmoud.'

'Mahmoud what?'

Nagpal shrugged. 'That's all we know him by.'

'Do you know where he lives?'

Nagpal nodded, but Ginger could see the shock of what had happened was getting to him.

'Go back to the Land Rover and have some more water. Wait for me there. Call the police, and ask them to go to the gate guard's house to check on his whereabouts.' Ginger thought it unlikely that kidnappers would bother to take an old man. It was far more probable that he'd been paid off or warned off his post the night before. Or maybe he'd simply run away when the intruders had arrived. They needed to find him – he was possibly the only eyewitness to what had happened.

Nagpal nodded and turned towards the gate.

'One other thing,' said Ginger. 'Do you know if there have been any threats to the office or to Vinke or Bakker personally in the last few weeks? Did they ever mention anything suspicious?'

Nagpal blinked. 'Like what?'

'People watching them, people following them – anything that gave them pause for thought.' He was starting to wonder if this attack was somehow linked to the assault in Marja, and whether Well Diggers was now facing an escalation of threat.

Nagpal shook his head. 'Nothing. They said nothing to me.'

After Nagpal had left, Ginger went back over the house once more, this time taking photographs of every room. He knew from experience that once the police arrived the scene would be compromised, and he wanted his own record before that happened. He took pictures of Vinke's body from every angle, and of the ground at the front of the house.

It was as he went to the opposite side of the body, closer to the wall, that he noticed something sticking out from underneath Vinke's shoulder. He dropped down onto his haunches for a closer look. It was the toe of a sneaker, well-worn and grimy, protruding from under the body. Vinke must have fallen on it. Being careful not to disturb the body in case there was an IED underneath it, he stuck a pen under the shoe's laces and drew it out ever so slowly. The white rubber rim and blue canvas were grey with dirt, and when he flipped it over, he saw that the sole was virtually worn through at the ball of the foot and rubbed down at the heel.

He looked down at Vinke's feet, but the Dutchman was wearing a pair of trainers – and he could see they were several sizes larger than the sneaker. Vinke was a tall man, and this certainly wasn't his shoe. Bakker was just as tall, so likely not his either. He went back to the Land Rover.

'Got any clean plastic bags in here?' he asked.

Nagpal shook his head.

'A large envelope?'

Nagpal passed him an empty brown envelope from the back seat. It would do as an evidence bag – it's not as if there would be any forensic facilities down here in Lashkar Gah. He photographed the sneaker and stuck it the envelope. They would need to find out who it belonged to. It was probably just chance that Vinke had fallen on it, but it still needed to be checked out.

Once he'd stashed the shoe in the back of the Land Rover, he felt he'd done all he could. It was time to call the boss.

Thankfully, Anholts picked up on the first ring, but his voice told Ginger that he was puzzled by the call.

'Mr Jameson, what can I do for you?'

Ginger took a breath. This wasn't a message that could be garbled. 'We've got a developing situation down here. Lars Vinke is dead, murdered by the looks of it, and Tomas Bakker is missing. I have reason to believe he may have been kidnapped.'

'Jesus Christ. Where are you and when did this happen? What makes you think Bakker has been taken?'

'There's no sign of him at the house, where we found Vinke's body, and no sign of his demise. The gate guard is also missing.'

'What about the cleaning woman?'

'She wasn't there at the time. Nagpal has sent a message to her home not to come into work. We don't want the property disturbed.'

'Have you had a ransom demand or other communication?'

'Nothing so far.' He discounted the nightletter they'd found pinned to the door. Nagpal had assured him it was nothing unusual. 'Am I right in my understanding that Well Diggers has no K&R insurance?'

There was silence at the other end of the line. It was all Ginger needed.

Finally, Anholts spoke. 'Jameson, how the hell did this happen? You were employed to ensure that my staff were protected from things like this.'

'Yes, and I was putting new security protocols in place. Protocols that should have been in use already.' There was no way he was going to let the bastard shift the blame onto him. It rested squarely on Vinke's dead shoulders.

'You need to bloody find him – and fast – or you'll be out of a job. After the Marja attack, this is the last thing we need. We could lose our financial backers…'

Ginger wasn't impressed. For Anholts it was all about the optics and the money. Not the fact that a man's life was on the line.

'I'll do what I need to do,' said Ginger, 'but I'm going to need men and money.'

'Sure. You have my full authority to handle the situation. Get what help you can from the local police – for what it's worth. And call me the moment you hear anything from the kidnappers. If they make any financial demands, I'll have to inform the Dutch and British governments.'

'The UK government won't pay a ransom,' said Ginger. He had no idea about the Dutch, but most western governments took a hard line, at least in public – a couple were rumoured to slip money under the table. 'Do you have any sort of contingency fund, and if so, how high can I go?'

Ginger could virtually hear the man shaking his head. 'Nothing. Our budgets have been reduced in recent years – we barely manage to finance our operations.'

This was bad news for Bakker.

'Stijn, can I make a suggestion?' He used Anholts's first name deliberately to put himself at the same level as the man.

'Go ahead.'

'I know someone, Alasdair MacKenzie, an ex-colleague who worked anti-terrorism in the Met. He's done their hostage negotiator course, and he has some experience in matters like this. He's based in Kabul.' Ginger wasn't entirely sure of the extent of Mac's hands-on experience with kidnappings, but it was a fuck of a lot more than his. Which was zero. 'I'd like to bring him in.'

'Okay. Sounds like a plan.'

'It'll cost you.'

'Not as much as a ransom, though?'

'I'll get in touch with him and let you know.'

As he finished the call, he heard vehicles drawing up in the street outside. The police had arrived.

Ginger had already met Commander Gulwal of the Lashkar Gah Central Police. Nagpal had taken him to the police station a few days earlier to make the introductions. When Ginger informed the tall, skinny police chief that he would be doubling the number of men he hired from him for security details, Gulwal's face had broken into a wide-mouthed grin, showing off a set of giant discoloured teeth that could have benefited from the attention of an orthodontist.

Nagpal had translated what he said. 'I think, Mr Ginger-jan, we are going to be the best of friends to you.'

Ginger had grinned back. 'As long as you can make a decent bloody brew, you could be right.' He still felt scarred by the gallons of bitter green tea he'd been subjected to in the office of Major Jananga, his contact within the Kabul police.

This morning, however, there was no grin on Gulwal's face as Ginger met him at the gateway to the compound. A handful of Gulwal's men stood behind him, craning their necks to see beyond Ginger's bulk. Nagpal came up to join them so he could interpret.

'You told him on the phone what we found?' Ginger asked Nagpal.

Nagpal nodded, at the same time listening to something Gulwal was saying.

'He wants to see the body, and he wants his men to search the house.'

Ginger looked at the ragtag band of men that accompanied the police commander. None of their uniforms matched, and their weapons, ex-Soviet AK47s, looked older than the men holding them. He felt thankful he'd been able to check over the property before they arrived and stomped through it. He wondered how trustworthy they were, and whether their presence would help in any way at all. He decided to keep the discovery of the sneaker to himself.

'Of course,' he said, stepping out of the way so that the police could enter the compound.

Gulwal walked towards the body, stopping a few feet away from it and holding up an arm to prevent his men from going any closer.

'He wants to know if you've checked it for IEDs,' translated Nagpal.

Ginger shook his head. 'Not yet.' It was something he was happy to leave to Gulwal and his men.

Gulwal barked an order at one of his subordinates, who jogged out of the compound to their vehicles. He reappeared a moment later with a coil of rope. The usual discussion ensued at increasing volume, but Gulwal had the last word. The man handed the rope to one of his colleagues, who passed it on to someone else, like some macabre game of pass the parcel. Ginger wondered how long this was going to take. But Vinke had nowhere to be in a hurry, so maybe it didn't matter.

The policeman who now held the rope passed his AK to his colleague and walked with exaggerated caution towards the body. Gulwal waved everybody else back towards the gate of the compound.

'We're to wait outside,' Nagpal explained to Ginger.

The rest of the men, Gulwal and Nagpal went out onto the street. Ginger leaned into the doorway, watching the now lone policeman with the rope. As he walked, he tied a sliding loop in one end of it. When he was within a couple of feet of Vinke's body, he paused. He stepped sideways and then bent forward. Ginger watched, his mouth falling open, as the man then attempted to lasso Vinke's right arm, which was hanging out a couple of inches from the back of his body. Realising the man's plan, Ginger stepped back behind the protection of the compound wall. It meant he couldn't see any more, but he'd rather that than have his head blown off if there was an IED underneath Vinke's body.

He heard the man's footsteps hurrying back across the ground in front of the house. He appeared in the gateway, carefully paying out the rope behind him with enough slack not to disturb Vinke's arm. Ginger took a step back to allow the policeman to shelter with him behind the wall.

Once he was out of the line of any blast, the man gave the rope a hefty tug.

Ginger shut his eyes tight in expectation of an explosion, but there was nothing but a dull thud as the body rolled onto its back, away from the wall of the house.

The policeman peered around the side of the compound entrance and started to speak excitedly. Gulwal added his opinion and the police surged forward, crushing each other in the gateway in their rush to get back into the compound.

'All is okay, I think,' said Nagpal.

33

'That's one way of putting it,' said Ginger, as he watched Gulwal's men excitedly trample the crime scene. One of them squatted by Vinke's body, now lying on its back a foot or so out from the wall, and inspected it more closely. The limbs, stiff with rigor, maintained the position they had when it was resting on its front, making it look awkward and uncomfortable, not that Vinke would be feeling anything now. The rest of the men piled into the house as Gulwal shouted orders at them.

No scene-of-crime protocol, no crime-scene suits, no police photographer, no pathologists taking charge.

He took some pictures of the front of Vinke's body and a couple of close-ups of the bruises on his throat, but he felt out of his depth. It was time to call Mac.

34

Day 1

Chapter 6

Kabul

'If you haven't found a body, then you have to assume Bakker is alive. And if Bakker is alive, someone's holding him.' Alasdair 'Mac' MacKenzie's eyes lazily followed his girlfriend Baz around their shared room in Le Monde Guesthouse as she threw clothes into an open suitcase on the floor. He should have been packing too, but he'd stopped to take a quick call from Ginger Jameson.

'What makes you say that?' said Ginger.

'He's missing. You're in Lash. It's not like when a bloke goes AWOL in Blighty. At home it's just a matter of working out which bar he's holed up in or who he's shagging. But Lash... no bars, no girls – there's literally nowhere he could be. Ergo, someone's got him.'

Baz held up two bikinis, one Dayglo orange, the other a multicoloured tropical print, each somehow smaller than the other.

'Both,' mouthed Mac. They were heading out to Dubai for two weeks' R&R. Hot sand, cold beer and afternoon sex. Mac couldn't wait.

'Yeah, that's what I reckoned, too,' said Ginger. 'I've got the local cop shop searching the city for him, but it's not looking good.'

'They'll probably be less than useless. Have you seen the governor?'

'Going over to his office in a minute.'

'Good. He'll have ears on the ground, and if you're lucky he'll know who's got your man. If you're even luckier, he'll

37

broker a deal to get him back – but it'll depend on his relationship with whoever's holding Bakker. I take it you haven't had a ransom demand yet?'

'Nothing.'

'Listen, when they get in touch with you, the first thing to do is to demand a proof-of-life video. No point paying a ransom for a dead body.'

'That's part of the problem,' said Ginger. 'Well Diggers hasn't got bloody K&R insurance.'

'Christ, what sort of cheapskates are they? If you've got no ransom, you're not going to get the guy back. Not unless one of the governments steps in with the cash.'

'How likely is that?'

'Not likely, but I think the EU might have some sort of secret slush fund for cases like this. Get your boss to put out feelers – there's an EU delegation up here he can talk to.'

'Cheers. I'll tell him to get on it.'

Baz looked at him and tapped her watch meaningfully. Javid was supposed to be taking them to the airport in forty minutes and Mac hadn't even started packing. He nodded at her. Time to wind up the call.

'Thing is,' said Ginger, 'I could do with a hand on this. Someone who's had a bit of experience in dealing with hostage situations.'

'Sure, mate. Always at the end of the line for you. Call anytime.'

Baz glowered at him, and he gave an apologetic shrug.

'Actually, I asked my boss. I've got budget for you to come down here, a bit more hands-on, so to speak. Given you're between contracts, it'll be a nice chunk of extra dosh.'

Two weeks of sun, sea and sex, or two weeks in Lash sorting out Ginger's problem?

Mac sighed. 'Any other time, Ginger, I'd jump on it. But I'm just off to Dubai with Baz. Haven't had a proper break in over a year.'

There was a pause. Then, when Ginger spoke, Mac could hear an undercurrent of desperation in his tone. 'I gotta tell you, Mac, I'm floundering here. I need this job to work out for me. Just a few days should sort it out. Then you'll be on your way to sunny Dubai.'

'Let me call you back.' Mac hated what he was about to do.

'There's a Louis Berger flight to Lash taking off in a couple of hours...'

'I'll call you back.'

Baz was standing at the end of the bed, glaring down at him and shaking her head.

'Don't do it, Mac,' she said, her voice barely louder than a whisper. He knew how much she'd been looking forward to this holiday. Their first holiday together as a couple.

Mac rubbed a hand over his mouth and chin, as if it could stop him from saying what he was about to say.

Baz's eyes filled with tears. 'Bastard,' she said, but without real venom.

'I'm sorry. I'm so sorry, love.' Mac got up from the bed and pulled her into a hug. 'But I've got to go, just for a few days. Ginger's a mate and he's in trouble. One of the guys he works for has been kidnapped. A man's life is on the line.'

Baz sniffed and nodded her understanding.

'Listen, it should only take a couple of days, and I'll get the next LB flight back here and come straight on to Dubai. You go ahead – you can do the shops without me trailing around behind you. We'll still have the better part of a week and a half.'

'I'll stay here till you get back. Then we'll go together.'

'Whatever you prefer,' said Mac. She knew the score. She'd been out here in Afghanistan for as long as he had, covering the war on terror as a reporter for the *Baltimore Sun*. When your mate needed you, you dropped everything – even your first holiday with the hottest girl on the planet.

'I'll rearrange the tickets and the hotel,' she said, 'so let me know soon as you can when you're flying back up.'

Mac called Ginger back.

'On my way, so secure a seat on that flight.'

'Thank Christ,' said Ginger. 'You take off at midday. I'll owe you for this, big time.'

'Yes, you bloody will, you bastard. See you this afternoon.'

Fourteen days until his new contract started. Four days in Lash, ten days in Dubai. That was plenty long enough for a holiday.

Chapter 7

Lashkar Gah

Mac spotted Ginger leaning against a dusty Land Rover as soon as he clambered down the plane's steps onto the rudimentary airstrip. Ginger Jameson had been his assistant while he'd worked at the Afghan police training academy the previous year, and after they were both 'let go' for their overzealous pursuit of an international arms, drugs and antiquities smuggler, they'd kept in close contact. You couldn't have too many friends in Afghanistan was the way Mac saw it.

Ginger waved him over, his boyish features cracking into a wide grin.

'Hell, am I pleased to see you.'

They gripped hands momentarily, until Mac let go to punch Ginger in the upper arm.

'Great to see you too, chum.' He looked round. 'Who are they?'

A group of four or five westerners were handing their cases over to be stashed in the aircraft's hold, then climbing the steps to board.

'Well Diggers' expat staff. Anholts, the country manager, called them back to Kabul until we find Bakker and get proper security up and running.'

'Just as well – gets them out of our hair while we sort it.'

On the drive into town, Ginger filled Mac in on the details of what had happened. They sat in the back of the Land Rover, while Ginger's interpreter, Darab, sat up front next to the driver.

41

Mac looked out of the car window with interest as he listened. The outskirts of Lash weren't dissimilar to the outskirts of Kabul – the usual patchwork of dusty roads lined by rows of compounds, all surrounded by high walls so you couldn't really get a sense of the properties or people inside. However, the scale of the two cities couldn't be more different, and without the roadblocks and gridlocks of the capital to contend with, they were in the centre of Lash in ten minutes.

'Still nothing from the kidnappers?' he asked when Ginger finished speaking.

'Not a dicky.' Ginger shook his head. 'There was a nightletter pinned to the compound gate, but Nagpal, our logistics guy, checked – they were pinned all across the neighbourhood.'

'But you're sure the one Well Diggers received was the same? Could be a smart way of delivering a more personalised message.'

'Jesus,' said Ginger, rubbing his hand across his forehead. 'I'll get Nagpal to take another look at it.' He pulled out his phone. 'Hi, Nagpal… you still got that nightletter?' He listened for a few seconds. 'Can you do us a translation? Could be important.'

'What now?' said Mac when Ginger had disconnected the call.

'I'm not sure what else we can do at the moment. The governor couldn't have been less interested – he said he knew nothing about it and hadn't heard any rumours. The police are supposedly searching for Bakker, but I'm not holding my breath.'

'Let's go straight to the scene,' said Mac.

'Not much to see… the body's been moved to the morgue at the Italian Emergency Hospital.'

'It'll give me a feel for how things could have gone down.'

The house on Herat Street was empty now – Vinke and Bakker had been its only residents – so Mac was surprised to see an old man sitting on the side of the road in front of the locked compound doorway when they pulled up.

'Who's this?' he said.

'Darab,' said Ginger to the interpreter, 'ask this man what he's doing here.'

Darab gave Ginger a puzzled look. 'Mr Ginger, this is Mahmoud. He is Mr Vinke's gatekeeper.'

The mysterious guard who'd been missing first thing was now waiting patiently to get back to his post.

Ginger pulled a key from his pocket and unlocked the compound door.

'Tell Mahmoud to come in,' Mac said to Darab. 'We'll need to ask him some questions about what happened.'

The air inside the house smelt stale and the surfaces already looked dusty. Apart from some dirt trodden in near the front door, there was little sign that the police had come and gone earlier in the day. There was no forlorn crime-scene tape flapping in the wind, no traces of the silver fingerprint powder Mac would have expected at a British crime scene. It didn't even look like they'd searched the house very thoroughly, though with the attackers coming from outside, maybe there wouldn't be much to find. But you didn't make assumptions like that – that was sloppy policing.

The house itself, while large and well-furnished by Afghan standards, lacked personality in the way expat rentals often do. There were no photos or ornaments, and the few houseplants looked as if no one took proper care of them. Clearly, Bakker and Vinke were not exactly homely types.

Mac took a cursory look around, in case anything obvious had been missed. Upstairs, he peered into the two bedrooms in turn. 'Which room is which?' he said to Ginger, who'd come up behind him.

Ginger shrugged and went into the messier of the two rooms. He looked around for a couple of minutes. 'I think this is Vinke's room – I'm pretty sure I saw him wearing that shirt,' he said, pointing to a pale yellow short-sleeved shirt that lay crumpled at the foot of the bed. 'D'you think the fuckers grabbed him up here?'

Mac studied the mess – a tangle of discarded clothes, books stacked by the bed, a couple of empty glasses on the nightstand and shoes kicked off by the wardrobe.

'No, this just looks like normal shit admin to me. No sign of a struggle.'

He went across the landing to what must be Bakker's room. It was the complete opposite – tidy to a fault. The bed was made, shoes lined up in pairs under the window, clothes precision folded and neatly piled on the wardrobe shelves. Surfaces clear of clutter. 'Military background?' said Mac.

Ginger shrugged. 'Not that I know of. But it's either that or OCD.'

Mac opened the drawer of the bedside table. There wasn't much in it. A wristwatch, stopped. Nail clippers. A wrist support bandage in a box, unused. A few loose condoms. A box containing pills.

Mac scooped up the condoms and held them up. 'Don't imagine he had much use for these in Lash.' He dropped them and picked up the meds instead. He read the label. 'Zoloft. Any idea what that's for?' He opened the packet. The information sheet was missing, and half the pills in the blister pack were gone.

'Not a clue,' said Ginger.

Mac slipped the meds into his pocket. 'Let's see what Mahmoud's got to say for himself.'

Through Darab, they instructed Mahmoud to sit on one of the chairs by the kitchen table. He looked around the room, and then frowned at Ginger and Mac. Mac realised why.

'No one's told him what happened yet,' he said to Ginger.

'But he should have been here last night. And, for that matter, first thing this morning. He lives on the property. Nagpal and I got here at just after nine, and we were here until when I phoned you at – what was that? Ten thirty, elevenish? Why wasn't he here then?'

'Darab, ask him whether he was here last night, and where he's been this morning.'

44

Darab turned to the gatekeeper, and they spoke for a couple of minutes in Pashto. As Darab mentioned Vinke and Bakker's names, the man's face registered a look of shock and then he let out a theatrical moan. He shook his head and agitated the prayer beads on his wrist.

Darab spoke in English. 'He didn't know that Vinke is dead or that Bakker is missing. He got a message yesterday from his home village – his mother was taken ill and he needed to see her.'

Mac studied Mahmoud's stricken features. He would have described Mahmoud as an old man, and was surprised that he had a mother still alive, but a harsh life under the Afghan sun often made men appear older than they were.

'He travelled back there yesterday afternoon and stayed the night at his family home. Mr Vinke had given him permission to do so.'

'I'm sorry,' said Mac. 'Please tell him that we hope his mother recovers soon.' But he had to wonder. Conveniently out of the way when the assault had gone down.

Darab passed on the message and it elicited another bout of moaning from Mahmoud.

'*Insha'Allah, Insha'Allah.*' If Allah wills it.

'Ask him if he noticed anything suspicious in the last few days – people watching the house, if anyone visited and argued with either Vinke or Bakker...'

'Ask him about nightletters,' said Ginger. 'There was one tacked to the door this morning, but Nagpal said that's pretty routine.'

Darab questioned the man again, and this time Mahmoud seemed to have plenty to say. Mac and Ginger waited patiently until he ran out of steam, then they looked at Darab.

'No, nothing has been out of the ordinary in any way,' said Darab.

'He took his time telling you that,' said Mac.

Darab waved a dismissive hand through the air. 'He's a super-stitious old man, and he likes to talk. He moaned about the nightletters – he's worried that the Taliban will gain power again.'

Mac glanced at Ginger and wondered how much they could trust the translator. But it was a conversation that would have to wait until Darab wasn't around.

'Just one other thing – give me a moment.' Ginger ducked out to the Land Rover and got the envelope with the sneaker in it. Being careful not to touch it, he shook it out onto the kitchen table. 'Is this his?'

Mac could tell by the way Mahmoud looked at the shoe that he'd never seen it before.

Darab confirmed it. Mac glanced down at Mahmoud's feet. They were old and gnarled, with protruding bunions. He was wearing sandals made from an old tyre, and Mac doubted he'd be able to get his foot into the sneaker.

He and Ginger took a cursory look around the rest of the house, mainly for Mac to get the lay of the land. Then Mac took some time to examine the outer door of the compound. There were no signs of forced entry.

'So, if Vinke had given Mahmoud the evening off, presumably the gate would have been bolted from the inside?'

'You'd have thought,' said Ginger.

'Which means either Vinke or Bakker opened the gate to the attackers – in other words, they knew them – or possibly the attackers came over the wall.'

They walked along the inside of the perimeter wall, looking for heavy footprints in the dirt as a sign that someone had lowered themselves over it. They found nothing.

'Let's look outside,' said Mac. 'Maybe they drove a vehicle up to the back of the compound and used it for a leg-up.'

But the Well Diggers compound backed onto a similar compound in the next street, with a shared back wall. And likewise, the side walls were shared with the two neighbouring compounds, so there would be no way of surreptitiously breaching the property from the sides or the rear.

'I guess either Vinke or Bakker let them in, then,' said Mac, as they stood outside the gate. 'Right, time to take a look at the body.'

Chapter 8

Lashkar Gah

The Italian Emergency Hospital – or to give it its full title, the Emergency Surgical Center for Civilian War Victims – was a new facility that had recently been opened by a European charity. It existed, as the name implied, to treat the casualties caught up in the crossfire of the country's enduring internecine strife. It also housed the city's only refrigerated morgue, where Vinke's body now resided.

Mac knew from his experience in Kabul that an Afghan post-mortem was a post-mortem in name only. Without the forensic facilities required to analyse tissue and fluid samples, any conclusions drawn by Afghan medical examiners were generally based on visual acuity or, to put it more bluntly, guesswork. And although the place was clean and bright compared to the morgue he'd visited in Kabul, the charity that ran the hospital quite rightly spent its budget on helping the living, rather than analysing the dead. Ginger had told him that it looked like Vinke had been strangled. Mac was no medical expert himself, but he still felt it would be worth examining the body to see if it could tell them something more.

An orderly in a white coat led them through the hospital to the morgue at the back of the building when Darab explained why they were there. He unlocked the morgue, pointed to a stainless-steel drawer, and left them to it.

'Fuck, we didn't even have to show ID,' said Mac, shaking his head.

Ginger shrugged. 'There aren't that many Europeans down here and they mostly work for NGOs. It's not like they're expecting a gang of British body snatchers, is it?' He pulled open the drawer and Mac drew back the sheet which covered the body inside it.

They gazed down at the chilled carcass that had once been Lars Vinke. His limbs looked stiff and awkward with rigor. Ginger had only known him a week, and Mac not at all, but they still stood for a moment in respectful silence. There but for the grace of God...

Mac spoke first, leaning over the body so he could examine the bruises on the neck. 'You were right, chum – certainly strangled.' There were blue-green finger marks ringing Vinke's throat, and they suggested that the killer had known what he was doing, applying enough pressure in the right place to block off Vinke's airway, and probably snapping his hyoid bone in the process.

'Poor guy didn't stand a chance,' said a voice behind them – Italian accent with a definite American twang. 'I'm Doctor Marchesi.'

They turned round to see a short, dark-haired medic standing in the doorway.

'Hi,' said Ginger. 'Chris Jameson, and this is my colleague Mac MacKenzie. I'm head of security at Well Diggers. Lars Vinke was our project manager.'

Marchesi nodded. 'Listen, guys, we don't have facilities or the time for a full autopsy, but I took a look at him, and I can give you a quick rundown on what I know.'

'Thanks,' said Ginger.

Marchesi joined them by Vinke's corpse.

'Do you have any idea who did it?' he said.

'No, but whoever it was has also taken one of my blokes.'

Marchesi let out a low whistle. 'Right, you're looking for a big man – tall, I mean. Certainly over six feet.'

'How do you know?' said Ginger.

Marchesi held a hand a couple of inches above Vinke's throat. 'Look at the size of these handprints.' They were much larger than Marchesi's hands. 'He was strong, too. It's not that easy to strangle someone – you have to hold that grip for four or five minutes, and the victim will probably be struggling, at least for the first minute or two. And this Vinke wasn't exactly small himself.'

'Can you tell us anything else?' said Mac. 'Time of death?' An accurate time of death would be useful – just on the off-chance that the bloody useless police stumbled upon a witness.

'When the body came in at eleven this morning, it was – and in fact still is – in peak rigor mortis.'

'What does that tell you?'

'Rigor starts to come into effect approximately four hours after death, maybe quicker in this heat. It can take up to eight hours for the body to become fully stiff, like he is now, and that can last for up to two days.'

Mac frowned – he hadn't signed up for a bloody science lecture. He just wanted answers.

'What it means is the latest he probably died, for rigor to have set in before he arrived here, is six this morning. However, it could have been several hours before that. When was he last seen alive?'

'Apart from whoever did it and Bakker, the missing man, we think it must have been when he dismissed Mahmoud, his gatekeeper. About four or five yesterday afternoon,' said Ginger.

Marchesi nodded. 'So, definitely sometime during the night. Lividity on the body is fixed, which narrows the time frame slightly – it suggests that he likely died before two or three a.m. If I had lab facilities, I would probably be able to give you a more accurate estimate, but that's all I can offer.' He shrugged.

That was life in Afghanistan – they had to make do with what was available, and it wasn't what Mac had been used to in the Met.

'Thanks, Doc,' said Mac. He pulled the sheet back up over Vinke's face. Although they might report Vinke's death to the local police, it would really be up to them to solve it – if such a thing was even possible. The most likely way was to find whoever had taken Bakker. He might still be alive and he had to be their priority now. Mac felt certain that finding Bakker's abductor would also lead them to the man who killed Vinke.

They headed for the HAVA building. It was gone five by the time they got there, but Nagpal was still working, so Ginger made the introductions.

'Jagvir Nagpal, this is Mac MacKenzie. He's a K&R specialist.'

It was hardly how Mac would have described himself, but he let it go. Building confidence was an important way of gaining co-operation, and he and Ginger would need all Well Diggers' staff to be fully on board.

'Good to meet you,' said Nagpal, sticking out a hand. It wasn't the usual Afghan greeting, but Mac saw from Nagpal's turban that he wasn't the usual Afghan. He knew a couple of Sikhs up in Kabul, but he hadn't realised there were still Afghan Sikhs living in Helmand.

'You too.' Niceties over, it was straight down to business. 'Have you got that translation of the nightletter for us?'

'It's here,' said Nagpal, handing over a sheet of paper covered in neat handwriting. 'I was going to type it up for you, but I haven't had a moment yet.'

'No worries,' said Ginger. He and Mac studied the text.

By the Name of Almighty Allah The Most Merciful
The Most Compassionate
Notice from the Holy Warriors of Afghanistan
Aslam Alaikum Wa Rahmatullahi Wa Barakatuho to
all honorable Moslems of Afghanistan.

We have the honour to inform you those disgraceful and
aggressive missions of infidel and puppet Karzai admin-
istration are deployed to invade Afghanistan demanding
your respected votes and pulling the wool over your eyes.

They are planning to make use of this sacred nation for US-backed invasion as well as to achieve their vicious goals and spreading Christian thoughts via your sanctified votes. They intend to undermine your determined and religious beliefs and they have already started spreading Christianity in this holy country in secret. Our objective is: Casting votes to those is assisting heathens and if you do so, then there is no difference between you and infidel Jews as stated in one of the verses of holy Koran: 'Muslims, don't pick friends from a Jewish or Christian community because they are friends to each other and if you do so, then there is no discrepancy between you and Jews/Christians and Almighty does not guide the tyrants.'

Mohammad Bin Ali Shoukani saying that the reason for prohibiting being companion with Jews/Christians is not to deal them friendly as friendship, association, social intercourse and any assistance even as cooking, driving, safeguarding etc. Anyone doing so for the livelihood of the family is religiously authorized to be executed.

As mentioned in one of the verses of holy Koran, while the infidels are seeking your alliance and amity, avoid it. Anyone committing is considered similar as Jew/Christian and will be painfully tortured in hell and this is the final stage of sin ousting a Muslim to infidelity.

Note: Anyone not acting upon these religious instructions will be faced soon its consequence Insha'Allah and everyone has responsibility or answerability of his/her own.

Islamic Revolution of Taleban
Shura of Scholars

'Wow,' said Ginger. 'They're not messing around, are they?'

'They want to scare us away from working with you,' said Nagpal.

'So, do you think there's a connection between this and what happened in the house?' said Ginger, turning to Mac.

Mac paused, running a hand through his hair and scratching. 'We can't discount it... but it doesn't seem that likely for a number of reasons.'

'Go on.'

'First, cause of death. Manual strangulation's not a Taliban MO. Gunshot wounds, stabbing, a cut throat... but not the way Vinke died.' He counted off the reasons on his fingers. 'Second, what's with killing one and taking the other? Vinke was more senior, so would be the logical hostage to take, if they only wanted one.'

'If they knew that,' said Ginger.

'It wouldn't have been hard to find out. And third, radio silence. Terrorist groups like to crow about things like this and the Taliban are no exception. They would at least put out a ransom demand.'

'There's been nothing,' said Nagpal. 'I've been monitoring all the company's email addresses and no one has received a phone call.'

Mac shook his head. 'It's not the Taliban. The local Talibs haven't been attacking aid projects and NGOs, so this would be a departure from their usual TTPs.'

'TTPs?' said Nagpal.

'Sorry – tactics, techniques and procedures. No reason for them to do that.'

'But if it's not the Taliban, who the hell is it?' said Ginger.

Mac shrugged. 'Who else is operating down here? Not the Haqqani Network. Unlikely to be AQ – they're a spent force in Afghanistan. Maybe some jumped-up local gangsters...' He looked at Nagpal.

'Plenty of those around here,' he said.

'No information from the governor's office yet?' said Ginger.

Nagpal shook his head. 'I spoke to his deputy less than an hour ago. They claim they haven't heard a thing.'

'You don't believe them?' said Mac.

Nagpal scratched the side of his neck for a couple of seconds and pursed his lips. 'I think they would tell us maybe if they knew something. Probably not everything. It would depend on how they could work it to their advantage. But to have heard nothing at all...' He threw his hands in the air, palms up. 'Afghanistan is like a leaky bucket. No one can mind his own business, and everyone has a cousin who's involved. There are always rumours – the game is knowing which ones to listen to.'

It did seem strange to Mac that there was nothing – no communication from the kidnappers themselves, nothing turned up by the police search, no chatter... They had no leads to follow and in an operation like this time was critical.

The longer Bakker was held, the less likely he was to get out alive.

If he even was still alive.

Chapter 9

Lashkar Gah

The Afghan National Police HQ in Lashkar Gah didn't formally advertise itself with any signage, but the phalanx of blue-uniformed men, smoking and gossiping just outside the gate, was something of a giveaway. They stared insolently as the Well Diggers Land Rover pulled up in front of the compound gate, and none of them seemed keen to take on the responsibility of finding out why the two westerners and a Sikh might be expecting to gain entrance.

It reminded Mac of the first time he visited the Police HQ in Kabul, when a row had broken out at the gate. Some things were the same up and down the country – stray dogs pissing against your vehicle, scorpions lurking at the bottom of your bed, and lazy policemen throwing their weight around.

Nagpal, who was driving, opened his window and let rip a stream of invective.

The policeman nearest to the gate came over to them at a slow stroll, cradling his AK in a way that Mac could only interpret as menacing. He replied to Nagpal just as aggressively.

'You've told him we've got an appointment with Commander Gulwal, have you?' said Ginger.

When the policeman heard the name Gulwal, his attitude suddenly changed.

Two minutes later, the steel gates in front of them swung open and they were allowed to drive into the compound. Nagpal parked the Land Rover at the end of a row of police Hiluxes and they got out. Mac looked around. The compound comprised two single-storey, cream-coloured buildings. Between them was a small patch of garden, incongruously planted with rows of scrubby rose bushes. There was a young police cadet watering them. He watched them sullenly, but carried on with his chore.

'Hello, hello, Mr Ginger,' came a shout from one of the office doorways, as Commander Gulwal emerged. This was the full extent of his English, but he beckoned them over and they followed him into his office. It was a large room, but cluttered with furniture – there were two battered desks, half a dozen plain wooden chairs and stacks of cardboard boxes that seemed to serve as filing cabinets. On Gulwal's desk there was a small blue-and-white vase of faded and drooping rose heads, no doubt from the garden outside.

'*Salaam alaikum.*'

'*Salaam alaikum, chutor asti?*'

'*Alaikum a'salaam.*'

Once the interminable round of greetings was done with, and Nagpal and Gulwal had asked each other about the health of their families, they were able to get to the point of the meeting.

'Can you ask the commander if the search has turned anything up yet?' said Mac.

Nagpal translated the question, and Mac could see from Gulwal's body language when he answered that he was obfuscating.

'His men have searched the streets around the Well Diggers house and questioned all the neighbours who might have heard anything.'

'And?' prompted Mac.

'Nobody saw a thing,' said Nagpal.

'Does he believe this, or does he think that people are frightened to talk?'

The commander looked affronted.

'His men are trusted in the community and if anyone knew anything, they would find out about it.'

Somehow Mac had no doubt of that, but it had nothing to do with how much the people of Lash trusted their police force.

Gulwal carried on talking.

'Although he understands how distressing this is for you, to have a man missing, he also has to point out that tying up his men in a door-to-door enquiry is costing him money he doesn't have,' said Nagpal.

'What happened to the money we gave him? That's what it was for,' said Ginger, his cheeks reddening.

Nagpal gave him a pained look. He was quite right – they didn't need this to turn into a confrontation. Mac held up a placatory hand.

'Tell him we think he is better placed to help us find our man than the governor or the NSD. His men have stronger ties to the community here, and they are more likely to hear some gossip that would give us a lead.'

Nagpal translated, and Gulwal shifted in his chair to face Mac. The flattery had worked. He asked Nagpal a question, and Mac heard his own name in the answer as Nagpal explained who he was and what he was doing here. Gulwal nodded along with the answer and then spoke.

Nagpal said, 'The commander thinks that a sum of money put up as a reward would perhaps draw out the information you need.'

Of course it would. With most of it ending up in Gulwal's pocket when one of his cousins came in with a spurious story. It was something Mac had been expecting, and he'd had Ginger call Anholts on the way over to get approval for a reward to be offered. They'd agreed to put forward half the amount Anholts had approved to test the water.

Gulwal looked put out when Nagpal translated the offer for him. He shrugged, then spoke at length.

'He would like to know when you will deliver the money.'

'When he delivers some useful information,' said Ginger.

'Please thank him for all the help he's given us so far,' said Mac quickly, privately reflecting it had been next to nothing.

57

Perhaps a meeting with the governor would yield better results. After all, time was running out for Bakker, and so far they didn't have a single bloody clue as to where he was or who was holding him.

Nagpal was clearly a consummate diplomat in his translations. By the time they left Gulwal's office, the commander was all smiles and promises, assuring them that it would only be a matter of hours before his men would recover the missing westerner. Mac doubted it.

It was nearly dark by the time he and Ginger got back to the house Ginger had been billeted in. It was two streets away from the house Vinke and Bakker had shared. When Ginger had first arrived, there had been a Belgian and an Italian engineer already living there, but they were back in Kabul for the time being, so there was plenty of room for Mac to stay.

Mac felt like it had been one hell of a long day. He'd woken up thinking he was going to Dubai, having never even heard of Tomas Bakker or Lars Vinke. Now Vinke was dead, and Bakker had been missing for almost twenty-four hours. And he was here in Lash, while Baz sat fuming back in Kabul.

'Next move?' said Ginger, putting a very welcome bottle of Corona on the table in front of him. It came from the case Mac had brought down with him on the flight.

Mac was tired.

'Fucked if I know – all out of options.' He took a swig of the beer. Cold, crisp, reviving. 'We'll speak to your staff tomorrow. If they have nothing, we wait – for a demand from the kidnappers or for a lead. Then we fucking go for it.'

Chapter 10

Kabul

Baz Khan wandered out into the garden at Le Monde Guesthouse with a resigned sigh. So much for their vacation. The hotel was cancelled, the flights were postponed. Now she was stuck at a loose end until Mac got back from his little adventure. She'd taken leave from work, which meant the news desk wouldn't be expecting any copy from her, and she'd been left twiddling her thumbs, with no one to have fun with.

It was stinking hot, the mercury nudging forty with not a breath of wind, and there was no air-conditioning in the room upstairs. Sweat made her kurta stick to her back, and although she was wearing her lightest pair of pants, it seemed mad not to be in shorts and a tank in this heat. She wandered over to the one patch of dappled shade, thrown by an ancient walnut tree. On the scrubby grass under its low-hanging branches, she could just discern a patch of scruffy grey-brown fur.

'Lobo,' she called.

The fur moved and turned into a young wolf cub. He stood lazily and came towards her, sniffing the air to pick up her scent. She held out a hand – he liked to be scratched under his chin.

'You've grown again,' she said.

She tickled his neck for a few seconds, but then the animal's body stiffened and he drew back, baring his teeth. There was a sound behind her, and she looked round.

'Garry, hi.'

'You know he's gotta go?' Garry was the manager of Le Monde, and he'd been gifted Lobo by the guesthouse owner, a

Panjshiri called Khudus, a couple of months earlier. Garry had brought him to live in the guesthouse garden. Back then, Lobo had been a tiny abandoned pup, and Baz had helped Garry care for him, feeding him milk through the night until he graduated onto minced meat. Now he was munching his way through a couple of chickens each day.

'I know. He's not a dog.'

'Too right he's not. Look what he did to me last night.' Garry held out a hand and Baz saw a nasty-looking gash across the back of it.

'He's challenging you for the alpha male spot.'

Garry laughed, then gave her a questioning look. 'Hey, I thought you'd be gone by now.'

Baz frowned, her mood dipping as she was reminded of her own desertion.

'Mac's gone down to Lash to do a favour for a friend – we had to postpone. Do you think you should get some shots for that bite?'

Garry scowled, gave a quick shrug and went inside.

Back upstairs, Baz tipped her vacation packing out on the bed. That had been a waste of time. And now she had three or four days to kill. But she wasn't going to sit around moping. There were stories she could be chasing. She dug under the pile of bikinis, T-shirts and shorts to find her phone.

'Logan?'

'Yo, my favourite woman in Kabul.' Logan's voice was loud and brash – and his familiar accent made Baz feel at home.

'Hi, second favourite guy,' she said.

'Oh, harsh, babe!' They both laughed. 'What can I do for you?'

'You busy? Working?'

'Can take it or leave it.'

'Fancy a short trip – three or four days?'

'Where?'

60

Baz took a deep breath. Was she about to do something stupid?

'Kandahar.'

'Hmm... What's happening there?'

'You heard about that Canadian journalist that got snatched? Brad Kaminski? I thought it might be worth going down there and digging around a bit. Write it up for the paper.'

'Like, you'll need to consider these things, Baz. There are no flights currently to or from Kandahar, so you'd be looking at a road trip. The road from Kabul to Kandahar is five hundred klicks through some real bad country. Then, when you're done, five hundred klicks back again. Kandahar city is crawling with Talibs, militiamen and narco gangs. Brad Kaminski isn't the only westerner to be grabbed there. A Turkish engineer and a couple of UN workers have also been kidnapped this year. You go down there, you'll be wearing a target on your back.' He paused to let it all sink in. 'But if you still wanna go, I'm your guy.'

'Sure, I still want to go. I'll pay you, of course.'

'Damn right you will. I'm not heading down there for free. Not even for you.' Baz heard the pop of a bottle top in the background, then a gulping sound as Logan drank. Beer, no doubt. 'When d'you wanna go?'

'Tomorrow, if you can fix it up.'

''Kay. I'll see if I can get us onto a USPI convoy – there's usually one heading out on a Tuesday.'

'USPI?'

'US Protection and Investigation. Del Spier's outfit. They escort convoys of construction materials up and down between Kabul and Kandahar. It's the safest way to travel.'

'How much will it be?'

'I'll come back to you. If the convoy's full, I might have to pull some strings, pay a bit more. But I'm in with them pretty good, so it shouldn't be a problem.'

It wouldn't be a problem for Baz – the paper would pay for it.

'Logan, you're a star. Let me know what time I need to be ready.'

'Sure. It's a six- or seven-hour drive, so it'll be early.'

Adrenalin spiked as she disconnected the call. She knew Mac wouldn't be happy with her plan, but he was busy. He didn't even have to know until afterwards. She opened their shared wardrobe and pulled out her camera bag to check she had all the kit she might need. She pulled her trusty Nikon D2H from the bag, balancing the familiar weight of it in her hands. It felt good. She felt good. This could be the breakthrough story she'd been looking for.

Day 2

Chapter 11

Lashkar Gah

Following a request from Mac, Nagpal had gathered all the local Well Diggers staff in the large open-plan office that doubled up as their meeting room. There were three engineers, Nagpal's assistant, Vinke's assistant, and assorted drivers, household staff and translators, including Darab. All of them were men. When Ginger and Mac went into the room, there was already a heated discussion going on between Nagpal and a dark-eyed young man in a grimy green *peraahan* and baggy trousers.

Nagpal shut down the conversation on their arrival.

'This is Pasoon,' he said. 'He was Lars's driver, and he's scared now that he'll be out of a job.'

Mac shrugged. It wasn't really their problem, but he could sympathise with the young man. 'Look, Vinke will have to be replaced and the rest of the staff will be back from Kabul soon.'

Ginger nodded. 'Tell him his job's safe for now. Tell all the staff that.'

Nagpal relayed what Ginger had said and the vibe in the room became instantly more mellow.

The purpose of the meeting was to question the staff to see if they knew anything at all about what had happened.

'We need to find out why Well Diggers is being targeted,' Mac had said, over breakfast. 'If we know why, it'll give us a steer on who it might be.'

His plan was to initiate a group discussion in the hope that a consensus might arise, and after that he and Ginger would talk to each staff member individually, in case any of them had any sensitive information that they wouldn't want to mention in front of the group. They would use Nagpal to translate, rather than Darab – as a member of the Sikh community, Nagpal stood apart from the tribal and family loyalties that could have a bearing on what one member of staff might say in front of another.

Now, once everyone was seated and those that wanted it had a cup of tea in front of them, Mac got Nagpal to ask them if they could think of any reason for the attacks or, indeed, any links between them.

Nagpal translated their answers.

'They are westerners and this is a western NGO – that in itself is enough for some people to target Well Diggers,' said one of the engineers.

'What people?' said Mac.

The man shrugged. He wasn't a local – he'd moved down from Kabul to take the job. 'Southern Afghanistan has always been less accommodating to foreign occupation,' he said. In other words, he had nothing specific to offer.

'We're no different to the rest of the country,' said Vinke's assistant, who was a native of Lashkar Gah. 'Mostly this is a welcoming place, but the growth of the opium trade has attracted criminals and gangsters.'

'Do you think this could be linked to the narcos?' said Mac.

One of the other engineers shook his head. 'What we were doing was helping the narcos – the poppy growers were bene-fiting from the restoration of the *karez* system. It wouldn't make sense for them to frighten us away.'

He had a good point. It was difficult to limit the advantages provided by Well Diggers to the legitimate farmers, when more and more of them were turning to the lucrative crop of poppies. Since it sold for nearly four hundred dollars a kilo, growing wheat or okra simply couldn't compete. And the drug barons were more than happy to provide impoverished farmers with the poppy seeds on credit.

'Yes, but when you help one narco, you make an enemy of another,' said a colleague.

One of the drivers spoke up, grinning, and Nagpal laughed.

'He said an old Afghan proverb might help – don't dig wells for others, for you will fall into one yourself.'

'Too right,' said Ginger, with a wry smile.

An engineer shook his head in disagreement.

Nagpal summarised his words. 'He doesn't see that the two incidents are linked. Vinke was a confrontational man – he often argued with staff here and with the people the project came into contact with. He could have insulted someone important.'

'Christ,' said Mac in Ginger's ear. 'That's quite an accusation.'

'Who does he mean by that?' said Ginger, directing the question to Nagpal.

Of course, the guy went quiet. He was in a room full of colleagues. Anything said in here would no doubt get churned through the local rumour mill, and that could have consequences.

Mac made a note of the man's name, Tanvir. He would be one of the first they would want to talk to. Mac's general impression was that Vinke was not well-loved by his staff, but that Bakker was. They were definitely more anxious about finding the head engineer than they were over who had murdered their boss. That in itself was interesting, but none of it had given them any leads.

'If anyone can think of a person or people who might have reason to hold a grudge against Vinke, please let us know. Were there any disciplinary actions taken? Have there been members of staff let go or sacked for any reason?'

'I can look into the records,' said Nagpal. 'There have been replacements made, and the previous staff members might bear looking at.'

Ginger held up the sneaker he'd found under Vinke's body, now in a clear plastic bag. 'Anyone recognise this? It was in the garden of Vinke's house. Maybe it belongs to one of you, or one of the staff that came and went to the house.' He wasn't going to tell them that he'd found it right under Vinke's body.

They all shook their heads and no one claimed the shoe. If it didn't belong to any of the staff, then maybe it had belonged to one of the intruders. It could have come off in the struggle.

'Does it belong to a man or a woman?' said Vinke's assistant.

Nagpal's mobile rang and he glanced at the screen, then held up a hand to the assistant so he could take the call. He nodded and said something, then disconnected.

Mac looked his way.

'That was Commander Gulwal's assistant. He has some news for us.'

'What news?'

Nagpal rolled his eyes. 'Not something the assistant would say over the phone. We have to go to Gulwal's office.'

'Fucking power play,' said Ginger. 'We gotta dance to his tune.'

'Of course we do,' said Mac. 'Okay, break up this meeting – we'll talk to people individually when we get back.'

Nagpal said a quick word to the rest of the staff, then he, Ginger and Mac made their way downstairs.

–

When the three of them arrived at Police HQ, Gulwal was outside, deadheading the rose bushes with the care and attention of a proud parent. He bent towards a branch of blousy pink flowers and breathed in deeply, inviting them to do the same.

'*Salaam alaikum*, Commander,' said Mac. He turned to Nagpal. 'Please tell him his roses are splendid. A labour of love in this heat.'

'A memorial to fallen colleagues,' came the reply. He beckoned them once more to follow him into his office.

'I understand you have some information for us,' said Ginger, once they were settled inside and the round of greetings had been completed.

The smile left Gulwal's face and his expression became serious. He spoke for a minute, pointing and gesturing. Mac waited patiently for Nagpal to get a chance to translate. Every conversation took twice as long and of course was filtered. At least when he'd worked with the police in Kabul, the major had spoken English.

'One of the commander's men came to him this morning and said he'd heard a rumour about a westerner that had been seen, out alone, very early yesterday morning.'

'Where?' said Ginger.

'On the empty land by the riverbank, to the south of the city.'

The Well Diggers house was south of the city centre.

'Where was he going? Did he get a description of the man?' Ginger's rapid-fire questions had already flashed through Mac's brain.

As Nagpal translated the questions for Gulwal, Mac turned away from the two Afghans and murmured to Ginger, 'We need to talk to the policeman directly to get the details. This is like a game of bloody Chinese whispers.'

'I agree,' said Ginger.

'The description that came back was just that the man was European. That's enough here in Lash – you just don't see westerners wandering about on their own, without drivers, interpreters or escorts.'

'Ask him if we can talk to the policeman in question. We'd like to hear from him and see where the man was seen,' said Mac.

He and Ginger didn't need Nagpal's translation to understand that this was going to be a problem. There was a lot of head shaking and hand gestures before Nagpal turned back to them.

'That won't be possible. The policeman in question has gone off duty now and returned to his village.'

'What about the witness? Could we have his name and details?'

Gulwal practically laughed when this was put to him.

'The man making the claims was an addict. He was down on the riverbank smoking opium. The commander thinks you should discount anything he says – after all, if this was your man, it wouldn't seem that he has been taken. In which case, where is he now?'

That might be a valid point, but it simply meant they had to dig deeper.

'We can't totally discount it,' said Mac. 'It's our only lead so far. Please ask the commander for the precise location, so we can make our own enquiries.'

Gulwal shrugged at this request, then gave Nagpal the information they wanted.

'I know the place,' said Nagpal, as they walked back to the Land Rover. 'It's a patch of wasteland, well known as a place where drug addicts congregate.'

'Right, let's go,' said Ginger.

It didn't make sense to Mac. A westerner wandering about by the Helmand River at dawn. No contact from whoever had taken Bakker. Could he have escaped his kidnappers? If so, they needed to find him before anyone else did.

They had no time to lose.

Chapter 12

Lashkar Gah

Lashkar Gah lay some eight kilometres north of the confluence of the Helmand River and the Arghandab River. Mac had looked down at them as the Louis Berger aircraft had come in to land – both waterways were wide and meandering, with gravel shores and sandbanks, and lush green vegetation on their margins. The Helmand ran down the west side of the city, the Arghandab coming in from the north-east, and just to spend time by them provided a sense of relief from the dust, dirt and dry winds that seemed ubiquitous throughout the region. For the children of Lashkar Gah, they were playground and swimming pool rolled into one, for adults they offered cool walks and recreation, and for the less fortunate – the homeless, the drug addicts and petty criminals – there were places on the riverbank to congregate and prey on those even less blessed.

Nagpal knew the place that Gulwal had described to them. To the south-west of the city centre, a narrow sandspit ran parallel to the east bank of the river for maybe five hundred metres. Along this stretch, the vegetation came close to the shore, offering shady nooks and crannies where a person could shelter from the heat of the day. This was where Gulwal's officer reported speaking to an itinerant opium addict, and now Mac was determined to track the man down to see if they could glean more details from him.

They parked the Land Rover as close to the riverbank as possible and then, leaving their driver to watch the vehicle, continued on foot. A narrow path wound down towards the water through a grove of date palms and almond trees. Mac took a deep breath. The trees smelt sweet, but there were undercurrents of fetid water and human excrement as they got closer to the river.

'How will we know our man?' said Ginger.

This would be a problem. Gulwal hadn't given them a physical description of the man, and all they knew was that they were looking for a homeless addict who hung out along this stretch of shore.

'We'll just have to question any likely candidates we come across. The guy the police spoke to might not be the only person who saw the westerner, anyway.'

They emerged from the trees onto a gravel foreshore, littered with detritus that Mac didn't want to look at too closely.

'Nagpal, if we find anyone, can you question them without giving away that we're looking for a European?' said Mac. 'Then if they mention having seen a westerner, we'll know they're not just parroting our question straight back at us.'

'Sure,' said Nagpal. 'I can just ask them if they've seen a stranger down here.'

Ginger dug into his breast pocket and pulled out a photo of Bakker. 'We won't show them the picture until they've given a convincing description.'

'And don't mention the bloody reward, or we'll get no end of porkies,' added Mac.

'Porkies?' said Nagpal. His English was good but didn't quite extend to rhyming slang.

'Porky pies, lies, stories,' said Ginger, with a grim smile. 'The shit people will say when they get a sniff of money.'

They were walking up the riverbank in the direction of the town centre. So far, they'd seen no one, but then Mac spotted movement through a patch of bushes to one side. He pointed, then put a finger to his lips. They didn't want to scare off whoever it might be.

Ginger nodded as Mac waved him forward so they could approach the clump from either end. Nagpal waited just behind Mac, watching closely.

'*Salaam*,' said Mac, peering through a gap between two bushes, expecting whoever was there to try and break away in the opposite direction.

Ginger stood as a block if that were to happen.

But they needn't have worried.

'*Salaam*, Karwan?' The voice was slurred, the words forming slowly in the man's mouth.

Mac stepped forward into a small clearing to show himself. 'I'm not Karwan.'

A young man was lying on the sandy ground, practically tucked under a scrubby thorn bush to make use of the shade it afforded. His hair was matted and filthy, his skin mottled. He was clearly an opium addict – and his hugely dilated pupils told Mac he'd taken a recent hit. Christ knew how he managed to feed his habit. Maybe he'd been a *bacchá bazi*, a dancing boy, making money by prostituting himself to older men, but his addiction had already ruined his looks, and there would always be someone younger to take his place. Though frowned upon, the practice went on all over Afghanistan. It sickened Mac, but the mostly corrupt police forces simply took money from those involved instead of trying to stamp it out.

The youth stared up at Mac, just as Ginger and Nagpal appeared behind him. He was too addled to be frightened, but he struggled into a sitting position, clutching a small cloth bag of belongings to his chest. No doubt he expected to be robbed or beaten.

'*Salaam alaikum*,' said Mac, keeping his voice low and calm. He glanced back at Nagpal. 'Ask him if he's the one who saw a stranger here yesterday morning.'

It was a mistake, to take his eyes off the boy. There was a scuffling sound, and by the time Mac had turned his head back, the kid was barrelling past Ginger and ploughing right through a stand of spiky hawthorn bushes, heading away from the river.

'Fuck! Jesus Christ!' roared Ginger, grabbing at his right arm. 'He fucking shivved me.'

Mac saw a glint of metal in the sunlight as the boy put space between them. Blood was running between Ginger's fingers. Nagpal shouted something, but the kid wasn't going to stop and listen, so Mac launched himself in pursuit.

For someone who had appeared to be high on opium, the boy could run fast. But not fast enough – stamina seemed to be an issue, and after twenty or so metres, he slowed down to a jog. Mac sped up and tackled him, diving low and wrapping his arms around the kid's thighs to topple him to the ground. He prayed that the knife would be knocked out of his grasp, or that he'd be winded, but as they both fell, he could see his quarry's arms flailing round like a windmill, the silver blade still flashing. As his weight hit the dirt, he felt a sharp stone dig into his hip – the pain was intense, reverberating through him. The boy grunted loudly as he was winded. As he gasped for air like a landed fish, Mac pushed himself up onto his knees and moved his grip to pin the kid to the ground. He shuffled forward so he could use his body weight to keep the boy still. Then he grabbed the arm which held the knife and slammed it against a large stone. The boy's grip stayed firm, even as he fought for breath. Mac slammed the knife arm down again and again, and finally the boy's grasp weakened, and the blade skittered away on the gravel.

By now, Nagpal had caught up with them.

Mac was panting, and he wasn't going to make the same mistake twice. He kept his attention trained on the body beneath his. As the addict replenished his oxygen, he was starting to struggle.

Nagpal came closer and bent down to talk to the boy. Mac had no idea what he said, but the kid stopped moving. Everything was quiet, apart from two sets of laboured breathing.

'Okay,' said Mac. 'We're not here to hurt you. We just want to ask you some questions.'

Nagpal translated and the boy replied to him, his voice rising to a whine.

'He wants money,' said Nagpal.

'Little shit,' said Ginger, catching them up, his ashen face crumpled with fury. His shirt sleeve was drenched with blood.

Mac sighed and considered standing up to release the boy, but thought better of it, and remained in place, pinning him to the ground. He pulled a twenty-dollar bill from his trouser pocket and dangled it in front of the boy's face. 'Tell him he can have this if he just tells us what he saw.'

'He says he doesn't know what you're talking about,' reported Nagpal a few seconds later.

But Mac had seen the hunger flash in his eyes when he'd seen the twenty. The kid was yanking their chain. He used one knee to apply pressure to the kid's upper thigh – an implicit threat.

'He saw a man here yesterday. I need him to describe him.'

The boy shook his head.

'He says it was just a man.'

'But a westerner?'

'Sure. He thinks so.'

'He thinks so?' said Ginger. 'Bakker has red hair and pale skin. You could hardly mistake him for a local.'

'Could have been a local with a penchant for henna,' said Mac. Plenty of Pashtun men used henna to redden their beards, but a local would probably be wearing a turban or the squat felt hat called a *pakul*, whereas westerners generally went bare-headed or wore baseball caps.

Nagpal translated and the boy shook his head emphatically, speaking at some length.

'I think he's just saying what he thinks you want to hear now,' said Nagpal. 'Repeating back whatever I say to him – and he's changed his mind twice about the colour of the man's hair.'

'Ask him where he thinks the man was going or what he was doing,' said Mac.

'He was running down the shore,' Nagpal reported back. 'The boy saw him through the bushes. It was just getting light.'

'And he was wearing?'

'Western clothes.' It was hardly a satisfactory answer, but then they didn't actually know what Bakker was wearing when he went missing, so it made no difference. None of what the witness said sounded particularly convincing.

Mac released the pressure and moved to one side as the boy wriggled free. As they both clambered to their feet, the boy held out a hand for the money.

'Don't give it to him,' said Ginger. 'He hasn't earned it.' He still sounded furious.

But Mac handed over the note. He knew it would vanish into the hungry maw of the narco economy, but at least it would buy the kid a few more minutes' oblivion from his shitty life.

Ginger glared at him. 'Twenty dollars and a ruined shirt. All for a fucking junkie's pipe dream.' He shook his head and turned back towards the riverbank. 'Come on, I need a beer.'

'And a tetanus jab,' said Mac with a grin.

Chapter 13

Kabul

Baz was ready and waiting at seven when Logan rolled up outside Le Monde in his Toyota Surf. Javid had already shifted her backpack and camera bag to the compound gate, and he quickly helped her load them into the Surf's trunk, squeezing them into the small space not taken up by gas cans, bottled water, a gun case and Logan's own backpack.

'Miss Basima-jan,' he said as he slammed the back of the vehicle shut, 'are you sure you're not wanting me to accompany you to Kandahar?'

Since she'd first hired him as her driver a year ago, Javid had taken on the self-appointed role of guardian and protector. It was sweet, and she was fond of him, but sometimes his attention was suffocating.

'No, Javid-jan. Your wife and family can't spare you. I'll be with Logan, so I'll be absolutely fine.'

Javid gave Logan a suspicious glare through the Surf's side window. He barely trusted Mac to take her anywhere, and in his view travelling alone with Logan was a step too far. But Baz knew she would be way safer with Logan – ex-US Special Forces, armed with a Beretta and an AK, and ready to use both – than with Javid and his hand-me-down Makarov.

Baz laughed. 'Stop worrying, Javid. I'll be back in three or four days, okay?'

'*Insha'Allah*,' said Javid, a grave look on his face.

'That guy thinks he's your father, right?' said Logan, cracking a grin as she climbed into the front next to him.

'He wishes, but he's actually younger than me,' said Baz, waving her protector away as Logan started the engine.

'Right, let's gun it. The convoy leaves from the USPI office in Wazir Akbar Khan District at eight, and if we're not with them, they'll go without us.'

Even at seven in the morning, the traffic in Kabul was stacking up. Minibuses bringing workers into the centre, battered jingle trucks piled high with produce for the city's markets, cars, taxis, bikes, scooters, night soil carts – all were jostling for position, trying to jump the lights, and simply didn't care if they blocked another driver's path. Lane discipline was replaced with lane drift, and the only way they communicated was with their horns.

'Jesus H. Christ,' muttered Logan under his breath, as he slammed on the brakes to avoid hitting a woman on a moped who'd just cut across in front of them. 'Doesn't anyone in this godforsaken place take a driving test?' Hitting another car on the way to work seemed to be a badge of honour.

They made it to the USPI office with less than a minute to spare. The convoy was lining up under the direction of a small, burly Hazara. He stood in the middle of the street, shouting orders and waving his arms to direct a succession of colourfully decorated jingle trucks into position behind a black Hilux that literally bristled with armed men. The trucks were painted in bright shades of red, yellow and green, and festooned with ribbons and the numerous small bells that gave them their name. The roar of the engines almost drowned out the tinkling bells, and Baz could hear the grating hoarseness in the Hazara's throat as he tried to make himself heard over the din.

Getting out of the Surf, Logan gave the man a wave and he came over. Introductions were made – his name was Aaban – and he collected Baz's 120-dollar tariff for joining the convoy. They were slotted in behind a second Hilux of armed men, mostly clutching AK47s with the odd PK machine gun thrown into the mix, and in front of a large tanker. There were three escort vehicles in all, one at the front, one in the middle and one bringing up the rear, protecting half a dozen lorries. The rear escort vehicle was a Toyota technical – so called due to the heavy machine gun mounted on the back.

'Sweet,' said Logan, surveying the armaments. 'What a darling!'

Baz look across at him. 'What are you talking about?'

'Look there, it's a Soviet DShK,' he said, pointing at the technical. 'Afghan's machine gun of choice since 1979. Commonly known as a Dushka, which means darling in Russian.'

They got back into the Surf, and Baz realised they were the only private car in the convoy.

A moment later, Aaban climbed into the lead Hilux and waved an arm out of the window to signal they were on the move.

'Let's roll,' murmured Logan, gunning his engine impatiently.

Baz felt a flutter of excitement, tinged with anxiety, deep in her belly. The unknown lay ahead of them – the long, dangerous road from Kabul to Kandahar. Five hundred kilometres on Afghanistan's notorious ring road. Bandit country, according to Logan. The first 150 klicks were through the mountains to Ghazni, a highway that was busy enough to make it relatively safe. But after that they would be into the barren stretches of the notorious Tarnak Valley – no man's land.

Baz tried not to think about it. They would be fine. The jingling bells and bright colours made the convoy seem more like a carnival procession, and for a moment it felt like the first day of vacation, with Logan chewing gum at the wheel beside her and Boz Skaggs on the stereo competing with the noises of the city as they drove out of Kabul.

As expected, the road to Ghazni was busy with traffic in both directions, most of it freight – tankers, lorries hauling battered, rusty containers, jingle trucks, lumber wagons and hay carts – all spewing filthy engine fumes, the drivers raucous with their horns, cursing out of their open windows and many of them quite openly smoking *chars* – hashish joints – as they drove.

The convoy made regular stops to allow the truckers to refill from the gas cans they all carried with them, or to relieve themselves. Baz was the only woman on the convoy, and mostly the men didn't realise she was there, so several times she had to look away as drivers urinated or worse, right by the side of the road where they'd stopped their trucks. When she needed to go, she scurried up an embankment and disappeared behind a large boulder, leaving Logan standing just below to make sure she wasn't followed.

After a couple of hours, they reached Ghazni, where the convoy picked up two more jingle trucks at a brief stop. But Aaban wasted no time in getting them back on the road and as they left the town behind them and the landscape became drier and harsher, Baz sensed the carnival mood of earlier melting away.

'Keep your eyes peeled on the sides of the road up ahead,' said Logan, 'and let me know if you see anything – anything at all – that seems suspicious.'

'Sure.' Baz took a drink of water nervously. Had she been wise to suggest this trip? She still hadn't told Mac about it, and now she wished she had. What if something happened before she had the chance to speak to him again? But she couldn't call him now. She glanced over at Logan. He looked relaxed, drumming his fingers on the steering wheel in time to the music, his own gaze intent on the road ahead.

Nothing would happen.

That was the point of travelling in a convoy. If there were any bandits out there looking to make a quick buck from stealing someone else's goods, they'd target the drivers who were foolish enough to set out along this road on their own. The USPI convoy was travelling with twelve heavily armed guards – they weren't to be messed with.

At around lunchtime they stopped for Dhuhr prayers. Baz and Logan stretched their legs and ate a light meal of naan and fruit, and Logan stood guard while the men prayed. The heat was brutal and there was no shade anywhere. Sweat beaded on Baz's forehead and the back of her neck, and the body of the Surf was too hot to lean against.

'Last leg,' said Logan, as they climbed back into the vehicle.

Baz's seat felt hot as she sank onto it. There was no way of cooling it down. 'My God, I'm going to take a long cold shower when we get to the guesthouse.'

Aaban waved and the convoy roared into life again. Down here, the scenery was monotonous. The road followed the bare trickle of the Tarnak River as it wound between low hills of parched ochre. A few scrubby bushes dotted the riverbank, and small villages, ringed by almond trees, came and went at ever-increasing intervals. As they jingled through the dust, they were the only vehicles on the road, and the only living thing Baz saw in an hour was a buzzard circling high above them, black wings spread in a piercing blue sky.

'What the fuck is that?' Logan's urgent question snapped Baz out of her reverie.

She peered through the dusty windshield at the road ahead, though her view was blocked by the trucks between them and the lead Hilux. But a dark column of smoke was rising into the air just beyond the next bend in the road.

'That's trouble,' said Logan. 'Get my AK off the back seat.'

Baz twisted round and grabbed the AK. She also pulled her camera bag between the seats and got out her camera, hanging it around her neck. She knew from experience that putting on her journalist's hat when things got hairy was one of the best ways of staying calm.

She held the AK between her knees, ready to hand it to Logan at a moment's notice. It wasn't like any AK she'd ever seen, as the weapon had been heavily modified. It had a collapsible telescopic butt from an M4 and sported a Picatinny rail with a fancy optical sight. Hardly surprising – Logan was always incredibly particular about the kit he used. She'd once asked him why he favoured an old AK over a more modern American M4, and he'd told her it was because AK ammunition was easier to come by – the whole damn country was awash with it. However, he'd made that AK into the best weapon it could be.

The convoy had slowed down now, and she could see Aaban holding up his hand to bring them to a halt. The technical sped up past them on the road's opposite lane, stopping to confer with the first vehicle.

'If it all kicks off,' said Logan, 'crouch down in the footwell until I tell you to get out. I'll try and get us close enough to some rocks for cover.'

It all kicked off.

Chapter 14

Kandahar–Ghazni Highway

The Surf was rocked by the shockwave from a huge explosion. A burst of flames and soot-black smoke spewed skyward, and before Baz had regained her equilibrium the ratter-tat-tat of automatic gunfire sounded up ahead.

Logan threw himself out of the vehicle.

'You drive,' he yelled, running around to the passenger side and yanking open Baz's door. 'They're going to need our fire-power.'

Baz leapt out and ran around to the driver's seat. She revved the engine, swerved the Surf out of the line of the convoy and drove as fast as she dared up to where the two Hiluxes and the technical were roaring off ahead of them. As she fell in behind the technical, Logan gave a thumbs-up to the guy manning the Dushka. He responded with a two-fingered salute.

Baz concentrated on driving as fast as she could, with enough precision to keep them behind the protective cover of the vehicles ahead. Logan opened the passenger window, braced his legs in the footwell and leaned out, holding the AK in the firing position. The column of black smoke ahead was larger now and as they rounded a bend in the road, Baz could see orange flames licking up through the base of the column. The source was a stricken oil tanker that had jackknifed across both lanes, the back end of it now a roiling inferno. Two men lay in the road close by, but Baz couldn't tell if it was the explosion that had knocked them down or gunshot wounds. Two other men were crouching in the lee of the cab, taking fire from somewhere ahead of the tanker.

The Hiluxes and the technical fanned out to create a row some twenty feet back from the tanker. Men streamed out, firing, the Dushka providing cover for them as they ran towards a rocky outcrop on the left-hand side of the road. Whoever had taken out the tanker was still shooting – as far as Baz could tell, incoming fire was hailing down on them from at least three separate positions. She could see why they'd chosen this particular spot for an attack – the rocky bluffs had narrowed the road into a gully, which had now been turned into a kill zone.

'Get round the back of the car,' shouted Logan, firing from behind the cover of the front wheel and the engine block.

Baz jumped out on her side, crouched low and scurried to the rear end of the Surf. Logan came back on his side, and they squatted, panting, out of the line of fire for now.

'Who is it?' said Baz, taking the lens cap off her camera.

Logan shrugged. 'Could be the Taliban wanting to disrupt oil supplies. Could be robbers wanting to jack the tanker. Or the settling of a tribal score.'

'You're kidding? They take things that far?'

'And further,' muttered Logan, breaking cover at the side of the vehicle to let off a round in the direction of the top of the bluff.

Baz stood up and edged her head above the line of the Surf's roof – she needed to get a series of shots of the burning tanker and the firefight that surrounded it.

'Fucking get down,' spat Logan. 'Or d'you want the top of your head blown off?'

As he said it, a round whistled past Baz's ear, and she dropped like a stone. She'd got some pictures, but her heart felt like it would explode as adrenalin flooded through her. Her hands were shaking too much for her to review the images she'd taken – that could wait until later. For now, she just wished it was over.

Logan carried on firing intermittently, and as Baz's heart rate returned to normal she lifted her camera above the roofline of the Surf to fire off some more shots using the motor drive. God knows what they'd show – but that was how you got an award-winning shot.

'Shit. The guy on the Dushka. He's down.'

Baz peered cautiously around the side of the Surf. The young man who'd given them a confident salute just minutes ago was slumped over the rim of the technical, blood gushing from a stomach wound that, given their situation, would almost certainly be fatal. The priority now was to win the firefight, and as she watched, the nearest of Aaban's men dropped his AK and sprang onto the back of the utility vehicle. He unceremoniously shoved his compadre to one side and took control of the Dushka, showering round after furious round across the hillside. Baz helped Logan replenish his magazines from the spare rounds in the back of the Surf, and he kept up the pressure on the attackers.

The return fire was slowing and then stopped.

Aaban, who'd been firing from the cover of a jagged boulder halfway up the slope, shouted something and held an arm up in the air.

There was a minute's silence as the men waited. Nothing happened and the silence stretched into two minutes. One of the men who'd been behind the tanker shouted something to Aaban, then stepped out from his cover.

He drew no fire.

The attackers were either dead or had fled.

Aaban's men let out a cheer of relief and quickly ran to give attention to a couple of wounded men. Baz broke cover to take pictures of the aftermath, as Logan jogged over to Aaban for a conflab. A couple of the gunmen were directed to climb the bluff to check for stragglers, but the word quickly came back that there were three dead men, and they'd heard the sound of a vehicle receding in the distance, its dust cloud visible through binoculars as it headed into the wilds of the desert.

They were safe. For now.

Baz went across to the two men who had been firing from behind the tanker. They had moved well away from their vehicle now, and were bent over the bodies of the two shot men lying in the road. The tanker fire was still burning with a fierce intensity and the surrounding air was scorched and fume-laden. As Baz got closer, she saw that one of the stricken men was struggling for breath. They were trying to help him, but then a long wail from the older man told her that they hadn't succeeded.

'My son, my son,' he cried in Pashto. The rest of his words were a jumble of distress that Baz couldn't understand.

The younger man clutched the victim's body to his chest, tears streaming down his face. Baz guessed he must have been the dead man's brother.

She squatted down in front of him. 'Who did this to you?' she said, speaking in Pashto.

The kid looked up at her, his startling blue-green eyes shimmering. He glanced down at the dead man and swept black hair back from his forehead. The man had the same turquoise eyes, now staring emptily at the sky.

'Do you know?' said Baz.

He nodded. 'I know. It was Turyalai Khan. He was here. He shot Said.'

'He's from another tribe?'

He looked at her with disgust. 'Tribe? No. He owns three tankers. He wants to take our business from us.'

Baz could hardly fathom it. If this was the way business rivals behaved to each other, what hope was there for peace at any level? But the fact that people had to run these sorts of risks daily to operate a business or make a living needed to be documented. Taking photographs of such distress to turn it into a news story seemed horribly intrusive, but how else would the world know what was happening here, in this country where God came to cry? Baz blinked back her own tears and continued snapping until she felt Logan's arm around her shoulder, and he led her away.

'Come on, let's get going.'

Baz looked around. The convoy was in disarray, the road was blocked by the tanker, and Aaban seemed to be involved in several high-volume arguments with different drivers.

'What do you mean?' she said.

'We'll hit the road. We can get round the tanker, but most of the convoy can't. They're arguing over whether to try to move it, or whether to turn back towards Ghazni.'

'You mean continue to Kandahar on our own?'

'It's just over an hour's drive away. Maybe less, because we'll be able to move faster.'

'But it won't be safe. What if those attackers are still out there?'

Logan cracked a grin and brandished his AK. 'Come on, babe, lightning doesn't strike twice. We're no threat to their trucking operations – we'll be fine.'

'*Insha'Allah*,' said Baz under her breath.

Chapter 15

Lashkar Gah

Nagpal checked the company's email accounts and Mac checked the internet, but both of them drew blanks. There was no message from Bakker's kidnappers, no messages from the police reporting any new leads, and nothing from Governor Khaliq's office, even though Mac was sure he knew more than he was letting on.

They were back at the HAVA building and Mac felt as if the day so far had been a complete waste of time. They'd stopped off at the Italian Hospital on their return from the riverbank – Ginger's bicep now sported a couple of stitches – and they'd sent one of the drivers to fetch a clean shirt from the house. At least the guy had managed to miss the regimental wings tattooed at the top of Ginger's arm, so that was something to be thankful for.

'Just because there's no message from any kidnappers, it doesn't mean he's not being held,' said Ginger, pulling on the fresh shirt carefully over his bandaged arm. 'After all, it's either that or he would have turned up dead.'

Mac thought for a second. 'The Taliban are pretty efficient at making their demands known.'

'So maybe it's not the Taliban. Maybe it's some other group who need money or want to frighten the shit out of the interfering westerners. What do you think, Nagpal?'

Nagpal tugged on his beard as he considered it. 'I think you could be right. The governor's cousin, Feda Khaliq, is a vicious man, and certainly Lars's enemy. But he's not the only candidate.'

'Do any of the local narco gangs have form?' said Mac.

'Form?'

'Sorry – have they done it before? Kidnapped any westerners?'

Nagpal shrugged. 'I think there have been kidnappings that have gone wrong. Westerners have definitely ended up dead.'

That killed the conversation, but then Nagpal dug a folder out from under a pile of papers on his desk. He held it out to Mac.

'Here – this is a list of staff who have left in the past year. Some for benign reasons, but I've marked a couple of the names – workers who Lars sacked or who left after a disagreement with him.'

Mac took the folder. 'Anything so bad that they would want to come back and kill him?'

'It's probably unlikely,' said Nagpal. 'The disputes are petty. But we have to also remember how valuable a job with a western company can seem. Working for Well Diggers confers a certain status and pays much better than working for an Afghan business.'

Mac opened the folder and looked at the list of names. They meant nothing to him but he supposed it might be worth their while to check these men out.

He was starting to feel despondent about the whole case, but luckily salvation came in the form of lunch. Nagpal had sent his assistant out for bolani – soft naans, warm from the griddle, filled with potatoes, spring onions and a blend of herbs and spices that was different depending on which roadside food stall they came from.

Mac bit into his, savouring the mix of flavours. It was scant consolation for their lack of progress, but pleasurable enough to enjoy for five uninterrupted minutes.

Apparently, even that was too much to ask.

Darab, the interpreter, appeared in the doorway. 'Can I speak with you?'

'Sure,' said Mac. 'Come in.'

'I think I have heard something that you might want to know.'

Ginger pointed him to one of the empty chairs and then came round to stand behind where Mac was sitting at a desk.

Mac swallowed the last of his bolani. 'Go on.'

'I have a cousin who lives in Sayed Sermohammad Kalay.'

'Where's that?' said Mac.

'South of Lash,' said Nagpal from the other side of the office, 'in Garmser District.' He pointed to an area on the Perspex-covered map of Helmand Province that graced the wall above his desk.

Darab looked at Mac for permission to continue. Mac nodded at him.

'When I was talking to my cousin last night, he said something that sounded strange to me. He said that he'd seen a westerner on the road heading south.'

'How did he mean on the road?' said Mac. 'Not walking, surely?'

'No, not walking,' said Darab with a shake of his head. 'He said he saw the man sitting in the back of a Surf.'

'That is odd,' said Ginger.

'Why?' said Mac.

'Because the countryside south of Garmser is pretty much a no-go area for westerners,' Ginger replied. 'And if anyone did need to venture down there, they wouldn't go without a proper escort. You'd want at least three vehicles, better four or five.'

'That's what my cousin thought,' said Darab. 'And the way the man was staring out of the car window. There was fear in his eyes.'

'Did your cousin describe him?'

'A westerner. That's all.'

Mac frowned and looked at Ginger.

'He's not wrong,' said Ginger. 'A westerner in Garmser would stick out like a sore thumb.'

'Can your cousin ask around, see if there's any chatter in the area?'

Darab's eyes narrowed as he shook his head.

Nagpal intervened. 'That would be asking a man to put himself in danger. If he happens to hear something, we'll know, but he's not going to draw attention to himself by asking questions.'

Darab gave him a look of gratitude.

'Fair enough,' said Ginger.

'Thank you, Darab,' said Mac. 'It's good information.'

Darab left the office.

'So what d'you think?' said Ginger. 'Is it a lead?'

'It's a lead,' said Mac. 'The question is what we do with it.'

'Get digging,' said Ginger.

'Nagpal,' said Mac, twisting in his chair to face him. 'What does this suggest to you? Any clue in this as to who might be holding him?'

'Garmser is an important area for opium cultivation,' said Nagpal. 'The Helmand River runs south through the district before it heads away to the west. The different narco factions fight for territory along the fertile river plain. To the south and east of this lies the Registan Desert – the Dasht-e Margo or Desert of Death – stretching to Bahram Chah on the Pakistan border. All of that area is under the control of Akhtar Jamali.'

'The Baloch drug baron, right?' said Ginger.

Nagpal nodded.

'What about where Bakker was seen? Who controls that area?'

'Sayed Sermohammad Kalay is in the north-west of Garmser District, only about forty kilometres south of here. The village falls under Governor Khaliq's protection, but it lies on the main road south, and we don't know that Sermohammad was their final destination.'

'And the cultivation of opium in that area?'

'The governor's cousin, Feda Khaliq. Who Lars Vinke had a poor relationship with.'

'Do the Taliban also have a presence?'

'There are local pockets, but they're not well organised. The region relies on the opium trade, and although the Taliban will turn a blind eye to it, it still means the local community is more loyal to the tribal leaders who control the poppies.'

'Makes sense,' said Mac. 'You don't bite the hand that feeds you.'

He turned over the facts in his mind. The dots were all there to be joined, except for one thing. Having killed Vinke, what was their purpose in taking Bakker? Where was the ransom demand or the video of his execution? What would a particular narco faction have to gain by what had happened?

'I think we need to confront the governor,' said Mac. 'If his cousin is holding Bakker, he'll know it, and take some advantage from it. If he says he can't help us, then we can be sure that it's not Feda who's behind Bakker's abduction.'

'And what then?' said Ginger.

'Then we head south and start hunting.'

—

Governor Wadaan Khaliq glared at Mac through narrowed eyes. Certainly, he'd agreed to speak with the Well Diggers contingent, but at the same time, he hadn't been well pleased at having his afternoon interrupted.

Mac, Nagpal and Ginger were shown into the cavernous meeting hall of the governor's office. There was a long, low table running down the centre of the room, lined on either side with intricately designed Ersari rugs and floor cushions. Khaliq himself sat on a low chair made of carved wood with a braided leather seat – ensuring that his head would be higher than any of his guests. He was already a tall man, and his silver beard and black-and-white striped turban gave him an air of authority.

Greetings had been exchanged, and tea had been served before Mac carefully brought the subject of conversation around to the missing man. Nagpal translated his words into Pashto, causing the governor's hawk-like features to darken.

'He wants to know why you think your man is being held in Garmser.'

Mac explained.

Khaliq shrugged.

'He says your witness was probably mistaken.'

Mac watched Khaliq closely every time Nagpal spoke to him, but ultimately the visit proved a waste of time.

'He didn't have a fucking clue,' said Mac to Ginger, as they climbed back into the Land Rover. 'We're on our own.'

'Nagpal, can you lean on Darab for more information?' said Ginger.

Mac didn't wait for Nagpal's answer. He was mentally totting up what they'd need to mount a rescue mission. Manpower. Weapons. Information. Now was the time to secure the first two of those, while they waited for the third. Because as soon as they had a clearer steer as to where Bakker was being held, he wanted to be ready to go.

And there was one man who could help them. It was time to call Logan.

Chapter 16

Kandahar

The cool water was a balm, and Baz stood under the soft rain of the Continental Guesthouse's shared shower for far longer than she knew she should, given that clean water was a scarce commodity in Afghanistan.

The rest of their journey had been thankfully uneventful, and she and Logan had rolled into Kandahar late in the afternoon, the sweat dried on their bodies and the smell of the tanker fire still hanging inside the car. They went straight to the Continental and checked in. This was the place that Brad Kaminski had been staying in before he went missing, so she'd be able to start digging into what had happened as soon as she'd washed away the grit and grime of the journey.

She dried herself slowly. She knew she ought to ring Mac and let him know where she was. But she still felt shaken up from the events on the road, and Mac would be furious with her for making such a risky journey. Not to mention the fact that any show of sympathy from him would have her in tears, so she decided to put the call off for a couple of hours, until after dinner.

Dressed and refreshed, she went to find Logan – who was, as she expected, already in the Continental's tiny honour bar drinking beer like it was a cure-all for the rigours of the day.

'Better?' he said, as he opened another bottle and held it out to her.

She took the offered drink, her fingers wrapping round the cold glass gratefully.

'Sure.' She nodded. 'Yup, I'm fine.' She was telling herself as much as him.

'Spoken to Mac yet?'

'Later,' she said. 'He's probably busy.'

Logan looked surprised by this, but he didn't say anything.

It was time to change the subject. 'I need to find René Hausmann, the photographer who was with Kaminski when he was snatched.'

The boy who'd showed them to their rooms was perfectly willing to give up Hausmann's room number when Baz flashed a five-dollar bill in front of his nose, and ten minutes later she was knocking on the French Canadian's door.

'*Entrez.*'

She nervously pushed open the door, unsure of the reception she would get.

René Hausmann was sitting on his bed sorting through camera equipment, but he stood up as she came in.

'Yes? Can I help you?'

'My name's Baz Khan. I'm a reporter for the *Baltimore Sun*. I want to write a piece about Brad Kaminski, and I wondered if you would talk to me?'

'*Merde!*' Hausmann looked away to one side, and Baz saw a jagged red scar, still fresh and raw, stretching down the side of his ear and onto his jawline.

She stood her ground. This was her job.

Hausmann processed whatever thoughts he was having and turned back to her. 'Sure, sure, we can talk. A story about Brad will put more pressure on our government to get him back.'

Baz stepped into the room and closed the door. 'You think they're not doing enough?' She'd seen the grainy video shots – Brad Kaminski, cowed and beaten, on his knees with his hands tied in front of him, flanked by armed, masked Talibs.

Hausmann shrugged. 'They say they won't pay the ransom the kidnappers are demanding.'

'But that's just in public, surely. Behind the scenes it will be different...' No one could be sure of that. 'Can you tell me what happened when they took him?'

Hausmann retold the story which he must have told a dozen times already – how he and Kaminski were visiting Karqa Sharif, the Shrine of the Cloak of the Prophet, where Mullah Omar had famously donned the cloak said to have been worn by Mohammed and proclaimed himself Commander of the Faithful, leader of the Taliban. Hausmann's voice was almost devoid of emotion, as if he had to disconnect himself from the events.

'Mullah Omar and the Prophet's cloak is the thing of legends, and we just wanted to see where it happened. It would have made a great story. We didn't mean any harm, but while we were there an old guy came over to us and started shouting. It seemed like he wanted us to leave. Brad told him to get lost, and he went away.'

Baz's heart sank. These idiots had been blundering around one of the Pashtuns' holiest shrines with no sensitivity. 'Then what happened?'

'After about ten minutes, he came back with a group of men – black turbans, black robes. A couple of them were armed, and they all seemed angry. We were about to leave anyway, so we tried to defuse the situation by turning our backs on them and walking away.' He paused for a second, his throat dry. 'They came after us. I heard their footsteps quicken and I broke into a run. I managed to get away, but Brad wasn't so lucky. One of them grabbed him, then they were all onto him. I didn't know what to do. If I went back for him, they would have taken me too.'

'And your head?' said Baz, pointing to the wound on the side of his face.

Hausmann shook his head. 'One of them ran after me, grabbed for me. I stumbled and we both fell – I don't quite know how this happened. I think he hit me with his pistol, but

96

I managed to get away. I kicked him hard as I got to my feet, so I was able to escape.' He dropped down to sit on the edge of the bed.

Telling the story had drained Hausmann, and Baz wasn't surprised. It must have been terrifying to realise that his colleague hadn't got away. How could he not be blaming himself? But at the same time, she wasn't entirely sympathetic. They shouldn't have just turned up at the shrine. They should have asked for permission to visit, which they probably wouldn't have been granted. Baz knew that a Canadian Broadcasting Corporation crew had been allowed to film in the grounds, but that was only because their security consultant had known whose palms to grease with a hefty wad, and even they hadn't been allowed inside the shrine.

'What paper do you and Brad work for?'

'We don't. We're freelancers.'

Inexperienced idiots, in other words. But Baz knew better than to let her feelings show.

'Thanks for talking to me. I'll do a story, and maybe it will add to the pressure on your government to get Brad back. But I'm sure they'll be working behind the scenes anyway.'

Hausmann snorted. 'If they are, I know nothing about it.'

Of course he didn't. He wouldn't be included in the loop in a million years.

–

She found Logan in his room, beer in hand, and a lingering smell of *chars* on the air.

'Find your guy?' he said.

She nodded. 'Prize idiots, running around where they had no right to be.'

Logan's phone buzzed on the bedside table. He picked it up and looked at the screen. 'Mac,' he said to Baz. 'Hey bro, we got here safe – just!'

'Where? What are you talking about?' Baz could hear a tinny rendition of Mac's voice.

'You didn't tell him?' mouthed Logan.

Baz shook her head.

Logan held out the phone to her.

'Hi, guess who?' she said. She couldn't help the huge grin on her face.

'Baz? You're with Logan? What's going on? Where are you?'

'Kandahar.'

'What the fuck?'

'I wanted to come down here and report on the Kaminski kidnapping.'

'But you were going to go to Dubai.'

'I changed my mind.'

There was silence at the other end of the line as he digested her words. When he spoke again, he sounded pissed.

'What did Logan mean that you only just got there safely?'

Shit.

'It was nothing. We came down with a USPI convoy. It was fine.' Time to distract him before he dug deeper. 'What did you want to talk to Logan about?'

Mac sighed. 'All right, we'll talk about your adventures later. We're putting together a rescue mission – our kidnapped man was spotted about forty kilometres south of here. Logan's got an in with Governor Khaliq, who I've already pissed off, so I want him to sort out a contingent from Khaliq's militia to accompany us.'

'Okay. Catch you later.' She handed the phone back to Logan, relieved that she'd avoided having to go into the details of the tanker attack.

Chapter 17

Lashkar Gah

'So that's it then,' said Mac, leaning back in his chair and putting his feet up on Vinke's desk. 'We've spoken to every member of the local staff and none of them have offered us jack shit that we can use.'

Nagpal raised a quizzical eyebrow, but it was clear that he understood what Mac meant.

'We'd better move onto that list of people who've left or were sacked.' It all seemed a bit desperate to Mac, but where else could they turn?

Ginger scanned the current personnel list. 'Wait.'

'What?' said Mac.

'We've never spoken to Nazanina, have we?'

'Who's Nazanina?' said Mac.

'She cleans the expat houses,' said Nagpal. 'She doesn't come into the office.'

'She sometimes stays at the houses,' explained Ginger. 'She wasn't there the night that Vinke was killed, but we should still question her. She might have seen something leading up to it in the days before.'

Mac shrugged. 'It's possible. How often does she clean the houses?'

'Every day, of course,' said Nagpal.

'Really?' Ginger shook his head. 'I don't think anyone's cleaned the house we're in.' He glanced over at Mac.

'No,' said Mac. 'That beer you spilled on the floor's gone tacky now.'

'That's odd,' said Nagpal.

'Where does she live?' said Ginger.

'She sleeps in the kitchen at Vinke's house some nights, and goes back to her family home from Thursday to Saturday each week. I sent her a message telling her not to come back to Vinke's for the time being, so that's probably why you haven't seen her.'

'But the night he died?' There was a sudden urgency in Mac's voice. 'Wednesday night? She would have been there, right?'

'There was no sign of her that morning,' said Nagpal. 'I just assumed she'd gone back to her village that night – or she would have been there.'

'For fuck's sake – we need to find her and ask her if she was there. She might be the only witness to what happened.'

Nagpal's face darkened. 'If she had witnessed it, do you think the killer would have left her there alive?'

'You think they might have taken her along with Bakker?' said Ginger.

Mac shook his head. 'She'd have no value to them. But...' Mac sucked in air through his lower teeth.

'What?' said Ginger.

'Nagpal, what do you know about Nazanina? Could she be in some way involved?'

'Come on, an old woman?' Ginger raised his hands in disbelief.

Nagpal leaned forward in his chair. 'Not so old – she's about forty-five, a widow.'

'What's her background? Could she have links to whoever took Bakker? Remember, someone opened the door to the killer.'

'Her clan lives in Gereshk.' Nagpal shrugged. 'I can't say who they're connected with or loyal to.'

'And she could have let them in under duress,' added Mac. 'We need to find her and talk to her. Can you undertake that, Nagpal?'

Nagpal nodded. 'Yes, I'll make enquiries.'

'And keep us posted if you find anything out,' said Mac.

Some intelligence on what happened that night might give them a much-needed steer for the rescue mission. Otherwise, they were pissing into the wind.

–

It was a troubling thought, and one that stopped Mac from sleeping. There was no air-conditioning in the Well Diggers house, and the heat was crushing. But it wasn't the blanket of hot, heavy air that oppressed him. His mind wouldn't stop churning, tumbling thought over thought like a cement mixer. What if? What if? What if…? He didn't know Tomas Bakker, and Ginger had only met him fleetingly, but Bakker's life was probably in their hands. If – and it was a huge if – the man was still alive, the decisions Mac took in the next few hours would be crucial. And not only for Bakker. He would be putting Ginger in danger, and himself too. A hostage rescue mission was an action of last resort – of course, negotiation and bargaining were always preferable. Hostage retrieval via ransom payment or prisoner exchange was a dangerous game, but they didn't even have that option. So instead, they were looking at what could easily be construed as a suicide mission…

The film of sweat covering Mac's body turned ice cold without offering relief from the heat. He felt feverish. He lay with his eyes shut, willing himself to sleep, but his body twitched and he couldn't get comfortable. More than once he sat bolt upright, wide awake and listening for a sound he thought he'd heard, balanced on the thin line between sleep and waking. But there was nothing but the low thrumming of the cicadas in the garden outside.

He forced himself to lie down again. He closed his eyes.

He wished he'd never come down to Lashkar Gah, because he had a feeling that something – he didn't know what – was going to go badly wrong in the days that followed. He'd had these feelings before, call them premonitions if you like, and they'd always played out...

A ferocious banging on the door pulled him out of the black tunnel of sleep he'd finally slid into.

What the fuck?

It was still dark. Rolling off the side of the bed onto his feet, he grabbed his pistol off the bedside table, then squinted at the luminous dial of his watch.

Four in the fucking morning?

He stumbled across the bedroom, almost tripping on his discarded desert boots. As he opened the door, the landing light went on, practically blinding him. Ginger was heading for the top of the stairs, brandishing his Stechkin in one hand.

'Jesus Christ, what's going on?'

'Fucked if I know,' said Ginger, taking the stairs two at a time.

Mac blinked and followed him down. The knocking sounded even louder and then he heard a woman's laugh and a man's voice with an American accent.

'Come on, you fuckers, open up!'

'Logan?' said Mac, as Ginger reached the door and pulled it open.

Logan practically fell across the threshold.

'Bro! Good to see you. I was getting worried we'd come to the wrong house and the door would be opened by a guy with a gun.'

Ginger was rendered speechless as Logan slapped him on the back.

But Ginger's surprise was nothing compared to Mac's shock when Basima Khan followed Logan through the door, laughing and throwing her backpack down in the hall.

'Hi, guys!'

Mac gritted his teeth and tried to hold back, but he couldn't.

'What the actual fuck? What are you doing here?'

Baz's laughter died in her throat and her eyes opened wide. 'Mac?'

Logan and Ginger turned to look at him, their smiles dissolving.

A tide of anger surged through Mac's chest as he turned towards Logan. 'What the hell were you thinking?'

'Dude, calm down...'

Logan's words fell flat as Mac turned his back and strode away down the hall.

Day 3

Chapter 18

Lashkar Gah

'Jesus, Mac!' Baz came after him. She was furious, but not as furious as he was.

Ginger hustled Logan away to the kitchen, taking on the role of peacekeeper.

Mac went into the living room – somewhat dazed by the sudden arrival, and still seething. 'Are you telling me that you and Logan just drove through the night from Kandahar to here?'

'No, we freaking teleported! Of course we drove. It's not like there are any flights.' Baz's eyes flashed and she stepped up to Mac's chest, her fists clenched by her side.

'Don't you have any clue how dangerous that could have been?'

'We got here.'

Mac put a hand over his eyes and sighed. Then he pointed towards where Logan had disappeared through the kitchen door. 'Well, *he* sure as hell knew how dangerous it was. What an idiot.' He turned his back on Baz and stormed through to the kitchen.

Logan turned towards him, his hands raised in supplication. 'Whoa! I get it, Mac, but give us both some credit. We've been out here long enough to know what we were doing.'

Mac didn't respond.

Baz came in. 'You know, you don't own me, Mac,' she said. 'I can think for myself and make my own decisions.'

Mac shook his head. He was starting to feel calmer, but he still didn't like it. 'Okay, but you could have let us know you were coming. Just in case anything happened...'

'Beer anyone?' Ginger was holding a couple of bottles out, but the atmosphere was still tense.

'Mac, I'm sorry. But when you asked for my help, I knew I had to get here. And I wasn't going to leave Baz on her own in Kandahar.'

Mac blinked at him. 'You drove at night.'

'Yeah, in the small hours. We kept our lights off and we didn't see another vehicle.'

'But if you had...'

'But we didn't,' cut in Baz. 'We're here now, okay? Just get over it.'

Dawn was breaking, and somewhere in the distance Mac heard the cry of a lone muezzin calling the faithful to their first prayers of the day. There was no point trying to get some sleep now – they might as well get on with everything that needed doing.

'I'm going for a shower,' he said, intentionally not catching Baz's eye as he left the room. But he was secretly pleased when she followed him up the stairs.

–

Logan had brought ground coffee. It wasn't quite enough to appease Mac's anger but, accompanied by an apology, it went part way. The jolt of caffeine banished the hangover left by a night of very little sleep, and Mac was starting to feel semi-human again as he sat at the kitchen table making a list of kit they'd need for any rescue mission.

Logan was on the phone to someone, speaking Pashto with loud enthusiasm.

'Come on, bro,' he said to Mac, clipping his phone back onto his belt where he habitually wore it.

'Where to?'

'You'll see.' He led the way out to his Surf.

'No driver? No terp?' said Mac, climbing into the passenger seat.

'Not needed. I know where I'm going. You forget, I've been here before.'

Ten minutes later, they pulled up at the gate to the governor's office.

Logan opened his side window, and shouted something in Pashto to the nearest guard. Mac fully expected a rebuff or at least a lengthy argument, but the man saluted and then grinned. As if by magic, the gate opened, and they rolled into the building's forecourt. Logan parked up, got out and bounded up the steps. He seemed to know exactly where he was going. Mac followed, dumbfounded.

At the top, two guards pulled open the heavy, carved wooden doors, but before Mac and Logan could enter, Governor Wadaan Khaliq stepped out.

'Logan-jan, my brother, my brother,' he called with his arms outstretched. It was the first time Mac had heard the governor speak English. When he and Ginger had been here, he'd only spoken in Pashto and Nagpal had translated.

Logan stepped forward into the governor's embrace, patting him on the back, and then the two men kissed each other's cheeks, once, twice, three times.

'*Salaam alaikum*,' said Logan, finally free of the embrace.

'*Wa'alaikum salaam*,' said Khaliq.

'Wadaan-jan, it is an honour for me to come to your office once more,' said Logan. 'You and your family are in good health?'

Khaliq pressed his hands together, beaming. 'We are, thank you, Logan-jan. And can I ask about your family? Are your parents well?'

'They are very well indeed, thank you.'

'May the eye of God stay on all those that you hold close to your heart.'

'Thank you.' Logan made a small bow. He turned towards Mac. 'Wadaan-jan, I believe you have already met my close friend Mac MacKenzie.'

The governor nodded. 'Yes, yes. Mr Mac, you are well?'

'Yes, thank you, sir,' said Mac. 'And you?'

'Yes, thank you. Now, come in. We have much talking to do.'

As they followed him into the building, Mac nudged Logan in the ribs. 'I see you two know each other.'

Logan laughed. 'Like I said, I've been here before.'

Khaliq turned back to them as they walked through the vast entrance hall and said something to Logan in Pashto. He led them through another door into a medium-sized room that appeared part office, part sitting room. It was more lavishly furnished than the meeting room Mac had been in on his previous visit, and glass doors on the opposite side overlooked a courtyard garden with a fountain in the centre.

'Please to sit down,' said Khaliq, pointing them to a pair of wooden-framed sofas piled high with *kilim* and Ersari cushions. 'I will order tea.'

A servant was hovering in the doorway, and Khaliq barked an order at him before sitting on one of the sofas. Mac and Logan took the other one.

'My brother, I'm so pleased to see you again,' said Khaliq. He turned towards Mac. 'You must know that Logan-jan and I have had many adventures together.'

Mac could only guess.

'I came down here with Wadaan-jan from Nad-e Ali in 2001, when he overthrew the Taliban who were holding the city and became the Governor of Helmand,' said Logan by way of explanation. He made it sound like nothing more than a walk in the park, but Mac knew there had been ferocious fighting and copious bloodshed before the transfer of power had been effected. He couldn't help but wonder exactly what part Logan had played in it.

The servant came back with a tray of tea – the usual green and bitter concoction, but now Mac knew the trick of sucking it in through a sugar cube, which at least made it bearable if not quite palatable. The conversation turned to the business of the day and for that the governor elected to speak Pashto. Mac couldn't follow what was being said, but there seemed to be plenty of agreement between the former brothers in arms, and Khaliq nodded more often than he shook his head, which had to be a good sign.

There was a pause as Khaliq momentarily ran out of steam. Logan turned to Mac.

'The governor has heard reports that a western man is being held in the village of Najibullahkhan Kalay.'

'Where's that?'

'About seventy klicks south, on the Helmand River.'

'Does he know who's holding him?'

'A breakaway Taliban cell – scoundrels who don't know what they're doing.'

Khaliq added emphasis with what Mac thought was probably a string of curse words.

'They're idiots and they are making everyone look bad,' he said in his stilted English.

There was more discussion. Mac sipped his tea and tried not to grimace.

'Right,' said Logan. 'My brother Wadaan is happy to help us retrieve the westerner with militia and vehicles.'

Khaliq grinned, nodding his head as Logan spoke. 'It is important for me to show these Talibs who holds the power in Helmand Province. My men will aid your mission and crush your enemies.'

It was weird – the governor seemed a completely different man from the one he and Ginger had their audience with. Then he'd been stern and disinterested in their problem. Now, under the extraordinary influence of Logan, it seemed he couldn't do enough for them.

'Thank you,' said Mac, bowing his head. 'Your contribution will ensure our mission is a successful one.'

'I will be sending with you my best men,' said Khaliq. 'I will also provide a guide who knows the area well and who will be able to direct you to where your man is being held. Pasoon will be waiting for you at Bost and will guide you from there. When do you want to leave?'

'As soon as possible,' said Mac. The longer Bakker was in captivity, the less likely he was to emerge alive.

Khaliq stood up, so Mac and Logan followed suit.

'My men will be ready at noon.'

'We'll rendezvous with them at Bost, at the shrine of the glass coffin, at 1230 hours,' said Logan.

'Good, they will be there.'

Mac glanced at his watch. It was gone ten already. He and Logan needed to get a plan in place, sort out their own weapons and inform Ginger's country manager in Kabul what they were doing.

'*Manana*, Wadaan-jan,' said Logan, once more embracing the governor as he thanked him. '*Daera manana. Jor' aw Rogh Ose.*'

'And good health to you too, my friend. When you return, we'll share some stories of the old days, yes?'

'You betcha,' said Logan. 'It's a date.'

And then, to Mac's utter amazement, they bumped fists.

Chapter 19

Qala-e Bost

It took Mac, Logan, Baz and Ginger half an hour to drive south from Lashkar Gah to Qala-e Bost, where they were to pick up Pasoon and an escort of the governor's best militiamen. They were all wearing body armour – ceramic plates which slotted into nylon plate carriers. The three men's were plain black, but Baz's was bright blue with the word 'Press' stamped on front and back. Over these, they wore ops vests, though none of them had the premium brand, Blackhawk. Instead, theirs were cheap Dawood Shams knock-offs – but they would serve just as well. There were plenty of pouches for their AK mags. Or in Baz's case, various camera accoutrements and spare batteries. The back of the Surf was loaded up with petrol, water, food – four days' worth of Meals-Ready-to-Eat, or MREs – med packs, a toolkit, and a range of basic vehicle parts. A pair of spare wheels was chained and padlocked to the roof rack, along with a bright red safari jack. Logan wasn't taking any chances of a vehicle failure out in the danger zone.

Baz had insisted on coming with them. 'Reporting on things like this is my job,' she said when Mac gave a slight frown.

'Okay, sure, but bring your flak jacket.'

Now they were sitting in the back of Logan's Surf, watching the countryside slip by out of their respective windows.

As they reached Qala-e Bost, their driver took a sharp left turn off the main road, and Baz saw ahead of them the legendary fortress that had stood overlooking the Helmand Valley for more than three thousand years. Now it was crumbling and deserted, but in its heyday it must have been an intimidating sight to the medieval tribesmen that roamed the area. Vast walls of ochre brickwork towered above the surrounding countryside, and Baz recognised the famous archway that featured on the hundred-Afghani banknote.

She craned her neck at the structure as they drove past, but there was no sign of the governor's men. Heat shimmered on the road ahead, and the only living creature in sight was an old man squatting in the shade of a courtyard wall.

'We're not stopping here?' she said to Logan, who was in the front seat next to the driver.

'Uh-uh,' said Logan, with a shake of his head. 'We're meeting them at the shrine – a few kilometres further on.'

Ten minutes later, they drew up in front of a squat brick building and parked up at the end of a row of four Hilux SUVs. It wasn't quite what Baz had been expecting – of the shrine or the militiamen.

If she hadn't known beforehand, she wouldn't have guessed that the dozen or so men lounging in the shade by the side of the shrine were the governor's crack troops. With their ages ranging from probably fifteen to fifty, the ragtag bunch of men were in mismatched uniforms, with sandals on their feet, and shemaghs wrapped round their necks, despite the heat. They didn't exhibit any sort of military discipline, and several of them were smoking what looked like joints – confirmed by the smell as soon as she climbed out of the Surf. The youngest, a teenaged kid lacking the de rigueur beard or heavy stubble of his companions, was striking poses with his AK, as if ready to shoot the strangers.

An older man shouted at him, and he lowered the weapon.

Logan went over and started talking to the guy who seemed to be in charge, so Baz took the opportunity to peer into the doorway of the shrine. Ginger and Mac were standing a few feet away.

114

'Jesus, if these are Khaliq's best men, I dread to think what the rest are like,' said Ginger.

'What were you expecting? A fucking parade?' said Mac.

Baz turned back to study the group again. They looked more like a bunch of narco heavies, and given that the governor's brother was Feda Khaliq, the region's biggest opium grower, that's probably what they were. Was Logan really happy to rely on these hoodlums to help them scoop up Bakker from under his kidnappers' noses? It looked like Mac thought the same, and his doubt showed on his face as Logan walked towards them.

'Don't underestimate them, Mac. I've fought with a few of these guys, and they know one end of their AKs from the other.'

'Talking of which…' said Ginger. The militiamen were supposed to have brought extra AKs and munitions for him and Mac.

'They're sorting them for us,' said Logan. He pointed at the older man he'd been speaking to. 'That's Commander Ibrahimzai. He's in charge. And the little guy standing next to him is Pasoon. He'll be guiding us to the compound where Bakker is being held.'

The teenage kid and another young militiaman were digging into a large metal trunk in the back of one of the Hiluxes.

Logan turned to Baz and pointed at the doorway of the shrine. 'We're going to be here a while – we'll need to check the weapons they give us. Why don't you take a look inside? It's some of the weirdest shit I've ever seen.'

'Sure,' said Baz, as the guys wandered over to the Hilux to look at the weapons. She'd heard of the shrine of the glass coffin, and it could make a good local colour piece for the paper at some future point.

'Whose body is it?' she called back to Logan as she stood on the threshold.

Logan laughed. 'Literally no one can remember.'

It seemed hard to believe that this was a venerated shrine. There was no sign on the outside, or any form of religious decoration. Just a small brick and mud building, hardly taller than a man. Baz ducked and went inside. A low, vaulted corridor led downwards into pitch black. Not particularly enticing, but the air was cool, so she ventured further.

Switching on the small torch that she'd crammed into one of the pockets of her ops vest, she walked on to the end of the short tunnel. Its brickwork walls were pale and unadorned, the uneven stones casting craggy shadows ahead of her. It was silent down here, apart from the soft gritty crunch of her boots on the floor. She couldn't hear the chatter of the men outside, and it suddenly felt as if she were all alone, somewhere at the edge of the world.

At the end of the passage, a stone archway opened out into a small, low-ceilinged room. Baz stood on the threshold, casting the thin beam of light around the space in front of her. In the centre of the room, something reflected brilliantly, and Baz shivered. This must be it – the famous glass coffin for which the shrine was named.

She stepped forward and concentrated the torch on the shadowy glass box. Inside she could make out a lying figure, and as she peered down at it, she realised it was the desiccated form of a human corpse. The skin was like boiled leather, stretched over jutting bones, and the figure was naked apart from a grimy loincloth draped around its waist. Its face was pinched and pointed – sunken cheeks, a gaping mouthful of brown teeth, and huge hollow eye sockets staring up at her.

Baz gasped and stepped back, hitting something that hadn't been there before.

She screamed.

Hands clutched her shoulders. 'It's okay, Baz. It's all right – just me.' Mac's calm voice reassured her, and she laughed. Nervously.

'Damn!' she said. 'This is like something out of a horror movie.'

'Come on,' said Mac. 'Time to go.'

Heart still pounding, Baz followed him out into the bright, sharp sunlight. Logan and Ginger were stashing weapons into the back of the Surf, and the militiamen were climbing into their Hiluxes.

Baz wondered what the rest of the day held for them. Najibullahkhan Kalay was still a fair distance south from where they were, and they were pretty much at the limit of where it was deemed safe for westerners to venture. Sure, they had the governor's men. But they were on a mission that would bring them into conflict with a Taliban cell. She watched as the kid with the Kalashnikov climbed into a vehicle, slammed the door shut behind him and then half emerged to sit on the open window rim, calling out excitedly as the convoy of Hiluxes started to move.

Would he still be alive by the end of the day?

The air-conditioning kicked in and Baz shivered. She felt as cold now as she had in the dark and silent tomb just moments before.

Chapter 20

Najibullahkhan Kalay

It was only another fifty kilometres to Najibullahkhan Kalay, the village where Bakker was apparently being held, but the journey took longer than Mac would have expected, even allowing for an afternoon prayer stop. The road was rough and several times they were delayed by agricultural vehicles blocking their way.

Naturally, the governor's militia were having none of this and would stream out of their Hiluxes, brandishing their AKs and shouting loudly to intimidate whatever poor unfortunate was the cause of the problem. More than once, they simply bull-dozed a smaller vehicle off the road. Logan's Surf was towards the back of the convoy, and they would watch the proceedings without getting involved. The less attention they drew to themselves the better, as far as Mac was concerned, and it was his opinion that they would be better served if the militia commander reined in his men and proceeded through the area with more caution. After all, these were to all intents and purposes Feda Khaliq's men, and this wasn't a part of Helmand that he controlled.

Logan was talking with Pasoon, the guide supplied by the governor, in the front. Periodically, Baz translated some of what they said, but Mac spent most of the drive drinking in the alien landscape. The road followed the river course as the Helmand wound south before swinging towards the west through Nimroz Province and crossing the border into Iran, and it formed a green corridor through the surrounding desert.

The basin through which it flowed was a patchwork of small fields, and as soon as they were south of Garmser it became abundantly clear that one crop dominated.

Poppies.

The west knew all about the Afghan poppy fields, from which Helmand alone supplied more than ninety per cent of the world's heroin. But where Mac had been expecting fields of red, the flowers of the opium poppy were not only more deadly than garden poppies at home, but also, he was surprised to discover, more delicately beautiful. Huge drifts of lilac and white petals fluttered in the breeze, a sea of soft pastels where it was easy to imagine lying down and falling into a dreamless stupor. Morpheus, god of sleep, couldn't have imagined a bed more lovely, and his name had been hijacked for the seedpods' sticky brown resin – morphine, the precursor of heroin. The precursor of misery and death.

Mile after mile after endless mile. Pink and purple brush strokes, broken here and there to skirt around small villages or rocky outcrops, and beyond the strip of fields, the blank canvas of the desert stretched away to the horizon on either side. An alternate sea of sand, rock and grit in a single shade of ochre.

'Mac? Hey, dozy...'

Logan's voice snapped him out of his private world.

'How much further?' he said. It was late afternoon and they'd been on the road for several hours.

'We're getting close,' said Logan. 'Here's the plan. We won't go into the village when we arrive. The main road bypasses the settlement completely, so they'll have no idea we're in the vicinity. Pasoon believes Bakker is being held in a compound on the eastern edge of Najibullahkhan Kalay. It's a tiny place, just a handful of houses, and we don't want to give ourselves away before we need to. We'll lager up off the road a few klicks north until 0300. Then we hit.'

'Lager up?' Baz had been listening with wide-eyed interest.

Logan explained. 'We'll find a wadi or some rocks, a lying-up point where we can circle the vehicles without being seen from the road.'

Mac had his own questions. 'Pasoon *believes*? I thought we were working on solid intel.'

'No intel is solid, especially down here,' said Logan. 'But Pasoon grew up a couple of villages away, and he still has contacts. He's putting his life in danger by bringing us here.'

Or putting our lives in danger if we've been wrong to trust him, thought Mac. He couldn't help but have a bad feeling about this whole little jaunt.

'So why's he doing it?'

'The Taliban aren't popular down here. They killed men from Pasoon's village, and this bunch aren't even proper Talibs. They use it as a label of convenience to do whatever they want. The local community wants shot of them. Also, money. He'll be well paid for his services.'

Logan took over from the driver and drove the Surf up to the front of the convoy so he and Pasoon could scout the way to a good resting spot.

An hour later, the guide pointed to a dusty track that turned off the road to the left. A wooden bridge took them across a canal and a hundred metres beyond that the road passed a tumbledown building and petered out. Logan carried on driving across the uneven ground, the Surf throwing up a dust cloud in its wake. Mac turned to look out of the back window. The Hiluxes behind them churned up even more.

'Talk about advertising your presence.'

'It'll settle in a moment,' said Logan. 'And we'll be out of sight from the road in a couple of minutes. Then we can find an LUP and hunker down for a few hours. Najibullahkhan Kalay is about ten clicks to the south, so we'll keep going until we're due east of the village. Pasoon thinks there's a dry wadi somewhere round here that will give us good cover.'

Once they were a safe distance from the highway, Logan called the convoy to a halt. He had a quick word with

Commander Ibrahimzai, then linked his BGAN to his laptop and fired it up. Mac had heard of BGAN but had never seen one, and Logan quickly explained that the comms device worked in conjunction with the Inmarsat satellite system to give him internet access no matter where he was in the world. This allowed him to access Google Earth on his laptop, and a minute later he and Mac were scouring the landscape for a suitable lying-up position.

'There,' said Mac, pointing to a craggy feature a few kilometres to the south of their current position, and due east of the village. 'That wadi looks like it might work.'

Logan fed the latitude and longitude into the GPS in the Surf, and they jolted across the stony terrain for another half-hour. Occasionally Mac got glimpses of the road in the distance, but there was very little traffic other than agricultural vehicles and the odd jingle truck. Most of the time all he could see was desert and boulders. But at least they were in front of the convoy and not eating someone else's dust.

The wadi came into view, steep-sided and deep enough to give them cover, but they had to drive along the edge of it for a couple of kilometres before they found a suitable access point down onto the dry riverbed. Logan called a halt at the top and sent two of the militiamen down on foot to check they would have no company round the next bend or two. Once they had the all-clear, the procession of vehicles rolled down the slope into the gully. With the sun low in the sky, the banks of the wadi cast deep shadows, allowing them to park up where the windows and doors would be less likely to cause reflections. Of course, it didn't seem any cooler in the shade, but Mac knew that as night fell the temperature would become a fraction more comfortable.

Logan and the commander organised a sentry roster — three men at a time, one on the lip of the wadi and one at each end of their encampment. The rest of the crew made a priority of checking, dry cleaning and double checking all the weapons. Ginger counted out five full magazines for each man with an AK, which they loaded into their green canvas Chicom chest rigs. Unlike the Well Diggers contingent, the militiamen sported no body armour and had little protective gear of any kind. Two of them were sorting out RPGs and spare rockets, while another two had armed themselves with PK machine guns. Using Baz to interpret, Ginger arranged for one of the PKMs to stay with him at the final rendezvous guarding the vehicles, along with both the RPG guys and one rifleman, while the rest of the team hit the compound. He organised the PKM and one of the RPGs as a fire support group, covering the village, with the rifleman and the second RPG covering their rear.

Mac was sitting on the rim of the Surf's open boot, wiping down his own AK, when Baz wandered across to him.

'Quite a little scalping party you've put together,' she said. 'D'you really think you'll need all this firepower?'

Mac laid the weapon down in the base of the boot, allowing Baz to stand between his knees and rest her head on his chest.

'Better to have more than we need than too little.'

'You'll be careful, won't you?' she said, nervous fingers twisting into the hair at the back of his neck.

Mac always felt jittery before heading into the critical phase of an op, and it was something he considered essential. The one time he thought he knew it all and wasn't nervous was the one time when disaster had struck and lives were lost. Lives that he was responsible for. Now he knew better than to take luck for granted.

'I'll be careful. And you make sure you stay well back until we give the signal that it's safe.'

This was part of the deal he'd struck with Baz. She wasn't to come charging in after them with her camera, but once the action was over and they were on the way out, she could get some shots of the hostage rescue. He knew it was important to her, and being in on the scoop could make a big difference to her career.

'Of course.'

'Promise?'

'Yes, Jesus, Mac – I promise.'

Mac heard footsteps crunching towards them and looked round. It was Logan.

'Time for some shut-eye, kids,' he said. 'We're going in pre-dawn, just before the first prayer call, when the baby Talibs are all tucked up sleeping. That means scouting out the compound a couple of hours before that to see how many guards they have and what their patrol routine is. If your weapon's ready, have some chow and then get some sleep.'

'The peace before the storm,' said Mac.

Logan nodded. 'Shit's about to get real.'

Mac wondered how many ops like this Logan had been involved in, and with whom.

Chapter 21

Najibullahkhan Kalay

Mac had found it hard to sleep the previous night, but now his training kicked in. He regulated his breathing to slow his heart rate and cleared his mind of the thoughts that had plagued it for the last twenty-four hours. It seemed like only minutes had passed when Ginger came and tapped on the window of the Surf, where he and Baz were sleeping.

Mac was instantly awake and alert. He squeezed Baz's shoulder and she opened her eyes.

'Rolling out in five,' said Ginger, as Mac lowered the window.

Mac drank some water and took a quick piss behind a rock. It was now or never. Around them, the militiamen were climbing into their vehicles, clutching their weapons. The vibe had totally changed from earlier in the day. No more smoking and joshing around – the men were quiet and focused. Maybe Logan had been right when he told Mac not to underestimate them.

Logan and Pasoon climbed into the front of the Surf. The American started the engine and led the convoy out of the wadi. At the top, they stopped for a word with the man who'd been guarding the rim. All seemed fine, and he got into the Hilux behind them. No headlights. They drove at a low and steady speed to minimise engine noise.

Mac explained to Baz what would happen. 'We've identified an abandoned caravanserai on the eastern edge of the village,' he said. 'This will be our final rendezvous – the FRV – and also the emergency rendezvous, should everything go tits up. That's where you'll wait until we're on our way out. You'll be safe as we'll have a protection party of Ginger and four men stationed there, including one of the PKMs to give covering fire. If anything at all goes wrong, we'll fall back there and then drive hell for leather.'

'But don't worry,' said Logan from the front, 'nothing's going to go wrong.'

Twenty minutes of desert driving brought them back to the small canal they'd crossed when they'd moved out to the desert earlier.

'The FRV is about a kilometre further on, on the other side of the canal,' he said, slowing down to a stop. 'We'll just send some scouts in to check it out.'

He waved to the Hilux behind. Two of the militiamen jumped out and scurried forward. Their job was to check that the caravanserai was indeed empty. The last thing they wanted was to blunder into an encampment of Kuchi tribesmen, with their camels, goats and half-feral children. Mac watched as they worked their way methodically down the track, looking carefully from side to side for any sign of danger.

The rest of the men waited in their stationary vehicles for a tense fifty minutes, but there was no noise, and then one of the scouts appeared and gave them the thumbs-up. All-clear. They could proceed towards the centuries-old structure. It had been built to give shelter to travellers and that's what, in effect, they were.

They drove on along the side of the canal until they came to another bridge, just wide enough for the Toyotas. The sound of their tyres on the wooden slats gave Mac cause for concern, but the track on the other side simply led into the empty baked mud structures of the caravanserai – there were no inhabited buildings for several hundred metres, just a series of dried-out fields that would give the PKM a clear field of fire. If it was needed.

Ginger and the militia drivers worked together to position the vehicles in the best formation for a quick getaway. Rather than driving back into the desert, once – if – they had retrieved Bakker, the plan was to hit the main road and drive fast. It would be the most effective way to put space between them and any Taliban pursuers.

But when Mac checked with Ginger how things were going, Ginger didn't sound happy.

'I'm none too sure about these PKMs,' he said, drawing Mac to one side. 'I took a quick shufti at them and the chrome inside both barrels is worn to fuck. God knows when the barrels were last changed, and we don't have any spares. They're more than likely completely shot out.'

It wasn't exactly reassuring, but there was nothing they could do.

'We'll just have to take our chances with them,' Mac said.

While Ginger sorted their exit and got one of the PKMs into a suitable position, Mac, Logan and the commander took on scouting duties.

The village lay due west of the caravanserai. It was completely dark, but they could see the outlined rooftops of several large family compounds and a handful of smaller houses. It was surrounded by a patchwork of fields, irrigated by the canal that ran between the village and the main road. Beyond the village, about a mile away across more fields, the broad sweep of the Helmand River formed a barrier on the other side of which the land once again became desert.

Pasoon had told them that the compound taken over by the Taliban lay on the eastern edge of Najibullahkhan Kalay – in other words, on the side they were approaching from. It was the middle property in a row of three, but they didn't abut each other – there were narrow alleys between the high mud walls on either side. The main gateway into the compound faced the village, naturally, so their approach was from the back. The questions that needed answering were whether or not there was

126

a rear gate into the property, and the number and position of any guards.

They approached the village as quietly as they could, sticking to the shadows and giving any buildings that looked inhabited as wide a berth as possible. The trick was to stay off the stony pathways and tracks, on which their boots crunched, and to find stretches of damp, muddy grass along the edge of the canal, where they could walk in silence. Once they were level with the middle compound of the three, they ducked down behind a low, crumbling wall to study their target.

The first thing of note was that there was no back gate in the wall. That meant going around to the front, either by way of the alleys between this compound and its neighbours, or by going right around the row of buildings and coming up the village street they fronted onto.

Mac knew better than to start a discussion in their current position – they would finish their recce and then fall back to the FRV to finalise their move and brief the rest of the militia. For now, they worked in silence.

Logan pointed to the roof of the house, then shook his head. There was no guard post up there, which was a plus. But they needed to take a look at the front, so they could assess how they were going to breach the entrance. Mac made a looping gesture with his arm to suggest that they should go around the southern edge of the village and recce the front of the compound. Logan nodded, and Mac broke cover from behind the wall. The other two followed him, but before they'd gone more than a couple of paces, Mac heard the unmistakeable sound of a cigarette lighter being flicked.

'Down,' hissed Logan in his ear, and within a split second they were back behind the wall, crushing themselves to the ground to make sure they couldn't be seen. The slow drip of adrenalin that had kept Mac on his toes turned into a flood, and he had to spend a couple of seconds calming his breathing and bringing his heart rate down.

Feet crunched on stony ground and Mac peered carefully around the edge of the crumbling brickwork. A man emerged from the side alley that lay between the middle and the southernmost of the three compounds. He was smoking a cigarette and had a Krinkov slung over his shoulder.

What a grade-A fucking amateur. He'd lose a valuable second, maybe two, possibly even his life, getting his weapon into a firing position if anything happened.

As he turned the corner to patrol along the back wall of the compound, his face showed in the moonlight. He was just a kid, maybe fifteen or sixteen, doing a man's work – and the chances were that this evening he'd die for it. It was an unsavoury thought, but Mac focused on it. It might be the kid's life or his own, and if he had anything to do with it, he was going to come out on top.

Anyway, the fucker was all right for now. They weren't going to take him out and announce their presence. The most important thing about this recce was that they shouldn't give themselves away – the element of surprise would be their most effective weapon, so they'd keep their powder dry until H-hour when, in seventy minutes hence, all hell would be let loose. Mac hoped the boy would finish his patrol and then maybe fuck off somewhere else in the village – but it didn't seem likely.

The sentry tossed his cigarette to the ground as he rounded the corner of the compound to head down the other side alley back to the front. Mac watched the stub as it smouldered, then went out. They needed to wait a few more minutes before making their move – give the kid time to get inside the gate before they came through the village to survey the front.

When you're watching ground zero before a raid, and the adrenalin's surging through your body, every minute seems like an hour. Every breath rasps loud and every heartbeat feels like thunder in your chest. Mac's hands were sweating. He wiped them, one at a time, on the seat of his trousers – he couldn't afford for his grip to slip if he needed to raise his AK.

After enough time had lapsed, they quietly and swiftly made their way through the shadows, skirting the bottom end of the village and then coming up to the compound from the front. There were no lights on in any of the buildings – villages this far south were rarely connected to the electricity grid. Sometimes they had rudimentary power supplies generated by waterwheels on the Helmand River, but there were no tell-tale wires suggesting that was the case here.

However, as they approached from the front, Mac heard the low hum of a diesel engine. Someone in one of the properties had a generator running, and as they got closer to the middle of the three, it became apparent it was this one. Before getting any closer, they crouched in a dense black shadow and studied the compound. Its wall was easily three metres high – it would be preferable to go in via the entrance than having to scale the wall while carrying weapons.

The main entry point was a double wooden gate, wide enough for vehicles to pass in and out. Mac reckoned it wouldn't be too hard to blast it open with shotgun rounds fired into the hinges. More concerning was what they would find behind the gate. The paucity of any intelligence on how many men there were inside the compound and how heavily they were armed was of real concern. They had no information on the layout of the buildings or the footprint of the rooms within the buildings, and of course, no clue as to where exactly Bakker was being held. From the moment they blew open that gate, they were heading into unknown territory with an undocumented enemy presence.

But there weren't any other choices on the table, and they were going to have to take what they could get.

They scouted some way up the street to take a closer look, but Mac couldn't find anything more to help them. He touched Logan's arm, then softly tapped the face of his watch. It was time they got back to brief the rest of the team. Logan nodded and they jogged on silent feet back to the caravanserai. Once inside the shelter of its walls, Logan had a quick conversation with Ibrahimzai. Then he turned to Mac.

They spent ten minutes comparing notes and formulating an operational plan. Kinetic entry. A team to hold the gate and secure the compound. A team to do the smash and grab. Logan translated to the commander, who added his own suggestions at intervals. Baz listened intently.

'What signal will you give me when it's safe to come forward?' she asked Mac.

'When you see us running towards you.'

'Seriously? That's too late. I want to get some shots of you actually bringing him out of the compound.'

'Sorry, Baz. Too dangerous.'

The militiamen were lined up, with the two men who would blow the gate in the lead position.

Logan looked at his watch. 'T-minus two. Take a deep breath.'

Mac gave Baz a swift kiss on the lips. 'See you on the flipside.'

She looked up at him, eyes wide, but didn't say anything. Then she stepped back to get out of their way.

'H-hour. We're outta here.'

And they set off at a jog, in tight formation, into the unknown.

Chapter 22

Najibullahkhan Kalay

They ran forward in complete silence. Every man knew what he had to do when they reached the compound – there would be no time for questions or second-guessing decisions that had already been made. They were reliant on surprise, speed and superior firepower, and there were question marks over the last, as they had no idea how many men there were within the compound.

Mac and Logan led the way out of the caravanserai, splitting into two streams of men to go down the alleys on either side of the compound. Two men peeled off the cohort in each alley to watch the back and secure the route out once they'd grabbed Bakker. Mac led four of the militiamen to the gate – their mission was to gain entry, immobilise the guards and lock down the compound, while Logan and the remaining three of the governor's men waited to one side, ready to surge through the gate to breach the main building, take out remaining personnel and free Bakker.

Mac signalled to two of his team. They stepped forward, AKs slung behind them, with pump-action shotguns raised, one aimed at the gate's upper hinge, the other at the lower hinge. Beyond the gate, there was no sound but the uneven chugging of the generator, hopefully enough to cover the scuffle of boots on gravel. Mac took a deep breath, then counted them down with his fingers.

All hell broke loose.

With the hinges pulverised by the shotgun blasts, Mac's other two men were able to shove the gate out of the way. It fell inwards with a loud splintering noise. The thundering of the militiamen's boots across the wood was greeted by a howl of surprise from the doorway of the main building. A man emerged, brandishing a Krinkov, but immediately dropped to the ground, taken out by Commander Ibrahimzai as Mac's team fanned out across the empty courtyard.

Mac swiftly scanned the landscape. Directly opposite the gate stood a two-storey house, with a covered terrace running along the front. This was where the man who'd just been shot lay bleeding out on the bare cement. The building's upstairs windows were shuttered, and above them, a low railing topping the wall suggested there was a roof terrace. Two vehicles, a Surf and a technical, were parked, nose to tail, on the left-hand side of the building. To the right, underneath an open-sided lean-to, sat the ancient generator, louder now they were closer.

Another man, the sentry they'd seen patrol the outer wall earlier, came at them from between the side of the house and the parked vehicles. He opened fire, but immediately took a hit from Mac's AK – his muzzle dipped and all his rounds hit was the stony ground.

Behind Mac, Ibrahimzai set up the PKM gunner and a rifleman to guard the compound entrance, while he and the other militiaman on the team moved forward to check around the vehicles for any more shooters. As Mac waited for them to reappear, ready to give cover if any shots came from the upstairs windows, he heard them slashing tyres to prevent pursuit. As they came round the corner of the wall, he waved at them to provide cover while he checked the other side of the house where the generator was.

As he came up level with the side of the lean-to, there was a roar and a giant of a man with a huge belly and a long black beard emerged from behind it, brandishing a pitchfork.

A pitchfork? What the actual fuck?

Mac raised his AK and opened fire – but nothing. The fucking piece of Soviet shit was jammed. The pitchfork giant was bearing down on him. He dropped the AK to hang on its sling and smoothly transitioned to his Browning, which was in a thigh holster on his right leg.

Firing three rapid shots, he felled the man with a couple of chest wounds just as the prongs of the pitchfork came within inches of his neck. The prongs clattered against his useless AK as the giant crashed to the ground, the third round clipping the side of his head and dislodging his black turban on the way down.

'*Allahu akbar, Allahu…*' He coughed on his own blood as his lungs filled up. The words turned to a gurgle in his throat as he drowned.

Mac was breathing heavily, holding the Browning out in front of him as he scanned the area for further threats. Nothing. He holstered the pistol and lifted up the AK. He removed the magazine and racked the cocking handle back to clear the chamber. The unfired round ejected, and he replaced the magazine and cocked the weapon. But could he trust it now if he needed it again? He decided to stick with his pistol, at least while they were still inside the compound.

Satisfied that the courtyard and gate were secured in Ibrahimzai's capable hands, Mac joined Logan on the concrete terrace. So far, this had taken less than a minute. The compound was silent, and there were no noises from beyond the walls to suggest that they'd roused the neighbours. He nudged the fallen gunman with his foot. The man was dead. A Krinkov lay by his side and Mac swooped down to pick it up, swinging the malfunctioning AK round to his back. He quickly removed the Krinkov's magazine and, finding it empty, replaced it with one of his own.

Then he lined up as third man in the stack, behind and to one side of Logan and one of the militiamen, catching his breath so he would be ready to spring into action again. Logan waited in the doorway, hardly breathing at all as far as Mac could tell. He was holding his AK with his right hand, and he reached back with his left to count down with his fingers.

Three. Two. One.

Zero.

With a hefty kick, he slammed the door back against the inside wall, then flattened himself against the wall on the other side, using his AK to cover the left half of a large square room. The second man in the stack flew in and scanned the right-hand side of the area, sweeping his Krinkov in a wide arc. The room was empty.

Mac came through the door. Directly ahead of him, at a perpendicular, a flight of mud-brick stairs led up to the next floor. Mac heard a shout from above and running footsteps. He pointed his weapon, ready to blast away the lower legs of anyone who attempted to come down.

Meanwhile, Logan, keeping flat against the side wall of the room, made his way around the perimeter to a position from where he could fire directly up the stairs. At the same time, the militiaman took up a position by the door to ensure no one could follow them inside.

Suddenly Logan let off a burst of rapid fire, aimed towards the top of the stairs. There was a cry and then a body tumbled forward, catching a round from Mac's borrowed Krinkov as he sprawled headfirst and crashed to the bottom of the staircase.

'Going up,' yelled Logan, signalling Mac to stop firing.

He leapt over the man's body and took the stairs two at a time, ready to fire in a split second if anyone at the top had the dumb idea of coming at him.

The stairs turned a corner, at which Logan took up a covering position, pointing the barrel of his rifle up towards the landing. Mac ran past him and then stopped, crouching on the top step but one. His heart hammered and his lungs burned – his chest felt fit to burst. Finger taking up first pressure on the trigger, he listened. Silence. All he could hear was his own breathing. But he'd learned well enough never to trust a silent house, so he waited longer. If there was anyone up here, he would draw them out. Behind him, he heard Logan slowly making his way up, step by step. He came level with Mac and then indicated with a jabbing finger that he would go right and Mac should go left.

Somewhere, in one of the bedrooms, a floorboard creaked.

Mac nodded and once again Logan counted down from three with his fingers.

In unison they emerged from the staircase, back to back, sweeping the top landing, weapons primed. Mac kicked open a bedroom door. There was a man sitting on the bed, struggling to get a magazine into his weapon, but messing up with nervous fingers. He dropped it and immediately raised his hands. Mac stepped forward, his Krinkov trained on the man's head, and with one foot kicked the guy's AK away to the far wall.

'On your knees.'

The man looked at him blankly. He was wearing nothing but his underpants, and in a shaft of moonlight coming through the window, Mac could see a girlie mag lying on the bed. Dirty little fucker had been cranking one out. It was all Mac could do not to burst out laughing.

'On your fucking knees!' Mac knew he wouldn't understand English, so he gestured with the barrel of his gun. Then the punk understood him and dropped forward from the side of the bed to kneel on the floor. He didn't have a hard-on now. Mac took a step backwards and bumped against Logan in the doorway.

'Jesus Christ, Mac, we're not taking any prisoners.'

Logan elbowed him out of the way, stepped forward and executed the man with a burst of fire before his victim even understood what was happening. His body dropped to the floor with a thud, blood flooding out of half a dozen bullet wounds.

'There's one more room up here,' said Logan, quickly loading a fresh mag. 'Door's locked, so I reckon we'll find Bakker on the other side of it.'

'Come on then, let's get him.'

Mac strode down the landing to the other end, where there was a single door leading off to the left. He tried the handle – it was indeed locked.

'The guy on the stairs was probably on guard duty. Key's probably in his pocket.'

'No time,' said Logan. He hammered the door. 'Bakker? Are you in there?'

They listened, leaning against the door, for a reply, but there was nothing. If Bakker was in there, he could be gagged, unconscious or dead. Or maybe he wasn't even there at all.

'If you can hear us, get away from the door. We're going to shoot the lock.'

There was still no answer.

Mac switched the Krinkov for his Browning and raised it to take aim, hoping to hell that Bakker was nowhere near the door. Logan stepped back and Mac braced himself – in the confined space of the upstairs landing, the noise would be piercing.

He fired.

There was a whip-crack of metal against metal as the bullet ploughed into the lock.

Mac raised his boot and launched a hefty kick, snapping the door open.

He peered into the pitch-black room, the shuttered windows not letting in a glimmer of light. His eyes, already accustomed to the dark, discerned the outline of a figure slumped against the far wall. It moved, a slight twitch, accompanied by the grunt of someone with a gag in their mouth.

Logan came up behind him and shone a torch into the room, lighting up a pathetic figure. The man was filthy, clothes ripped, gagged, hands bound behind his back, blond hair caked with blood and a bruised face. He was chained to an iron ring that had been crudely set into the wall with cement. Above the gag, Mac could read panic in his eyes.

But something didn't stack up. He looked nothing like the photo of Tomas Bakker in his Well Diggers personnel file.

Mac blinked and looked harder. 'Who the fuck are you?'

Chapter 23

Najibullahkhan Kalay

'Brad Kaminski,' said Baz, elbowing her way past the two men so she could get a couple of images of how the Taliban had held him captive. Then she ran forward, falling to her knees in front of him.

'Can you get a light?' she said, over her shoulder to Mac and Logan. 'And some water.'

Mac ignored her requests and strode across the room. He grabbed her shoulder and spun her round. Anger and adrenalin made him rougher than she'd ever seen him.

'What the fuck, Baz? You were meant to stay at the FRV with Ginger.'

'Sure, and miss the biggest scoop of my life?'

'Or die for the sake of a photo?' said Logan, from the other side of the room.

'Look, I don't work for you two. I'm a free agent.' She turned her attention back to Kaminski, who was clearly in a bad way. 'I got Amu to bring me over. We were careful.'

'Amu?' said Mac.

'One of the governor's men,' said Logan. 'He's solid – she was in good hands.'

Mac gave her an incredulous look. 'You could have got him killed too.'

But Logan's shoulders were shaking with mirth. 'Man, you've got some balls for a girl.'

Baz would have laughed at that, but she was more concerned with undoing the gag that was preventing Kaminski from speaking.

Mac bristled. 'Come on, we need to get out of here. The gunfire will have woken the whole village.'

Baz finally got the gag undone and gently peeled it away from Kaminski's face. His mouth was a bloody mess, and he was missing his two front teeth. It looked as if someone had struck him hard with a rifle butt or something similar. He didn't speak, but the look of gratitude and relief he gave Baz said it all.

Logan came over to them with his pistol out.

'Baz, wait outside for a minute.' Kaminski's eyes widened with fear again. Logan squatted down in Baz's place. 'It's okay, dude. I'm going to shoot that ring out of the wall.'

He holstered his pistol for a moment and pulled a knife from a leather sheath strapped to his calf. Moving to the other side of Kaminski, he used it to hack through the leather camel hobbles that secured the Canadian's wrists.

'Cover your ears,' he said.

Kaminski complied, wrapping his arms around his head and facing away from the iron ring. The chain was about a metre long, so he was able to shift his legs well out of Logan's firing range. It took a couple of shots, and some brute force, but a minute later, Logan had the iron ring clattering to the floor. Mac swooped in from the door, pulled Kaminski to his feet and then bent underneath him to hoist him into a fireman's lift across his shoulders.

'I'll lead,' said Logan, putting his pistol away and raising his AK again. 'Baz, you guide Mac down the stairs. He might not be our man, but he's still one hell of a precious burden.'

Baz carried on taking photographs of the rescue. This was gold. They'd almost certainly saved Kaminski's life and the story would be even bigger when accompanied by candid photos of the rescue mission.

'Coming down,' yelled Logan in Pashto, to alert the militiamen downstairs.

Mac had to turn sideways to manoeuvre Kaminski down the narrow staircase. Baz went just ahead of them, guiding Mac around the corner on the stairs and making sure that Kaminski's head didn't smack against the wall. She wondered if he was married, and if his parents were still alive. Somebody, somewhere, would be getting some very happy news the next morning.

They came out onto the concrete terrace at the front of the house. Commander Ibrahimzai came across to them, leaving two of his men posted at the gate.

Baz listened to their hurried conversation, translating for Mac in a low voice.

'All quiet?' said Logan.

'So far,' said Ibrahimzai. 'But the gunfire will have woken people. We should move fast.'

No one was arguing with that.

'Here, let me take him,' said Logan, turning to Mac.

They swiftly transferred Kaminski from Mac's shoulders to Logan's. The Canadian was compliant. Baz could tell from his spaced-out expression that he was in shock. He didn't speak, apart from a couple of grunts of pain. His face showed that he'd taken a serious beating at some point – no doubt there were other injuries on his body. But those would have to wait until they'd got away from Najibullahkhan Kalay.

The commander called to the militiamen that were still in the compound. He sent two out to check with the perimeter guards and scout the route back. The rest waited silently just inside the gate. They were back within minutes with nothing to report. Ibrahimzai sent one of them to the left-hand alley to pick up the guards on that side, and the rest of them set off down the right-hand alley, gathering the two guards there. Once they were all mustered at the back wall of the compound, they were ready to cross the five hundred metres of open ground to the FRV. They would move in pairs, leaving two of the militiamen back to maintain a rear guard against anyone coming up either side of the compound to impede their getaway.

'Wait, there's a light,' said Baz, pointing to where she could see a soft glow emanating over the wall of one of the compounds on the other side of the village.

There was no way of telling whether someone was getting up in response to the noise of the raid, or simply because it was approaching the time for morning prayers. But they had to assume the former.

Ibrahimzai barked an order at two of his men to go back down the side of the compound to check out what was happening in the village. Logan pulled a Motorola VHF radio out of his ops vest.

'Golf, this is Lima, we're exfiling to you. All complete, plus one. Over.'

'Roger, out,' came the crackling reply.

He stowed the radio back in its pouch. '*Di di mao!* We're outta here.'

It was time to go.

Ibrahimzai and Mac led off, scanning the terrain in front for threats, ready to respond in a heartbeat. Logan and Baz were tucked behind them, jogging at a steady pace. The weight of Kaminski across Logan's shoulders seemed to make no difference to him, but then it hadn't escaped Baz's notice that despite the beer and the *chars*, the American kept himself pretty damn fit. The rest of the militiamen formed a phalanx around them, each covering their arcs, with the tail-end Charlie facing the rear.

Five hundred metres of open ground. No distance for a casual stroll. But this seemed like the longest run of Baz's life. The settlement now lay to their left. The light she'd seen had gone out, or had possibly been obscured by another building. It was dark between the houses, despite the first glimmer of dawn on the distant horizon. All was quiet.

Until the sudden cry of the muezzin erupted, calling the faithful to prayer, waking the rest of the village to discover a scene of carnage. A gasp caught in Baz's throat, and it seemed as if her skin was suddenly a size too small as every muscle contracted in shock.

Eyes front. Keep moving. Almost there.

Somewhere behind them an engine roared to life.

'Run,' hissed Logan. 'Faster.'

All the men picked up their pace, and their previous tight formation drifted apart.

Baz glanced up at Kaminski, bouncing roughly on Logan's shoulders. His face was a grimace of pain.

Still running, Logan turned to the side just enough so he could see what was coming.

'Zigzag,' he shouted at Baz. 'Run in a zigzag.'

Baz looked round and wished she hadn't. A light-coloured technical had come around the far end of the village and was speeding towards them up the track bordering the canal. There was a machine gun mounted on the back of it, and a heavily bearded man was fiddling with an ammo belt as they jolted over the stony ground. Baz prayed the damn thing was jammed or broken or simply stuck long enough for them to gain the cover of the caravanserai.

Ahead of them lay the choke point. They had to get across the canal and the bridge was narrow. If he got his gun working in time, the machine gunner would be able to pick them off like ducks in a row as they crossed it.

Commander Ibrahimzai took the bridge first, running in a low crouch.

The technical immediately opened fire. It was hardly any distance behind them now, and still coming up fast. Baz heard the whistle of rounds slicing through the air and the stench of propellant was sucked deep into her lungs with every breath, making her cough as she ran.

As Ibrahimzai threw himself headlong onto the ground on the far side of the bridge, there was a flash from within the caravanserai. Ginger's crew was returning fire. There was a loud crack, then the hiss of a rocket ripping the air apart. A shriek of fear sounded somewhere behind her, but as she turned to look, the rocket thudded into the ground to one side and just ahead of the technical. The warhead exploded, showering everything with sand and gravel, but doing no real damage.

'*Allahu akbar!*' whooped the gunner at the near miss.

In front of her, Mac was running across the bridge, and Baz could see bullets splintering the wood beneath his feet. It would be a miracle if he made it across.

'Go, Baz,' yelled Logan, shoving her onto the wooden structure.

She ran crouched low, trying to weave from one side to the other, though there was virtually no room to do this. A figure appeared above the mud wall of the caravanserai and immediately opened fire with a PKM. The noise was intolerable and the air was getting smoky. Her feet thundered on the wooden slats. She was nearly at the other side. Nearly there. Another step, another two.

It felt like someone punched her in the back, just underneath her right shoulder blade. She stumbled and tripped, flying forward, a shockwave of pain radiating through her.

What the fuck?

Then she realised. She'd taken a hit.

She lay on the ground, winded. As she struggled to breathe, she felt as if she'd just gone ten rounds with a heavyweight champion. Pummelled.

But thank God for the body armour.

'Mac,' yelled Logan as he ran past her, Kaminski still riding high on his shoulders.

She finally managed to get some air into her lungs. The PKM gunner had stopped firing. She could hear the rest of the militiamen storming over the bridge. There was no more machine-gun fire coming from the technical. Wincing with the effort, she sat up and twisted around to look behind her. The technical had come to a stop. Its windshield was shattered, its driver slumped over the wheel. But more importantly, the

143

machine gun stood idle. The gunner was missing. Then she spotted him, lying several feet behind the vehicle, where he'd fallen in the hail of bullets, his white kameez now scarlet.

One of the militiamen bent down by her side.

'Are you hurt?' he asked her in Pashto.

She shook her head and tried to heave herself to standing, but it was too painful.

Mac appeared at her other side.

'Come on,' he said. He pushed one arm under her shoulders and the other under her knees, and the militiaman helped him to stand up bearing her weight.

Baz looked up into his face. It was ashen and taut with worry.

'I'm okay,' she said. 'Just a hit on my plate.'

'I thought I'd lost you for a second,' he said through gritted teeth. 'If that had been a round from the Dushka, it would have cut right through your body armour. You were lucky – it must have come from a Krinkov or an AK.'

'I'm sorry,' she said, and she really meant it. But she'd got her story.

By the time they got behind the cover of the walls, Baz could hear other technicals approaching from the direction of the village. The PKM gunner let rip once more.

Their own vehicles were revved up and ready to go. Logan was carefully helping Kaminski into the back of the Surf. Mac assisted Baz in from the other side. Seconds later, the four Hiluxes and the Surf streamed out through the ancient gateway and hit the main north–south road. They turned north and accelerated away.

Baz twisted painfully in her seat to look behind, but no one was following them. Perhaps the fate of the first technical made the others less keen to engage.

Her shoulder throbbed and she felt suddenly exhausted. Despite knowing she should keep her body armour on until they were safely back in Lashkar Gah, she couldn't resist taking off her ops vest, unstrapping the plate carrier she was wearing and sliding out the back plate. The material of the carrier showed a slight rip – she would hardly have noticed it if she hadn't felt the impact of the bullet on her back. But the black nylon cover of the ceramic plate itself had spalled and shredded from the impact. She peeled the material away, expecting to see a slug embedded in the ceramic, but instead all she could see was a slight impression – a dimple in the surface showing where the round had hit the plate and simply bounced off it. And if she hadn't been wearing the plate... Fuck, she'd probably be dead.

It was a sobering thought, and she hurriedly put the plate back into the carrier and strapped it to her body again.

Dawn had turned the eastern sky the palest shade of tangerine. They were still driving at speed, and the road was empty in both directions. Baz turned to the man in the seat beside her. He was leaning forward, his face in his hands, and she realised he was crying. She stretched out a hand to his forearm.

'It's okay, Brad. You're safe. We've got you and we're gonna get you home.'

He raised his head to look at her, his eyes beaming.

Mac turned round to look at them both.

'Just one thing,' he said. 'If you're Brad Kaminski, where the fuck is Bakker?'

Day 4

Chapter 24

Helmand River Valley

They drove fast, without stopping. Mac felt the familiar drop in his mood following the adrenalin high of the action, but Logan still seemed to be buzzing, cranking up the music and drumming his fingers on the steering wheel as he drove.

'Man, that was something,' he said, as they cleared the last reaches of Najibullahkhan Kalay. 'You did real good. That guy with the pitchfork, he nearly took you out.'

'You saw?' said Mac.

'Yeah, as we came up to the house. I would have taken a shot, but you were blocking him.'

Mac rubbed his eyes. They felt gritty. It didn't sit particularly comfortably with him, killing another human – even though he knew the man would have shown no hesitation about doing the same to him. He drank some water and wished he could sleep, but Logan needed his eyes on the roadsides.

Baz was doing what she could for Kaminski in the back of the Surf. She gave him water, which he drank greedily, and food, which he was only able to pick at. She tried to give a couple of flesh wounds a cursory clean, but really they needed to be checked over by a doctor as soon as possible. Something that would have to wait until they reached Lashkar Gah.

Though none of his injuries appeared life-threatening, the Canadian reporter was almost certainly suffering from emotional shock. He didn't speak and every bump in the road seemed to make him fearful, gripping the edge of the seat with white knuckles and constantly looking around for threats. Dehydrated and confused, he seemed to be taking little comfort in the fact that he'd been rescued – and was probably finding it difficult to process what was happening.

Mac twisted in his seat to look at Kaminski. The man was shivering.

'Baz, can you reach into the back and grab a survival blanket?'

Baz nodded and unclipped her seatbelt so she could delve into the space behind her. She spent a minute rifling through Logan's trauma pack until she found a polythene-wrapped silver blanket.

Mac turned back to the road ahead.

'What the hell is that?'

Beyond Ginger's vehicle, which was leading the convoy, it looked as if the road was blocked by a military checkpoint. It certainly hadn't been there when they'd come down the highway the previous day. He grabbed the Motorola from the console between his and Logan's seats.

'Golf, this is Mike. Am I seeing a fucking mirage or is that a Brit checkpoint up ahead?'

'Mike, this is Golf. You're not seeing things – it's real.'

Ginger's Hilux was slowing down.

'Ain't no Brits in Helmand,' said Logan. 'Weapons ready – I don't like this.'

What the hell was going on? They were only a kilometre and a half out of Najibullahkhan Kalay – it seemed like a lot of interest for one small village.

Mac pulled the Krinkov he'd taken in the raid out of the footwell. The armed men at the checkpoint seemed to multiply, emerging from a couple of WMIKs and a six-wheel Pinzgauer all-terrain vehicle, as if they were expecting trouble.

'Mike, this is Golf. Can confirm visual on 1 Para personnel.'

Mac craned his neck to the side to see beyond the Hilux. Ginger was right. He could now see a couple of men wearing maroon berets, with red DZ Flashes on their sleeves. Curiouser and curiouser.

'Doesn't make sense,' he said to Ginger over the radio. '1 Para aren't even out here, are they? And they certainly don't have Pinzgauers.'

There was a moment's silence as Ginger thought. 'Shit. Heard a rumour they just deployed out here to support UKSF ops.'

So they'd stumbled into the middle of something big, some sort of covert Special Forces operation.

The Para at the checkpoint waved them to a halt.

'Fuck me backwards, it's the Head.' Mac could hear trepidation in Ginger's voice over the radio. What did he mean? What was the head?

Ginger got out of the lead vehicle and Mac followed suit, walking forward to join the conversation.

'Hey, Head, didn't expect to see you out here.'

'Fuck! The ginger minger, as I live and die.' Mac didn't care for his tone – dripping with menace and sarcasm. 'Didn't think we'd see you again. After what happened.'

Ginger's face darkened with anger. Mac knew there'd been some sort of trouble at around the time Ginger left the regiment, but he'd never pried into the exact details.

'You know it had nothing to do with me,' said Ginger through gritted teeth.

'That's where we'll have to agree to disagree. Anyway...' The Head, conscious of Mac hanging on their every word, clearly wanted to steer things onto a different subject now. He looked at their convoy, taking particular interest in Logan, who was now standing outside his vehicle, leaning nonchalantly on the driver's door. 'Quite a band of renegades. Mind filling me in on exactly what you're up to?'

Mac stepped forward. 'Yes, chum, I do mind. None of your bloody business.'

This wasn't the answer the Head was expecting. He gripped his rifle a little tighter. 'Listen, mate. We're on an operation and we don't need a bunch of amateurs like you fucking it up for us. A hostage's life could be on the line, so I need you to get the fuck out of here.'

Realisation dawned on Ginger's face. 'You're here for Kaminski, aren't you?'

The Head gulped air like a fish gulping water. 'How the hell...'

Mac laughed out loud. 'Right, you might as well pack up and go home.' He turned to Ginger. 'Why's he called the Head? Not on account of his brainpower.'

'No chance,' said Ginger. 'It's because of the size of his fucking head. Like one of those bloody orcs in *Lord of the Rings*.'

It was the Head's turn to fume. He glared at Ginger with undisguised hatred. 'You saying you got Kaminski?'

'Could be,' said Ginger.

The Head's eyes widened. 'Stay here a mo, I've got to get the boss down here.' Turning his back on them, he spoke quietly and urgently into his radio. Mac heard the crackle of someone replying, but he couldn't make out what was said. The Head turned back to them. 'Right, my boss wants a word. He'll be here in a moment.'

'Fine,' said Mac. 'We'll wait.'

The Head pursed his lips with a frown, looking at Mac as if he was stupid. 'Of course you'll bloody wait.'

Mac looked back towards the Surf and gave Logan a nod to tell him everything was cool. But that didn't mean they wanted to hang around long – they needed to get Kaminski some proper medical treatment, and for all they knew, the guys they'd hit might have got themselves together to come after them by now. He looked at the WMIKs and the Pinzgauer that formed the British cordon. If anyone was coming for them, at least the odds were now stacked in their favour.

At that moment, another dusty WMIK came up past the convoy and drew to a stop. A bearded figure emerged, heavily laden with field gear, all coated with fine desert moon dust.

The only clean thing about him was the UCIW, a shortened version of the M4, that he was holding as naturally as if it was an extension of his right arm. There was something familiar about his walk.

'Mac?'

'Sharky?'

'Jesus wept.'

'You're like a fucking bad penny, turning up wherever I go,' said Mac, slapping Paul 'Sharky' Benchley on the shoulder.

'More like your lucky charm!'

Mac had worked counterterrorism with Sharky in London back in the day, when he was in the Met – and this was the second time he'd run into him since arriving in Afghanistan.

'What are you doing here?'

'Not the way it works,' said Sharky. 'I get to ask the questions.' He turned to the Head. 'Can you get a brew on for everyone?'

If it was possible, the Head looked even more furious than before. 'Sure, boss.' He slouched off, muttering grumpily.

Sharky watched him go, waiting until he was out of earshot.

'That little turd causing you problems?' he said, eyeing up Mac and Ginger.

'Nothing we couldn't handle,' said Mac.

'So whose is the Pinzgauer?' said Ginger. 'Not your standard British-issue kit.'

Sharky laughed. 'Sure isn't. It's on loan from the Kiwis. 1 Para Support Group are trialling it.'

'Sweet,' said Ginger, staring at the vehicle with undisguised longing.

'Okay,' said Sharky, his expression turning serious. 'Now tell me if what he said is true. You've rescued a hostage from the Taliban? Who the fuck are you working for?'

'I work for Well Diggers,' said Ginger. 'One of our blokes has been taken...'

'So you mounted your own rescue? Jesus Christ.' He looked at Mac. 'You can't have been thinking straight.'

Mac shrugged. 'Successful mission.'

'Apart from the fact we picked up the wrong guy,' said Ginger.

Sharky looked incredulous.

'Yeah, faulty intelligence,' said Mac. 'We hauled a man out, but he turned out not to be our man.'

'So who did you get?'

'Canadian journo – Brad Kaminski – taken down in Kandahar a couple of months back.'

Sharky's shoulders started to shake, and he let out a deep rumble of laughter. He clapped Mac across the shoulders.

'Thanks, mate. You've just done my job for me. Where is he?'

Chapter 25

Helmand River Valley

Sharky took Kaminski off their hands, still grinning that they'd done his work for him, though some of his crew were less than thrilled at having missed out on the action. They had a medic with them, who immediately inserted a drip into Kaminski's arm to rehydrate him and counter the shock. He was also able to take a closer look at the worst of the Canadian's wounds.

Over a quick brew, Mac introduced Logan to Sharky, who knew of the mercenary by reputation, and the two of them promised to meet up in Kabul some time to trade war stories.

'Okay, everyone, time to head out,' said Sharky, tossing the dregs of his tea into the roadside dust. 'Doesn't look like they're sending anyone after you, or we would have known it by now, but I wouldn't waste any time heading north if I was you.'

Mac shook his hand and accepted his gratitude graciously. But inside he was seething. He'd risked all of their lives on a piece of dodgy information and while Sharky was happy, they were back at square one.

'What the fuck do we do now?' he said to Logan, Ginger and Baz, as they climbed back into the Surf and fell in behind the British contingent. They would drive in convoy as far as Lash, where Sharky would carry on towards Kandahar to hand Kaminski over to the Canadians at KAF – Kandahar Airfield, the biggest staging centre in the region.

'Even if we get better information on where Bakker might be,' Ginger said, 'this little jaunt has probably blown the whole

Well Diggers budget, because the governor will still expect to be paid.'

'Surely it's time for the Dutch government to step in,' said Baz. 'With money, if not with manpower?'

'I'll have to talk to Anholts when we get back,' said Ginger. 'Basically, I've fucked up.'

'Not your fault,' said Mac. 'What were the chances that the westerner who was spotted wasn't our man?'

'Almost as bad as a dry hole,' muttered Ginger, referring to a rescue mission in which no hostage is found.

They slumped into silence, exhausted, deflated, all wondering what would come next. No one wants to return from a rescue mission empty-handed, even if it had been a success of sorts.

—

The drive back up to Lash seemed long, but at least it was uneventful. After waving Sharky and his team off once they'd crossed the Helmand River at the edge of the city, Logan drove back to the Well Diggers house.

'Jeez, I need a beer,' he said, following Mac and Ginger inside.

Baz limped in behind him. 'Tell me about it,' she said.

'How are you feeling?' said Mac. He'd been pleased that she'd had the distraction of looking after Kaminski, at least for a bit, so she couldn't dwell on the fact that she'd taken a hit and what might have been if she hadn't been wearing body armour.

'Bruised, battered.' She smiled at him. 'Lucky to be alive.'

He shook his head. He couldn't afford to take her on any more missions if she kept putting herself in danger. But now wasn't the time to get into it. Now they all needed a beer and some food, and a good night's sleep once they'd had a chance to unwind.

Ginger called Nagpal to see if he could organise a delivery of food from one of the local restaurants, and he did one better by arriving with another crate of beer and the assurances that an order of Kabuli *palaw* was on its way – a popular Afghan dish consisting of rice and mutton, with raisins and grated carrot.

He joined them on the shaded terrace at the back of the house.

'So where do you think Bakker might be?' he said, once they'd filled him in on what had happened.

'Fuck knows,' said Ginger. 'You've clearly not heard from the kidnappers?'

Nagpal shook his head. 'Nothing.'

'We've missed something,' said Mac. 'The man can't have vanished into thin air. Someone, somewhere, knows where he is.'

'If he's still alive,' said Logan, tossing his empty beer bottle into a bucket and reaching across the low table in front of them for another. It was a thought that no one had wanted to voice.

'Whether he's alive or dead, there's got to be some information out there,' said Mac. 'Nagpal, who haven't we spoken to? Where are we with Nazanina?'

'She hasn't come back to work, so we'll probably have to go to her – she's at a family compound somewhere in the countryside. I'm on it.' Nagpal took a long drink of beer, and looked thoughtful. 'Maybe...' he said, wiping his mouth with the back of his hand.

'Maybe what?' said Logan.

'Okay, you remember our list of people who left the company?' said Nagpal, putting his bottle down on the table.

Mac had completely forgotten about it, probably because he didn't think it would lead to anything. 'Sure,' he said. 'Why?'

'I think we should follow up on one of them. About a year ago, there was an argument at the other house which resulted in Vinke sacking one of the gate guards.'

'You surely don't think that this was an act of revenge for something as trivial as that?' said Mac.

Nagpal pulled a face. 'Not trivial. The man lost his living. He supported his whole family on what he earned from Well

Diggers. That sort of insult can only be settled by the spilling of blood.'

'You're kidding,' said Mac.

Nagpal frowned and shook his head. 'No. It's part of the Pashtunwali – the code of life. *Nyaw aw badal* – even a mere taunt, a *peghor*, counts as an insult.'

'Shit. I wish you'd mentioned it sooner.'

Nagpal shrugged. 'It might just be a waste of time.'

'Don't forget,' said Logan, exhaling an odorous cloud of smoke from the *chars* he'd just lit, 'Afghan society is tribal – and vengeful. Do you know what happened to him, Nagpal? Did he issue any threats?'

'It was a year ago. Lash is big enough, but there aren't many jobs as soft as being a gate guard at a western compound. If he wasn't able to find work, he might still be blaming Vinke. And that would call for the shedding of blood.'

'We need to find him and talk to him,' said Ginger. 'What was his name?'

'Said Wali Gul.'

Mac remembered the name from the list Nagpal had given him.

'Do you know where he lives?' said Baz.

'His family are from Kandahar – the Hotak tribe, I think. I can check his address in the office records.'

Despite feeling wrung out from the events of the past twenty-four hours, less than an hour later Mac found himself sitting next to Nagpal in the front of one of the Well Diggers Land Rovers. Ginger sat in the back, but for once Mac had managed to persuade Baz that she shouldn't come. She needed to rest, and it wasn't going to be much of a story for her – they were just going to question Said Wali Gul about his whereabouts on the day of Vinke's death. Mac didn't expect much would come of it, but they had to try everything. Time was running out for Bakker.

'It said in the records that his family lived in Loy Bagh. It's a run-down area of farmland on the other side of the river.'

'You've got his address?' said Ginger, leaning forward between the seats.

'No, not a street address. Just a rough indication – the streets aren't named and the houses aren't numbered. When we get there, we can ask around if anyone knows the family.'

It didn't seem very precise, but Mac knew it was the Afghan way. He just hoped they weren't setting out on another wild goose chase.

Once they were across the river, the buildings thinned out and the roads became narrower. They drove through a patchwork of tiny fields, tended to by women and children. Instead of the large walled compounds of the city, the dwellings were small, mostly built of mud, without doors or windows. Despite their poverty, the women wore brightly coloured shalwar kameez, while their children sported a mixture of traditional and western-style clothing, all grubby and worn out, handed down through an endless succession of siblings and cousins. The little boys stared with wide, dark eyes as the Land Rover rumbled past on the rough tracks, while the little girls hid their faces in their mothers' clothes, already knowing better than to look strangers in the eye.

A few kilometres north of the main river crossing, Nagpal brought the Land Rover to a halt in a more built-up, but no less poverty-stricken, area.

'I think he should be living somewhere around here,' he said, climbing out of the vehicle.

Mac quickly checked his Browning and got out too. He hoped he wouldn't need it. After all, they were just here to ask a few questions. If they actually found the guy.

Nagpal walked towards the nearest house, a small, squat building made of mud bricks. A goat bleated loudly as Ginger pushed it to one side so he could come round the Land Rover. The air smelt of livestock and raw sewage. Mac hoped they would find the man quickly. The light was fading now, and this wasn't the sort of area he wanted to be wandering around after dark.

'*Salaam alaikum*,' called Nagpal, to alert anyone inside of their presence and make it clear that they were friendly.

There was no response. Only the bleating of the goat and the sound of their boots on the stony ground.

He said it again, louder this time.

A small boy, maybe five or six, peered round the edge of the doorway, the two middle fingers of his right hand stuffed firmly in his mouth.

Nagpal stepped forward and squatted down in front of him. He asked him something in Pashto, but the boy's intense blue-green eyes widened with fear and he ducked back inside the house.

Mac sighed. This was getting them nowhere. He looked around to see if there were signs of people at any of the other nearby dwellings. A teenage girl ducked out of sight, and Mac knew better than to attempt to talk to her.

Then a man appeared in the doorway of the first house, taking the boy by the hand. Nagpal straightened up with a groan, rubbing the small of his back. The man gave him a hostile stare – Mac supposed it wasn't every day that a Sikh and two westerners appeared in his village and accosted his child.

Nagpal took a step back to lessen any threat he might have presented.

'*Salaam alaikum, chutor asti?*'

'*Alaikum a'salaam.*' The man's tone was gruff.

Nagpal spoke and Mac heard the name Said Wali Gul in amongst the words.

The man shook his head vehemently, with a torrent of words. But he rubbed the side of his nose with his index finger, a sure-fire tell that he was lying as far as Mac was concerned.

Nagpal turned back to him and Ginger. 'He says he doesn't know where Said lives. He hasn't heard of him.'

'Ask him what tribe he's a member of,' said Mac.

This set off a lengthy conversation that in due course turned into an argument. The little boy tugged his hand out of his father's and went back inside. Mac could feel the tension growing, and beside him, Ginger stiffened, his hand drifting down to rest on the grip of his holstered pistol. Mac looked at him, giving a slight shake of his head. There was no point spooking the bloke.

The goat meanwhile had wandered off around the side of the house. A sudden sharp bleat and a scuffling of feet caught Mac's attention. An angry shout.

'*Waa, ásha ásha!*'

Someone was running away.

Without thinking or waiting, Mac set off after whoever it was. If the person had reason to bolt on hearing whatever Nagpal and the man were saying, the chances were that this was the man they were after. And if he was running away, it suggested he had something to hide.

As he came around the mud hut, Mac saw a figure dressed in dark clothing disappearing into the gap between two more houses. He pelted through the filthy back yard, shoving the protesting goat out of his way, and ducked into the space where the man had disappeared. He could still hear the footfalls thudding somewhere ahead and he was determined to catch up.

There he was, charging across a turnip field. The ground was softer, but the knee-high plants impeded Mac's progress, and the distance between them grew.

'Hey, stop!' yelled Mac.

The man glanced back over his shoulder, but carried on running.

'Wait, I just want to ask you some questions.' He didn't even know if the man would understand him.

It made no difference. The runner was determined not to get caught. He disappeared into a grove of stubby trees and Mac crashed after him, the low branches scratching his face and catching in his hair.

'Fuck!'

Emerging from the trees some twenty metres further on brought Mac onto a narrow dirt road. He looked in both directions – there was the bloke, to the left, still running.

Mac's chest was burning, and every breath was a struggle. But he wasn't going to give up. He was going to catch the bastard if it killed him.

Chapter 26

Lashkar Gah

The man was running south along the narrow track between the fields that they'd driven up just minutes before. It was about a mile to the bridge that would take him across the river and into the main part of the city. Mac realised that if he hadn't caught the fugitive by then, the man would be able to evaporate into the warren of narrow streets and alleyways – and with darkness falling quickly, there would be no hope of tracking him through the shadows.

In other words, it was now or never.

He cursed himself for having neglected his fitness as he felt the burn of lactic acid in his calves and thigh muscles. But he wasn't going to stop.

In the dusk, the fields had become featureless expanses of grey and sepia interspersed with the squat black silhouettes of the mud-built houses. None of them had the luxury of light, though the smell of woodsmoke from their fires hung on the air. Mac could hear nothing but his own breathing and the crunch of his boots on the gravelly surface.

Where the hell were Ginger and Nagpal? Surely they would have come after him in the Land Rover by now.

A dog barked close by. It ran at him, snarling, giving chase through instinct. A man called out to it, but the dog took no notice, jumping up at Mac's legs, trying to get a grip with its teeth. As its jaws scraped his flesh, Mac smashed a fist at the side of its head and it lost balance, sprawling away behind him with a whimper. He hated doing it, but in a country where rabies was endemic, he wasn't taking any chances.

Mac pressed a hand against his thigh, still running. His jeans were intact, the damage would be no more than a graze. But the encounter had cost him a couple of valuable seconds. His quarry had reached the road, and was turning onto the bridge now. In moments, he would disappear into the urban landscape.

Mac pushed on harder, regardless of the fact that if he actually caught up with the man, he'd be too winded to even talk to him, let alone tackle him.

After the silent run through the fields, the dull roar of traffic on the main road sounded louder than usual. The runner ahead of him was silhouetted over and over by the headlights of the cars coming towards them. He glanced back, checking to see if Mac was still in pursuit, picking up his pace when he saw that he was still being chased.

Ginger, where the fuck are you?

There was no pavement on the bridge, just a foot-wide strip of pebbles, litter and automotive detritus at the side of the carriageway. Mac leapt over a shredded lorry tyre, almost tripping on a strip of twisted bumper as he did. Cars whizzed past him within touching distance, the fumes from their dirty exhausts catching in his throat, depleting the oxygen he needed so desperately to keep going.

The man had reached the far side of the bridge now and was heading into Lash. Where was he going? Mac wondered if he had a destination in mind, or was simply running because someone was chasing him.

Mac was halfway across the bridge, but the gap between them never seemed to lessen.

A sudden stitch stabbed under Mac's ribs, making him gasp with pain and slow down to a jog. He pushed both fists against the affected area, gritting his teeth, but it did no good. It felt as if a piece of string had been threaded through his viscera and was being pulled tighter and tighter.

Gasping for breath, he stumbled, just as a car coming towards him swerved to avoid a piece of debris in the road. Headlights blinded him as he felt himself falling. There was a sickening crunch as he collided with the vehicle's nearside wing. He felt himself being thrown clear with a rush of air. Then he crashed against the concrete side wall of the bridge, and was sucked into a maelstrom of pain and darkness.

Chapter 27

Lashkar Gah

As Mac disappeared towards the back of the house, Ginger turned to Nagpal. The argument between him and the man was becoming heated, both gesturing with their hands and talking over one another.

'What's the problem?' said Ginger.

Nagpal gave the man a final admonishment and turned back towards the Land Rover. Giving the villager a last glance over his shoulder, Ginger followed the Sikh.

'That man' – Nagpal sounded exasperated – 'it turns out he did know Said Wali Gul. But Gul is dead. He fell ill a few months back, a tumour in his stomach that couldn't be treated.'

Ginger wondered what sort of rudimentary healthcare had even been available to Gul. Was it something he would have died of if he'd been in Kabul, or in a western country with advanced healthcare? It was a moot question, anyhow. Gul's death ruled him out as a suspect in Vinke's murder.

They reached the Land Rover. There was no sign of Mac. Whoever he'd chased after, it wasn't Gul and so not someone they'd even be interested in. Just a villager who'd taken fright and probably didn't speak English.

'Mac? Hey, Mac, come back.' Ginger's shouts cut through the quiet village but elicited no response. He got out his phone and called Mac's number, but it just rang through.

Nagpal blasted the Land Rover's horn.

They waited.

Still Mac didn't come back.

Ginger was growing impatient. 'Can we go down that road?' He pointed to a lane leading off in roughly the direction Mac had disappeared. 'Maybe we can catch up with him.'

'Sure,' said Nagpal.

Dusk was falling, and Nagpal switched on the headlights as they bumped along a rutted track out of the village. Ginger scanned the countryside as the mud-walled compounds gave way to fields again, but there weren't any people around now. The women workers had finished for the day and had taken their children back to their impoverished homesteads.

After going straight for about a mile, the track came to an irrigation canal and took a sharp turn to the left. In every direction, the fields were flat and the crops low – if Mac had still been running around here, surely they would have seen him by now.

'Come on, let's go back to the village,' said Ginger. 'He's not out here.'

He'd probably chased the man around the houses without going far, and would now be wondering where they'd got to.

They returned to where they'd stopped originally. The man they'd spoken to had disappeared. There was no sign of the little boy, and even the goat had been tethered for the night.

There was no sign of Mac either.

Ginger got out and roamed between the houses for a few minutes, shouting Mac's name. Nagpal hit the horn a few more times.

Mac wasn't in the village, and he hadn't been out in the fields beyond. Where the hell could he be?

Nagpal was looking round nervously. 'What do you want to do, Ginger-jan?'

Ginger shrugged. They couldn't leave without Mac. 'Let's drive slowly back towards the main road, see if we find him.'

He tried the phone again. Mac didn't answer. Ginger couldn't believe that he was still running after the bloke – it was now more than twenty minutes since they'd taken off. Had he caught the man? Were they tussling somewhere nearby? It was possible that Mac's phone had fallen out of his pocket while he was running. Or maybe it had run out of power.

They trundled slowly along the track, between more fields, punctuated here and there by the walls of small, isolated compounds. Ginger kept trying the phone and Nagpal sounded the horn regularly. They stared out of the windows at the dwellings they passed.

Nagpal stopped abruptly and jumped out of the vehicle. Ginger watched as he banged aggressively on the doorway of one of the compounds. After a moment, it opened a crack and Nagpal spoke. Ginger couldn't hear what he said.

Seconds later Nagpal was climbing back into the car, shaking his head.

'Sorry, it was nothing. I saw a man was watching from the roof of that house, so I asked him if he'd seen people running. He hadn't.'

'Do you believe him?' said Ginger.

'I think so. He'd have no reason to lie.'

Ginger wasn't so sure. When it came to the local population, he had no idea who to trust and who not to, so his default setting was to trust no one.

By the time they reached the main road, it was dark. Ginger got out of the Land Rover and walked up and down by the side of the road, calling Mac's name again and trying his phone.

Nothing.

'Right, back to the village.' He wasn't going to give up. Mac couldn't have vanished into thin air. 'We'll door knock every house until we find him.'

Nagpal nodded his assent, but he didn't look happy as they drove back down the track.

'I'll speak to the villagers, though I doubt they'll tell me much.' He fingered his steel bracelet. He was a Sikh, while the villagers were Pashtun.

For a small village, it took longer than Ginger expected to knock on the door of every house and ask the occupants if they'd seen a westerner nearby, or if they knew anything about the man he'd been pursuing. Ginger waited by the Land Rover, while Nagpal spoke with each family. Then he came back and told Ginger what had been said. But apparently nobody had seen or heard anything. Even at the original house, the man they'd spoken to first time around claimed no knowledge of the man Mac had set off in pursuit of.

'What do you think has happened?' said Nagpal, as the two of them sat in silence in the Land Rover, wondering what to do next. It was gone ten p.m. and Mac had been missing for more than three hours.

Ginger tried Mac's phone again, though with no expectation of getting an answer.

He exhaled a long breath. 'He's got lost. He tripped and fell, knocked his head. He caught up with the bloke he was chasing and they fought. He lost his phone. He fell in a canal or in the river. I don't have a fucking clue.'

'Maybe he chased the man back into Lash,' said Nagpal. 'Maybe he's gone back to the house or the office.'

Ginger shook his head. 'He would have called us.' Mac would know they would be searching for him and waiting for him at the village. He could only conclude that something untoward had happened. He guessed Mac was lying in a field or a ditch somewhere nearby – and now it was night, it would be virtually impossible to find him.

'We need to organise a search party,' said Ginger. 'Men and torches.' They couldn't afford to wait until the morning – Mac might be injured. His life might be in danger.

'Where from?'

'Won't these villagers help us?'

'They don't have torches,' said Nagpal. 'We have one torch in the back of the Land Rover. It's not enough.'

Ginger thought for a moment. 'Call Logan, the other drivers, the interpreters and the rest of the local staff. Ask them to come here and to bring torches. We'll search through the night until we find him.'

Nagpal didn't look particularly convinced, but he got on the phone.

Ginger climbed out of the car. The night was clear, and the air was still warm. That at least was in Mac's favour. There were no lights in the village, and the only sounds were the cicadas and the occasional bleat from the goats tethered between the houses. He lit a cigarette and smoked it slowly, as slowly as he could. Because when he finished it, there was one more call he had to make.

A call he didn't want to make.

The cigarette tasted like shit anyway, so he dropped it and ground it out with his heel. He got out his phone and located the number.

'Hey Baz.'

'Ginger?' She sounded puzzled.

'Baz…' Seconds passed.

'What is it?' Her voice was laced with anxiety.

'It's Mac. We've lost him.'

Day 5

Chapter 28

Location unknown

Mac's mouth was dry. It tasted of blood. He ran his tongue along his upper teeth until it hit a jagged edge, sharp enough to cut the soft flesh. The metallic tang intensified as blood flowed from the gash.

Bloody hell!

There was a gap where one of his front teeth should have been. Beyond that, a cloth was bound tightly round his face, gagging him.

Fear kicked in.

Half-awake jumped to fully awake with a surge of adrenalin. His eyes felt sticky and gritty. He opened them but saw nothing. His eyelids and lashes brushed against the fabric of a blind-fold. All five of his senses bombarded him with information. It was still dark, he guessed. Either that or the blindfold was incredibly effective. He was lying down but he was moving, bumping roughly against a cold, hard surface. Metal. The smell of exhaust fumes and the thrum of a diesel engine explained the movement. The noise of the tyres on the tarmac didn't seem muffled, making him guess he was in the back of an open truck, rather than inside a closed van. However, he could feel the weight of a covering of some sort. Fabric, from the way it hugged the contours of his body. Maybe a tarpaulin. Pain in his wrists told him he was bound. Chafing around his ankles confirmed it. He flexed his muscles to move, but all he managed was to amplify the magnitude of the pain that seemed to rack every sinew of his body.

He had been running. He remembered running through fields, along a dirt track in the dusk. He had been chasing someone, a man. He'd just wanted to ask a few questions, so how had he ended up hog-tied in the back of a truck? Who had done this and where were they taking him?

His instinct was to shout for help, to draw attention to himself, but the gag prevented that.

Think, damn it!

The truck was moving at a steady speed, in a constant direction. No stopping at junctions or turns, no roadblocks. No traffic jams. They were out of the city, which suggested one of two options – either they were travelling on the main road north, which would eventually hit the ring road, giving a choice of heading east to Kandahar or north-west towards Herat, or they were heading south towards Garmser and beyond that the poppy fields and the barren expanses of the Dasht-e Margo, the so-called Desert of Death where temperatures could reach as high as forty-six degrees at this time of year. Mac didn't fancy either option.

More questions crowded his brain, heedless of the fug of a possible concussion.

Why?

Why would someone take him? For a ransom. Why else? He couldn't think of any other reason. Ockham's razor dictated that the most obvious explanation is usually right. But that didn't appear to have held true in Bakker's disappearance. There had been no ransom demand for him. But if they had Bakker, why did they need him?

For God's sake. His mind was jumping to unwarranted conclusions. He didn't even know if it was the same people. His ending up here, in the back of this truck, was pure opportunism. No one could have predicted their visit to Loy Bagh, or that he would give chase to a random man. Bakker, on the other hand, had been lifted from the Well Diggers compound. There was nothing random or opportunist about that.

174

Mac's mind spun. With every mile driven, he was getting further and further away from the prospect of any help. He knew that Ginger and Nagpal would be searching for him, but their only chance of finding him would have hung on their seeing what happened or finding an eyewitness on the spot. Mac couldn't really say how much time had passed since he'd been captured, but as they had evidently left Lash behind, the chances were he was on his own now.

He was securely bound and he'd sustained some injuries, although he couldn't remember how. The extent of those injuries was unknowable – at this moment every part of his body seemed broken and in pain. He couldn't really assess where he was worst afflicted until he was able to move. The sharp spike of tooth in his mouth had ripped his tongue to shreds, but though its constant irritation loomed large, he doubted it was the worst of his problems. His right knee burned and throbbed, and if he couldn't run or walk on it, he would have no chance of escape.

He flexed his fingers and a stab of pain shot up his left wrist. *Goddamnit!*

He needed to work his way out of his bindings, but the rope was so tight around his wrists and ankles that he was losing feeling. There would be no wriggling free. The alternative was either getting the knots untied – and that seemed unlikely – or finding something sharp that he could rub the rope against like a saw.

Despair washed through him. What were the chances of doing that?

His mind drifted as he lost focus, the hum of the engine and the constant rattle of the truck mesmerising him into a stupor.

Time passed and still they drove on.

The huge jolt of a pothole made Mac's jaw snap shut and his mouth filled with blood from another slash of the broken tooth against his tongue. He swallowed, feeling sick, but the gag prevented him from spitting the blood out. He desperately needed water, and a mouthful of blood was no substitute.

But he was awake now, and furious with himself for losing attention. His head ached like there was a hammer drill working inside his cranium, and he had to reluctantly accept the fact that he might have concussion. Another thing to add to the list of obstacles to his escape. Just when he needed his wits about him more than ever before.

He slowed his breathing to control his erratic heartbeat. He needed to stay calm. Apply logic to the problem.

The road was far bumpier now than it had been before. So they'd reached a point where the tarmac gave way to a compacted dirt surface. The air seemed dry with dust, catching at the back of his throat with every intake of breath, supporting this hypothesis. Now he could feel the heat of the sun through the tarpaulin that covered him. Day had broken.

The inertia in his body told him he was lying longitudinally on the truck bed, with his head towards the front, in the direction of travel. The sun would still be to the east of the sky, rising higher and moving round to the south as the day wore on. Mac was curled up on his side, and the sun definitely felt hotter on his back than his front. That meant they were driving south. He felt sure of it.

It wasn't a happy realisation.

By now, they must be deep into narco territory, probably passing through the wide swathe of poppy fields that stretched along the Helmand River. With the demise of the Taliban, the area had fallen back into the hands of the rival warlords and criminal gangs who worked together to bring in the bulk of the world's opium crop. This was no place for a westerner. Down here, he would be seen as nothing more than a commodity, with a certain monetary value – and when his captors realised he was an Englistani, his value would drop. The British government wouldn't countenance the payment of a ransom and, between jobs, Mac didn't even have a supportive employer with K&R insurance to step into the breach.

Fuck. Fuck.

He should never have changed his plans. At this moment, he should have been lounging by a pool in Dubai, drinking cocktails with Baz…

The thought of her made his breath catch, and a coughing fit added to the brutal damage the broken tooth was inflicting on his tongue and lower lip. He had never felt so wretched, so without hope.

And still the truck drove on into the searing heat of the day.

Chapter 29

Lashkar Gah

Nagpal drew up outside the Well Diggers compound and waited for the gate guard to open up for them. Ginger couldn't wait. He jumped out of the Land Rover and slipped through the narrow gap in the opening gate, then ran across the parking area to the house.

Baz appeared at the front door looking dishevelled. She clearly hadn't had a wink of sleep.

They both spoke at once.

'Is he back?'

'You've found him?' Her voice was a mix of hope and desperation.

Ginger looked down, shaking his head. He couldn't bear to meet her eye. 'I'm so sorry, Baz.'

Baz pursed her lips and turned her head away. Ginger could tell she was trying not to cry. He followed her inside the house, as Nagpal pulled the Land Rover in to park.

In the kitchen, Baz stood leaning against the table. She'd brought her emotions under control, and now she looked angry and exhausted.

'I don't understand what's going on,' she said. 'Fill me in on the details.'

Ginger took the steel saucepan they used in lieu of a kettle off the stove and went to the sink to fill it with water. He'd been up searching the city streets all night and he needed coffee.

'When we were searching for the gate guard, Mac spotted something and darted off. He was running after someone.'

'Who?'

Ginger shrugged. 'No idea – maybe he thought it was the guy we were looking for. They both just disappeared.'

'And?'

'We waited for a while by the Land Rover for him to come back, then we went searching for him.'

Baz shook her head, a look of incomprehension on her face. 'What was he thinking?'

Ginger slammed the saucepan onto the stove, sloshing water over the side of it. 'I just don't know. We've driven around for hours, through all the villages on that side of Lash. We stopped and asked people if they'd seen him. We kept going back to where we last saw him.'

'And his phone?'

'Not answering.'

'I know,' said Baz, with a sigh. 'I've been trying to get through to him all night.' She brought both hands up to her face and rubbed her eyes.

Nagpal came in and sat down at the table without speaking.

'Where's Logan?' said Ginger.

'Out searching for Mac,' said Baz.

'Someone has taken him,' said Nagpal. He looked across the room at Baz. 'I'm sorry – but we would have found him or he would have come back here by now. I think we've got to face the facts.'

Baz dropped into the chair opposite him. 'So what can we do? I can't just sit around waiting for his body to turn up.' There was a tremor in her voice.

Ginger felt like shit. He was responsible – he'd persuaded Mac to come down here and get involved in the search for Bakker. Now both men were missing, without a single clue as to who had taken them or where they might be. He understood all too clearly why so few of the private contractors he knew were interested in coming to work down here.

The door opened and all eyes turned to see Logan coming in.

'Nothing?' said Baz.

'Nothing, I'm afraid,' said Logan. 'Coffee would be good,' he said, in Ginger's direction.

Ginger ignored him. 'I need to call Anholts,' he said. He went through to the living room, judging it would be a call better made out of Baz's earshot.

But the entire call turned out to be a waste of breath.

'That man is not my responsibility,' said the country manager, when Ginger had filled him in on all that had happened. 'Bakker, yes, but not your friend.'

'We need to find both of them,' said Ginger.

'And how do you propose to do that?' said Anholts. His voice seemed devoid of any sympathy.

'I'll need to hire a team of militiamen from the governor,' said Ginger. 'They can search the villages far more effectively than we can, and they'll have informants across a far wider network.'

'And all this is going to cost how much?'

'As much as it takes. There are two lives at stake here.' Ginger was finding it hard to keep the anger out of his voice.

Anholts snapped. 'The contingency fund is already gone – you threw that away rescuing the wrong man. I can take some money from next year's budget, but that will have to be made up.' He paused, but Ginger remained silent. 'This is going to put us out of business.'

'And that's more important to you than saving their lives?'

'Of course not. But the people we're working for, if we can't carry on with our work, their livelihoods will suffer. Our demise will drive them into the arms of the narco gangsters, as there will be no legitimate way for them to make a living.'

'Forgive me, but the threat to Bakker and MacKenzie is more acute. That's what I've got to deal with.'

'Sure, I get it. Go and ask the governor for help. If he demands money, tell him we'll pay him when next season's grants come through.'

Ginger hung up. As if that was going to work. Khaliq financed his operations through his family's poppy-growing profits. He didn't give a shit about the lives of two western do-gooders and there was no way he was going to lift a finger without a hefty wad of cash up front. Or...

He went back into the kitchen.

'Logan, Khaliq owes you a favour or two, right?'

Logan pulled a face that didn't really answer the question, but Ginger couldn't blame him for keeping his cards close to his chest.

Baz looked from one to the other of them closely. 'Jeez, guys, this is Mac. Don't play games. Logan, if you can call in favours from anyone, anywhere, just do it, okay?'

She rushed out of the kitchen and slammed the door.

Ginger felt helpless.

'Sure, sure,' Logan called after her. 'I'm on it.'

—

They drove to the governor's office, only to find that he was receiving visitors at the Bost Hotel – by Afghan standards, a rather luxurious hotel on the banks of the Helmand River. Khaliq had requisitioned the place for his own use after he won control of Lashkar Gah and declared himself governor following the fall of the Taliban.

The hotel was situated approximately half a kilometre from the governor's office along East Bost Avenue, and the road between the two properties was closed off at either end by militia checkpoints. Logan conferred with the captain at the checkpoint at the office end of the road and then returned to where Baz and Ginger were waiting in the Land Rover.

'He's going to call the hotel and check if the governor will see us.'

'What will you ask him for?' said Baz, leaning forward from the back seat.

'Intelligence, primarily,' said Logan. 'Men, if we need them.'

'Of course we need them,' said Baz. 'We need boots on the ground, searching.' There was an edge of hysteria to her voice.

'Which will be more effective if we can get some intel first,' said Ginger.

'Listen,' said Logan, 'nothing goes on in Lash without Khaliq or his cousin having a finger in the pie. I'm confident he'll know something.'

Baz sat back in her seat. Ginger could feel the strength of her glare via the rear-view mirror.

The captain raised the barrier and waved them through, speaking briefly with Logan through the vehicle's open window as they passed.

'Good,' said Logan. 'We're on.'

Three minutes later they parked up in front of a sprawling two-storey building on the riverfront. Built by the Americans in the 1950s as a club house for a legion of expat engineers and their families, the Bost Hotel may have seen better days but it could still be seen as the standard bearer for the dreams of Lash becoming a modern garden city. Beds of gold- and rust-coloured chrysanthemums bordered the parking area and uniformed guards stood to attention as they walked through the wide double doors into the bullet-pocked lobby. Every seat was occupied by bored-looking men, either alone or whispering together in groups, and Ginger guessed this was the queue for an audience with Wadaan Khaliq – who alone had the power to settle scores, grant permits or give his blessing to whatever venture they were here to talk about.

An officious Pashtun with a red hennaed beard came out from behind the reception desk to ascertain who they were, as if it wasn't obvious given that there were no other westerners in the place.

'Come, come,' he said to Logan, pointedly ignoring Baz, who'd put on a hijab as soon as they'd drawn up outside.

They were shown into the hotel dining room – a cavernous salon with bow windows overlooking the hotel's swimming pool and the river beyond. There was no one swimming or sunbathing by the pool, which on closer inspection Ginger realised was empty. A set of cricket stumps painted onto the broken tiles at each end indicated its more recent function. Still, the room they were in was well-furnished with rugs, heavy pleated curtains pulled back from the windows, solid wooden furniture and garish chandeliers, probably imported from Dubai.

'Logan-jan, my brother!' Wadaan Khaliq came towards them with arms outstretched.

'*Salaam alaikum*, Wadaan-jan,' said Logan. He dipped his head in respect, then stepped forward to shake the governor's hand, and was finally swept into a back-slapping embrace.

'*Salaam alaikum, chutor asti?*' said the governor as they broke away from each other. He glanced at Ginger, and switched into English. 'I hope you and your family are well and thriving?'

Ginger realised this was a huge sign of respect and he had to wonder again exactly what had transpired to put Logan in such a venerated position.

'*Alaikum a'salaam*. We are all blessed, thank you,' said Logan. 'And may I ask after your family and your beautiful children? They're well too?'

'*Insha'Allah*. Allah is watching over us always with his beneficence.' He turned to Ginger and held out a hand. 'It is good to see you again, Mr Ginger-jan.'

'*Salaam alaikum*,' said Ginger. 'I hope that you are well and that your family is all good.' He knew what was expected of him.

'Indeed, indeed,' said the governor. He turned to Baz and spoke in Pashto, though he didn't extend a hand to her.

She smiled and answered him, but Ginger could see that the extended round of niceties was taking a toll on her. Every minute was valuable, but they couldn't risk upsetting the governor by cutting short the formalities.

'Come, sit,' said Khaliq, leading them to a grouping of low, cushioned chairs by one of the curved windows. 'Tell me how I can be of service to you, my friends.'

Now they were getting down to business, the conversation switched back into Pashto. Ginger listened without understanding, but he heard Logan mention both Bakker and Mac, gesturing with his hands to get his points across. The governor listened without interrupting, then spoke in return for several minutes. Baz was biting her lip, as if she wanted to say something but was holding back. Certainly, it would be better to leave matters to Logan – he had the governor's ear, and expecting Khaliq to conduct business with a woman would be out of line. In fact, they were stretching that line to breaking point by even bringing Baz with them – but she'd been absolutely insistent on coming.

Finally, after more discussion, during which Ginger had to keep dragging his eyes away from the view of the river to try and look attentive, some agreement appeared to have been reached. He would have to wait until they were back in the Land Rover before Logan and Baz could reveal what had been said, but he gathered by the tension still showing in Baz's jaw that she wasn't particularly happy.

They shook hands again, bowed some more and Logan and Khaliq engaged in their usual round of brotherly love. Finally, Khaliq led them out into the lobby, where he made another effusive show of leave-taking. The same groups of men were still waiting to see him, and they looked on impressed. It was rare for a high-ranking Afghan official to show such respect to westerners. What had Logan done for him?

Back in the car, Baz was spitting nails. 'I call BS,' she hissed, as Logan reversed them out of their parking spot.

'Chill, Baz,' said Logan. 'He's good for his word.'

'Like to fill me in?' said Ginger.

Logan outlined the conversation as they drove. Khaliq had apparently promised them unreserved help – he would put his most reliable intelligence officer in charge of finding out who was holding the two men, and once they had that information, his forces would be at their disposal.

'For sure,' said Baz. 'That's when we never hear anything from him again. I know his type. Promise the world with no intention of delivering.'

'Drop it, Baz,' snapped Logan. 'Wadaan Khaliq and I go back a long way. And him walking us out in front of so many people means he has to come good on his promise. If he'd stayed in the dining room when we left, then I'd know nothing was going to happen in spite of what he said. I trust the guy.'

'Good for you.'

Silence reigned for the rest of the drive back to the Well Diggers compound. Ginger chewed the inside of his cheek, wondering which of them was right.

Only time would tell. And that was the one thing they were rapidly running short of.

Chapter 30

Location unknown

Dried blood stinks. Especially when it's plastered across your mouth and nose in the form of a gag, soaked with your own blood over a number of hours. Dried sweat stinks. Diesel fumes stink. Even though Mac feared he would throw up at any second, his mouth was as dry as the thousands of square kilometres of burning desert that made up the southern reaches of Helmand Province.

Where the hell are you taking me?

He'd passed out at some stage but now he was awake again, in his own private hell. The heat under the filthy tarpaulin was unbearable – he felt as shrivelled as a bit of crispy bacon. The thought of which brought on another urge to vomit. But if he did that the gag would probably see to it that he suffocated.

It wasn't quite the glorious end he'd imagined for himself.

Breathe slowly. Calm yourself down.

He was too angry to be completely calm, but cold rage would be of more use to him than hysteria, so he did everything he'd been trained to do to get a grip. Focus on breathing. Think about one problem at a time. Find a solution, then move onto the next.

The intensity of the heat told him it was midday or later, which meant they'd been driving south for six or seven hours. If there had been any stops, it wasn't while he was conscious. Which meant they must stop sometime soon. He needed water and whoever was in the driver's compartment would know that.

A dead hostage has next to no value and very quickly becomes a dangerous inconvenience.

He considered his options. Limited options. Severely limited options. He couldn't shout for help because of the gag. Assuming that he could somehow loosen it enough to call attention to himself, it was doubtful that anyone would hear him, or if perhaps passing through a village they did hear him, he could be almost certain that no one would help him.

Escape didn't seem much of an option either.

Engaging with his captors?

Do you think they'll speak English, stupid?

Wait for release and rescue. And pray to a God he'd long since stopped believing in.

The road was rougher than before, with bumps and potholes that jarred him against the metal truck bed again and again. He braced himself between the side of the truck and something solid that jutted out on one side, but it didn't help much. His head juddered against the floor, magnifying the pain he was already suffering, but he couldn't find a way of moving his arms up to act as a buffer.

The distraction of hearing voices raised in the vehicle's cab did little to take his mind off his predicament. Try as he might, he couldn't hear any recognisable words or place names – there was nothing that gave him a clue as to who they were or where they were taking him. Instead, he concentrated on rubbing the side of his head against his shoulder in an effort to shift the blindfold up enough to allow him to see. It was tied tightly at the back of his head, and as he pushed at it, he felt a sharp jag of pain behind his left ear – there was a swelling, where he'd taken some kind of knock.

Eventually, a chink of light became visible at the bottom of the dark cloth. It seemed bright after so long in darkness. He could only open his eyes a slit and he couldn't really see anything, but for all that, it was welcome. He continued worrying at the material and, as the gap widened, he was able to open his eyes further. Underneath the light-coloured tarpaulin he could see the dim outline of his body. His clothes were filthy and stained with blood, but it didn't jog his memory as to what had happened to him. However, he was now able to see, so he pushed against the side of the truck until he could lever himself up into a sitting position. The cover fell away from his upper body and he blinked, screwing up his gritty eyes against the unforgiving glare of the sun.

He took a deep breath, relieved to be out of the fetid air trapped under the canvas. He looked round, steadying himself against the side of the truck and tilting his head back so he could see under the edge of the blindfold. Poppy fields. As far as the eye could see, a bright tapestry of purple, pink and white flowers, wilting in the heat as if they'd taken a dose of their own sap. Helmand's wealth by the hectare, but no sign of human life. The fields would become busy with workers once the petals had dropped and the resin could be collected – but for now the precious crop seemed abandoned.

It was a disquieting sight, beautiful as it was, and Mac wished he was anywhere else but here. The mere fact of being western put his life in danger, and he was miles from help or a safe haven.

They passed through a small village – a handful of mud dwellings crowded round a solitary well. It was quiet, deserted. The midday heat drove everyone indoors. There wasn't a single stray dog sniffing for food or a kid scratching in the mud. Even without the gag, there would be no point shouting for help in a place like this.

The truck slowed down, then stopped. Mac quickly lay down and closed his eyes, feigning unconsciousness as he listened for what would happen next. The doors on both sides of the cab creaked open, and the truck bed rocked as two people climbed out. Their voices became more distinct out in the open – the men were speaking Pashto, the dominant language in Helmand. Footsteps crunched round to the back of the truck. A hand prodded Mac's arm, but he didn't respond. The owner of the hand shouted something to his mate, then pulled the tarpaulin back over Mac's body, covering his head and roughly tucking it round him to stop it drifting off again. Mac hardly dared breathe.

The two men walked some distance from the truck. They were quiet for a minute, but then he heard a quiet muttering of prayers. Midday or afternoon prayer time, he wasn't sure which, but it meant a ten-minute window during which their attention would be focused on something other than their prisoner.

He took a split-second decision.

Taking a deep breath, he pushed himself upright into a sitting position. He looked around quickly, but the truck's cab blocked his view of the men. Good. It was difficult to move, even more so to do it without making a noise, but he shuffled on his arse to the edge of the truck bed and peered around the side of the cab. There they were, about four metres away from the vehicle, kneeling on their prayer mats with their heads bent low to the ground, luckily facing in the opposite direction to him.

Now was the moment to break free. It was a plan that would rely on a huge dollop of luck, but if he could get out of the truck, and if they got in and drove off without checking the back... He didn't dare to hope, and he had no time to think about what he would do after that.

Long shot? It was his only bloody shot.

The problem would be climbing over the side of the truck with his hands tied and his ankles bound together. Climbing wasn't in fact an option. He looked over the edge. It was about a metre drop to the ground. He sat up tall and leaned on the side, then swung his legs round to push himself up onto his knees. The ridged surface was painful to kneel on, but he wasn't hanging around. He bent forward at the waist to lean over the side, and pushing up with his feet, launched himself out of the vehicle head first.

The drop wasn't long enough to twist his body round, but he managed to tuck his head to one side and land on his left

189

shoulder. The ground at the side of the road was strewn with stones and as he rolled onto his side, he heard a familiar snap. He'd broken a collarbone before so the immediate explosion of pain was no surprise, but crashing to the ground had winded him, adding another layer to his agony.

He lay in the shadow of the truck, waiting for breath. Surely the men had heard him crashing to the ground?

A few feet from the road, the edge of the nearest poppy field might offer shelter. The plants were densely packed and the flowers stood about a metre tall. If he could get in among them…

He knew it was a stupid idea. He wouldn't be able to get any distance and his captors would easily see the disturbance he'd cause to the poppies. Better to roll underneath the truck, between the wheels, and hope they'd drive off without checking.

He could breathe now, but even the tiniest move precipitated a flare of pain at the front of his shoulder as the snapped ends of his collarbone rubbed together. He'd broken out in a heavy sweat, and all four of his limbs felt like jelly. Moving anywhere was a huge challenge and time was running out.

With a final '*Allahu akbar*', the men finished their prayers. He heard them getting up and rolling their prayer mats. Then their footsteps approaching the vehicle.

He was halfway under the truck when the form of one of the men blocked out the sun above him. The man let out an angry cry and lunged for him. Mac tried to roll away, but it was a wasted effort. Within seconds, a hefty kick in the ribs made him yelp with pain. The other captor came running round to see what was going on, and the two of them shouted excitedly as the second one joined in with the kicking.

'Wait… stop…' But through the gag, the words sounded like grunts.

They didn't stop until they were ready to. It was the most effective form of communication. He'd done something wrong.

He was being punished for it. After a minute of relentless attack, finally one of them said a word and they both stepped back to look at their handiwork. There was a bit of a discussion, then each one of them grabbed an arm and manhandled him back into the truck.

Part of Mac wished they'd finished the job. Oblivion seemed far preferable to this. He'd been a bloody idiot, driven by panic and fear, and all he'd achieved was to make matters worse for himself.

As he lay panting in the back of the truck, the two men argued. Then one picked up a coil of nylon rope and passed the end of it twice around Mac's waist. He threaded the other end around the rusted chrome light bar that ran along the back of the cab and tied it securely. There was no way Mac was going to be able to throw himself out of the truck now.

Desperate for water, Mac made a sound in the back of his throat. They had already turned away from him to get back into the cab. Mac made the noise again, louder and more forcefully. One of the men, the shorter of the two, who was dressed all in black and wearing a *pakul* hat, turned back towards him. Mac shook his head and moaned. How could he explain his need to them? Gagged, hands tied behind his back, there was no way to communicate.

The other man, tall and skinny, in a grubby, cream-coloured kameez with a black-and-white patterned *keffiyeh* wound around his head, said something, then headed round to the passenger side. A couple of seconds later, he tossed a water bottle over the back of the truck to his partner. The short man unscrewed the cap, tugged down Mac's gag, and held the bottle to his lips.

It was the first moment of consideration his kidnappers had shown him.

He drank for as long as the man held up the bottle, pleased to clear the taste of blood from his mouth.

The man finally snatched the bottle away and screwed the cap. He tossed it in the back of the truck – there was no way

that he or his fellow abductor would drink from it now after
the infidel had contaminated it. Mac didn't care – he was just
grateful to have assuaged his thirst.

'Thank you... *mn'n'na, mn'n'na.*' It was literally the only
word of Pashto he knew.

The two men ignored his thanks, climbed back into the
vehicle, and the driver started the engine.

As they drove out of the village, Mac saw an old man
watching surreptitiously from a doorway.

Thanks for your help, mate.

The sun was lower in the sky, but the heat was just as fierce.
And on they drove, ever southwards.

Chapter 31

Location unknown

The water bottle rolled from one side of the truck bed to the other as they went over bumps and potholes in the road. It was the most subtle form of torture imaginable. Mac was thirsty again within twenty minutes, and watching the water sloshing around inside the plastic only made matters worse. He would rather have been blindfolded.

Of course, that wasn't true. He was now tied in such a way that he was sitting upright, with his back against the cab. He could hear *pakul* and *keffiyeh* talking or – more often – arguing in the front, but more importantly he could now see where they were going. As they drove, the poppy fields thinned out and the bland desert landscape came closer to the road. Eventually all signs of human enterprise disappeared and the road and the river parted company. Mac knew from having studied the map of Helmand before their mission to Najibullahkhan Kalay that from here on there was nothing but desert until they reached the villages along the southern border with Pakistan – but that was more than a hundred kilometres away.

Surely they weren't going to drive on through the desert all night?

Hopes of being rescued faded. No one would venture down here. No one would even realise this was where he was being taken. And if he did manage to escape somehow, there was nowhere to go. He'd die of thirst, alone in the desert. Anxiety gnawed at his empty belly, and with each kilometre they travelled, panic bubbled closer to the surface.

Inside the cab, a sat phone chirruped.

One of the men answered – he didn't know whether it was *pakul* or *keffiyeh*, as he hadn't fixed their voices yet. There was a one-sided conversation, followed by a lengthy argument between the two men. Then the truck screeched to a halt and both men got out to continue their argument over the bonnet.

Their words meant nothing to Mac, but one of them sounded angrier, while the other seemed to be more placatory. He wondered who'd called them, and what had been said that had kicked off the row.

The two men climbed back into the truck, making it rock, and slammed their doors. The engine started and, to Mac's surprise, the driver executed a fast three-point turn, churning up a cloud of dust as he revved the engine bad-temperedly. They were going back the way they'd come. Could Mac dare to hope that there had been a change of plan, and that they were taking him back to Lash?

Now they were driving faster than before, and inside the cab, *pakul* and *keffiyeh* were still arguing. Mac wondered which one of them was in charge. Maybe *keffiyeh*, as it was he who'd made the decision to give Mac a drink. But maybe he was just the more humane of the two.

Whatever hopes Mac had harboured during the hours of being jolted in the back of the truck like a sack of potatoes were summarily crushed when, without any warning, they took a sharp left turn off the road onto a dirt track. Mac was slammed sideways against his bindings, and then back the other way as the truck straightened. Now they were heading north-west. Mac tried to picture the map of Helmand in his mind, but he couldn't remember any side roads off the main road heading south. God knew where they were headed, but it wasn't back to Lash.

Mac looked around, trying to pick out features in the landscape that he might be able to remember easily, even if travelling in the opposite direction, but the land was dry and barren, and none of the rocks were different enough from each other to stand out. It made it impossible to estimate how far they had travelled and unlikely that he would recognise this stretch again if he needed to. The rutted track made for harder going. They had slowed down and the constant bumping and jarring exacerbated every one of Mac's injuries – his tooth, his collarbone, his knee. Sunburn on his face, scalp and the back of his neck was now an added factor, and his mouth was as dry as it had been before the water.

A steep incline down heralded a change to the landscape. They were descending into a river valley. Back at the Helmand River along the stretch that turned west? Mac felt too disorientated to feel sure, but he was damn certain there weren't any other sizeable rivers in the region. As they reached the flat plain through which the river snaked, once again there were areas of irrigation, and once again they found themselves passing by pink and purple poppy fields.

The sun had turned into a fiery ball on the western horizon, but the heat had hardly abated and Mac's clothes were stiff and salt-stained with sweat. He was losing valuable hydration and starting to feel light-headed. They passed through two tiny villages, and it struck Mac that down here, his captors evidently saw no need to hide their trophy. A few kids, an old woman and the ubiquitous donkeys all ignored him, if they even noticed him. Perhaps the sight of kidnapped westerners had become commonplace to them, or perhaps they valued their lives enough to pretend they'd seen nothing. Either way, he wasn't going to find help in these remote communities.

A sudden lurch and a change of sound from the tyres made Mac straighten up. The track they were on forded the river to cross over to the northern bank. A few splashes of water hit him on the arms and torso, but nothing like enough to cool him down. Then they were driving on gravel on the other side, until they picked up another rutted track.

The interminable drive went on.

All the time he'd been strapped to the light bar, Mac had been straining against the nylon rope that held him in place, and working his wrists against their bindings. If only he could get one hand free, he might be able to reach the bottle of water. He might be able to loosen the other hand and untie his feet. Even escape. But the knots held tight, and he felt he was making no progress at all. Any chance of escape wouldn't come while he was still in the back of the truck, so now he longed for them to arrive at wherever they were going. What they had in store for him, he couldn't guess, but he'd had enough of this hellish journey.

Eventually, as the sun was finally slipping away behind the low hills to the west, he heard *pakul* and *keffiyeh* arguing again. The truck slowed down – they were coming into another village. This settlement was larger than the previous few and there was even a handful of walled compounds. Mac guessed it was the southern stronghold of one of the narco barons. His heart fluttered as adrenalin surged, and as they made a turn off the track, fear bubbled up through his chest. Perhaps he could do with the journey lasting longer after all.

They came to a stop, and there was a hurried conversation which included a third voice. He heard the creaking of heavy hinges, and they pulled forward, through a gateway into a walled compound. A man closed the gates behind them, staring at Mac with undisguised disdain as he passed. He was heavily bearded and in traditional dress, with a Krinkov slung over one shoulder.

When the truck stopped, another two men appeared and, shouting excitedly, untied Mac from the light bar and dragged him out of the truck. Their eyes shone as if they were unwrapping a longed-for Christmas present, making Mac feel like a turkey ready for the oven.

'Speak English?' he said, looking from one to the other, as they dropped him unceremoniously on the ground. More men emerged from the compound building and gathered round to stare. 'Do any of you bastards speak English?'

Maybe it wasn't the right way to phrase the question, but Mac wasn't expecting a reply. What he got instead was a kick in the ribs, though whether this was because the boot's owner understood what he said or simply wanted to shut him up, who knew?

Pakul and *keffiyeh* were out of the truck, and Mac watched as an older man with a white beard drew them to one side. They spoke for a few minutes and then a large wad of US dollars changed hands.

He'd just been sold, presumably to the highest bidder. He hoped he was worth the money.

Chapter 32

Location unknown

Fear was overtaken by fury as Mac realised that he was simply a meal ticket to *pakul* and *keffiyeh*. There was nothing political about his abduction. They were a pair of criminal opportunists who'd seen a chance to make what was, for them, big money. He'd been snatched, trafficked and sold, placed in the hands of people even less scrupulous who would no doubt try and sell him back to his own country.

Problem was, it was a trade the UK government didn't care to participate in.

As *pakul* and *keffiyeh* climbed back into their truck and turned it round to leave the compound, the man with the white beard barked an order. One of the others squatted down at Mac's side, drew a knife and cut through the rope that was binding his ankles. He grabbed hold of Mac's left upper arm and yanked him to his feet, making Mac yelp with pain from the pressure this put on his broken collarbone. Starbursts flared in front of his eyes and he felt light-headed. He bit down hard on his bottom lip to anchor himself. He needed to keep his wits about him, now more than ever.

As White Beard gave more orders, Mac looked around the compound. It covered a large area, and the house at the centre was big – two storeys, and though crudely built it certainly wasn't a farm worker's hovel. There were a couple of additional, smaller buildings, one of which appeared to be a stable or livestock barn, and one which had small, high windows and a heavily padlocked door. Two battered Toyota Hiluxes and a technical were parked close to the main gate, along with several Hando motorcycles – the ubiquitous Honda knock-offs, ridden all over Afghanistan. And so far Mac counted at least seven men, all carrying Krinkovs or AKs, as well as a variety of pistols in holsters or simply shoved into waistcoat pockets. He would have his work cut out if he was to make an escape bid on his own.

But most interesting of all, running along one of the side walls of the compound, under the charred and blackened wooden covering of a lean-to, stood a row of four huge firepits. Oil drums were suspended above two of the fires, which were gently smouldering. The stench of chemicals wafted towards him. Beside the firepits were rows of empty oil drums, discarded iron pans, stacked barrels of chemicals and cans of solvents. A teenage boy with a scarf wrapped round his mouth and nose was stirring the contents of one of the drums with a long stick.

Mac knew immediately what he was seeing. This was a heroin lab. Not content with the profits to be made from smuggling raw opium over the border into Pakistan and Iran, Afghanistan's drug barons were increasingly bringing the manufacture of heroin in-house to enhance their profits. Ten kilos of opium could be transformed into one kilo of heroin – worth far more than ten times the value of the raw opium. It took little skill, and the chemicals involved, though illegal, were easily available, so why not keep a bigger slice of the pie to themselves? And who was going to stop them, when they could pay off the government officials and police who might have challenged them? It made perfect sense.

The man who'd pulled him to his feet prodded Mac in the back, and Mac tore his eyes away from the heroin still. The men were all making their way into the house. It was getting dark now. The gates to the compound had been bolted and a couple of guards had been posted just inside. Mac followed his captors through the door, hoping the fact that they'd paid good American dollars for him meant they'd want to keep him alive.

Like most Afghan houses, a small vestibule led into a large communal room, where the men now congregated. The floor was carpeted with overlapping handwoven rugs, and the tapestry-hung walls were lined with seats made from giant floor cushions. Apart from that there was no furniture, and the small windows were set high up, allowing just enough light during the day, while keeping out the heat of the sun. Now it was getting dark, the room was illuminated by a single bare bulb hanging from the ceiling. The exposed wiring, crudely stapled to the wall and ceiling, showed that electricity had been a recent addition to the house. Somewhere outside Mac could hear the hum of a generator.

An old man jostled the chattering men out of the way to lay out a large, food-stained tablecloth in the centre of the floor. It was time for the evening meal. Mac was shoved down onto a floor cushion in the corner of the room. Were they going to allow him to eat with them? He could smell cooking, and his dry mouth started to water. It was more than twenty-four hours since he'd had anything to eat, and while a day of high anxiety meant food had been the last thing on his mind, now he could smell it he realised how much he needed sustenance.

The younger men leaned their rifles up against the walls and sat down, talking loudly among themselves while they waited. The old man and the teenage boy who had been stirring the heroin outside brought in plates piled with rice, huge, charred naans and bowls of stewed chicken in a thin-looking broth. The men fell on the food as if it was their first meal of the day, but Mac, with his hands still tied behind his back, was unable to join in.

At least the bastards could give him something to drink.

He cleared his throat. The men ignored him. He tried again, louder this time.

'Water,' he said. He didn't know the Pashto word. His voice sounded cracked, and it was difficult to form the word as his slashed tongue was swollen and the geography of his mouth felt alien. They certainly didn't understand what he was saying.

'Water.'

He said it louder this time, and when White Beard finally deigned to look in his direction, Mac made a drinking gesture. White Beard looked away and spoke to a younger man with glossy black hair swept back from his forehead and a dark, luxurious beard. Some discussion ensued, and as both men occasionally glanced in his direction, he guessed they were talking about him. The discussion turned to an argument, but White Beard prevailed with a sharp finality. Black Beard said something to the man next to him, who stood up, cramming a last piece of bread into his mouth, and came across to Mac's corner.

He gestured with a hand for Mac to stand.

Mac struggled to his feet as quickly as he could. His shoulder was still burning and the last thing he needed was more manhandling.

'Water?' he said again, earning himself a slap across the jaw from his new keeper.

The man pulled a pistol from his shoulder holster and hustled him out of the room. Mac paused in the small vestibule, not knowing if he was supposed to go up the flight of stairs that led to the first floor or out through the door.

The man shoved him with the muzzle of the pistol. It was through the door, and Mac felt the heat hit him again as he stepped out into the darkened courtyard. His keeper shouted something to the two guards at the gate and they laughed.

Mac received another shove in the back, but he didn't know where he was supposed to be going. Had he been brought out here so he could be shot? That didn't make sense, given that they'd just paid for him, but this logic didn't stop the bitter taste of fear from flooding his mouth. He stumbled on the uneven ground.

He'd never felt so helpless or so vulnerable in his life, and in a rush of thoughts he wondered if he'd ever see Baz or his parents again, or get back to Scotland, or...

The man lost patience with him and grabbed hold of his right arm, and suddenly Mac was thankful for small mercies and fully back in the moment. He was being frogmarched towards the squat building with the padlocked door he'd noticed earlier. His captor let go of him to undo the lock and then shoved him roughly inside. He followed him in and rebound his ankles.

As the man turned to leave, Mac made one last appeal for a drink of water. The man said something he didn't understand and slammed the door behind him. Enveloped in darkness, Mac waited for his eyes to acclimatise. The small windows high in the walls let in a glow of moonlight, and eventually Mac was able to discern dark silhouettes in the room around him. Not furniture – they were all square. He felt with his hands. Boxes and crates. He was in a storage room. He sniffed. There was the tang of chemicals on the air, and he guessed this was where the ingredients for the heroin-making enterprise outside were stashed.

And now his makeshift jail.

He was exhausted and weak. Without giving it much thought, he sat down on the pressed mud floor, resting his back against the door. If they didn't give him food or water, he wouldn't be of much value to them for long. And by the same token, if he didn't get sustenance, he wouldn't have the strength to mount an escape attempt.

The sound of footsteps approaching on the ground outside made him tense all his muscles. Someone was coming towards the hut, so he scuttled from where he was to a position resting against a crate opposite the door.

He heard the noise of the padlock being released and the door creaked open. A torch shone in his eyes, temporarily blinding him.

'Bread. Water,' said a husky voice from behind the light.

'You speak English?'

There was no reply, but the light showed a hand reaching forward to place a plastic bottle of water and a metal plate with a folded piece of naan just inside the doorway.

'My hands,' said Mac. There was no way he'd be able to open the water bottle with his hands still fastened behind his back.

The man said something in Pashto, but he stepped into the room and swiftly cut the rope from Mac's wrists.

It could have been an opportunity to attempt an escape. He could have knocked the bloke over and gone for the door. But he'd already suffered the failure of one unplanned escape attempt. This would be too risky – there were two armed guards at the gate, and he was weak, injured and disorientated. He wouldn't stand a chance.

Instead, he rubbed his wrists where the ropes had chafed, and thanked the man.

'*Mn'n'na*, thank you.'

He would bide his time and wait for a better chance.

That might never come, but at least he had some bread and water.

Day 6

Chapter 33

Lashkar Gah

Baz didn't sleep a wink, and nor would she until she knew Mac was safe. And that might never happen because he might already be dead. Hot tears slid down her cheeks until she swiped them away with the back of her hand. Her eyes stung and her skin felt dry. There was a constant lump in her throat, making it hard to swallow water and virtually impossible to eat.

'God, you look like death,' said Ginger, putting a plate of soft naan and a steaming cup of tea in front of her. 'Get this lot down you or you'll collapse.'

He meant well, but it didn't really help. Logan had tried to make her eat the previous evening, but after a few mouthfuls she'd had to run out of the room to vomit. Her gut ached with hunger, but nothing was going to stay down.

'He's been gone thirty-six hours now,' she said. She didn't need to add what this implied. Ginger would know well enough. Each day, no, even each hour that passed meant a successful outcome was less likely. Successful meaning Mac getting out of this alive. Logan had offered her sedatives to take away the edge and she'd been sorely tempted, but that would feel like deserting Mac when he needed her most – and even if there didn't seem to be anything she could do for him, just sitting vigil was important.

Ginger sat down opposite her and started scraping Marmite onto his naan. The smell made her want to barf – weird English food that she'd never understand. She took a sip of the milky tea he'd made.

'So what's the plan?' she said, giving him a direct look.

He avoided making eye contact. 'We wait for intelligence from Khaliq.'

Baz slammed her fist down on the table in frustration, making the cups and plates jump. 'That's not a goddamn plan. That's doing nothing.'

Ginger didn't have a response, but catching the end of the exchange as he came into the kitchen, Logan did. 'Come on, Baz. This is how it goes in these situations. You wait and wait and wait. Then word comes in and suddenly you're off.'

Baz sighed. 'Sorry, guys. It's just...' The words dried up.

Ginger reached across the table and squeezed her hand.

The sound of the outer gates opening and a car driving into the compound caught their attention. Logan went to the window. 'It's Nagpal.'

A minute later, he came into the kitchen, starting to talk almost as soon as he was through the door. 'I asked around about Nazanina, and I got some information.'

'Nazanina?' said Baz.

'She was the housekeeper and cleaner at Vinke's house. She went missing after the murder.'

'She's a suspect?' Baz's eyebrows went into vertical lift-off.

Nagpal shook his head. 'No, no, but she might have seen something.'

'Then why would she disappear?'

'She would be frightened,' said Nagpal. 'If she told us anything about the killers, they would come after her.'

'So what information have you got?' said Logan.

'Tirich, my driver, told me she's a member of the Barakzai tribe. Her son and his family live in Gereshk. That's where she's most likely to have gone.'

'Someone needs to go and question her, straight away,' said Logan.

Nagpal looked at Baz. 'Will you come with me?' he said. 'It will be better if there is a woman present. Her family won't be happy for her to talk to a man, even someone from the company which employs her.'

Baz shook her head. 'I'm sorry, Nagpal. I can't. We might get some information on Mac… I should be here.'

Logan frowned. 'Baz, this might be just the lead we're waiting for. If she knows anything about who's holding Bakker or killed Vinke, it might also lead us to Mac. He could have been taken by the same people.'

Baz considered for a minute. If the same people were responsible for both abductions, that was true. But what if Mac was being held by someone different? She hesitated to say yes.

'Please go with him, Baz,' said Ginger. 'It's got to beat just sitting here doing nothing. And we'll call you if we hear anything from the governor.'

'How far is Gereshk?' she said to Nagpal.

'About seventy kilometres,' he said. 'If we go this morning, we can be back this afternoon.'

'You promise you'll call?' Of course they would.

—

Tirich drove them, with an armed guard sitting next to him in the front. The road between Lash and Gereshk was notorious for shakedowns and bandits, and Nagpal didn't want to take any chances. Logan had offered to come with them, but Baz persuaded him to stay behind in case a lead on Mac's where-abouts came in. They all knew that if this happened, a rescue mission would need to move fast. So Ginger and Logan stayed behind at the Well Diggers compound, gaming out a variety of scenarios while they waited for a call from Khaliq's number two.

They took the road north-east from Lashkar Gah until it hit the ring road, where they turned west. It was an uneventful journey, and just over an hour after leaving the city, they came to the outskirts of Gereshk – a moderate-sized town that was dominated by the ruins of an ancient Mongolian fort on the banks of the Helmand. As soon as they'd crossed the bridge over the river into the town centre, an argument broke out between Nagpal, Tirich and the guard over which way they should go to find the somewhat vague address Tirich's contact had given them. Although Baz could understand what they were saying, she chose not to get involved, having not the slightest clue about the geography of the place.

'We should be taking this main road past the factory and then turn south towards the mosque,' said Tirich.

The guard shook his head vehemently. 'No, no. I know the city well. It will be quicker to go south before the factory and then west to the edge of town.'

Nagpal had another opinion, and so it went on. But ultimately, Tirich was driving the Land Rover, so they went by his chosen route and finally reached a scrubby area where the rows of walled compounds started to peter out.

'This is the place,' said Tirich, pulling up outside a mud-walled compound that looked identical to the scores of others they'd driven past to reach it.

'How do you know?' said Baz.

Tirich looked round with a grin. 'Miss Basima, you're just going to have to trust me. I have counted the roads and the houses to bring us to the right place.'

Baz wondered if the Afghans would ever get around to naming their streets and numbering their compounds, but somehow she doubted it. She put on her hijab and took a last swig of water before venturing out of the Land Rover into the fierce midday heat. As Nagpal knocked on the gate of the compound, she wondered if the housekeeper would even be here and whether she'd have anything to tell them. It was probably all a wild goose chase. She checked her sat phone, desperate to hear news from Ginger and Logan, but there was nothing.

A young man opened the gate in the wall and eyed them suspiciously.

Speaking in Pashto, Nagpal introduced himself and Baz, and then stated their business. 'We are from Well Diggers in Lashkar Gah and we're looking for Nazanina.' They only had a first name for her, but this was hardly unusual in Afghanistan where a significant proportion of the population only used a single name.

'Why are you looking for her?'

'Is she here?' said Nagpal.

Baz stepped forward. 'We are worried for her. She hasn't come back to work and we'd like to see if she's all right.'

The man stepped back to allow them to enter the compound.

'My mother is here,' he said. 'She no longer works for Well Diggers, but I will ask her if she'll speak with you. Please wait.'

He closed the gate and walked across the open space of the compound to a small, single-storey dwelling. Baz looked around. There were a couple of young goats wandering about, stripping the last few leaves from some scrawny shrubs. An ancient scooter was parked by one wall, but there was no other vehicle. They clearly couldn't afford a car.

After a couple of minutes, the man reappeared and beckoned them into the house.

They were introduced to two more men, cousins apparently, but there was no sign of Nazanina. The men asked them some more questions and Nagpal again repeated what had been said at the gate. Green tea was served, and finally Nazanina's son said he would bring her in. Her relatives were obviously uncomfortable with the prospect of letting her speak to a man who was a stranger to them, even if Nazanina knew him from her work at Well Diggers. Baz flashed Nagpal a warning look to tell him that she would do the talking when Nazanina arrived, and he gave her a small nod of understanding.

The woman who came into the room was neither as old nor as poorly dressed as Baz had been expecting. She was probably in her mid-forties – old by Afghan standards – but to Baz, she looked strong and fit. Her shalwar kameez was of decent quality, and it made Baz realise how working for a western NGO must have afforded her far more than the rest of her family, up here in rural Gereshk. So why had she run away?

'Nazanina, my name is Basima Khan. I work at the Well Diggers office in Kabul.' A white lie, but she needed to reassure the woman.

Nazanina nodded but avoided eye contact. She didn't seem comfortable, so Baz knew she had to be careful if she was going to elicit any useful information.

'You worked for Lars Vinke and Tomas Bakker, and I know you had a message not to clean their house, but you haven't been in to clean the other houses for several days either. Are you sick?'

The woman shook her head, then glanced sideways at her son.

'Talk to them,' he said quietly.

'I'm not sick,' said Nazanina.

'Can you tell me why you haven't come to work?' said Baz. 'Did something happen?'

Nazanina looked down into her lap where her hands were twisting nervously together.

'Please tell me if you saw something.'

Nazanina pursed her lips and nodded her head. Then she found her voice. 'It was the last night I was working at Mr Vinke's house. I had finished cleaning the kitchen and I was getting ready for sleep.' Nagpal had told Baz about the small sleeping alcove just off the kitchen.

'Where were Mr Vinke and Mr Bakker?'

'Mr Vinke was in the living room. He would read every evening after his meal, late into the night.'

'And Mr Bakker?'

'He was out, but as I was sweeping up, he arrived back.'

'Then what happened?'

'I think Mr Bakker was drunk.' She looked apologetically at her brother, as if it had been her fault. He frowned.

'Do you know where he had been?' said Baz.

Nazanina shook her head. 'It happened once before, but I don't know where he went. He entered the living room, and I heard them arguing. They were speaking in Dutch so I couldn't know what they were saying.'

'Did someone else come to the house?' said Baz. She needed to know if Nazanina had seen the attackers.

Nazanina looked surprised by the question. 'No. I don't know. The argument got louder. Mr Vinke was shouting more and more. Mr Bakker went to the front door and went out and Mr Vinke followed him out.'

'You were watching?'

'I heard it – the voices, the door opening. They argued and I heard another voice join them, and more arguing. I could hear the sounds of a fight coming from outside, so I hid in my sleeping place.'

'Did you recognise the other voice?' said Baz.

Nazanina shook her head.

Nagpal showed her the sneaker in the plastic bag. 'Have you ever seen this before?'

The woman shook her head again.

Baz wanted to clarify what she'd said. 'Bakker and Vinke were fighting outside the house? Are you sure of this?'

'I don't know who was fighting. There was another person there.'

Baz looked at Nagpal. What she was saying didn't seem to tally with what they thought had happened.

'The other voice – was it a man?' said Nagpal.

'I went to hide in the place where I sleep. I didn't hear any more.'

'What about in the morning?' said Baz.

'When I got up, the house was quiet, but the front door was still open.' She covered her face with her hands, unable to speak.

'And?' Baz felt bad for prompting her when she knew what Nazanina must have found outside.

'I went out. Mr Vinke was lying on the ground. He was dead.'

'You're sure he was dead?' said Nagpal.

Nazanina gave him a withering look. 'I am sure.'

'And what about Mr Bakker?' said Baz.

'He was gone. I checked inside the house, but I knew. It was so silent. Like a grave.'

Things didn't seem any clearer, and Baz felt frustrated. Nagpal looked at her as if he wasn't sure what to do next.

'You're sure you didn't know the other person who was there?' said Baz.

'You can believe what my mother says. She doesn't lie.' Nazanina's son clearly thought the conversation had gone far enough. He turned to Nagpal. 'She will not be working for your organisation any more, but you still owe her last week's wages.'

'Of course,' said Nagpal. He drew his wallet out of a pocket and counted out several twenty-dollar bills. 'Here's her wages, and also some extra.' He handed them to the brother who pocketed the money. Baz wondered if Nazanina would see any of what was rightfully hers, but now wasn't the moment to intervene.

They were shown out and as they walked across the compound to the gate, Baz voiced what they were both struggling to believe.

'What do you think, Nagpal? Do you think she didn't know or see the third person? Or could she be trying to protect someone?'

Nagpal didn't have an answer.

Chapter 34

Location unknown

Mac's breakfast was bread and water, brought by a different guard this time. If he was going to be here long, it was a diet that might become challenging. But at least this visit came with added benefits – a scuffed plastic bucket for him to use as a latrine. And he was even given a moment of privacy with his hands untied so he could make use of it.

He took the chance for a split-second survey of the small storeroom, now that it was light, but he couldn't see anything useful and there wasn't time to delve into the boxes and crates stacked up against two of the walls. The guard returned to retie his hands, in front of him this time, which meant he could at least sit up with his back leaning against the wall without crushing them.

Left on his own again, he slumped forward to rest his head on his knees. Despite a couple of hours of fitful sleep, he still felt exhausted – probably due to the pain from his injuries. His head throbbed, his shoulder burned, his lower back complained with every movement and his knee was still hugely swollen and barely mobile. He was a mess.

He closed his eyes and zoned out, wishing he was anywhere but here. Wishing he was with Baz in Dubai, or even just back in Kabul. His mind was suddenly populated with people he knew – people he'd been in the Met with, boys he'd gone to school with, folk from the village, ancient relatives – all sorts of characters he hadn't seen in years, and now he wondered if he'd ever see any of them again. His mum and his dad. And places – from the familiar landscapes of his childhood to places he'd briefly visited and wanted to return to.

Would he ever see anywhere beyond the confines of this small room again?

Get a fucking grip.

If there was one thing Mac knew, it was that he couldn't afford to give in to despair. He needed to channel all that emotion into anger, and then use his anger to fuel his survival. Because he was going to bloody survive this. And he was going to see all those people and places again. He wouldn't let these fucking scumbags win.

Making a plan would distract him from obsessing about bad outcomes, and if he was to have any chance of successfully outwitting his captors, he would need a bloody good plan.

First, inventories. An inventory of his injuries, so he could form a realistic picture of what he might be able to do, and then an inventory of what was in the storeroom, in case there was anything that could prove useful.

He felt his knee gingerly with both hands, wondering how bad it was. No way of telling without an X-ray. But if he was going to get away, he needed to be able to run, and as things were, he could hardly stand and bear weight on that leg. However, he could flex the joint, albeit painfully, which suggested it wasn't broken. That was a plus.

On the other hand, his collarbone was a nightmare. His arm should be in a sling and immobile for several weeks for it to heal properly. He didn't have that luxury, and he could only hope that whatever happened to it over the next hours or days could be corrected later with surgery. It also meant that every movement of his body caused a sharp stiletto of pain, distracting him, making all his muscles tense up and his eyes water.

The bump on his head was the size of an egg, and tender to the touch. He was still suffering intermittent headaches, though the pain wasn't as severe as when he was being jolted up and down in the back of the truck.

The important thing was not how much he was suffering, but what he could do to alleviate the impact these injuries would have on any opportunity he found for escape, however unlikely that might be. Some strapping for his knee could certainly make a difference. Painkillers and anti-inflammatories were a remote hope – even if his captors offered him any meds, he didn't trust them enough to risk taking them. A sling wasn't practical, but with his wrists bound together, he could use his right arm to support the weight of his left arm and take pressure off his left shoulder. It wouldn't do much in terms of healing, but it was a way of minimising the pain.

He spent an hour examining the piles of boxes, crates and jerrycans.

There wasn't much that would prove useful, but some of it was interesting and had Mac scouring the depths of his memories back to chemistry A-level and the things he'd learned since about drug refining and bomb making. His captors held a good stash of petrol in here for their vehicles, and a large quantity of the chemicals used for heroin manufacture – acetone, ammonium chloride, sodium carbonate. Some things he recognised from the labelling on the containers, others by their smell. There were plenty of other compounds that he didn't recognise. It seemed they were running quite a cottage industry here.

In one corner, there was a basket of tar-like blocks wrapped in clingfilm. Raw opium – the dried resin from the poppy seedheads, ready for processing into heroin. For a split second, Mac considered taking some of it. He knew it could be eaten, and it would relieve him from the grinding pain in his shoulder and the throbbing in his knee. But he couldn't afford to be fuzzy-headed, and the last thing he needed was a drug habit to contend with on top of everything else.

There were no tools in the storeroom, and nothing that he could use as strapping for his injured leg. He sat down against the wall again, feeling useless and tired. The anxiety

217

he'd managed to tamp down by assessing his surroundings came surging back, and despite the build-up of heat in the room, he shivered.

He couldn't just sit here and passively wait for whatever was going to happen. He still needed to devise a plan. Escape seemed unlikely, so maybe he should try and parlay with his captors. If he could make them believe that his employers would pay a high ransom to have him back, perhaps he could persuade them to take him back to Lashkar Gah. Trouble was, that idea wouldn't work – because when they arrived at Lash, there would be no grateful boss waiting with a suitcase of dollars. At which point he'd probably be paid off with a bullet.

With his watch and phone missing – probably currently residing in *pakul* and *keffiyeh*'s pockets – Mac tracked the passing of time by watching a small square of sunlight move across the wall opposite the window. He'd quickly dismissed the high window as an escape route. There was no way he would be able to squeeze through it, which was maybe why his captors had chosen to incarcerate him in here. But it was a window to the outside, and through it he might be able to see some of what was going on in the compound. He'd counted seven men, including White Beard and Black Beard, when he'd arrived the previous day, but he couldn't be sure that was the total number. He needed a more accurate head count.

It took him nearly a quarter of an hour to push a large wooden crate from the other side of the room to the wall beneath the window. His ankles were still bound, so he could barely shuffle, and pressing against the wood, even with his right shoulder, was agonisingly painful for his collarbone. Furthermore, he only dared to edge the crate across the rough floor a little at a time – he couldn't afford for anyone outside to hear what he was up to. After each push, moving it a few inches, he would sink down against it, panting, until he got his breath back and the stab of pain in his shoulder receded.

Once the crate was in place, Mac faced the challenge of climbing up onto it with his feet tied together. He started by sitting on top of it, then bent his knees to draw his feet up. His injured leg complained, making him grit his teeth. Mustering all his willpower, he twisted his hips so he could push his feet round to the side, shuffling his arse to the edge of the crate to give himself space to transfer his weight onto his knees. It was more difficult than he had thought, and his right knee was almost too swollen to bend under him. He grunted with pain, then bit his lip hard to stifle it.

His already filthy shirt was now drenched with sweat from the exertion, and for a moment he felt light-headed. Kneeling up, using his forearms to steady himself against the wall, he was finally able to raise his face to the window.

He was looking straight into the sun, and it blinded him. He blinked and looked away, realising that this meant it was lower in the sky than at midday – so, late afternoon.

Time flies when you're having fun.

When his eyes got used to the glare, he looked out at the section of the compound the window overlooked. It wasn't much of a view. He could see the back wall of the main house, and just to one side of it he could see two of the heroin factory firepits. The kid he'd seen before was at work again, stirring the contents of the oil drums, mesmerised by what he was doing in a way that suggested, despite masking his face, he was breathing in too much of the drug-laden fumes. Dope Boy – that would be his nickname.

The sound of a car engine caught Mac's attention, but he couldn't see the vehicle in question. It revved a couple of times. Then there was the crunch of tyres on gravel. Someone was going somewhere. He listened for the opening of the gates, but couldn't hear anything over the sound of the engine. However, once that noise became more distant, he heard the gates slam shut behind it. Now, there was at least one person less in the compound. Maybe more.

Footsteps were approaching from the front of the house.

He sunk back down onto the crate. He didn't want to get caught looking out of the window, in case that led to his captors blocking it off. He dropped to the floor, causing a spike of pain to travel from his knee to his hip, and as quietly as he could he shoved the crate away from its position under the window.

The door opened. The guard who'd brought his breakfast stared at him from the threshold. Mac was sitting on the floor with his back against the shifted crate. He looked up. The man looked barely seventeen years old, his requisite beard just bumfluff and his face unlined, but he held his pistol casually, with a confidence born of familiarity. He could have been an insurgent for a couple of years already. Pistol Boy. In his other hand, he held a bottle of water and a piece of folded bread.

Mac held out his bound hands.

'Untie me.'

Pistol Boy looked at him blankly, until Mac shook his wrists and motioned an attempt to pull his hands apart.

The lad said something in Pashto, put the water and naan down on top of the crate and shoved his pistol into the pocket of the woollen waistcoat he wore over his shalwar kameez. He undid the rope tied around Mac's wrists.

'You speak English?'

No answer.

Mac pointed at the bucket in the corner to convey that he wanted some privacy. Rather than leaving the room, the boy simply shrugged and turned sideways. He got out his weapon again and made a show of passing it from hand to hand, reminding Mac of what might happen if he tried anything. It was pure bravado – the kid was anything but alert.

Good.

Mac stood up with difficulty and took a leak. He couldn't see a way of leveraging any advantage out of this encounter, so when he'd finished, he picked up the naan and water and sat back down against the crate.

The water tasted stale, and the bread had no flavour at all. Pistol Boy watched him with a look of impatience. Mac wondered how many hostages he'd had charge of. Bakker maybe? He wondered if it was possible the Dutchman was being held in the same compound. Mac drew out the meal for as long as he could, just for the sake of having his hands free, but after a few minutes his guard started shuffling and tutting.

Mac's temper flared.

'Fuck you!' he said, sprinkling crumbs down his front as he spat out the words. 'I need someone who speaks English. I need to wash. I need clean clothes.' He pulled the collar of his shirt to one side to show the bruising on his upper chest. 'I need a doctor and medicine.'

Pistol Boy stared at him blankly.

'Fuck you!' he said again.

The pistol butt hit him across the side of the head, smashing him to the floor in an explosion of stars and static. Mac gasped like a fish landed in the bottom of a boat.

Pistol Boy might not have understood much English, but apparently he knew what 'fuck you' meant.

Chapter 35

Gereshk

Baz was confused after talking to Nazanina. Could she really tell them nothing about the attack at the Well Diggers house that night, even though she'd been there? How was that possible?

'Why would she lie to us?' she said, as she and Nagpal hurried out through the gate of the family's compound.

'Fear of reprisal, maybe,' said Nagpal. 'If it was the Taliban, they could have sent a threat to her via her imam. Maybe she thought it would be safer to make up…' He stopped talking mid-sentence.

Baz looked up to see why.

The street that had been deserted when they'd arrived at the compound was no longer empty. Tirich and the guard they'd brought with them were still sitting in the Land Rover, just across the road, but a group of three men were leaning against a Toyota Hilux parked a little further along. One of them was pointing at her and Nagpal, saying something to the other two.

'Come on,' said Nagpal, quickening his pace.

'What is it?' said Baz.

Before he got the chance to answer, one of the men shouted something at them in Pashto. Baz didn't catch the words, but she could tell it wasn't friendly.

'What's going on?' she said to Nagpal in English, so the men couldn't understand.

'Sorry,' said Nagpal in a low voice. 'It's my fault.'

'What do you mean?'

The three men were approaching them now.

'Hey, Sikh, get out of our city,' said one, making a rude hand gesture that Baz had seen plenty of times before in Chicken Street in Kabul.

'You're not welcome here. You're an infidel, an insult to Allah.'

Tirich had started the engine of the Land Rover, while their guard had wound down his window. Baz could see that he was holding his rifle in readiness.

Damn! This was escalating fast.

'Heh, what are you doing, travelling with a Pashtun woman – you know that's *haram*.' Forbidden. The man who spoke picked up a stone from the street and rolled it from hand to hand threateningly.

Because of her looks and her hijab, they'd made an assumption that she was a Pashtun. She stepped forward to block the man's path, ignoring Nagpal's hand on her arm, trying to draw her back.

'I'm not Pashtun. I'm American,' she said in English first and then repeated it in Pashto. 'I'll travel with whoever I like. Please move out of our way.'

The men burst out laughing at her show of bravado, but they didn't move. They stood their ground between Baz and Nagpal and the Land Rover. Beyond them, Baz saw the guard get out of the vehicle, his AK pointing towards the ground. He slammed the door behind him to catch the men's attention.

They turned to look at him, but the fact that he had a weapon did nothing to deter them. Every Tom, Dick and Harry in Helmand carried an assault rifle.

Tirich got out of the Land Rover now and leaned on the driver's door. 'Get lost, you sons of donkeys.'

The man with the stone raised his arm and threw it. Tirich ducked, but it glanced off his forehead, leaving a wide, red gash.

'Goddammit,' said Baz, a tide of anger rushing through her.

One of the men turned back to her and, stepping forward, gave her a sharp punch in the stomach. Winded, Baz stumbled backwards into Nagpal, who only just managed to save her from falling on her arse.

A shot rang out. The guard's rifle pointed at the sky, but he slowly lowered it, training it on the man who'd thrown the stone. Tirich had a hand pressed to his forehead, but his face was awash with blood.

'Come on,' wheezed Baz, still fighting for breath.

She and Nagpal scurried past the men and back to the Land Rover.

'Get in the back,' she shouted at Tirich. 'Nagpal, help him.'

She climbed into the driving seat. The engine was still running. Beyond the three men, she could see more men emerging from compound gates and jogging down the road towards them. The shot had alerted them to trouble in the neighbourhood, and the strangers were cast in the role of villains.

The guard fired another warning shot into the air, then climbed into the passenger seat.

'Drive,' shouted Nagpal, as the posse closed in on them.

Baz threw the Land Rover into gear, and they shot forward. She had to swerve violently to miss the stone-thrower, then she sped up the road towards the T-junction at the end.

'Which way? Which way?'

'Left,' said Nagpal.

'Right,' said the guard.

'Fuck!' She took a fast right, tyres almost skidding on the gravelly surface, and immediately saw that it was a dead end. She slammed on the brakes and executed a three-point turn.

'Are you okay, Tirich?' she said, not daring to glance round at the speed she was driving.

'He'll be fine,' said Nagpal, sounding calmer now. 'Cuts to the head always bleed a lot.'

She slowed down. No one had followed them. Tirich directed her back to the main road, where she swapped places with Nagpal, happy to let him take on driving duties back to Lash.

'What the hell was that about?' she said, once she'd applied a couple of butterfly stitches from the Land Rover's first aid kit to Tirich's cut.

In the front, Nagpal shook his head. 'It's nothing. I'm a Sikh, and the Taliban declared us heretics.'

'But the Taliban are no longer in control,' said Baz.

'They're not in government, no. But down here in the south, there's a strong insurgency and they have plenty of sympathisers.'

'Do things like that often happen?'

'More often than I would like. Many Sikh families have left Lashkar Gah for Kandahar or Kabul – and even more have left Afghanistan altogether.'

'And what about you, Nagpal? Will you leave?'

He glanced around at her. 'I'm an Afghan. This country is my home. I won't let them drive me out.'

Baz checked her phone. In all the commotion, she'd momentarily forgotten they were waiting for word on Mac. But no matter. She hadn't missed a call or a message.

Day 7

Chapter 36

Location unknown

It was more than forty-eight hours since he'd been taken.

Mac chewed this fact over in his mind like a stick of Wrigley's. It meant it wasn't looking good for him – he could be here for the long haul or, more likely, he could wind up dead. He wondered if they'd sent a ransom demand yet and, if so, who they'd sent it to. He tried to remember if he'd been carrying any form of ID when they took him, because no one had asked him for his name or who he worked for. He'd had a small wallet with cash – dollars and afghanis – which usually would also have included a couple of business cards. But he'd run out, so there was nothing to tell them who he was.

Presumably they'd want to recoup their investment in him somehow. If not by demanding a ransom, then by selling him on to some other group.

You can't feel fear continuously. The body can't sustain it. So now, a couple of days into captivity, Mac found his mood swinging between fear, frustration and boredom, always with an undercurrent of anxiety that snaked through his gut and wracked his back with tension. He slept on the hard floor. They'd given him a threadbare blanket, which he wound round himself tightly for both warmth and to provide a layer between him and the pressed dirt beneath him. His clothes were stiff with sweat and his body smelt rancid – though not as bad as the latrine bucket in the corner, which went unemptied despite the fact that he was now suffering dysentery from the well water they were giving him to drink. Diarrhoea and stomach cramps were an unwelcome addition to his catalogue of injuries. He barely slept at night and felt exhausted all day.

He would have given his right hand for a shower, a bed and a set of clean underwear.

This morning, he'd spent an hour watching over the back of the compound, but he'd only seen Dope Boy doing his chores as usual. Occasionally he heard voices towards the front of the compound, but he couldn't see what was going on, and he had a feeling that maybe there were fewer men here than there had been on the evening of his arrival. The generator hummed on and off, but he didn't hear any vehicle movements.

He got down off the crate and lay on the floor. A fly buzzed over the bucket in the corner, but he didn't have the energy to swat it. He felt feverish and the heat of the day was only just beginning to kick in.

Counting helped. He closed his eyes and counted – up to five thousand, down from two thousand, in threes, in twos. He constantly lost count, but that didn't matter. It was a way of quieting his mind, and letting slip some of the tension for some of the time.

He was dozing when the door slammed open.

Mac blinked as a shaft of sunlight cut across him. He sheltered his eyes with the crook of one arm and looked up. It was Pistol Boy, but Black Beard quickly pushed past him and said something in rapid Pashto. He looked down at Mac with an expression that combined disgust and pity.

'Come, come,' he said, gesturing with his hands for Mac to get up.

As Mac, still tied at the wrists and ankles, struggled to get onto his feet, Pistol Boy grabbed his left arm and pulled him up. The kid meant to help, but the sudden movement ground the broken ends of Mac's collarbone against each other. Mac let out a yelp and Pistol Boy let go of him. On his feet now, Mac slumped hard against the wall, gritting his teeth against the biting pain. Black Beard gave him a questioning look and Mac inclined his head towards his shoulder. Black Beard touched it tentatively, making Mac grimace, and then felt the ridge of where the bone was broken. He spoke to the lad again, then turned back to Mac.

'Come, come.'

The two of them led Mac out of the storeroom and round to the front of the house. They made slow progress as Mac limped along behind them, but his knee held up better than he had feared, confirming to him that nothing was broken there at least. He followed them into the main room, and Black Beard indicated that he should sit down on one of the cushions along the wall.

A moment later, White Beard came into the room, accompanied by a man that Mac hadn't seen before. From the deferential way White Beard waited for the other man to seat himself, it was clear that he was the old man's superior in whatever organisation they belonged to. The newcomer was probably in his forties. He wore a pristine white turban and shalwar kameez, a stark contrast to the sun-baked darkness of his skin and neatly trimmed black beard. Mac noticed that his shoes were hardly worn – this wasn't a man who spent his time in the rural villages of southern Helmand. So what was he doing here?

He returned Mac's stare. '*Salaam alaikum*,' he said.

'*Alaikum a'salaam*,' said Mac. What was the etiquette when talking to one's kidnappers? Polite greetings and small talk?

'My name is Akhtar Jamali.' He had switched to English.

Dope Boy came into the salon, carrying a tray with glasses of tea on it. It gave Mac a moment to think. The name Jamali was familiar for some reason. He took a glass of pale green tea – perhaps it would help settle his stomach. Then it came to him. Akhtar Jamali, the narco warlord who controlled swathes of the poppy cultivation in the southern reaches of Helmand Province.

Shit!

231

This man was no rank amateur when it came to kidnapping, and he would expect to make good money out of a westerner.

'What is your name?' said the warlord, once Dope Boy had retreated.

'Alasdair MacKenzie.'

'English?'

'Scottish.'

Jamali frowned at him. The distinction meant little. 'I hoped you were American.'

There was nothing Mac could do about that.

'The UK government won't pay a ransom,' said Mac. 'You're wasting your time with me.'

'Every government pays ransom money,' said Jamali. 'The British are no different. They pretend to be special, they pretend they're above trading bodies, but they'll pay. Tell me who you work for?'

'I'm between jobs.'

Jamali's brow lowered further and he turned to say something to White Beard.

'If you are not employed by someone, what are you doing in our country?'

'Like I said, between jobs. I start a new job in Kabul soon.' Mac was damned if he was going to tell them who he'd be working for.

There was more conferring.

'So what were you doing in Lashkar Gah?'

'Looking for someone.'

Jamali nodded at Black Beard, who was standing sentry by the door. Black Beard lunged forward and hit Mac across the side of his face with his pistol butt. He overbalanced sideways, but struggled back to sitting as quickly as he could.

'Tomas Bakker, a Dutchman. I'm searching for Tomas Bakker. He was abducted in Lashkar Gah a week ago. He works for an NGO called Well Diggers.'

White Beard shook his head. He whispered something in Jamali's ear, his eyes sliding sideways to judge the reaction to his words.

'We know nothing of this man,' said Jamali, but the slight nod of his head made Mac wonder if this was really the case. 'We settled our score with Well Diggers on the road in Marja District.'

So that's who'd been responsible for the attack that had resulted in Ginger having the job now.

'I know Governor Khaliq — he's helping with the search.' Mac hoped this would buy him some clemency, but how wrong could you be? It earned him another swipe from Black Beard's pistol. Clearly there was no love lost between Khaliq and Jamali.

When his head stopped swimming, he drank some of the bitter green tea. Jamali was engaged in a whispered conversation with White Beard. Mac had the distinct feeling his fate was being sealed and he didn't like it.

'Listen, I need water to wash in and clean clothes. I'm ill and I need a doctor. I need a mattress and bedding.'

Jamali barely glanced at him. He was looking at the doorway to the room, where a teenage boy was standing, leaning against the door frame.

'Akhtar?' said the youth, beseechingly.

'Khalo!' Jamali's expression softened and he said something in low, guttural Pashto. Mac realised what the youth was — his face was almost feminine and his eyes were heavily rimmed with kohl. This was *bacchá bazi* — he was Jamali's dancing boy, a form of male prostitution that was widespread among the gangsters and warlords. It infuriated Mac — Khalo was hardly more than a child. These boys would be used for sex until they reached eighteen or nineteen and then cast aside for being too old, probably already with an opium habit to feed.

The boy nodded and disappeared, seemingly mollified by whatever had been said to him. Jamali watched him go with undisguised lust, before turning his attention back to the business at hand.

233

'I need to see a doctor. I'm no good to you dead,' said Mac.

This, finally, made the warlord look up. His mouth twisted in a cruel smile. 'That's for me to decide, Mr MacKenzie. It will be up to me if you live or die.'

Two more men came into the room. The first of them was carrying a tripod and a video camera. Under Black Beard's direction, they set it up opposite where Mac was sitting. Mac had studied hostage videos and ransom requests when he'd done his police negotiator training with the Met. It seemed surreal now to be the subject of one himself. He thought quickly – what information could he surreptitiously pass on while they were filming him?

Once the camera was set up, Black Beard had him stand up and held a piece of paper in front of him. It was a message for him to read, written in crudely formed letters. Mac knew the drill – he would read it as slowly as he dared while at the same time tapping out a message in Morse code with one forefinger against the back of his other hand. This had to be done with just the tiniest of movements, hardly flexing his finger at all. He couldn't afford for any of his captors to notice.

Black Beard gave an order to the man operating the camera and Mac saw the tiny red light go on above the lens. It was recording. Black Beard shook the paper. It was time for him to read out the message.

'My name is Alasdair MacKenzie and I will be killed if you don't pay up.' His legs felt weak and shaky. He wondered how long he could stand for. 'I will be killed if you cannot arrange the transfer of one million dollars, as you will be instructed. If you do not believe the men who are holding me, if you do nothing to help me, they will cut off my fingers one by one and send them to persuade you. My blood will be on your hands if you don't make this payment.'

It was a chilling message, but as he read it out, Mac was concentrating on spelling out two words with the smallest movements of his right index finger. H-O-O-K. This was a reference to his location – the Hook was the name given to the bend in the Helmand River where it turned from flowing south to meandering west, where he knew his original kidnappers had driven him. Then he tapped out J-A-M-A-L-I.

His head swam and he stumbled over his reading. 'Please do what... please do as...' He stopped to clear his throat, playing for time until he'd finished signalling the second word. 'Please pay this money or you will never see me again.'

The red light went out. The video was made. The bearded men argued, presumably over who to send it to. Would his secret message reach Ginger and Logan – and would it arrive in time for them to rescue him before Jamali started cutting off his fingers?

He was taken back to the storeroom. But some time later that afternoon, he was brought a bucket of cold water, a cake of soap and a towel, untying his wrists so he could wash, then resecuring them when they took the bucket away.

Thank you, Akhtar Jamali.

He was genuinely grateful.

Chapter 37

Lashkar Gah

Bleak. Desolate. Inconsolable. There was a hollowed-out pit of darkness at Baz's core that grew larger and more voracious with each passing hour. It gnawed at her, every waking moment. And with sleep hard to come by, exhaustion made her even more susceptible to the raging fear and anxiety that had her in its grasp.

Ginger and Logan did what they could to support her, but they had nothing concrete to offer. There had been no word from Khaliq's network of informers. Mac had as good as vanished into thin air, and Bakker was so long gone that all hope of finding him alive was rapidly fading.

'How can people just cease to exist like this?' said Baz. She and Ginger were up on the flat roof of the HAVA office building, looking out over neighbouring houses and gardens, and beyond them, the sprawling town in one direction and the glittering band of the Helmand River in the other. 'He has to be out there somewhere.'

'We'll find him,' said Ginger, but his words sounded hollow to Baz.

'Where's Logan?' She'd left the house to come to the office before he was up, and he hadn't appeared with Ginger.

'He's gone to the Bost to talk to the Governor's number two about men and equipment for a rescue. We need to be ready to move in a heartbeat.'

Baz hardly felt reassured by this. 'I'm going to make some calls,' she said.

She headed down to the Well Diggers office and sat down at one of the desks. She'd called virtually all her press contacts over the last forty-eight hours, asking them to talk to their sources and come back to her if they heard anything about captured westerners. Now she scrolled through her address book and decided to call them all again. She couldn't let a single person forget about Mac's predicament.

'Hey, Bob, how's things?'

'Carlos, good to hear your voice. Any news?'

'Hey Jen, just wanted to catch up...'

But no one had anything to tell her.

The office door slammed and she looked up as Nagpal came into the room. His normally pristine dark blue turban was askew on his head, and he was holding one hand to a graze on his cheekbone.

'Nagpal, what happened?' She leapt up and guided him to one of the threadbare chairs in the small reception area.

He sank down, resting his elbows on his knees, his head in his hands.

'Are you okay?'

When he lifted his head, she could see the extent of the cut on his cheek. 'I'm okay,' he said, but his voice was shaky. 'A man knocked me off my scooter on the way here.'

'You were in a traffic accident?'

Nagpal's face darkened. 'It was not an accident. The man was on a motorbike, and he came up close from behind. He drove me off the road and then sped away without stopping.'

Ginger listened from the doorway, having just come down from the roof.

'Is there a first aid kit anywhere?' said Baz, glancing across at him.

'I'll see what I can find.' He disappeared into the small kitchen and returned moments later with a glass of water, and a large red rucksack which contained the office trauma pack. He put the pouch down beside her.

'Why would someone do that?' said Baz, cleaning the blood from Nagpal's cheek with an antiseptic wipe.

Nagpal gingerly unwound his turban. Underneath it, his long hair was tied in place with a square of fine black fabric. Placing the metres of blue material and the black square onto the chair next to him, he let down his hair and gently felt his skull. The long, black tresses reached practically to his waist. He winced slightly. 'Ay, that's a bump. I took quite a knock when I fell off my scooter, but thankfully my *dastar* protected my head from serious injury.'

'Are you sure?' said Baz. 'Should we take you to the hospital and get a doctor to check you over?'

Nagpal shook his head and gave her a weak smile. 'I'm fine, Basima-jan. Really.'

'But what about reporting the man to the police?' said Ginger.

'Of course that would be a waste of time,' said Nagpal. 'The police here have no sympathy for us Sikhs. They treat us as very second-class citizens, even lower than the Hazara.'

'Could this be linked to what happened yesterday in Gereshk?' said Baz.

Nagpal shrugged. 'Things like this happen to Sikhs everywhere in Afghanistan, every day. As you saw, most Pashtuns view us as heretics, and even though the rules against us laid down by the Taliban are no longer in force, there are plenty who believe they still should be.'

He stood up and bent forward at the waist, pulling his hair up to the top of his head and twisting it into a loose knot. Baz watched fascinated – she had such problems getting her hijab to stay in place, she couldn't imagine having to wrap a turban.

'Can you pass me the *patka*?' said Nagpal. 'The black square.'

Baz passed it to him, and he used it to secure his hair in place. He spent a minute tucking in stray strands. Then he took up the long, blue cloth and folded it into neat pleats. Tucking one end between his teeth, he slowly wrapped it around his head several times, with each pass making sure that the pleats were flat and sharp. Finally, he took the tail from between his teeth and tucked it in at the back to hold all the layers in place.

'There, done,' he said.

'What about your scooter?' said Ginger. 'Is it repairable?'

'I think so,' said Nagpal. 'A shopkeeper saw what happened, and he let me leave the scooter at the side of his shop. I'll fetch it in a minute and take it to the garage.'

Baz carried on calling her contacts, while Ginger and Nagpal went to sort out the scooter. She made call after call, but still there seemed to be no one with any idea who might have snatched Mac. She checked the office emails constantly, as well as all the newsfeeds, for any word of a ransom demand, for either Mac or Bakker. But all the while, she couldn't stop thinking about what Nagpal had said, about the Sikhs being treated as second-class citizens. It outraged her. This was Nagpal's country. He'd been born here and lived all his life here – he was as much an Afghan as the Pashtuns and Tajiks that made up the vast majority of the population.

Of course, she knew well enough how minorities like the Sikhs and Hazaras were treated. Religious and tribal prejudice was rife – and it made her despair. It was what had caused her parents to emigrate to America. Her father was Tajik and her mother Pashtun, and neither of their families had approved the match. Tribal and ethnic loyalties were placed above loyalty to the country as a whole, and it was one of the reasons why there would never be peace or stable governance.

But twice in two days, Nagpal had come under attack for his religious beliefs. It was sickening, and she knew she had to write about it. Her role as a journalist was not only to report the news, but to raise awareness of what was going on in the country – Americans needed to understand the full complexity of Afghan society and politics if they were going to succeed in helping the country.

And maybe it would take her mind off what was happening to Mac, for a few short hours at least.

239

She put it to Nagpal, when he and Ginger came back into the office.

'Yes, I think that's a great idea,' he said. 'You know, under the Taliban, we had to wear yellow patches on our clothes to identify us as Sikhs, and fly yellow flags at our houses and businesses. This just made it even easier for people to harass us. And since then, it hasn't really got any better. Last month, my wife was frightened when someone threw rocks over the wall into our compound.'

'That's horrible.'

'Tomorrow, I'll show you the damage that's been done to the Gurdwara – our temple – and the desecration of our cremation ground.'

'Baz! Baz, you need to see this.' It was Ginger, shouting from the office next door.

'What?' She and Nagpal ran through.

Ginger pointed at an ancient television in the corner of the room. 'One of the guards just brought this video up,' he said, pointing at the screen. 'Apparently a Hilux drove by the front of the building and this was thrown out of the passenger window. It was in a plain envelope, addressed to Well Diggers.'

Baz stepped closer to see what he was talking about. The quality of the image was poor – fuzzy and lined – but she saw immediately that it was Mac, standing unsteadily, with his wrists and ankles bound. It might only have been two days since he'd gone missing, but he looked a shell of his former self, back bowed, favouring one leg, and his face showing several bruises. His hands were trembling – the man was terrified.

Bastards!

She caught the tail end of what he was saying.

'...the men who are holding me, if you do nothing to help me, they will cut off my fingers one by one and send them to persuade you. My blood will be on your hands if you don't make this payment.' He seemed unsure of what he was saying. 'Please do what... please do as...' He coughed. 'Please pay the million dollars or you will never see me again.'

240

'What the hell?' said Baz, as the screen fizzled to black. 'Let me see it again and call Logan here.'

They watched it over and over – while they waited for Logan and once he'd arrived – but it didn't make things any better. Finally, Ginger snapped off the television with the remote. Logan sighed.

'A million dollars?' said Baz. 'Where are we going to get that sort of money?'

Chapter 38

Location unknown

Time was passing, and Mac was losing hope that the ransom video would lead to a rescue attempt. Survival was going to be down to him, and him alone. Physically, he was hardly in shape to mount an escape – his knee was as swollen as ever, and he continued to suffer intermittent stomach cramps and bouts of diarrhoea. He had no choice but to continue drinking the dirty water they gave him in unwashed plastic bottles. It was a vicious circle of drinking water to stay hydrated, but knowing that water was causing his stomach problems. And a diet of stale naan was not really building his strength.

However, he was determined. He wasn't going to die here without putting up a fight. He watched through the tiny window, and spent hours stretching and flexing his muscles against his bindings for exercise. Now, whenever Pistol Boy came to bring him his rations, he was compliant and pretended to be weaker and more ill than he actually was.

In his mind, he rehearsed a daring escape plan. Daring because of the number of unknowns he would be dealing with. How many men? How many weapons? How could he get out of the storeroom? Getting out of the compound while surrounded by multiple hostiles was his biggest problem. Ideally, he would wait until the small hours, when most of his captors were asleep, but he could only get out of the storeroom by jumping whichever guard came with his evening food and water. So it would have to be early evening. And once he had set the plan in motion by ambushing the guard, he would have to commit to it one hundred per cent. As soon as he was out of the storeroom, it would be essential to minimise the amount of time that he remained inside the compound.

The main gate was always guarded by two men – he knew this as he could hear them talking and laughing through the day. Even at night, there were two men at the gate. He sometimes heard them speaking, and occasionally he would hear one of them snoring, but they would certainly still be awake at the time when he'd have to break out of the storeroom. They were armed, so he couldn't consider the gate as a route out.

That left him with one other option – he would have to go over the wall. And maybe his chance had come.

This morning, Pistol Boy had given him his breakfast in a rush, untying his hands and then hurrying away. He never came back to re-secure him. Left alone, Mac untied his ankles. Then he spent the rest of the morning watching and waiting. He still wasn't entirely sure how many men there were in the compound, certainly five at least, maybe more. In the afternoon, he visualised what he would need to do. He knew his chances of success were minimal, but if he rehearsed it in his mind enough times, he would be able to put his plan into action more fluidly.

For some reason, Pistol Boy was late with his evening meal. This suited Mac fine, as by the time he arrived it was almost dark outside.

Mac listened for his approaching footsteps, and took up position behind the storeroom door. When it opened, before Pistol Boy had the chance to look round for him, he raised his arms and smashed a full plastic jerrycan down on the kid's head. Pistol Boy crumpled to the ground like a rag doll, dropping his pistol with a clatter.

Mac pulled him inside and quickly closed the door, as quietly as he could. He hoped that no one had heard the noise of the falling gun or the thud of the can on the kid's head or, if they

243

had, they had not attached any significance to it. With his back resting against the door, he listened, waiting for any response to what had happened. After a minute of silence outside, he knelt down and checked Pistol Boy's pulse. The lad was out for the count, so Mac picked up his pistol, a Makarov, and searched his clothing for anything useful, helping himself to a battered pocketknife with a scarred wooden handle. Working as quickly as he could, he pulled the *keffiyeh* from around Pistol Boy's neck and ripped it into strips. This enabled him to tie the boy's hands, and to gag and blindfold him. Then he opened the door a crack and squinted out through the gap. In the twilight, the compound was full of shadows – in fact the entire wall that encompassed the heroin factory was in deep darkness. That was good, as this was his initial destination.

Opening the door a little wider, he slipped outside. He closed it silently behind him and found that he was able to snap shut the padlock. When Pistol Boy came round, he would be trapped in the storeroom – one less hostile for him to deal with. He peered cautiously round the edge of the small building. The guards on the gate were whispering about something, their heads bent close to each other. They were there to deal with external threats, and hardly took any notice of what was happening inside the compound behind them, and it didn't seem like they'd heard anything from inside the storeroom. Other than this, the place seemed to be deserted. He guessed that everyone else was inside, sharing the evening meal. How long would it take for them to realise Pistol Boy was missing?

He scurried across empty ground, trusting that neither of the guards would pick that moment to glance around. He was in luck, and a couple of seconds later he was out of their sight, with his back pressed against the rear wall of the house. He had moved carefully, and the sound of the generator had covered the noise of his feet.

Pausing for breath, he listened again. There was a shuttered window in the wall above him, and he could hear the sound of voices from inside as the men ate their meal. Good. This was his moment. He moved quickly in the shadows along the back of the house and then darted across to the far wall where the heroin factory was situated. Halfway to his destination, the generator suddenly shut down.

The compound went silent as the house was plunged into darkness. Mac's footsteps now sounded horribly loud in the empty seconds before the men inside started shouting. Confusion broke out, and Mac heard the guards running towards the house. Doors slammed, and then more people were running outside. Mac dived for cover behind an empty oil drum standing in the shadow of the high compound wall. Pain radiated from his knee up and down his leg, and he pressed himself into the ground as he waited for it to subside. He didn't know if his captors had heard him or not. The shouting and footsteps congregated at the generator – that would be their first priority, but then Mac heard a shout go up from the other side of the compound. Had someone discovered what had happened to Pistol Boy?

Holding the pistol up, ready to fire, Mac peered cautiously around his oil drum. He could see four men gathered at the generator, which was located along the side wall of the house, near to the front. They were about six metres away from him, all intent on the machinery, not looking around.

Someone shouted from the other side of the house, and there were more footsteps.

It was now or never. If they had discovered Pistol Boy, they would waste no time in hunting for him. He shoved the pistol into the back of his waistband and took a deep breath. Bracing himself against the inevitable pain from his shoulder and his knee, Mac clambered up onto an upturned oil drum next to the one he'd hidden behind. Once he was standing on top of it, he could reach up with his arms to the top of the compound wall. In his weakened state, it took supreme strength to pull himself up, his shoulder screaming as his broken collarbone took the strain, but fear gave him wings. Gritting his teeth, he swung his hips until he was able to hook his good leg over the wall, then he was straining every sinew in his body to heave his torso up and over.

Gunshots rang out around him, and a bullet clipped the baked mud brickwork inches from his face. Unable to return fire, Mac rolled over the top of the wall, staying as low as he could, then dropped down the other side. Even though he landed on his good leg, his injured knee gave way beneath him and he sprawled headlong onto the ground. But he couldn't afford to waste a second. As he regained his feet, he heard the creak of the front gate opening. The men were all shouting at once, and amid the noise he heard the sound of a car engine being started.

Without warning, AK fire rained down from above. Luckily he was hidden by the scrubby undergrowth that grew outside the wall. He pulled out the pistol from his waistband and looked up. Dope Boy was firing randomly into the field of poppies that abutted the compound. Mac didn't hesitate for a moment. He raised the pistol in a double-handed grip, took aim, and fired. Dope Boy fell away on his own side of the wall, and the firing stopped.

As the headlights of a Toyota technical swung round the corner of the compound wall, Mac dived headlong into the poppy plants. And then he ran.

Despite his knee, despite his shoulder, despite the stomach cramps, he ran as fast and as hard as he had ever run in his life. Because if he stopped, he was a dead man.

Chapter 39

Location unknown

Mac had no idea how long he was running for. It felt like forever, but in his weakened physical state, it couldn't have been long. He didn't dare stop. He hardly dared look back. Gunfire had erupted from the compound as he ploughed through the poppy field, but the night was dark enough to shield him. His captors were firing randomly and, though he heard bullets whistling past him, none of them hit their target.

After a few minutes, the shooting stopped. Mac dropped his pace to a jog. As he pushed between the waist-high plants, he realised he would be leaving an easily followed trail of destruction through the field. It had given him cover when he needed it, but now he had to move forward without leaving a trace. He heard more engines revving in the distance – they were coming after him in multiple vehicles, and that meant he couldn't use the road.

He crossed a second field of poppies much more slowly, slipping between the stems without breaking them.

An arc of light spread across the sea of purple and white flowers to one side of him and he dropped to the ground. A Toyota technical with hunting lights attached to its light bar was careening through the first field and gaining ground.

Fuck!

He crawled forward on his belly, gasping as his broken collarbone had to bear weight. But as he moved, the poppies swayed and shimmered above him, and he realised whoever was in the technical would be able to see his progress as their lights caught the movement. He lay still and listened as the vehicle came closer and closer. He was lying right in its path, but there was nothing he could do without giving himself away.

Should he stand up, hands raised, and turn himself in? At least they wouldn't run him over then – they needed him alive to be able to collect the million-dollar ransom. But it was only a fleeting thought. He wasn't going to give up that easily. He would take his chances.

The wheels thundered past him, clipping poppy plants that were just inches from his head. The men in the Toyota were shouting loudly – the driver had his window open so he could talk to the man standing on the truck bed, directing the lights and, Mac saw as the vehicle charged by, manning a machine gun. It went on another fifty metres or so, then took a sharp ninety-degree turn, crushing a wide swathe of flowering plants as it ploughed along the edge of the field. The driver clearly didn't care how much of the valuable crop he damaged. Mac supposed it was nothing compared to the prospect of losing the ransom.

He breathed a short-lived sigh of relief. He was by no means out of danger, but at least he hadn't been turned to pulp under the Toyota's wheels. He allowed himself a couple of seconds to gather his thoughts, but he couldn't afford to stay where he was. It was only a matter of time before they would come sweeping back and he didn't want to be like a startled deer in their beam of light.

He was several hundred metres from the compound now, which meant he was the same distance from the road. Without the position of the sun, he didn't know which way was north or south, east or west. He hardly knew which direction he should head in, apart from the logic of going north. If he could locate the Helmand River, he could stay close to its bank. But they had driven for hours from Lashkar Gah – he was hardly going to be able to walk all the way back.

The situation seemed hopeless.

He started crawling again. He needed to get out of the poppy field and find somewhere to hide until they gave up hunting him for the night. The sound of the technical had receded into the distance, so he raised himself up on his knees just high enough to peer over the tops of the poppy flowers. He was near the edge of the field, and there seemed to be a break of a few feet between this field and the next one. An irrigation canal? He crept forward, all the time listening for his captors' return.

It only took a couple of minutes to discover he had been right. A narrow cement canal ran between the poppy fields, a ruler-straight line in both directions as far as he could see in the darkness. The irony that it had probably been constructed by a Well Diggers project didn't escape him. But it explained the Toyota's change in direction – if there were any bridges over the channel, they would be footbridges, so it formed a barrier the vehicle couldn't cross.

The roar of the engine became louder again and he could hear the men, still shouting. The hunting light of the technical came into view, sweeping an area a couple of hundred metres from his current location. They were coming in his direction. He slipped into the water, taking care not to make a splash. Not that they would hear it if he did, but he couldn't risk the light catching the disturbance of the canal's glassy surface if he sent out a large ripple. Cool water rushed into his boots and soaked through his trousers in an instant. It felt like a balm to his swollen knee, but that wasn't his reason for doing it. He waded into the middle. The water wasn't deep, coming to halfway up his thighs in the centre, and the base of the canal was flat. Wading through water took more energy than walking on land but there was virtually no current, and it was at least deep enough to mean that even standing upright, his head didn't come above the top of the flower heads.

As far as he could surmise, the course of the canal ran parallel to the road. At some point, he'd have to choose a direction of travel, but right now, he needed to evade recapture and the Toyota was getting closer. He tucked the Makarov into a small hollow on the canal bank and sank down into a squatting position, so only his head was above the water. It meant he couldn't see where the vehicle was, but as the sound of its engine became louder, he started to see glints of light between the poppy stems. The beam was swinging back and forth across the field.

Mac breathed in and out slowly as the light grew brighter. With each swing of the arc, a strip of the canal surface was illuminated, and it was coming nearer with each pass. It was going to take split-second timing. If he went under too soon, he might need to come up again for air before the light had gone. Too late, and the bloke on the back would see ripples on the surface of the water.

The timing would be guesswork, and he had to make a bloody good guess. His life depended on it.

The light wheeled across the water towards him. He took a huge gulp of air, then sank gently to the bottom of the channel. He reckoned he would need to stay under for at least a minute to be safe, for the light to have moved on sufficiently for his resurfacing to go unnoticed.

The cool water enveloped his head, making all his muscles contract with the shock of it. He had to fight against his natural buoyancy to stay under. He felt around the bottom of the channel with his hands, but there was nothing to catch hold of. His body, lungs inflated with air, wanted to drift upwards. He could breathe out to counter this, but that would mean a trail of bubbles breaking the surface tension of the water. As he fought an unseen battle against the natural urge to surface, his lungs started to burn, craving more oxygen to fuel the fight.

As the light swept across his section of the canal, he closed his eyes against its glare.

One Mississippi, two Mississippi, three Mississippi…

Just a little longer. His chest was on fire, his muscles screaming, but he had to keep control. He couldn't burst out of the water, gulping for air. His emergence had to be just as controlled as his submersion.

The light passed, but still he held himself down. He wanted as much distance as possible between him and the Toyota before he resurfaced.

And then what?

Finally, it seemed completely dark. He slowly raised his face, nose and mouth breaking the surface first, sucking in much-needed air. He pushed towards the side of the channel, leaning against the sloping concrete, breathing softly until his muscles relaxed and the tightness in his chest released. The Toyota was long gone, engine noise receding in the distance, the sweep of the light cutting a swathe much further down the canal now.

He was alone, somewhere in the heart of Helmand's opium tract – a hostile environment where he didn't speak the language and where the paleness of his skin made him both contemptible and valuable. He was weak. He had no food or fresh water, but he had Pistol Boy's Makarov. He retrieved it from where he'd stashed it and checked the chamber. Three rounds left. The odds were stacked against him, but he started to walk along the canal. He needed to put as much distance between himself and Jamali's compound as he could before first light.

Only then could he afford to rest, if he could find some cover, and take stock.

On either side of him, the poppy flowers swayed in the breeze, as beautiful as they were deadly.

Day 8

Chapter 40

Lashkar Gah

Baz stared out of the window of the Land Rover, not listening to a word Nagpal was saying. He was talking about the problems faced by Afghan Sikhs who had fled to India. They were foreign refugees and not necessarily made to feel welcome. It was important information for the article she was writing, but how could she keep her focus on work when her mind replayed Mac's hostage video over and over again? Bloodied and broken, pleading for his life. A one-million-dollar price tag on his head, and no one stepping forward to pay.

Fuck the British government, with their 'we never pay' mentality. Surely a man's life was worth more than a measly million dollars? He'd been working for Well Diggers when he was taken, but Anholts had told Ginger in no uncertain terms that they didn't have the money – for Mac or for Bakker, if a ransom demand for the Dutchman ever surfaced.

'We're here,' said Nagpal.

Baz snapped to attention as Tirich pulled up outside a square two-storey building topped with a small gold dome. The white outer walls were daubed with graffiti and Baz could see that one of the wooden doors had been staved in.

Nagpal was frowning as they both climbed out of the Land Rover.

'The flag is missing,' he said, pointing to the top of a tall flagpole, 'and we have to paint over new graffiti nearly every week.'

Baz looked at the words daubed in red.

Infidel.

Heretics.

Death to Sikhs.

'Do the police do nothing?' said Baz.

Nagpal shrugged. 'They listen to our complaints and say they'll deal with them, but they do bugger all. Other issues are more important to them.'

Smoothing down her hijab, Baz followed him into the temple. They took off their shoes by the entrance, then went forward into the main hall. Nagpal bowed low and knelt to touch the floor with his forehead.

'This is the *darbar*,' said Nagpal, as he straightened up.

The room was virtually empty, devoid of any religious icons or statues. At one side there was a raised platform, covered by a fabric canopy.

'This should be where we keep our sacred book, the *Adi Granth*, but it has been desecrated and stolen too many times. Now our *Granthi* brings it with him when we meet for prayers, then takes it away again.'

Baz could see freshly painted patches on some of the walls.

'You've had graffiti inside as well?'

'Yes. The doors are always open, and people have come in the night. They don't want us to pray, and they don't want us to cremate our dead in the prescribed manner of our religion. Come, see how they've desecrated our cremation ground.'

They made their way back to the Land Rover, where Tirich was waiting for them. The cremation ground was a short drive away, on the riverbank near the edge of town. When they arrived, Nagpal pointed out the area.

'Look how people have dumped rubbish on the sacred ground. And now I hear that there is a plan to build on it, so we'll have to find somewhere else to cremate our dead. The Taliban banned cremation and made us bury our dead, and people think that ban should remain.'

As Baz took a wide-angle shot of the scene of devastation, she noticed the figure of a man melting back behind a tree on the other side of the cremation ground. He appeared to have been watching them. Nagpal had noticed him too and, exchanging a glance with Baz, he set off across the patch.

The man darted out from the copse and hurried back towards the road.

'*Wadrega!*' Nagpal shouted. Stop!

The man glanced back at them, but didn't slow down.

Baz caught up with Nagpal. 'Who is that? What's he doing?'

'I recognise him,' said Nagpal. 'He applied to work at Well Diggers. He wanted the job that I got, and I know he's very resentful of it.'

'What was he doing here?'

Nagpal looked sheepish. 'Sometimes he follows me. He wishes me harm, but he's not brave enough to do anything himself.'

Baz ran to catch up with the man. 'Hey, hey you!'

The man sped up to a run, emitting a stream of curses over his shoulder. He wasn't going to stop and talk to her. Before she could reach him, he climbed onto a dusty Hando and rode off at a speed that was hardly more than her running pace.

'*Kona ka dzha!*' he called as the distance between them grew. Fuck off.

'Nice,' said Baz, slowing down to a trot.

'That's the bike that knocked me off my scooter,' said Nagpal. 'Let's see where he goes.'

They ran back to the Land Rover.

'Follow that Hando!'

The Hando was no match for them — it was more of a problem persuading Tirich to hold back so the man didn't realise he was being followed. He rode towards the centre of Lashkar Gah, then turned north onto a narrow side street lined with food shops. Meandering from side to side to avoid piles of rubbish and puddles of bloodied water from roadside butchers' stalls, he carried on to the end of the road, then turned left into a smarter area of town.

'Slow down, slow down, he'll see us,' said Baz from the back seat.

'I could nudge him off,' said Tirich, 'to avenge what he did to you.'

'That's not a good idea,' said Nagpal.

Luckily Tirich didn't get the chance. Without warning, the Hando turned sharply and went through an open compound gate. The heavy wooden doors slammed shut behind him, leaving the Land Rover to carry on up the road.

'At least you know where he lives now,' said Baz. 'If he tries anything else, you can tell the police.'

'That would be a waste of time,' said Tirich. 'Do you know who owns that compound?'

Nagpal shook his head and, of course, Baz was clueless.

'It belongs to Akhtar Jamali, big narco boss. Not a man to be messing with.'

Nagpal smacked the heel of his hand against his forehead, then nodded. 'Now I understand. Of course, Jamali wanted one of his men working for Well Diggers.'

'Why?' said Baz, feeling she'd missed something.

'What better way to ensure someone else pays for the irrigation of his poppy fields?'

Chapter 41

Underground

Everything hurt. Mac was rolled up in a ball on a hard, concave surface. Stone. He couldn't stretch his legs – there wasn't room. He was cold and stiff, shivering. Feverish perhaps? His forehead was burning. His mouth was dry and had the rancid taste of extreme hunger. His lips were dry and chapped. His belly ached. He didn't want to open his eyes, but he knew he had to.

He blinked. Darkness all around him. He rubbed his eyes and tried again. Turning his head, he saw a circle of light, too bright. He looked away and waited for a few seconds. When he looked back at the circle, blinking, he saw poppies. As far as the eye could see, drifts of white and pink, bands of purple, shimmering in the glare of the sun.

Then he remembered. Running. Being chased. Wading along the irrigation canal for hours, then trudging along a track until, half-dead with exhaustion, he'd been forced to take cover by the approaching dawn. He'd found the outlet of a dried-up *karez* – an underground irrigation channel – and crept inside to hide.

Trying to ignore the objections of virtually every muscle in his body, he crawled towards the opening. He had no way of knowing how long he'd slept, but the sun seemed high in the sky. Late morning or early afternoon. He would have to stay hidden until dark – his captors would have spread the word in the surrounding area for people to search for him. No doubt there would be a cash reward for anyone who brought him back to Jamali's compound. There would be people in the fields and on the road, and he couldn't afford to be seen. Finding food and water would have to wait until nightfall, by which time he'd probably feel even weaker than he did now.

Situation hopeless.

He slumped back against the rounded stone wall. He couldn't quite see a way out of this alive. Even if the ransom video had reached someone, anyone, who might consider helping him, they'd first have to be able to make sense of his message. And if they could, it didn't tell them much, and they wouldn't know where to come searching for him. He had no hopes of the ransom being paid. Fucking powers that be would rather let a man die than give money to crooks and terrorists.

He needed water desperately. He couldn't afford to wait until sunset.

Though he couldn't leave the *karez* at risk of being seen, there was another option. The underground water channels formed a vast network underneath the land for miles around, taking water from aquifers on higher ground, usually meltwater from snow, and distributing it to be used in the irrigation canals that fed the poppy fields. Of course, they hadn't been built for this purpose. They'd been developed by the ancient Persians and had been used ever since. Each village had a *mirab*, or water bailiff, responsible for maintaining the *karez* system, for which the remaining villagers had to provide free labour.

He would have to go further into the *karez* until he found water.

He struggled to his feet in the low stone tunnel – too low for him to stand upright, meaning he had to walk in a crouched position. It only took a few minutes for his back to start complaining but he had no choice.

The dark tunnel sloped gently upwards, and he was able to find his way by keeping his right hand on the stone wall, carved out of the bedrock maybe centuries before. Every thirty or so metres there was an access well up to ground level which provided a small pool of daylight ahead that he could aim for. Just reach the pool of light, that's all he had to do. Then he could stop for a breather before setting out towards the next one. Some of these shafts had ladders up the side, but most of them were broken or missing.

Eventually he came to a junction with two branches leading in opposing directions. He chose the larger branch, simply because it allowed him to stand upright, so walking suddenly became easier. He had no idea if he was headed north or south, or where he would be when he finally emerged. He didn't care, as long as he was nowhere near Jamali's compound.

The slope in the larger branch was less steep and he felt as if he was making better progress. It was cooler down here than in the first tunnel, which told him he was deeper underground.

However, he was becoming dangerously dehydrated. If he didn't find water soon, it would get harder and harder to keep moving. Helmand had been suffering a drought, and the whole *karez* system was falling into disrepair. It was what had made Well Diggers' work so important, but after the recent spate of murders and kidnappings, Mac doubted they'd continue with their projects in the region.

He wondered if the round he'd fired at Dope Boy had hit its mark, or whether the boy had successfully dodged it when he dropped behind the wall. But the name said it all – he couldn't believe that Dope Boy was that quick-thinking, and it weighed heavily on him that he might have killed a kid who was already clearly being exploited. Was Akhtar Jamali pure evil or simply an opportunist making money in one of the few ways available in a country that had been at war for decades? Then he thought of his time spent in the Met, mopping up the collateral damage caused by the global drug trade, hunting terrorists who murdered innocent children, sending his own team into situations that got them killed. Jamali was evil, and Dope Boy was yet one more of thousands of victims who suffered because of a gangster's greed.

Without his watch and in almost constant darkness, it was very hard to judge the passing of time. It seemed like he'd been walking for hours, dry mouth, dry sweat on his body, but he was canny enough to realise it wouldn't have been as long as it seemed. Wondering how far he'd walked, he began to count the access shafts. Their frequency varied, but there was one approximately every thirty metres. So, thirty pools of light equalled nearly a kilometre. But he'd walked quite a way before he started counting them, then he lost count several times. And what did it matter how far he'd walked if he had no idea what direction he was travelling in?

He decided to rest while it was still daylight, because after dark he could come out of the *karez* tunnels and get the lie of the land. When he reached a side branch that contained a trickle of water, he dropped to his knees and drank. The channels carried meltwater from the mountains, fresh and clean in the winter, but stale and scarce in the summer drought, which was why most of the tunnels were dry. It tasted okay, and anyway, he hardly cared how clean it was. It was water, goddammit.

He slaked his thirst, then took his stinking clothes off to wash the sweat from his body. Though still exhausted and hungry, he felt one hundred per cent better and, moving back to the larger, dry *karez*, he curled up on the stone floor and went to sleep.

Chapter 42

Lashkar Gah

Baz stared at the two men across the kitchen table. Ginger's complexion was pallid – the situation with Bakker and Mac was taking a heavy toll on him. Logan looked healthier – possibly just because he tanned more easily. Baz could hear the chair legs rattling as one of his knees jigged up and down. His nerves were showing too. As for herself, she hardly dared face the mirror. There had been dark rings under her eyes last time she looked, and nothing had happened to make them any less pronounced.

They were supposed to be talking about what to do next, but the discussion had fallen silent. No one had any great ideas to share. Or even half-baked ones. Lunch plates in front of them on the table were hardly touched – no one had an appetite.

'I need a smoke,' said Logan, standing up and going outside onto the compound's parched brown lawn. The smell of hashish drifted in through the open door.

'How did your outing with Nagpal go?' said Ginger.

Baz shook her head. 'It's depressing, really,' she said. 'The way people will treat others, just because they subscribe to a different religion or come from a different tribe.'

'Of course,' said Ginger. 'But it's not about that. It's about scarce resources, and no one wants to share.'

'Maybe.' Baz didn't think it was that simple, but he had a point. 'We saw the guy that knocked Nagpal off his scooter. He was following us when we went to the cremation ground.'

'Seriously? Hope you went after the fucker.'

263

'We tailed him. Tirich wanted to knock him off his bike.'

This raised the glimmer of a smile from Ginger. 'But you told him no.'

'Of course,' said Baz. 'But, thing is, he went into a compound that apparently belongs to Akhtar Jamali. Nagpal said that the man had applied for a job here and got knocked back, and that Jamali wanted to get someone into Well Diggers to buy influence.'

Ginger looked surprised, then frowned. 'Rumour has it that Jamali has a finger in nearly every pie, at least south of Garmser, in the places where Khaliq's influence has never reached.'

'What are you saying?'

Ginger shrugged. 'Speculating... Perhaps Jamali has something to do with Bakker's disappearance.'

'But could Bakker have run off after arguing with Vinke? He might be out of the country by now.'

'Not without his passport, and that was still in his bedroom.'

'Only there hasn't been a ransom demand for Bakker, and there's been one for Mac. What if he's hiding out somewhere? Maybe staying with a friend – in Kabul perhaps?'

'Then we'd be wasting our energy trying to find him, and it would be a matter for the police.'

'I could give Jananga a call and ask him to put out feelers.' Major Jananga was the Kabul policeman she, Mac and Ginger had worked with after the murder of a British Army officer in Kabul's infamous tank graveyard the previous winter.

Ginger shrugged. 'Might be worth a try, but isn't he away on some course at the moment?' he said without conviction. 'Anyway, it still doesn't stack up. If Bakker was fleeing after committing a crime, he would have taken his passport. And he left medication in his bedside table, and money, other personal belongings. And the sneaker – don't forget about that.'

Baz sighed. 'Nothing seems to add up or make sense.'

She dialled Jananga's number in Kabul, but his deputy answered and told her the major was away in the Panjshir

Valley, visiting his sick mother. She put down her phone and rubbed her face with both hands, feeling freshly despondent. They seemed to be getting nowhere, chasing one dead end after another. Bakker had vanished in a puff of smoke, and Mac... Her heart clenched. She'd watched the ransom video a hundred times, as had Ginger and Logan. Surely the grainy image of Mac couldn't be her last sighting of him.

'There must be something we can do, Ginger,' she said. 'We can't just sit around here and let Mac die.' She stood up and slammed her fists on the table, kicking her chair over behind her. She was too angry to cry but she needed some way of venting her emotions.

Logan appeared in the doorway from the garden.

'Sure,' he said, his voice thick with *chars*, 'there is something we can do. Get Tirich and Nagpal over here. We'll go Jamali-baiting.'

Chapter 43

Underground

Mac woke up knowing that he hadn't slept long. The gritty base of the tunnel was uncomfortable, and his joints were sore and stiff. He drank water greedily, not knowing when he'd next get the opportunity. Wiping his mouth and chin with his good arm as he stood up, he set out walking in the direction he'd been travelling.

At least, he thought he was going in the same direction. But then he wasn't sure and doubled back on himself. Had he come across the branch with the water to the left or to the right of the main tunnel? He couldn't remember. He leaned back against the stone wall, his head spinning with hunger but his gut churning with anxiety. If he went the wrong way, he'd take himself right back to the environs of Jamali's compound, where everyone would be looking for him.

'Damn!'

His voice echoed more loudly than he expected in the stone vault, bouncing off the walls in either direction. He panicked. What if someone had heard? There was no one down here but him. But what if the sound had travelled up one of the access wells and there was a person nearby?

He needed to keep moving.

A flash of memory – the water had been up to the left – meant he could carry on with more confidence. Despite the gnawing hunger in his belly, he picked up his pace. He would have to come out of the tunnel to find food, and he wanted to make sure that was as far as possible from where he'd gone underground.

He didn't bother counting the access wells now, but he noticed the quality of the light changing as he passed from one to the next. The sun was getting lower in the sky, the light entering the shafts at a more acute angle, so less of it was reaching the bottom. As soon as it was dark, he would be able to climb one of the shafts – assuming he came to one with a ladder intact – and take a shufti outside. No point risking it before nightfall, not with a price on his head.

He walked on for what might have been another hour, mesmerised by each successive pool of light up ahead and the rhythm of his own footfall on the stone floor. He didn't come across any more branches or any more water. The height of the shafts he passed underneath seemed to be becoming shallower, and he wondered if he was getting near to the end of this particular branch.

It was only when the shafts of light in front of him abruptly disappeared that he surfaced back into conscious thought. No more access wells? Maybe the channel turned a corner – this had happened a couple of times before. Passing the last shaft, he walked on into the darkness, feeling more carefully with his hand against the tunnel wall in case of a curve or a sharp corner.

But it was his foot that hit something first, making him stumble forwards, arms outstretched to break his fall.

He didn't land on the ground, but on what felt like a pile of boulders.

Shit!

A collapse.

He felt around with his hands. The pile of boulders sloped all the way up to the top of the tunnel. Perhaps the walls of one of the access wells had caved in, or the tunnel roof. Whatever had happened, the path ahead was blocked, and Mac knew he didn't have the strength to move the boulders out of his way. He'd reached the end of the road and his only choices were going back to the last junction, an hour or so since – something he desperately didn't want to do – or coming out of the *karez* and bypassing the blockage overground until he found the next access well.

He made his way back to the previous well shaft and looked up. There was no ladder, and to climb the four or five metres to the top he would need to brace himself across the shaft and shuffle up. He didn't think his leg and shoulder would be up to this, so he carried on walking to the next access shaft. This one at least had a ladder propped against the side, but it looked ancient, and there were rungs missing. It didn't quite make it up to the top either. However, it was probably as good as he could hope for.

The light was dull now – dusk was falling – but Mac wasn't taking any chances. He sat and rested for half an hour until all he could see above him when he looked up the shaft was an inky sky speckled with stars. It reminded him of a planetarium he'd once visited as a kid, and now he wished he'd taken more notice of the constellations. If he had, he might be able to navigate by them now.

He struggled to his feet, stiff muscles complaining, empty belly cramping. He was thirsty again, and continuously light-headed from lack of food. That had to be his priority, but if he couldn't find something to eat, then what? He barely had the concentration to think ahead...

The first rung of the ladder gave way under his foot as he transferred his weight onto it. He crashed back to the ground, jarring his knee in an explosion of pain.

Fucking hell!

He took a deep breath and waited for the pain to subside, then he tested the next rung gingerly. This one held as he raised himself up slowly. The whole structure wobbled, but he didn't come crashing down, and so he cautiously brought a foot up to the third rung. The fourth cracked as he started to put weight on it, so he skipped it and went for the next one. As he climbed higher into the well shaft, he knew that if a rung gave way it would be more serious – possibly a death sentence if he crashed to the bottom of the shaft and broke both legs or cracked his head on a rock. There would be no one coming to his rescue.

It would be an ignominious end – dying of thirst at the bottom of a dried-up well shaft.

He took extra care with each successive step, ensuring a tight grip with both arms wrapped around the sides of the ladder as he moved.

Finally, he reached the top. There was a gap of about a metre to the lip of the well. Bracing himself against the other side of the narrow shaft, he clambered onto the top rung, and stretching upwards, he was able to raise his head over the edge.

He could see nothing.

That wasn't quite true. He could just make out the dark silhouette of a spiky bush. He looked from side to side. More spiky bushes. As his eyes became accustomed to the light, he realised that they were giant thistles. This was good – they would give him cover as he climbed out of the well. But it meant he had no idea of the landscape he was coming into – and whether he would be in immediate danger. He felt the back of his waistband. The pistol was still there. A small speck of reassurance, but not enough to prevent the cold sweat that broke out at the back of his neck.

He stretched up on the final rung of the ladder, placing his hands flat on the ground at the edge of the shaft.

It was now or never.

With a huge push, gritting his teeth against the pain in his shoulder, Mac crested the top of the well. At the very moment he pushed his feet off the top rung of the ladder, which let out a loud cracking sound, the bushes in front of him parted and a dark shape surged towards him. Mac threw himself forward as hard as he could to make sure he wouldn't fall back down the shaft, twisting his body to one side to roll out of the path of the oncoming…

A loud, prolonged bleat made him nearly jump out of his skin.

It was a goat, a bloody goat!

A goat that would have butted him back down the well shaft had he not had the presence of mind to shift to the side.

Panting from the exertion, Mac swore softly under his breath. He'd landed directly in one of the thistle bushes, and its bristling spikes were no joke. He felt like a pin cushion.

'Damn you!' he said to the goat.

The goat swore back at him – at least its loud bleating sounded angry.

'I'll have you.' Not caring about how much he ripped his clothes disentangling himself from the bush, he reached a hand to the back of his waist and pulled out Pistol Boy's weapon. Sitting up, he raised the pistol, taking aim at the goat's head. The animal's eyes glinted malevolently in the starlight, and it bleated again.

'Shhhhh…' If there was anyone within earshot, they were going to hear the racket the damn thing was making. Goats meant people – maybe a goatherd, maybe a village close by, and he didn't want to advertise his presence.

Mac lowered the pistol. He couldn't shoot it. It would definitely draw unwanted attention. He put the gun away and dug into the front pocket of his trousers. He still had Pistol Boy's pocketknife. God knows whether it would be sharp enough for the job.

Whether it was the glint of steel or the quickening of Mac's breath that alarmed it, the goat suddenly took fright and plunged back into the bushes. Mac dived after it, heedless of the killer spikes that ripped his shirt and trousers and rent deep scratches across his hands and forearms. The goat tried to run, but its progress was hindered by the plants. As soon as Mac got within reach of it, he took a flying leap to land on its back, snaking an arm around its neck as it stumbled underneath his weight. It landed on the ground with a crunch and a loud exhalation of breath.

Mac held it tight by the head with his left arm and with his other arm he slit the beast's throat. Thankfully the knife was sharp enough to do the job with one swift cut. He felt hot blood gushing out over his hands, and he yanked the head back.

The blood tasted simultaneously delicious and disgusting – salty, metallic and with the familiar goaty tang. He took three large mouthfuls, then, without warning, he was violently sick. He rolled off the dead animal and lay on the ground next to it, spitting blood from his mouth.

It didn't matter. He had goat meat to eat and he was a free man.

And suddenly he found himself laughing uncontrollably.

Even though none of it was remotely funny.

Chapter 44

Lashkar Gah

Despite being quite sure he wouldn't need it, Ginger took extra care checking and cleaning his Stechkin – the chunky Soviet automatic pistol he'd picked up in Kabul before coming to Lash.

Logan appeared in the kitchen, weighing a Baby Glock 27 in his right palm.

Ginger glanced at it. The Baby Glock was about half the size of his hefty piece.

Logan noticed him looking. 'Small but reliable, baby – it's all I need.' He stashed it into a shoulder holster under his arm, then pointed at the Stechkin.

'Jeez, bro, where'd you find that old dinosaur? Your target will die of shock when he sees you pointing that thing at him. You won't even have to pull the trigger.'

'Ha fucking ha,' said Ginger. He snapped a twenty-round double-stack magazine into place and tucked it into the back of his jeans, pulling his polo shirt down to cover the bulge.

'Just add jackboots and a leather coat, and you'll be a fully paid-up member of the KGB.'

'Fuck off, Yank! When I want your opinion, I'll give it to you.' He stuck his middle finger in the air.

'Hopefully you won't need either of them,' said Baz. 'The idea is to get information, not shoot people.'

Tirich was already gunning the engine outside, his eyes gleaming with delight at being included on the mission. 'Top getaway driver,' he'd said with a big grin, when they'd told him the plan. Nagpal was the only one of the crew who looked like he didn't want to be there.

'The man is already harassing me often enough,' he said to Baz. 'This is only going to make it worse.'

'You've got a point,' said Baz. 'He doesn't need to see you. He won't know who Ginger and Logan are, so he won't make a connection.'

It was agreed that Nagpal should stay at the office rather than going with them.

Finally, as dusk fell, Tirich, Ginger and Logan headed across town in Logan's Surf – this was not the time to use one of the Well Diggers' branded Land Rovers. Tirich was driving and would remain with the vehicle, leaving Logan and Ginger to either tail their quarry on foot or jump back into the Surf for a speedier pursuit.

'I still think we should have brought Nagpal with us to bait the bloke,' said Ginger, as they pulled up twenty metres down the street from the compound that Tirich had identified as belonging to Akhtar Jamali earlier in the day.

'Listen, we don't need Nagpal,' said Logan. 'Tirich knows what the guy looks like. If he sets foot out of those gates, we'll have him.'

'As long as he's on his own.'

Logan conceded this point with a nod, and lit a cigarette.

Ginger opened his window pointedly. They might be in for a long wait. They didn't even know for sure that the man was in the compound, let alone whether he was going to come out. But they could hardly knock on the door of Jamali's house and ask to speak to him.

Logan started talking to Tirich in Pashto. Ginger couldn't understand what the conversation was about, though on hearing the word *chars*, he could make a pretty good guess. Tirich laughed at something. Ginger leaned back in his seat and momentarily closed his eyes. What a clusterfuck. He should never have got Mac involved. In fact, he wished he'd never taken the bloody Well Diggers job. He should have stayed in Kabul, instead of coming down here to the Afghan equivalent of the Wild West.

He opened his eyes and fingered his weapon, staring intently at the compound gates, as if he could will them to open. They were running out of options, and the hope was that Nagpal's harasser might be able to tell them something useful. If Jamali was resentful that his man didn't get the job at Well Diggers, perhaps he'd taken a more menacing approach to getting the irrigation channels he wanted. And Hando man was a small cog in a larger machine – as Logan put it, he was someone they could lean on without stirring up too much shit.

Ginger's phone rang. The screen showed Nagpal's number.

'Nagpal-jan?'

The Sikh replied, sounding out of breath. 'Ginger-jan, you should come quickly. The man you are wanting to talk to is here.'

'Where?'

'He's following me on his bike, as I left work.'

'Where are you?'

'I'm stopped on North Khyber Road. He's a bit down the street from me.'

North Khyber Road was one of the main roads leading out of the city.

'Okay, take a left onto Nangarhar Street when you get there – we'll tuck in behind him, and as soon as we get somewhere quiet, we'll intercept.'

It was the end of the working day, and the traffic would be busy in downtown Lash, but if they could lead him into a quiet neighbourhood, they'd be able to cut in front of him and force him off the road.

Ginger relayed the contents of the call to Logan, who instructed Tirich to head straight for Nangarhar Street. Within five minutes they were in position parked at the side of the road, and a minute later Nagpal came past on his battered scooter. He gave no sign of recognition, but carried on puttering down the road. Seconds later, a red Hando came into view. The rider was in a khaki shalwar kameez, and he had a black cloth *lungee* twisted round his head in place of a helmet.

'That's him,' said Tirich. 'That was the man Miss Basima was running after at the cremation ground this morning.'

Letting another car go by first, Tirich pulled out and started following. Ginger leaned forward between the two front seats to keep eyes on the Hando and Nagpal's scooter. Nagpal led the way, right, then left, then right again, until they were nearly at the edge of town in an unremarkable residential area. The traffic diminished until it was just the scooter, the Hando and the Surf on a stretch of road that looked as if it would peter out after the last compound.

If the man on the Hando wondered where Nagpal was going, he seemed to have no hesitation in following him. Perhaps he too was waiting for a quieter neighbourhood to make his move.

'Now,' said Logan.

Tirich revved the engine and sped past the Hando, only to immediately cut in front of it. The man on the bike let out a stream of curses as he braked sharply. Tirich positioned the Surf to block his way. The man stopped and jumped off his bike. He let it drop to the ground and charged towards the driver's window, suddenly pulling himself up short as he saw Logan and Ginger emerging from the vehicle.

Leaving the bike lying on the ground, he started running. He was small and wiry, and made a sharp spin to disappear down an alley between two compound walls. As Ginger skidded on the sandy ground to make the corner, Logan overtook him, shouting at the man in Pashto.

'*Wadrega!* Stop!'

But the man kept running. There was no way he would stop and talk to two westerners.

Logan pounded after him, taking advantage of his height and longer stride to gain ground. The man had led them into a warren of alleyways, and if he'd had any sense, he could have melted into the shadows of a dark corner somewhere – it was twilight and of course there were no streetlights in Lash. However, fortunately for his pursuers, he didn't seem to be the sharpest nail in the box, and he kept running, panting noisily and skidding with each twist and turn.

Logan caught up with him and slammed a hand down on his shoulder, forcing the man to stagger. The beefy American hooked a foot round one of the Pashtun's legs, swiping the support out from under him. The man dropped heavily onto his knees with a sharp cry. Ginger caught up and stopped a couple of metres from the man, raising the Stechkin to stop any further attempt at escape.

The man wailed something in Pashto.

'Speak English,' commanded Ginger.

The man wailed even louder.

'He doesn't speak English,' said Logan. He started to question the man, briefly translating each answer so Ginger could keep up with what was being said.

'He says he doesn't know Akhtar Jamali,' said Logan, after the first exchange.

'Then ask him what he was doing in Jamali's compound.'

Ginger could tell by the man's tone that he was now backtracking.

'Jamali is a distant cousin of his wife, but he still claims he hardly knows him. It's BS,' said Logan. He spoke to the man again. 'His name's Arqam – it's a Baloch name. Jamali's tribe, in other words.'

The man spoke rapidly for a couple of minutes.

'He's scared of Jamali. He does what he's told. He works in a shop in the middle of town, but sometimes he has to run errands for Jamali or his men.'

'Ask him if he knows anything about Jamali kidnapping westerners.'

As Logan asked him, Arqam's eyes widened in fear. He shook his head. '*Na, na...*' He looked up at Ginger's weapon, but whatever he was scared of, it wasn't the Stechkin. Without warning, he pushed himself to his feet and shouldered Logan out of the way. As he started running again, Ginger lunged after him with a rugby tackle. He slammed Arqam to the ground, straddled him and pressed the muzzle of the pistol against his throat.

Arqam wailed.

'You fucking tell me what you know, you little bastard,' said Ginger. 'If you can help me, I might just let you live. If not, you and your family die.'

As Logan translated this, he pulled out his Glock and made sure that Arqam could see it – a double threat. If Ginger didn't do him harm, Logan would.

Arqam cried unashamedly and begged for mercy for his wife and children. Then he told them what he knew. There were rumours that Jamali was holding three westerners. His wife told him that was a lie, but he heard the guards referring to *kafirs* – infidels.

'What nationality *kafirs*?' said Ginger.

Arqam shrugged and reeled off a string of words.

Logan translated. 'American, Italian, Dutch. He's not sure.'

'Dutch?' said Ginger.

'He's just guessing,' said Logan. 'Making things up so we'll let him go.'

But Arqam swore he wasn't lying, and said some more.

Logan put a hand on Ginger's wrist and pulled it back so the gun was no longer against Arqam's throat. 'They were holding one man – English, he thinks – and that man got away. Jamali had several men executed for letting him escape.'

'Where? Where the fuck did this happen?' said Ginger, ramming the gun back hard against Arqam's throat.

Arqam coughed until Ginger released the pressure. Then he spoke.

Logan translated.

'In the poppy fields. Where else?'

Chapter 45

Location unknown

There were no cities, or even sizeable towns, south of Lashkar Gah in Helmand Province, and this meant there was no light pollution. Mac stared up at the endless black sky, following the shimmering trail of the Milky Way with his eyes. It reminded him of home where, on the west coast of Scotland, the skies were similarly clear.

But he couldn't pause for long. It was time to go.

He pulled himself out of the *karez* with newfound strength. After eating his fill of the goat's liver and part of the heart, he'd rested further along the *karez*, giving it time to digest. Now he was ready to set out across the dark expanses of the poppy fields, and this time he had a plan. During the day, he'd been able to work out the compass points from the movement of the sun, so now he knew which way was which. It was his intention tonight to relocate the river, and then follow its course north, while keeping on the furthest edges of the cultivated area to avoid the villages and farms along its banks. It would be one hell of a walk – he had no idea how far south of Lash he'd been taken. He suspected it would be a journey of weeks rather than days, and only possible if he could find more food and suitable hiding places along the way.

He'd stripped all the muscle meat from the goat and had tied it up in a pouch of goatskin he'd cut from the animal's back. But it already stank, and it wouldn't be fit to eat for long in the oppressive heat. He left the remains of the animal in the *karez*

– at some point a goatherd would realise one of his beasts was missing and start to search. And once it was found, they'd see that its death had been no accident.

With the pouch of meat slung around his waist, Mac surveyed the landscape. He'd emerged from a different access shaft than the one where he'd found the goat – he didn't want to risk that one again in case the goat had already been missed. Instead, he'd walked approximately a kilometre underground before climbing out.

This time, he came up in the heart of a poppy field. Around him, the stems rustled in the slight breeze, the flower heads closed for the night with petals furled tight. Cautiously, he raised his head above the level of the plants and looked around. He was on an area of flat ground beneath a ridge. Climbing to the top of the ridge, he could see the broad expanse of the Helmand glinting in the starlight, about three kilometres away. Any signs of human habitation – a couple of small villages, a lone compound – were down near the water. Up here there was nothing but fields.

Good. He would stay up on the hillside and cover as much ground as he could before finding a place to shelter just before dawn.

Reaching the edge of the field, he set off at a relaxed jog. He would run for as long as he could, then walk, all the time scouting – for humans, for water, for shelter. The ground was uneven and rocky, meaning he had to watch where he was placing his feet, but his eyes were already acclimatised to the darkness. He alternated between scanning the ground and scanning the horizon, thankful that his boots were sturdy and gave him good ankle support – and that the kidnappers hadn't taken them to incapacitate him. The idiots.

However, despite having eaten and rehydrated, Mac wasn't as strong as he'd hoped. The jogging soon took its toll on his knee and jarred his broken collarbone. Drawing in the deep breaths he needed to run made his mouth dry. He stooped down and picked up a pebble to suck on, to increase his salivation, but it didn't work for long. Eventually, he concluded that if he slowed down, he'd be able to preserve energy and hydration and carry on longer. A brisk march would still eat up the kilometres. Some at least.

Whenever he needed to pass a village below him on the riverbank, he took extra care to find cover, crawling along to stay below the level of the poppy plants or dropping back behind rocky outcrops on the hillside. He couldn't afford to be seen, and even though it looked as if everyone was asleep, he couldn't count on it.

Once, he heard the sound of a vehicle coming down the rutted track that hugged the river. He ducked out of sight behind a clump of thistles, watching through the thorny branches as a pair of headlights danced over the bumpy ground. As it passed, far below him, he identified the black silhouette of an SUV. One of Jamali's vehicles, out looking for him? Maybe he was being paranoid, but better to err on the side of caution, so he waited until it was completely out of sight before moving off again.

Every hour or so, he would sit down and chew on some of the goat's meat. The taste was strong and it already seemed rancid. When he'd been starving, it had been easier to eat. Now, not hungry but wanting to maintain his strength, he could barely bring himself to swallow it, and he was sorely tempted to dump it behind a rock. But he wasn't going to allow himself the luxury of dumping food just because he didn't like the taste. It would last until the next day before it was too off to eat, so he would persevere with it, even though every mouthful made him retch.

The landscape barely changed as he walked. The stars moved overhead as the planet turned, the moon rose, casting its silver glow over the fields and turning the Helmand into a mirror. But still, from the river basin to the top of the slope where he walked, the land was a continuous patchwork of fields, and the only crop was the barbed bringer of sweet dreams for its users and, for its growers, cold, hard cash.

Mac thought about the problem as he walked. How would the west ever persuade the Afghans to give up their most lucrative crop? From the field workers to the narco barons, there was no incentive to swap opium for okra. The numbers didn't add up, while demand for what they grew continued to rise as the unscrupulous found ever more ways to snag people on its golden hook.

Cursing, Mac stamped on a flower head that had drooped across his path. He understood how people got addicted, but there had to be some way of breaking the chain of evil that stretched from these beautiful flower heads to the filthy squats and piss-drenched alleys of Europe's cities.

He'd be damned if he knew the answer.

He trudged on, his legs beginning to feel tired and heavy, his mouth dry and his lips sore. He decided to drop down the slope to the flat valley floor to see if there were any irrigation canals. He desperately needed water if he was going to keep up this pace for another few hours. If only he'd thought to bring one of the empty plastic bottles from Jamali's compound. But there was no point in regrets. It was too late now.

Walking down in the valley meant being far more careful and by necessity taking wide detours to avoid villages and compounds. The progress he made was slow and still he didn't find any water. He was thirsty and he needed a drink.

Finally, on the very edge of a small village, he saw an enclosure of goats, penned in by a crude wooden fence. Goat's milk. Salvation. He'd occasionally milked a cow as a child, so how hard could it be to milk a goat? He allowed himself to go right down the slope until he was within twenty metres of the pen. It meant he was close to the road, and he prayed that he wouldn't hear an engine rumbling in the distance.

He waited for several minutes, his eyes scanning the village for signs of life. But dawn had yet to break and the early morning call to prayer was still some time away. Some of the goats were awake, silently chewing the cud, while a few were huddled together sleeping. As Mac crawled closer to the fence, one of them heard something and let out a derisory bleat of alarm. The sleeping goats stirred and a couple of them clambered to their feet to check out what was going on. Mac saw that one of them was female, with a heavy udder slung beneath her body. She would be his target.

Still trying to be as quiet as he could, he skirted the perimeter of the pen to find a rudimentary gate. It creaked as he pushed it open, and again when he closed it behind him. He dropped to the ground and lay still, once again assessing the surrounding area for signs of people, but apart from the occasional bleating of the now interested goats, there was nothing to be heard. The stench of goat was overwhelming inside the pen, made even worse when he inadvertently rested one elbow in a pile of dung.

Now was the time to act, but he felt some trepidation. Up close, the goats were larger than they'd appeared from outside the pen. They were milling around him and he was concerned that the increasing volume of their bleating would alert the village. He needed to be quick.

He picked out the large-uddered female goat and moved towards her on his hands and knees, making soft clicking noises with his mouth.

'Come on, you beauty,' he whispered as he reached out to grab the rope around her neck.

A male goat with stubby, hooked horns butted up against him with remarkable strength, sending him sprawling on the dirt. All of his injuries protested with sharp bursts of pain, but he was more intent on keeping hold of the nanny goat's tether as she tried to struggle free.

'Come on, darling. Just stand still for me.'

The goat twisted her neck from one side to the other, tugging against his hold. He sat up and pulled her in close to his chest. He was able to snake one arm around her neck and he held her tight. With his free hand, he grabbed for her udder, feeling for a teat to squeeze. She gave a loud bleat of protest, calling on her male protectors. He wasn't sure this could possibly work, with nothing to squirt the milk into except his mouth, but he had to give it a try.

The goat that had already butted Mac came in for a second shot on target. This time he crashed his bony forehead into Mac's bad shoulder. Mac flew backwards with a howl of pain, letting go of the female goat, which took full advantage to put distance between them. Cursing loudly, Mac attempted to stand. But the nanny goat had other plans for him and before he'd regained his balance, she charged. Her weight cut his knees out from under him and he crashed to the ground. The breath was blown out of his chest and his vision blurred. The bleating around him had reached fever pitch, but he still heard the creak of the rickety gate.

Then a female voice shouted angrily in Pashto. '*Sta noom sa de?*'

He sat up, blinking.

The voice belonged to a girl in a hijab and a brightly embroidered red dress. She was barely a teenager, but she was holding a hefty-looking wooden club above her head.

Mac rolled out of range and shoved a hand to the back of his waistband for the Makarov – only to find that it was no longer there.

Day 9

Chapter 46

Sar Banader

Mac lay on the stony ground, coughing out a lungful of dust and absorbing the kick in the gut that came with the realisation of failure. His freedom had been short-lived – a little over twenty-four hours on the run before being recaptured by a young girl with a big stick. He must have dropped the gun somewhere during the night, and now he was defenceless.

He didn't know what she'd said, but given that she looked quite capable of bringing her weapon down on his head, he assumed it was along the lines of 'hands up'. So he showed her the palms of his hands while remaining as still as possible.

Without taking her eyes off him, she yelled loudly a couple of times. He rightly guessed she was calling for help, as a moment later a man emerged from the nearest dwelling and came running towards the goat pen. He came through the gate and she quickly handed the club to him, talking in rapid Pashto. The man was much older and similar looking – her father probably. His arrival meant that any hope Mac had of being able to jump up and wrestle the stick from the girl was dashed. It was a pathetic idea anyway. Mac was lying on the ground, winded, injured, weak from dysentery, and exhausted. He was kidding himself if he thought he was in a fit state for heroics.

The goats were still bleating loudly, disturbed by this intrusion into their compound, but Mac was relieved to see that the man had lowered the club and now held it loosely at his side. He was wearing black trousers and a *kosai*, a white felt coat.

287

If Mac remembered rightly from his initial briefing when he arrived in Afghanistan, this would indicate he was a Kuchi – a member of the semi-nomadic tribes that herded sheep and goats across the country. He had a bulbous white turban and a pale woollen blanket draped over one shoulder.

'*Salaam alaikum,*' said Mac. His voice cracked and speaking set him off coughing again.

'*Alaikum a'salaam,*' said the older man. Then he said quite a lot more.

Mac sat up and shook his head. 'English? You speak *inglisi*?'

The man shook his head and the girl stared down at Mac with wide-eyed interest. She asked her father something and in the answer Mac heard the words Englistani and Jamali. His heart sank. They knew who he was, and now they would hand him back to Jamali's men and claim their reward.

The father waved the girl away and tucked the weapon somewhere inside his *kosai*. Then he helped Mac to his feet. It was getting light, and Mac could see the small village more clearly now – a cluster of mud houses with walled courtyards and flat roofs. The small fields closest to the dwellings seemed given over to vegetable cultivation, but there were still plenty of poppy fields stretching away beyond them.

The father beckoned Mac to follow him, while the girl scurried ahead. Feeling dejected and humiliated, Mac trudged after them. What was the point in trying to run? The man was fit and clearly had the upper hand. If he made a break for it, he could die here and now, or if he went willingly, he would no doubt die at some point later, when Jamali realised there would be no ransom forthcoming. It wasn't much of a choice, but it seemed to make sense to delay the inevitable.

The man led him to the edge of the village and into the courtyard of the small dwelling from which he'd appeared. He closed the gate firmly behind them, and the girl disappeared into the house. There was nothing but dried dirt, goat shit and a couple of scrawny chickens in the courtyard, and the house itself was a primitive construction made from mud, straw and wooden poles. Along one side of the courtyard, a low wooden structure sheltered a giant, sleeping Kuchi dog, its pale golden fur brindled with brown patches. It woke at the sound of their arrival, barking loudly and yanking at the short chain that secured it. The man spoke softly to it, and it settled back down on its haunches, eyeing Mac – suspiciously or hungrily, he couldn't be sure which. On the other side of the space, a lean-to wooden roof gave an area of shade for two low wooden chairs and a plain bench. The man pointed at one of the chairs, indicating Mac should sit down.

He did as he was told.

Creaking loudly, the door of the house opened a crack and the face of another young girl appeared, her head wrapped in a brightly embroidered shawl. The man shouted something at her and the door slammed shut. Mac looked away. He couldn't be seen to take an interest in the women of the household. But he knew he would be an object of immense interest to them – a bedraggled westerner, lost and alone, in a part of Helmand that rarely saw people from beyond the next village, let alone foreigners.

The man said something to him, then realising he was wasting his breath, he disappeared into the house.

Mac looked at the compound gate. There was no guard here and he wasn't tied up. There was nothing to prevent him from getting up and leaving. He had no idea what sort of reward Jamali would have put up for his return, but his host didn't appear to be that bothered by the prospect of it simply walking out of the door.

And this was the reason Mac stayed.

It seemed that the man who'd taken him in didn't view him as a captive. When he came outside again, he was carrying a tray. There was tea and a bowl of food – rice studded with nuts and herbs, a few beans and slices of soggy, over-cooked okra, with a piece of naan balanced on the edge. He put it down on the bench next to where Mac was sitting and made a gesture to encourage Mac to eat and drink.

'*Mn'n'na*, thank you.'

Mac sipped the green tea, and the bitter taste he usually hated seemed like an elixir. Then he fell on the food, eating it with his fingers in the traditional Afghan manner, savouring every mouthful. Across the courtyard, the dog whined. Mac formed a little ball of rice in his hand, stood up and took it to within reach of the beast, where he dropped it on the ground. The dog wolfed it down and the man, who'd been watching him with a concerned look, laughed out loud.

'Mantoo,' he said, pointing at the dog. The dog's ears pricked up at the mention of his name. Then the man pointed to himself. 'Obaid.'

Mac put a hand to his chest. 'Mac.'

The introductions out of the way, the man went back inside the house, leaving Mac and Mantoo to finish the food. The stinking pouch of goat meat must have fallen from his belt some time before, Mac realised with relief.

Mac sat back in the chair. Although the food had tasted good, his stomach cramped. He'd not yet recovered from the dirty water at Jamali's compound, let alone the effects of eating raw goat meat. Hopefully the rice and bread would settle things down a bit.

After a while, Obaid returned for the tray.

'*Mn'n'na*,' said Mac again, pressing both his hands together and bowing his head.

An older man, similarly dressed but with a white beard, came out of the house. He studied Mac and spoke to Obaid. Then he left the compound. Obaid took the tray inside and came back a few minutes later with a bowl of water and some rags. He put them down by Mac's chair, then reached out with one hand and touched Mac's left shoulder. Mac winced and Obaid nodded. He understood that Mac was injured. He did the same with Mac's knee and Mac nodded in return.

Obaid set to work. It seemed like he was something of a medic or a healer, or whatever these remote, rural communities relied on to tend to their ills. He cleaned up a number of minor abrasions and cuts, bandaged Mac's knee to give it support and fashioned a sling for him using a *keffiyeh* scarf. Once he'd finished, he brought a thin canvas mattress out from the house and put it in the deep shade at the back of the lean-to. The sun was climbing now, and the heat was already punishing, but Mac couldn't be invited inside the one-room house because, as a stranger, and an infidel at that, he couldn't be allowed to mix with the women.

He lay down to sleep, wondering what would happen next. Had he been right in assuming that Obaid wasn't going to hand him over to Jamali? And if he didn't intend to do that, what did he intend to do? Sleep overtook him before he had any answers, but minutes later he was woken up again by the opening of the compound gate.

Immediately alert, he sat up.

It was the old man returning. He came straight over to Mac, holding out something in his hand. Mac stood up and reached for it – a satphone. '*Mn'n'na, mn'n'na.*' With a rush of adrenalin, he dialled Baz's number.

Pick up, pick up…

Obaid appeared in the doorway.

Pick up, for God's sake pick up…

'Hello, who's this?'

'Baz, it's me.'

'Mac!' she practically screamed in his ear. 'Thank God. Where are you?'

'No fucking clue. Speak to my friend, Obaid.' He gave the phone to his host.

Obaid talked animatedly for several minutes, listened for a bit, then talked some more. Just as Mac was reaching the point of grabbing the phone from him, he held it out. Mac snatched it and pressed it to his ear.

Baz spoke quickly. 'Okay, you're in a village called Sar Banader. Obaid is no friend of Jamali's, who was holding you, but he knows there are search parties scouring the countryside for you. He wants rid of you ASAP.'

'I don't blame him,' said Mac.

'It will take us several hours to reach you – it's quite a bit further than Najibullahkhan Kalay. Sit tight.'

'Not going anywhere, babe.'

When Baz replied, he could tell she was crying. 'I was so scared, so scared. You're okay, right?'

Mac sniffed. 'Sure, I'm fine. A bit bashed about, but nothing that seeing you won't fix.'

'Put Obaid back on for me. See you soon.'

Mac handed the phone back to Obaid, mouthing his thanks as he did. Obaid listened to Baz, a large grin breaking out on his face. He said a couple more things, then disconnected and handed the phone back to the old man, who disappeared out of the gate, presumably to return the phone to its owner.

Mac looked up at the azure sky and took a deep breath.

They were coming for him.

The nightmare was nearly over.

Chapter 47

Sar Banader

Finally able to relax, Mac fell into a deep sleep on the lumpy mattress in Obaid's courtyard. Threadbare or not, it seemed a million times more comfortable than sleeping at the bottom of a *karez*, and the world disappeared for a few blissful, dreamless hours.

Mantoo's frenzied barking woke him, and he sat up, wondering what the commotion was. It was virtually dark now, and the fierce heat of the day had receded. As he looked around, he saw three men coming through the gate. Obaid appeared in the doorway, shouting to them. Two of the men glanced in Mac's direction, while the other made the gate secure with a couple of heavy deadbolts. He noticed that all three of them were armed with AKs, and that Obaid had a Tokarev pistol in his hand.

Obaid made a low, growling sound at the dog, and Mantoo stopped barking and slunk back into his shelter. Now, with the racket subsided, Mac could hear vehicles racing outside the compound. More than one. Beyond the wall, a barrage of shots was fired into the air, and men were shouting in loud, excited voices.

What the hell was happening?

Obaid gestured to Mac, urging him towards the house. Mac hobbled over to him as fast as he could.

'Jamali,' said Obaid. A single word that conveyed to Mac all he needed to know.

Obaid thrust his pistol into Mac's hands, then pushed him through the door into the house. A woman drew him inside – not either of the girls he'd seen earlier, but of an age that suggested she might be Obaid's wife. It wasn't a large room and it was set out in the usual Afghan manner – a carpet covered the floor with cushions all round it and against the wall. On one side, the goat girl and the younger girl sat huddled together. They looked frightened and Mac felt immediately regretful for having brought danger to their door.

Propriety now long forgotten, the older woman pulled him through the living area to a door at the back. They went into the sleeping quarters. The woman picked up a pile of bedcovers and motioned for Mac to hide himself underneath them. She covered her mouth with a hand, to tell him to stay silent. It wasn't something that sat well with Mac – hiding in a bedroom and letting others fight his battle, but he knew it would be better for the family if he complied. He was in the women's quarters, and Jamali's men wouldn't be allowed to come back here. Obaid and his relatives would be within their rights to refuse them entry.

He stretched out on one of the mattresses and pressed himself against the wall, and the woman threw the covers over him. It wouldn't fool anyone making a thorough search of the room, but in the dark, it would be enough for him to evade a cursory glance. He heard the door close as the woman left, and concentrated on regulating his breathing to be silent and shallow.

There was more shooting outside. A door slammed. A woman screamed. Heavy footsteps and voices. Mac clutched the pistol, hardly daring to breathe at all.

The door swung open and crashed back against the wall. People came into the room. A boot kicked him hard, and his cover was blown. He sat up fast, raising the pistol. A man he recognised as one of Jamali's gate guards was pointing a Makarov at him. More men were rushing in behind him. Obaid. The man with the white beard. Another of Jamali's men. All of them were shouting furiously.

Mac pulled the trigger.

In the small room, the sound was deafening.

Jamali's gate guard fell forward onto the floor.

Obaid had a pistol trained on Jamali's other man.

The old man said something sharp and the expression on the face of Jamali's man changed. He said something, and Mac could hear the scorn dripping from his voice. The old man raised his eyebrows, unimpressed. Without another word, Jamali's man allowed Obaid to escort him out of the room at gunpoint. Beyond the door, Mac could hear women crying. The men filed out, leaving him alone with the dead body of the gate guard. Mac grabbed the guy's Makarov and stuck it into the back of his waistband. Then he frisked the body for spare magazines but found none. Still unnerved from shooting the guy, he sat back down on the mattress, pondering what he should do next.

The house fell silent apart from the women weeping. Outside, Mantoo was barking ferociously. Obaid and a younger man came back into the room. Ignoring Mac, they picked up the dead body and carried it out. Mac stood up and followed them, watching from the door of the house as they took the body out of the compound. He noticed that the hinges of the compound door had been shot through. There was an angry conversation outside, then came the sound of engines starting and vehicles driving away. Obaid and the young man came back into the compound, their clothes stained with the guard's blood.

Obaid pointed for Mac to go back to the lean-to before they disappeared into the house.

He was alone, apart from Mantoo.

What the hell had just happened?

Chapter 48

Sar Banader

There was no way Mac could go back to sleep. The adrenalin that had flooded his body as he'd stared down the barrel of the gate guard's Makarov had made him hyper-alert. Pulling the trigger of his own pistol to take the man's life had left his hands shaking and his stomach roiling. Sure, he'd fired at people before, even hit them, but never at such close range, with the sole intent of killing. But it had been the guard's life or his own. No decision to be made – and he was relieved he'd been able to act in the moment. A second's hesitation would have been his last.

After a while, Obaid's wife came outside and brought him some food – rice and vegetables and naan again. He had no appetite, but he forced himself to eat it. He didn't want to be rude to these people. They'd defended him against Jamali's men, saving his life for a second time, and he had no idea how to express his huge gratitude to them.

He gave some of the rice to an appreciative Mantoo, wondering how long it would be before Baz, Ginger and Logan would arrive, and hoping they didn't run into Jamali's goons on the road.

Obaid came out of the house with the young man and started a temporary fix on the compound gate. Mac stood up and held out the Tokarev that Obaid had given him at the beginning of the raid. Obaid took it with a nod of thanks. Mac also had the weapon he'd taken off the gate guard, but Obaid and his assistant didn't need to know about that. He indicated that he wanted to help them, but Obaid pointed at his sling with a weary smile. It seemed there was nothing he could do, but he stayed with them, watching them work, passing pieces of wood to them when he got the chance, just to show willing.

He wished he had access to the satphone again, so he could warn Logan and Ginger about what had happened. He had no doubt that Jamali's men would still be in the area. They could bide their time, because it was obvious he couldn't shelter in Obaid's house forever. He wondered how long had passed since he'd spoken to Baz. Neither Obaid nor the young man were wearing a watch and he had no idea how to ask the time in Pashto.

When the gate was secure, Obaid called into the house for tea, and the three men sat in the lean-to drinking it in companionable silence. Mac felt bad for the chaos he'd rained down on them, and he'd make sure to let them know as soon as Baz was here to translate.

It was almost dawn when they heard the rumble of approaching vehicles in the distance. Obaid jumped to his feet and shouted instructions. The young man ran into the house, and moments later appeared on the rooftop, clutching an old pair of Soviet binoculars. Everything the Kuchis had appeared to be begged, borrowed or stolen. Meanwhile, Obaid gestured to Mac to hide in the shadows. The flurry of activity woke Mantoo, who set up barking again, no doubt waking the rest of the household and the whole village to boot.

Mac crouched in the darkness, trying to assess how many vehicles he could hear. Was it Jamali returning with reinforcements? It was certainly more than just Logan's Surf or one of the Well Diggers Land Rovers.

The man on the roof shouted something down to Obaid, then disappeared, and Mac watched as his host started to dismantle the barricaded door. That meant one thing. It had to be Baz and Logan. Mac ran over and started to help him as best he could with one arm. It only took a minute, and Mac was first out of the gate.

Logan's Surf was bumping down the track towards them, and behind him were two Toyota SUVs, bristling with armed men at every window, and a technical with a Dushka mounted on the back. Mac recognised them as the governor's men, and he blessed Logan for whatever he'd done for Khaliq that had made the man putty in his hands.

The Surf had barely pulled up in front of Obaid's compound when Baz was in his arms.

'Mac, oh Mac...' Whatever else she might have said was smothered in a kiss, Mac suddenly aware that he hadn't cleaned his teeth for days. But if it didn't bother her, it didn't bother him.

Logan slapped him hard on the back, nearly knocking them both over, but Baz wasn't letting go of him any time soon.

'Christ, mate, am I glad to see you,' said Ginger. Then he shook his head. 'This is all my fault, I'm so sorry...'

Mac pulled back from Baz's embrace slightly to talk to Ginger, who looked like he might cry. 'Fuck's sake, man, pull yourself together,' he said with a grin. 'I knew what I was getting into.' That wasn't strictly true, but there was no point in letting Ginger feel bad on his account.

The governor's men poured out of their vehicles and, under instructions from their captain, started setting up a protective ring around the property.

Logan and Obaid were deep in conversation, and Baz reluctantly let go of Mac to go and join them. Still talking, Obaid beckoned them into the compound, where Mantoo was loudly making his presence felt. Baz glanced over at the dog.

'Meet Mantoo,' said Mac, giving the Kuchi hound a chuck under the chin.

Baz burst out laughing.

'What's so funny?'

'Mantoo,' she said, 'you know what that means?'

Mac shook his head.

'Dumpling. The largest dumpling I ever saw.' Then she was laughing and crying at the same time, completely overwhelmed by emotion, and Mac gave her another hug.

'Sorry,' she sniffed. 'I'm just so relieved to see you.'

'Likewise, times ten,' said Mac.

Baz turned back to listen to Obaid and Logan.

'I don't understand what happened,' said Mac in her ear. 'Jamali's men raided the house and were about to take me. Then Obaid's old man intervened, and they left empty-handed.'

Baz's eyes widened, then she nodded her understanding. '*Melmestia*.'

'What?'

'It's the Pashtunwali code of hospitality. If you enter their house unarmed, they'll protect you with their lives. They won't break the code, and Jamali's men obviously realised that. They were willing to give their lives, and that's what saved your life.'

'Too bloody right it did.' That, and the fact that he'd lost Pistol Boy's weapon somewhere in the night.

Logan turned to face Mac. 'Jeez, you're a lucky guy, Mac. Obaid here says he found you inside a goat pen sprawled on the ground like a halfwit. And he had a lot of other, unrepeatable things to say about you too – but we'll let him off that.'

'Not quite such a halfwit. I bloody escaped from Jamali's compound, didn't I?' He looked at Obaid. 'Will you tell him that I thank him from the bottom of my heart, and that I owe my life to him?'

Baz translated and Obaid grinned and said something.

'He says you now have an honour debt to him that you can never forget.'

'Believe me, I won't forget any of this in a hurry.'

Logan was digging a hand into his pocket. He retrieved something and held it out to Obaid. Mac saw silver glinting in his palm and there was a jingle of coins.

Obaid gave a shallow bow and took what was offered. He held one of the coins up to the light.

'Christ,' said Ginger. 'Are those what I think they are?'

'Yup, sure are,' said Logan. 'Genuine Maria Theresa Thalers.' Mac had seen them before – Austrian silver dollars, used in trouble spots all over the world since the 1700s. 'Each one is worth about thirty bucks – I've given him nearly two hundred dollars' worth.'

'That's a fortune for him,' said Baz. She looked back at Mac. 'But I suppose you're worth it.'

'Some people seem to think I'm worth a million dollars,' said Mac.

Logan and Obaid were still talking in Pashto. Suddenly the smile fell away from Baz's face, and she was all ears.

'What?' said Mac.

She held up hand for him to be quiet while she carried on listening for another minute.

'Wow – Obaid knows where Bakker is. Apparently it's common knowledge that Jamali is holding another westerner.'

'Did he say where?'

'Bahram Chah.'

Mac looked at her, eyebrows raised. The name meant nothing to him.

'The opium bazaar, down on the border of Pakistan. Jamali's HQ. It's the seventh circle of hell compared to here.'

Chapter 49

Sar Banader

It was almost dawn by the time they rolled out of Sar Banader.

'We need to head out fast,' said Logan. '*Melmestia* might have saved your hide while you were a guest in Obaid's house, but Jamali's militia will be waiting for us somewhere out on the road.' He made sure each of them was armed as he rearranged the convoy, putting one of the governor's Hiluxes as lead vehicle, followed by the technical, with the Surf third in line and the other Hilux bringing up the rear. Obaid waved them off, presumably with a huge sigh of relief, and considerably better off than he had been before his daughter had discovered Mac in the goat pen.

Mac sat in the back of the Surf with Baz, suddenly overcome by the extreme exhaustion which follows days of living on adrenalin. He tried desperately to keep his eyes open – they weren't out of danger yet. He wouldn't feel absolutely safe until they were back in Lash. They were driving as fast as the road conditions allowed – the sooner they got out of this part of Helmand, the better.

'Tell me about it,' said Baz, resting her head against his good shoulder.

Mac wasn't sure he was ready to talk about everything that had happened yet, but it was one way of staying awake.

'I killed a goat and ate its liver,' he said.

'Ugh!'

'I walked miles underground through a dried-up *karez* system.'

'What can you tell us about Jamali?' said Logan. He wanted intelligence, not war stories, which was fair enough.

'I met him,' said Mac. 'He organised a ransom video.'

'We saw it, mate,' said Ginger.

'So you got my message?'

'Um, no?' Ginger turned round in his seat to stare at Mac.

'Morse code, with my fingers.'

Logan smacked the heel of his hand against the steering wheel. 'I wondered for a second, but the quality of the video was crap. Some ancient VHS that had been recorded over hundreds of times.'

A barrage of fire out of nowhere snapped them into hyper-alertness. Baz gasped and ducked down, scrabbling for the pistol she'd put on the floor by her feet. Logan started shouting instructions over his radio to the other vehicles. They all accelerated, as windows were opened and weapons were primed. Mac braced himself between the door and the edge of the seat, resting his elbows on the sill of the open window to steady the AK he had pressed into his shoulder.

'Up on the ridge over there,' said Ginger, pointing to where a low hillside banked at the edge of the road ahead.

The vehicle leading the convoy was the target as it entered the killing ground.

'It must be Jamali's men,' said Mac. 'They want to collect what they came for.' He watched in horror as the Hilux took an RPG hit and skidded off the track into a deep ditch. It teetered on the brink, one man returning fire, before rolling over onto its side. The driver must have been taken out. Bullets rained down on it and flames suddenly flared from the engine as another grenade detonated.

'Goddammit,' said Baz, as Mac pushed her head back down to keep her out of harm's way. She bobbed up again, taking potshots out of the window with her pistol.

'Two guys, two positions, as far as I can see,' said Ginger.

The technical with the machine gun let rip and Logan gunned the engine to take advantage of the cover it was giving them. He sped through the killing ground, while Ginger leaned out of the passenger window, spraying AK rounds up the hill. Casings flew out of the weapon, a couple of them hitting Logan on the arm and cheek.

'Hot brass,' he spat. 'Cut it out.'

'Better than a bullet,' shouted Ginger over the racket, as he carried on firing.

They were clear of the killing ground in ten seconds. The technical had pulled over and continued to fire to their rear, and the second Hilux swept up behind them. Logan carried on half a kilometre up the road, then stopped.

'Fucking amateurs,' he said, as he waited for the Hilux and the technical to stop beside them. 'Pretty sure our guys have wiped them all out now.'

He climbed out of the Surf to have a conflab with the captain of the governor's men.

'You okay?' said Mac, as Baz stretched her back after being crouched down low on the seat.

'Sure.'

But some of the men in the second Hilux hadn't been so lucky. Ginger and Mac grabbed the trauma pack from the back of their vehicle and went across to where two injured men were being given rudimentary medical attention by their colleagues.

'He's gone,' muttered Mac in Ginger's ear as they came close enough to see that one of the men was bleeding out from a wound that had nicked his femoral artery.

The other man had a fighting chance. He'd taken a bullet to the right side of his torso, near the bottom of his ribs. It was a sucking chest wound, damaging his lung, and bloody froth was being expelled from the entry and exit wounds. Ginger grabbed a couple of shell dressings and, stripping off their waterproof wrappers, he applied the wrappers to the wounds to create airtight seals. Then he placed the dressing pads over the plastic and secured it all tightly to the man's torso using surgical tape.

Mac set up a drip for the guy and administered a morphine shot.

'Should be okay, if we can get him back to the Italian hospital pronto.'

Logan came over to them.

'Here's the plan. The technical's going to go back and collect the bodies. That's non-negotiable, so I've told them to take the other Hilux for cover.'

Ginger looked at the man he'd just finished bandaging. His colleague with the leg wound was already dead, and one of the militiamen was solemnly wrapping a bloodstained *keffiyeh* around the dead man's head.

'This guy needs to get to hospital fast.'

'That's fine,' said Logan. 'He can come with us. We won't wait for the bodies. That was Jamali's best attempt to take us out, and I don't reckon we'll see any more trouble up the road.'

'Fair dos,' said Mac. 'You're probably right.'

He and Ginger carried the wounded man to the Surf and stashed the trauma pack. Baz was taking photos – although it might have seemed distasteful to shoot pictures of a man as his life ebbed away, Mac knew it was important for her to document everything that happened.

'Rolling out,' yelled Logan to the captain, as he started the engine.

The car doors slammed, and they were back on the road.

'Let's hope we can get this guy back in time to save his life,' said Mac.

'*Insha'Allah*,' said Baz, '*Insha'Allah*.'

Day 10

Chapter 50

Lashkar Gah

While the nurses prepped the injured militiaman for surgery, the duty doctor came in to take a look at Mac. Mac recognised him as the Italian American who'd shown them Vinke's body. Was that just over a week ago? It seemed like a lifetime had passed since then.

'Dr Marchesi, good to see you again.'

'At least you're alive, unlike the last patient we spoke about,' said the medic, with a wry smile.

He checked Mac over.

'Broken collarbone – no treatment, just rest. Sprained knee – no treatment, just rest. Dysentery and dehydration – ciprofloxacin, oral rehydration, rest.'

Baz gave Mac a look, and he shrugged at her. Rest wasn't a word in his vocabulary, especially not now that they had a lead on Bakker's whereabouts. They'd both grabbed a couple of hours' sleep on the drive back to Lashkar Gah, and that was going to have to suffice.

Logan was waiting for them in the hospital parking lot, catching forty winks behind the wheel of the Surf. Mac tapped on the window, and he sat bolt upright, blinking and reaching for his gun. Ginger woke up from where he'd been dozing on the back seat.

'Just us,' said Mac, as Logan opened the window.

'I need coffee,' said Logan.

But Starbucks hadn't made it to Lash, and coffee was a luxury that westerners in Helmand could only dream of most of the time. Baz reached into her bag and pulled out a can of Zamzam cola, Afghanistan's answer to America's other favourite drink.

'This do?'

Logan grinned. 'You're a girl after my own heart, Baz. When you get fed up with this one' – he nodded in Mac's direction – 'give me a call.' He snapped open the can and took a long drink.

'Sod off, chum,' said Mac. 'She's got better taste.'

They got into the Surf and Logan pulled out of the parking lot. Baz found another can of Zamzam for Ginger, who hoovered it down in a single gulp.

'Plan?' said Baz.

'Dropping you at the office, then Mac, Ginger and I are going to pay Khaliq a visit. We need to apologise for the loss of his men and then talk about a little trip to Bahram Chah.'

'And I'm not invited?' said Baz.

Mac laughed at her indignant expression.

'Boys' talk,' said Logan. 'Khaliq will be more forthcoming if it's just us three. I don't write the rules.'

Baz sat back in her seat with an indignant sniff.

'It'll give you time to file some copy,' said Mac.

'Sure, I know. But it's frustrating…'

They dropped her off at the HAVA building, then drove over to the Hotel Bost, where Logan had already ascertained that the governor was giving audiences. The security detail waved them straight through, and within minutes, they were shown into the hotel dining room, to find Khaliq staring wistfully out of the window at the slow-flowing river.

He turned round as they came into the room, and though his greeting was as warm as ever, it was not quite so effusive. He enquired after their families, and after Baz, and then pointed them to a seating area in one of the bow windows.

'Mac-jan, you have been injured, I see. I must offer you my heartfelt apologies that something so terrible could happen in my province. Jamali is an evil force, and I will be commanding my men to do all they can to expel him from our lands.'

The irony of this wasn't lost on Mac. He knew full well that Khaliq's interest in removing Jamali would be so that he and his brother Feda could take over the Baloch chieftain's opium empire. But he made the right noises in response.

'Wadaan-jan, we come to offer our apologies for the loss of your men this morning. We were attacked by some of Jamali's gangsters, and your militia were brave in protecting us, some of them even giving their lives to save ours.' It was an embroidery of the truth. The vehicle in which the militiamen had died had been caught unawares.

'My fighters are the lions of Helmand. There are no better men.'

Logan took a deep breath. 'This is why we are coming to you again for your help. While we were south of Garmser, we learned that the Dutchman Tomas Bakker is being held by Jamali in Bahram Chah. We want to mount an expedition to withdraw him.'

Khaliq's eyes sparkled and his mouth curled into a sly grin. 'Of course, there is nothing I would like more than to snatch his prize away from under his nose. It would be suitable vengeance for the loss of my men. What do you need from me, Logan-jan?'

–

An hour later, Mac, Ginger and Logan left the Bost Hotel having secured the promise of ten armed infantrymen, with vehicles, plus a four-man team on a heavy technical. The governor had also undertaken to speak to a contact in Bahram Chah to see if he could get precise details of where Bakker was being held, and who would also sort out a guide for them once they arrived in the vicinity. They agreed with Khaliq to liaise with his men immediately after midday prayers at the southern edge of the town. This gave them a couple of hours to eat, rest and sort their kit. It was a tall order, but in a hostage situation, every minute counted.

Logan sped back towards the HAVA building to pick up Baz. Then they headed to the house to make their final preparations.

'What the fuck did you do for Khaliq?' said Mac, unable to contain his curiosity any longer. 'It seems like he'll move heaven and earth for you.'

Logan grinned. 'We're sworn brothers, dude. I'd do anything for him too.'

'So spill – what's the story?'

'It was back in 2001,' said Logan, running a hand through his unruly, unwashed hair. 'I was down here, still a snake eater then' – Mac knew this was how the Green Berets referred to themselves – 'pushing back against the Taliban, chasing them out of Lash. Khaliq was moving in with his militia, looking to mop up and snatch the governorship.'

'So you were fighting on the same side?'

'My enemy's enemy is my friend, sure. US forces were lending support to anyone routing the Taliban. We didn't care about their politics or how they lined their pockets – those issues were for later. And for the politicians, not for us boots on the ground.

'There was a lot of house-to-house fighting, all over town. Khaliq's men were concentrating on taking the governor's office and the Bost. High casualties on both sides. We'd skirted round to come in from the south, while they'd entered town on the main road from the north. We were mopping up fleeing Talibs – they were running off to hide in the countryside and we wanted to stop as many as we could from getting away.

'Anyway, I don't know if you know this, but the Helmand Central Prison lies in that part of town, just south of the main bridge over the river, on the east bank. We were going right past it, so my boss had the bright idea of dumping our Taliban prisoners in the jail. Which of course meant liberating the prisoners who were already in there. It was stuffed with guys that the Vice and Virtue Ministry had deemed evil – you know, people who cut their beards too short or didn't go to the mosque enough, or who might once have talked to someone the Taliban didn't care for.

'We went in, guns blazing, shot the Taliban guards and freed the men inside, most of whom were either supporters of Khaliq or petty crims. They were in a sorry state, starved, tortured, whatever, but they scarpered pretty quick when they realised they were free. I was taking a bunch of our prisoners down to the cells when I came across this kid, still chained in shackles, barely able to walk, being dragged along by a Taliban guard who was holding a gun to his head, using him as a get-out-of-jail-free card.'

They were drawing up to the HAVA building now. Logan parked the Surf.

'Anyway, long story short, I shot the Talib in the head without harming the kid. Then I got the chains off him and carried him out. Turns out, it was Beroj Khaliq – the Gov's nephew and appointed successor. He told Khaliq that I had saved his life and ever since then, I've been an honorary member of the Khaliq family.'

'And Beroj Khaliq?' said Mac, as they got out of the vehicle. 'Was he okay?'

'Absolutely – he was fine. You'll meet him in' – Logan glanced at his watch – 'just under two hours. He's coming down to Bahram Chah with us in charge of the governor's men.'

Chapter 51

Southern Helmand

In an ideal world, one wouldn't travel at night in southern Afghanistan. In an ideal world, all roads would be smoothly tarmacked. In an ideal world, Mac would get eight hours sleep a night and three square meals a day...

Only it wasn't an ideal world. Far from it.

Beautiful, yes. The sky was like a fold of black velvet, the moon a disc of molten metal casting its light on the desert all around them. Sand and rock painted silver, chequered black with shadows... uninhabitable and uninhabited. There were no trees, no bushes, just a rutted track stretching ahead of them and trailing out behind. Five vehicles traversing the Registan Desert, a flat plateau also known as the Desert of Death. From time to time, the track vanished in the sand, resulting in a stop and a conflab between the drivers who knew the route, while Beroj Khaliq – a dark-eyed and handsome twenty-five-year-old – squinted at the stars, humming tunelessly until Logan pointed them in a new direction.

Mac wondered if Beroj ever stopped humming, and felt glad he wasn't in the same vehicle as the kid.

They'd left Lashkar Gah at lunchtime, taking the road south that led through Garmser and Najibullahkhan Kalay. Three Hiluxes, an ancient Russian GAZ-66 heavy technical with a ZU-23-2 automatic cannon mounted on the back, Logan's Surf, and twenty-four men and one woman, speeding through the poppy plantations as fast as the road conditions would allow.

Field workers and villagers stared as they roared by – and no doubt passed on what they'd seen to Jamali's informants in the area. They needed to stay one step ahead, so they barely stopped – only once for late afternoon prayers, and Logan didn't allow that until they had branched away from the river valley and were out in the empty desert. Some of the militiamen had muttered ominously about it, staring darkly at the westerners when they did stop, but Beroj had put them in their place with a volley of harsh words. It was clear that, despite his youth, he was completely in charge and would brook no insolence from his soldiers.

'I'm aiming for eleven hours,' said Logan. 'I'll be happy if we reach the edge of Bahram Chah by midnight.'

'And then what?' said Baz from the back of the Surf.

Mac had begged her to stay behind in Lash, but she'd put on her Kevlar body armour with PRESS stamped on the back and front, and climbed into the vehicle, saying, 'This is my job, buster, and I don't need your permission to come along.' Mac had backed off – there was no point in having a row over it, because she was right.

Logan cleared his throat. 'Hopefully, by then Beroj will have heard from Khaliq's contact in Bahram Chah. It's a small place, but we have to view it as entirely hostile. We need to know where Bakker is so we can go in cleanly, extract him, then get out again fast. On-the-ground information is critical.'

'And if we don't get that information?' said Mac.

'We'll get it,' said Logan.

With the moon almost full, and low in the sky, they were able to drive without using headlights, and when the track they were on completely disappeared, they sped forward across the stony ground in an arrow formation, with the Surf at the apex. It was a bone-juddering experience and Logan insisted that everyone in the vehicle kept their seatbelts on. Just in case.

Ginger and Mac were in the back, with Baz between them. The two men each had a set of binoculars, and they constantly

313

scanned the horizon for distant vehicles – it was certain that their presence would have been noted travelling south. There was also the risk of running into opium smugglers heading for the border with Pakistan or to sell their goods in Bahram Chah's notorious opium bazaar. Tirich was driving, with Logan next to him. Tirich concentrated on finding a straight line that avoided rocks and boulders, while Logan watched the horizon and tracked their progress on the map on his laptop. Every now and then he conferred with Beroj using a Motorola handheld radio.

'Take us down that wadi, just over there,' he said to Tirich, pointing in a more easterly direction. 'It'll give us good cover for the next fifteen klicks or so.'

The base of the wadi was more rock-strewn than the open desert had been, and narrower, so they were back to driving single file. To Mac, progress seemed slow, and he wondered if they really would reach their destination by midnight. The weapons and jerrycans of fuel rattled in the back, and it was hard to keep watch through the binoculars as they constantly banged and bumped against the top of his cheekbones and the bridge of his nose. Though it wasn't deep, there were plenty of shadowy crevices in the sides of the wadi – perfect places from which to launch an ambush. Even though he knew Jamali's men wouldn't have had time to get in position and wouldn't have known that they would drive down this particular dried-up water course, he couldn't help but feel twitchy about what lay in the unseen pools of darkness on either side of them.

A sudden flurry of Pashto chatter over the radios made Mac drop his binoculars into his lap. Tirich brought the Surf to an abrupt halt.

'What's happening?'

'Shhhhh...' said Logan, holding the Motorola closer to his ear to catch what was being said.

Baz spun in her seat to look behind. 'Oh crap!'

Mac looked round. The vehicles behind them were also stopped and the reason was easily apparent. One of the Hiluxes was tilted at an awkward angle – the driver hadn't spotted a dark-coloured rock in its path and had hit it. The nearside front wheel was buckled and twisted.

'Goddammit!' said Logan, opening his door and climbing out.

Mac watched as men spewed out of vehicles to assess the damage and discuss the chances of rectifying it.

'Set up a security cordon,' he said to Ginger as they both got out too.

Ginger went across to Beroj, but Mac could see that Khaliq's son was already instructing his men to form a perimeter. The militiaman in charge of the ZU was swinging it round in readiness for anything, and Mac and Ginger went across for a closer look.

'That GAZ-66 truck's probably older than you are,' said Mac.

'And ageing better by the looks of things,' said Ginger, laughing.

The GAZ-66s had an epic reputation for reliability, while the ZU on the back of it was a twin-barrelled monster with a two-mile range and a cyclic rate of 400 rpm.

'Gun's pretty damn impressive though,' he added.

Mac nodded. 'Just shows what the governor thinks of Logan, that he'll hand over the big boys' toys.'

They joined Baz and Logan at the stricken Hilux. One of the militiamen was lying on his back, examining the underside of the vehicle with a torch. He shuffled out and sat up, reporting to Logan and the driver.

Baz sighed. 'He says the axle is bent.'

'We won't get that fixed in a hurry,' said Mac, 'if at all.'

Thankfully nobody was hurt in the incident, and the decision was quickly taken to split the men and equipment between the other vehicles. Within half an hour, the two remaining Hiluxes, the GAZ-66 and the Surf were off again, cramped inside with extra bodies, lower on their suspension, the ride even bumpier than before.

It was long gone midnight and there were still miles of desert ahead of them before they reached the small border town where Bakker was apparently being held. The flat desert had given way to rocky hills and it took time to find the track that would take them through to the dry river valley that finally led to Bahram Chah. They drove in silence and the night seemed never-ending. But finally, the radio crackled into life once more. Logan spoke in Pashto for a minute, then issued some instructions to Tirich.

'That's it,' he said, turning back to Mac and Ginger with a grin. 'We've got what we need and we're meeting our local liaison in Khoni Bibi in fifteen minutes.' He checked his watch. 'Put your foot down, Tirich, and we'll make it.'

Day 11

Chapter 52

Khoni Bibi and Bahram Chah

Khoni Bibi was nothing more than a hamlet, sustained by a narrow trickle of water along a winding river valley. There were no fields of poppies down here, only rocks and a hot, dry wind that put grit in your eyes. Mac stared at the tiny, mud-walled compounds and wondered how people survived in such a harsh environment – and why they didn't simply go somewhere else.

The convoy arrived with a roar of engines, tyres crunching on the gravelly track. Dogs started barking, but no lights went on. Perhaps the handful of people that called Khoni Bibi home knew better than to show themselves to strangers in the night. This tiny dirt track was a smuggling route for opium leaving the country and armaments coming in, and the warlords and private armies of Helmand and Kandahar came and went freely through the desert to ply their illegal trade at Bahram Chah's notorious bazaar, just twenty or so kilometres further south.

Logan gave the command to stop over the radio, and the vehicles pulled up in an arrow formation in the centre of the village.

A tall man stepped out of the shadows of one of the compound walls. His clothes were black and so was the cloth *lungee* wound around his head. He had a heavy black beard and dark, scowling brows. This was their guide.

Logan climbed out of the Surf and Beroj quickly joined them. Beroj and the man embraced – they clearly knew each other. They spoke for a few minutes, then Logan and the guide came back to the Surf. Logan opened the passenger door and stuck his head in.

'Shift up,' he said.

There were already three of them on the back seat, but they crushed together and the guide climbed in.

'This is Sarbaz,' said Logan, getting into the front.

There was a polite round of *salaam alaikums*, and they were off. After twenty minutes, Sarbaz directed Tirich to turn away from the river course and into a narrow gully, following a barely perceptible track. Mac had to wonder how much they could really trust the man – he could be leading them straight into an ambush of Jamali's men. Loyalty in this part of the world came at a price, and Jamali might have offered him more than Khaliq. Or might have threatened worse.

As if he could sense Mac's thoughts, Logan turned back in his seat.

'Sarbaz is taking us through the hills to a safe position on the bluff that looks down on Bahram Chah. We'll use it as the FRV – final rendezvous point.'

'What happens then?' said Baz.

Logan looked out of the window. They were just cresting a low slope onto a rocky platform. The sky was getting light in the east – it was nearly dawn.

'We'll eat and rest for a couple of hours, final weapons check. I want Sarbaz to take me on a recce into Bahram Chah. Mac, you and Beroj should come too. We'll check out where Sarbaz thinks Bakker is being held, then come back here for final planning and briefing.'

'Seriously? You and I are going to walk through Bahram Chah in daylight? Talk about announcing our presence.'

Logan laughed. 'I am ze master of disguise,' he said in the worst French accent Mac had ever heard. 'A bit of black walnut juice on your face and a turban and even your mother wouldn't know you.'

'You're kidding?' said Ginger.

'Sorry, pal. You're gonna have to sit this one out. The orange beard is too much of a giveaway.'

It was a moment of levity, but there was no denying how dangerous it was going to be. Their only saving grace was that Bahram Chah was a crossroads, border crossing and trading centre. Strangers came and went daily, so as long as they kept their heads down and let Sarbaz and Beroj do any necessary talking, they might just make it out alive.

Half an hour later, the convoy was parked up in a bowl-like hollow just beneath the brow of one the hills which over-looked the notorious opium bazaar. Mac was lying on his stomach, studying the village below them through a pair of binoculars. For all its reputation, Bahram Chah didn't look like much – a cramped gathering of maybe a hundred walled compounds. The buildings were low, all single-storey, all built of the ubiquitous brown mud. He traced the path of the wide central street, part of it lined with rudimentary shops, but it was too early for the market to be in evidence. On the eastern edge of the settlement, he could make out a small mosque with a squat, brown dome – he'd heard the distant cry of the muezzin calling the faithful as they'd arrived. It seemed there were still some God-fearing folk in this den of iniquity.

Baz was lying next to him, taking photographs with a long lens.

'You'd hardly believe it, would you? One of the world's major opium-trading sites.'

'It's geography,' said Logan coming up behind them. 'Conveniently situated on the Pakistan border. Arms for opium, bombs for heroin. Millions of dollars changing hands via the *hawala* system, ending up in bank accounts in Switzerland and Dubai. And Jamali with a finger in literally every pie.'

–

Black walnut juice. Logan produced a little bottle of the stuff. It stank and it stung Mac's cheeks and forehead, but when he looked in the mirror on the Surf's sun visor, with the addition of a traditional turban wound round his head by one of Beroj's militiamen, he knew it would do. The shalwar kameez Logan had tossed at him a few minutes earlier smelled fusty and worn, but he couldn't deny it was comfortable in the heat – already searing despite the early hour.

They'd rested for a while, and had eaten MREs and stale naan, washed down with water. The village had come to life and the main street bustled with men – there wasn't a woman in sight. Trucks and SUVs came and left, leaving Mac wondering about their cargos, and he felt the familiar fluttering of nerves in his stomach that he always felt before embarking on a mission. He had a Browning tucked inside his shalwar, easily hidden in its capacious folds. Of course, it would be a disaster if he needed to use it on the recce mission, but he'd be a fool to enter hostile territory unarmed.

Logan was similarly disguised and looked so completely at home in his new persona that Mac guessed he'd done it a thousand times before.

'Remember, you're mute, okay?' he said to Mac, as they climbed into the Surf. 'If anyone approaches us, leave it to Beroj and Sarbaz to sort it out.'

'Mute?' said Mac.

'It's not that unusual – the Pashtuns suffer a high level of birth defects, and they don't have the luxury of western medicine to sort them out.'

They were going to drive round the back of the hill they were on and join the main track that came into the village from the north. No one would arrive in Bahram Chah on foot – it was in the middle of a goddamn desert, and the dusty Surf would easily blend in with the Hiluxes, Land Cruisers and ancient Mercedes used by the opium dealers and gangsters that frequented the market.

'When we get out of the car, we stay within sight of it. Tirich will remain behind the wheel and he'll keep the engine running at all times.'

'Do we know where Bakker is being held?'

'Sarbaz has a good idea – Jamali owns three compounds in the centre of the village and he believes it'll be one of those. He's had a cousin watching them, and we'll meet him in the bazaar for an intel update. Once we get a final fix, we can recce the site.'

They drove up the main street, slowing down as donkeys laden with hessian sacks – raw opium? – blocked their path, squeezing past jingle trucks that were openly loading or unloading crates of armaments in broad daylight. Mac's eyes widened as he saw stall after stall selling a jumble of small arms, automatic rifles and opium in various stages of production, along with precursor chemicals for heroin production, while merchants haggled over prices and men inspected weapons – Soviet and American, ancient and modern. A boy was hawking ammunition from a rug on the ground, and an old man was selling something in huge blue plastic barrels at the side of the road.

'What's that?' said Mac, as they trundled slowly past him.

'Fertiliser,' said Logan. 'Barrels of ammonium nitrate for bomb making.'

'Christ, what can't you buy here?'

'Peace of mind.'

Sarbaz said something, nodding his head slightly in the direction of an imposing compound wall.

'Jamali's headquarters,' said Logan.

There were two armed men standing outside the gate, and no doubt plenty more inside. They carried on driving.

A minute later, Sarbaz directed Tirich to take a turn off the main street. A middle-aged man in a long blue shalwar and a cream turban was striding up the edge of the road they turned onto. After fifteen metres, he stopped and Sarbaz said something to Tirich.

'It's his cousin,' Logan explained.

The Surf stopped and Sarbaz got out. Tirich drove further up the road, then pulled over. They waited while the two men

323

conferred for a minute or two. Then the cousin ducked into a nearby compound and Sarbaz returned to the Surf. He filled Logan in on what his cousin had told him.

'He thinks Bakker is being held at a compound on the edge of the village. It's not one of Jamali's main compounds – it belongs to an associate of his. But the cousin has seen armed men going in and out, some of whom he knows work for Jamali.'

'And what makes him think Bakker's in there?' said Mac.

Logan shrugged. 'A place like this has a very active rumour mill – and lately it's been going into overdrive.'

'So let's go and check it out.'

Chapter 53

Bahram Chah

Baz gazed down at the village through the binoculars. She couldn't see the Surf and she was starting to feel nervous. They'd been gone too long. She turned back to the huddle of vehicles. Ginger was sitting in the paltry patch of shade cast by one of the Hiluxes, dry cleaning an AK47.

'What's keeping them?' said Baz, plonking herself down next to him.

Ginger glanced up at her. 'You can't second-guess what's happening down there. A recce takes as long as it takes.' He concentrated on his work again.

Baz wandered around between the vehicles. There was no point just staring down at Bahram Chah – it wouldn't tell her anything about the recce. She drank some water and watched Beroj's men making their final preparations. They were a scruffy bunch, spanning a wide age range, but Baz knew better than to underestimate their prowess. Some of them had already seen off the Red Army, and they'd been fighting pretty much non-stop ever since. And even the younger ones would have seen more action than most of the US or Brit troops that were supposedly now giving them the benefit of their superior knowledge.

She checked her watch again, but hardly any time had passed since she'd last looked. These damn missions appeared to be ninety per cent waiting around, then one percent action, before nine percent getting the hell out of Dodge. They were in the ninety per cent stage of the process, and it seemed to be lasting forever.

The whine of a low-powered scooter engine coalesced in the distance. Nearly everyone at the FRV looked up and looked around. As the noise became louder, it was accompanied by the sounds of weapons being cocked, and several of the militiamen took up firing positions using their vehicles as cover.

'Get down, Baz,' hissed Ginger. He was kneeling at the back of the Surf, his AK trained in the direction of the engine sound.

She squatted down next to him. 'What is it?'

'No idea, but we can't take any chances. This place is crawling with Jamali's men and the longer we can avoid detection, the more chance there is of the mission succeeding.'

A small Hando came into view on the track that led up the hill. Baz sensed a frisson of tension as fingers tightened on triggers.

'Stop!' shouted the militiaman who Beroj had left in charge.

But the Hando was already skidding into a U-turn. The rider was a teenage boy, and Baz could see the whites of his eyes as they widened in fear. It was an idiotic manoeuvre to attempt, and on the gritty track his back wheel spun out from under him and the bike crashed down. He scrabbled desperately to get out from under it, but within seconds he was surrounded by a circle of AK barrels pointing at his head.

He gave an anguished cry, and Baz could see he was hurt.

'Stay where you are!' said the commander of the militia as the boy struggled to stand.

'Please, please, just let me go,' said the boy.

They were speaking in Pashto. Baz glanced over at Ginger, but it was so clear what was happening she didn't feel the need to translate.

Back on his feet, the terrified teenager tried to lift his bike. 'I promise, please, I promise. I won't say anything to anyone.' He didn't care who they were – he just wanted to get away.

One of the militiamen stepped forward and kicked the bike hard. The boy lost his grip of it and it crashed to the ground again. A shot rang out and the kid collapsed, clutching at his lower leg.

'What the actual?' said Baz, leaping up from behind the Surf.

'Leave it,' said Ginger.

But Baz certainly wasn't going to leave it. She strode across to the head militiaman and addressed him in Pashto. 'What the hell do you think you're doing? He's just a kid – there was no need to shoot him.'

The boy was writhing on the ground, moaning as he tried to staunch the blood flow from a bullet wound in his left calf. Baz squatted down beside him. The leader of the militia looked furious.

'We can't let him go back to the village and raise the alarm. It will put Beroj and the others in danger.'

'But you didn't have to shoot him. You could have disabled the bike and held him here without doing this.'

She ripped the fabric of the boy's kameez to get a better look at the wound, which was still bleeding freely. She was no medic, but it looked like a deep flesh wound. Not life-threatening, but the bullet had ripped through his calf muscle.

'Ginger,' she called, 'get me the trauma pack.'

The boy's head was lolling from side to side, and his eyes rolled back. He was about to faint. Ginger ran back to the Surf and pulled out the medical kit. They quickly put a tourniquet just below the boy's knee, then packed the wound and bandaged it tightly. He managed to remain conscious, though he was crying now. When they finished, he thanked Baz profusely, while still viewing the militiamen fearfully. They, however, had lost interest and gone back to their preparations.

Baz stood up and used a bottle of water to rinse the boy's blood off her hands. She glared at the commander.

'He's not one of Jamali's spies and he had no idea that there would be people up here. That's no way to have treated one of your own countrymen.'

The commander shrugged. 'I'm not paid to be kind or gentle. The boy is a threat to my men and my operation. You're American and you don't understand the way our country works.'

327

It felt like a slap in the face to Baz. Sure, she'd been born in America, but both her parents were Afghan. She loved the country and considered it her own. Too furious to waste breath arguing with him, she helped the boy to his feet and took him to sit in the back of the Surf. They were going to have to keep him here until the operation had been completed, but there was no need to be unkind. She gave him some water to drink and one of the MREs. The food didn't impress him, but he accepted a couple of painkillers, and thanked her again.

The waiting continued.

What the hell were they doing down there?

Chapter 54

Bahram Chah

Sarbaz gave Tirich directions as they drove through the village towards the compound that had been identified by his cousin. They passed the mosque that Mac had seen from the hilltop. Of course, it seemed bigger up close, but it was nothing like the mosques in Kabul or even Lashkar Gah. This one was mud-built like the rest of the buildings in Bahram Chah, with little thought for decoration or finesse.

Five minutes later, Sarbaz told Tirich to stop. He pointed at a compound wall further up the street they were on.

'How does he know this is the right place?' said Mac.

Logan questioned the guide. 'The gate in the wall is painted black.' Most of the compound gates were plain wood, crudely constructed. Whoever lived here possibly felt himself a cut above the rest of the villagers. An opium trader perhaps, or a weapons dealer.

They wanted to take a closer look, but on the deserted street it was likely that their presence would be noted.

'Drive past the place slowly, Tirich,' said Logan. 'Then see if we can find a road running along the back.'

When they approached, they could see no guards outside.

'All quiet,' said Beroj.

As they drew up perpendicular to the entrance, Mac took a breath. 'Stop.'

Tirich did as he was told and Mac studied the gate.

'It's not closed properly, is it?' he said.

'Damn right,' said Logan.

Bahram Chah didn't seem to be the sort of place where people left their doors unlocked so neighbours could pop in to borrow a cup of sugar. Especially not if you were hiding a western kidnap victim in your spare room.

Something was amiss.

They parked further up the road, and Logan and Mac decided to risk a recce on foot.

'Keep the engine running,' said Logan, as they left the vehicle.

They walked towards the compound, eyes scanning the road and nearby houses, ears listening intently for any sounds coming from within the walls. Everything was quiet. As they approached the gate, they drew their pistols. It stood ajar and, with Logan covering his back, Mac squinted through the gap. He could see a narrow strip of bare ground and the corner of a one-storey building. There were no sounds, nothing moving. He put his hand flat on the gate and softly pushed to widen the gap. No guards, no vehicles parked inside the compound.

'The house door is open too,' he said quietly. 'Shall we?'

'Would be rude not to.'

They slipped into the courtyard, closing the gate quietly behind them. Mac scanned the area in front of them – nobody. No response from the house. Nothing.

Logan pointed to one side of the area. 'Check the perimeter – meet me at the back.'

Mac went round one side of the house, Logan the other. The building had few windows, and Mac's side was shaded which would make it harder for anyone to see him. There were no signs of life, not even a dog or a goat. Logan shook his head when they met up moments later.

'Seems deserted,' he said.

'Let's go inside.'

Leading with their pistols up, the two of them covered each other as they went from room to room. There was little to see –

barely any furniture, just floor cushions and carpets. A cupboard in one of the rear rooms had been turned over, its contents spread on the floor, but if there had been anything of interest, it had already been taken. In the other rear room, there was a stained mattress against one wall, a latrine bucket in the corner and blood spatter on the floor.

'Shit!' said Mac.

'The bird's flown,' said Logan.

The sound of a car driving along the street made them both tense up.

'Let's get out of here.' Mac led the way back to the front door and scanned the courtyard. The gate was still shut, and the car engine was receding into the distance. They crossed the compound in silence, pistols up, and squinted out at the street. All was quiet apart from the Surf's engine softly idling, further along.

They slipped out of the gate and held their pistols out of sight in the folds of their shalwars.

'Fuck!' said Mac beneath his breath. 'What the hell do we do now?'

–

Back at the FRV, Mac felt despondent. Their only lead had petered out, and now they had a shot kid on their hands as well. They argued with Beroj and his commander over what to do with the boy.

'Just leave him up here, tied up, when we go,' said Beroj.

'But what if nobody comes up here and finds him?' said Mac. The boy seemed feverish – he needed proper medical treatment.

'Look, we're not taking him all the way back to Lash to the hospital,' said Logan.

'What if we drop him off in Khoni Bibi?' said Mac. 'That will give us enough of a head start, but he won't be left alone.'

It seemed like a reasonable plan, but in reality it was a side issue. The mission had been derailed. They had no idea now where Bakker was being held or if he was still alive, and Logan was loath to go down to Bahram Chah in daylight hours again.

'We've already pushed our luck, and we can't just snoop around the bazaar hoping to overhear something.'

'We should go down when it gets dark,' said Beroj. 'We can snatch one of Jamali's men and get the information we need.'

It was an easy guess how the intelligence would be extracted and Mac wasn't keen on the idea. Not least because torturing a man was never a quiet pursuit and they were out in the open. They could drive back several miles to be out of earshot, but he still wasn't convinced.

'We've got nothing else to go on,' said Logan.

'But what if the man we take doesn't know where Bakker is?' said Mac. 'We're running out of time. Can't Sarbaz try his cousin again?'

'It'll cost us,' said Logan.

'And?'

'And it might yield nothing.'

They'd reached an impasse. Mac went over to where Baz was sitting with the boy in the back of the Surf. It would be dusk soon, and they needed the cover of darkness for the extraction. That meant finding out pretty damn quick where they would be extracting from.

'How is he?' said Mac, taking the water bottle Baz held out to him.

'Not great. The painkillers have helped, but he's still terrified.'

'Tell him he's safe. We'll make sure no one hurts him again.' Mac opened the front passenger door and checked the glove compartment. There was a roll of dollars that he knew Logan kept as a contingency fund. He peeled off a couple of twenties and passed them back to Baz.

'Give him these and tell him to find a doctor when we let him go.'

'There are no doctors down here,' said Baz. 'But I've given him a course of antibiotics from the trauma pack.'

She handed the money to the boy, and he seemed well enough to snatch the notes and shove them inside his shalwar.

Beroj and Sarbaz came across to the Surf. Sarbaz leaned in and spoke to the boy.

'He's asking about the boy's family,' Baz whispered to Mac. 'And introducing Beroj – it seems that the kid's clan and Sarbaz's family are linked in some way.'

Of course, thought Mac. Everyone was related to everyone else.

Sarbaz asked another question.

The boy placed a bloodstained hand on the guide's forearm and said something to him with quiet urgency. Baz's eyes widened as she listened. When he finished speaking, she gestured to Mac to get out of the Surf. He went round and met her, Sarbaz and Beroj at the front of the vehicle.

'What was all that about?' said Mac.

'He said there's a marble quarry, about two kilometres north-east of the village,' said Baz.

Mac nodded. 'Sure, you can just about see it from here if you look in the opposite direction from Bahram Chah.'

'He told Sarbaz they're holding a westerner there.'

Chapter 55

Bahram Chah

They waited until darkness had completely shrouded the hills and valleys surrounding the village. There had been some debate as to how much they could trust the boy's words, but as Baz pointed out, he'd spilled the information unprompted – just grateful for a promise of safe passage and more money than he'd ever possessed in his life. So in the end, with no other leads in sight, Beroj and Mac had persuaded Logan that they could observe and then swoop if they saw anything that suggested he might be telling the truth.

'As long as we don't pick up the wrong freakin' guy again,' said Logan.

'Lightning doesn't strike twice,' said Ginger.

Logan let out a bark of laughter. 'Ha, I can show you the scars.'

But now wasn't the moment for more of his war stories. Using Logan's BGAN and laptop, they studied Google Earth images of the marble quarry. It lay almost two kilometres due east of the village, a gravel track winding up the hillside to where a pale, lozenge-shaped scar showed the extent of the blasting area. Close to the ground being worked, there was a large walled compound, which they presumed was used for storing the cutting tools, explosives and slabs of cut marble. A long rectangular building ran along one side of the inner wall, possibly a workshop or storage area. Beyond the compound, further down the hill from the quarry, there was a cluster of smaller buildings. They had no way of knowing from the aerial images what these buildings were – perhaps housing for quarry workers? They could make out a number of vehicles parked outside the main compound, but the image they were looking at wasn't live, so this detail was irrelevant.

Looking in the direction of the quarry from the FRV, Mac couldn't see any lights at all, but they didn't read too much into that. If there were people in the compound or the other buildings, they might have covered the windows to stop any light showing.

There was only one road to the quarry and that led directly out of Bahram Chah. To maintain the element of surprise, they were going to have to approach from the north on foot.

'So how are we going to get out?' Ginger had said when Logan proposed this. 'As soon as we appear, they'll call down to the village for backup. We don't know what sort of state Bakker will be in, and we might have to carry him.'

'He's right,' said Mac. 'We need vehicles as close as possible for the exfil. That gives us two choices – our drivers come in through the village to pick us up, then we have to run the gauntlet of Bahram Chah to get out again, or they come cross country to a point beyond the quarry and we drive straight out through the desert.'

They gamed the various options, debating how many men they would need for the exfil, and thus how many vehicles, and where the remaining vehicles and personnel would wait for them.

It was gone midnight when the GAZ-66 and two of the Hiluxes freewheeled downhill from the FRV in a north-easterly direction, away from the village. The assault group was Mac, Logan, Ginger and Beroj, with six militiamen, two machine-gun teams and the ZU team. Baz, armed with a long lens, had hitched a ride on the GAZ-66, but only after Mac had extracted a promise from her that she would stay back with the support group and not come into the quarry itself.

A dry riverbed ran through a series of shallow valleys, and following this would take them to a point directly north of the quarry. Despite the hilly ground between where they were now driving and the village, they didn't dare put on their headlights. In a landscape with no artificial light, a single flicker would announce their presence like a flare. So they had to drive slowly and several times they had to stop and get out to move rocks out of the vehicles' paths.

Logan was in the front Hilux, continually checking their position via GPS, steering them towards the FRV – the far side of the hill out of which the quarry was carved. Once they arrived, he and Beroj worked out a position for the GAZ-66 and the other Hilux, out along the eastern shoulder of the hill. This would be the fire support group or FSG, positioned so they could shoot down on the quarry buildings in case the team needed cover on their way out. It would also be an excellent position for Baz to take long-range images of the raid in operation. They would move into place once the team had completed their observation of the quarry.

Leaving Baz and Beroj with the FSG and drivers in the wadi, Logan, Mac, Ginger and the remaining militiamen now faced a one-kilometre march up the back of the rocky hill to set up an observation post at the crest. The entire surrounding area was barren of any plant growth – just rocks, gravel and sand. If they needed to find cover, it had to be afforded by the lay of the land, behind outcrops of rocks or by lying flat in narrow gullies. Mac hoped upon hope that it wouldn't come to a pitched battle. They needed to go in silently and cleanly, taking out any guards on the way in to stop them sounding the alert, extract the Dutchman and then beat a hasty retreat.

The hill was steep and they climbed in silence, each one with the butt of their AK tucked into their shoulder, ready to fire at a moment's notice, change levers set to fire and fingers millimetres from the trigger. Additionally, they each had a sidearm holstered under their arm or tucked in their belt in case of close combat. Without Beroj and his incessant humming, all Mac could hear was the crunch of the rock surface under their feet. He glanced up. As usual the sky was a panoply of stars, the moon still bright, though on the wane. A scuttling on the ground made him look down. It was a scorpion, scurrying out of the way of the tramping boots.

He remembered other missions, other raids – none of them had started out quite like this. But inside, he had the familiar knot of anxiety. What would happen when they reached ground zero? Would his reactions be quick enough for the perceived threats? Would they achieve the mission goal? Would he come out alive? Unscathed? He visualised what was about to happen, playing out scores of options, running the variables, the what-ifs. But he knew it wouldn't go down exactly as he imagined it, and the one thing that would protect him more than his gun would be his ability to make split-second decisions under pressure. It was always something he'd been pretty good at. But if that skill dried up in a situation like this, he was as good as dead.

Or, even worse, a member of his team would be dead. Quickly, he pushed the memories down. He needed to be here, in the moment, not wallowing in past mistakes.

As they reached the brow of the hill above the quarry, Logan held up a hand to stop them. From now on, absolute silence was essential. They all lay down at the edge, and Mac looked down at the quarry through the night-vision sight he'd attached to the AK's Pic rail. Logan, stretched out on the sand next to him, was doing the same.

The quarry was like a huge bite out of the hillside, and the main compound sat directly in front of the scarred vertical wall from which the pale marble was hewn. Beyond the mud-brick walls of the compound, about a hundred metres east towards the edge of the quarry, the cluster of smaller buildings revealed themselves to be tumbledown stables, presumably dating to a time when the marble would have been hauled down the hill on donkey carts. The shadows were too deep for Mac to be able to see inside them, but without doors, they weren't likely candidates for Bakker's captivity.

He swung his weapon back towards the main compound. The quarry face itself was a vertical drop, meaning they would have to go round one side or the other to reach the building. Skirting the eastern side of the marble works would give them the full support of the ZU. If they came down the other side, they would have the luxury of approaching from the back.

From their current position, Mac couldn't see the gate. He touched Logan on the shoulder and, using prearranged hand gestures, showed him that he was going to creep along the ridge of the hill until he could get an angled view of the front of the compound. He wanted to see exactly where the gate was, and whether there were any guards stationed outside it.

They remained in position, watching and waiting, for a couple of hours, in which time Mac counted at least five armed men coming in and out of the building to smoke or check vehicles in the courtyard. They all had AK47s or Krinkovs slung over their shoulders, but they generally seemed more interested in their cigarettes than seriously checking the area for intruders. Only once did a pair of them venture out of the gates, walk around the perimeter and check the deserted stables. But more tellingly, one man came out of the main building carrying food and water to a smaller adjacent hut within the compound. Bingo – the kid had been telling the truth.

Mac made his way back to where Logan, Ginger and the other militiamen were waiting. Logan raised questioning eyebrows. Mac held up five fingers, to indicate that he'd seen five men. Then he pointed to the smaller building and gave the pre-agreed sign for Bakker. They dropped back from the OP to the wadi and, in hurried whispers, worked out their final assault plan, deciding on a route in and calculating the arcs of fire from the FSG and how they would remain clear of them. Cold MREs and a snatched hour of sleep was as much of a refresher as they could afford to take.

Finally, two hours before the dawn call to prayer, when the guards would be at their lowest ebb or sleeping, it was H-hour – they were ready to go. Mac's mouth was dry as a huge rush of adrenalin surged through him. He watched as the FSG and the GAZ-66 moved out first, driving agonisingly slowly to keep the noise to a minimum. Once it reached its agreed position just below the ridgeline, the PKM teams fanned out on either side. Beroj radioed back that they were ready – they could reverse to the brow of the hill to bring the guns to bear on the quarry buildings at a moment's notice.

Logan acknowledged the message. The rescue team were crouched just below the brow of the hill, where they waited for several minutes to see if there were any signs that the men at the quarry had heard the vehicles.

Satisfied that all was quiet, Logan gave the hand signal to move out. The moon had set but there was no sign yet of the impending dawn, and they were able to take advantage of the absolute dark.

Just as they took their first steps down the hill, Mac heard a car engine starting up.

'Drop!' he hissed.

All six of them immediately ducked back down and stared through their optical sights or binoculars. Brake lights and reversing lights flared on a dark-coloured Mercedes saloon, parked at the centre of the compound. It made a three-point turn, ready to go out of the gate, then sat with the engine idling for a few minutes. A flurry of men emerged from the building, stopped for a minute to take leave of each other. Two of them got into the vehicle.

'Fuck, that's Jamali,' Mac whispered in Logan's ear.

'You sure?'

'I met him face to face four days ago. I'm sure.'

It certainly gave added credence to the boy's intel. Why else would Jamali be visiting a marble quarry in the middle of the night, if not to check on his other million-dollar treasure. Having lost one when Mac escaped, no doubt he was keeping closer tabs on Bakker.

Logan let out a low whistle as he watched the Mercedes pass through the gate and drive down the track back towards Bahram Chah. 'Three less guns to contend with. Maybe Lady Luck is on our side tonight.'

She'd bloody better be.

Mac stood up and held his AK at the ready.

It was time to retrieve their man.

Day 12

Chapter 56

Bahram Chah

Logan went over the top first. Mac followed approximately six metres behind him, then the militiamen, with Ginger bringing up the rear – all spaced out, single file, walking slowly, slowly to minimise the noise of their footfall. The initial objective was one of the tumbledown stables they'd seen from the top of the hill. This would put them in a good position in front of the quarry compound, facing the gate, with approximately fifty metres of empty ground to cover. As each of them arrived, they squatted down behind the low mud walls. Logan tasked one of the militiamen to remain inside the structure to give covering fire if they needed it.

Step one accomplished.

They waited, listening. All quiet.

Another hand gesture took them forward again. Next objective – the compound gate. It wasn't locked. Jamali's car had left a short while before, and with the typical arrogance of a lot of men with a lot of weaponry, security seemed slack. After all, there was no one for miles around who didn't already work for Jamali or was in his pay in one way or another. Bahram Chah was the beating heart of his opium empire, and no one would be foolish enough to take him on down here.

Except for them.

Mac cleared his mind of doubts, buttoning down his anxiety and just taking the buzz of energy the action provided. He was ready.

Logan slipped through the gate ahead of him, a length of piano wire looped in his fist. Mac listened. There was a scuffle, a stifled gasp. The slump of a body onto the ground. Mac stepped into the compound courtyard and squatted down over the garrotted guard to help himself to the spoils – a couple of magazines for the AK that lay by his side. Mac didn't bother to pick up the weapon, as he wouldn't be able to fire one effectively if he was carrying two. But Logan stooped down for it and slung it round his back, giving Mac a look. There was no point leaving a weapon for the enemy.

As the last two men came through the gate, Logan used hand signals to direct one of them to take defensive positions that would secure their way out. The last thing they needed was to lose access to the gate once they had Bakker.

Mac shuddered. Sure, it had been easy to get in… but now the hard part.

He, Logan, Ginger and the remaining militiaman moved quickly towards the small mud-built hut to which the guard had delivered food and water earlier. There was no guard here, but the rough wooden door was secured with a hefty padlock and chain. They formed a stack along the wall, and Logan gestured the militiaman forward. The man released a pair of bolt cutters that was slung over his back, and seconds later he caught the chain so it didn't rattle as it fell to the ground.

Logan eased the door open cautiously and Mac went through, pistol raised. There was no light inside and he quickly put a hand up to snap on the head torch he was wearing. Logan and Ginger followed him in and did likewise, and the three beams illuminated a hellish discovery.

The small room was almost completely taken up by a roughly constructed cage made of steel reinforcing bars welded together. It looked home-made. In one corner, there was something that looked like a pile of rags. Until it moved. Then whimpered.

Mac wanted to gag, so strong was the stench of human excrement.

'Fuck me!' said Ginger.

Mac had never laid eyes on Tomas Bakker before, but it was a sure bet that he looked very different now to how he'd looked when he'd disappeared less than two weeks ago. The Dutchman was completely naked, clutching at a ragged blanket, stained with blood and shit. His hair was sparse and his scalp bloody, and even now the nervous fingers of one hand were tearing at one of the few remaining clumps. His skin was sallow, his cheeks hollow and his eyes haunted. Keeping hostages naked was just another way of breaking them down.

'Get him out,' said Logan, snapping them back to the reality of the moment.

Mac looked for the cage door but there was nothing. On all four sides, every joint was welded.

'What the hell? How do we...?' Ginger rattled the structure but it was totally solid.

Mac looked round the room, the beam of his torch swinging as he moved his head. There was nothing, no tools, no discernible way of opening the cage. He went to the door, where the guy with the bolt cutters was standing guard, his AK47 pointing straight towards the entrance of the main building in case anyone came out to see what was going on.

Mac gestured for the cutters and the man turned his back to Mac, who quickly detached them. Seconds later, he had snapped through the first row of steel bars. The tool's compound hinge, if not making it exactly easy to cut through the tough steel, certainly got the job done. But each cut made a sharp clack, and Mac knew they had only moments before their presence was discovered. His arms ached, and his broken collarbone was screeching at him, so he passed the cutters to Logan.

Snap! Snap! Snap!

Bakker cowered at the back of the cage. He still seemed confused as the beams from the three head torches danced around the room. All he would be able to see were the lights,

345

rather than the faces underneath them, so he probably had no idea who they were.

'Tomas,' said Mac, squatting down at the side of the cage where the Dutchman was cowering, 'when we get the cage open, we're going to take you out. You need to come with us. Do you understand?'

Bakker stared at him blankly.

'Are you hurt at all? Can you walk?'

Still no answer. Then Bakker frowned. 'You're... you're English?'

'Yes, from Well Diggers.'

But that wasn't the right answer – Bakker cowered even further into the corner, hiding his face in the crook of one of his arms.

On the other side of the cage, Logan and Ginger were now levering a panel of the bars outwards, trying to open up a gap large enough for Bakker to crawl through.

Outside, a shot rang out, then another. Their position had been compromised – they were going to have to fight their way out. Mac raced round to the opening in the cage as Logan and Ginger strained to bend back the remaining metal. He went in on his hands and knees and reached out for one of Bakker's arms.

'Come on, chum, we're taking you home.'

Gradually Mac was able to pull the stunned man across the base of the cage. They helped him out, wrapping the stinking blanket round him as best they could, but it became immediately clear that he was too weak to walk unaided. Mac swore silently to himself. Having to half carry, half support the unresponsive Bakker was going to cost them precious seconds at every stage of the exfil. There was a battlefield stretcher in one of the Hiluxes, but a fat lot of good that would do them now.

Logan detailed off Ginger and the militiaman with the bolt cutters to take Bakker between them. He and Mac went to the door. Logan pointed a finger, indicating to Mac that he should lead the way out. Mac turned off his head torch and kept within the dark shadows of the doorway as he assessed the situation outside in the courtyard. Another of Jamali's men lay dead on the ground, while their own men were taking cover and exchanging fire with a couple of the narco gangsters who were sheltering behind a parapet on the roof of the building.

'Fuck, we need support from the FSG.'

Behind him, he heard Logan on the radio, alerting Beroj.

Mac calculated the odds. If they could make it across ten metres of the compound courtyard, they could find safety in the inky shadows of the surrounding wall. But then someone set off a flare, illuminating every corner of the space, even making Mac visible just inside the doorway. More shots rang out, one hitting the door frame beside him. Far too close for comfort. The militiaman at the gate tried to back out as fast as he could, but in the flash of light he froze like a startled rabbit. A long burst of fire, a truncated scream of terror, then nothing. He was dead before he hit the ground.

Logan shoved past Mac, stepping forward with his AK47 held high. He fired a long burst of tracer rounds at the roof of the building, lowering it for a second pass across the doors and windows. As if in reply to his overture, the ZU roared into life up on the ridge, spitting ordnance and chewing great chunks out of the mud structure.

Enemy fire evaporated as they reeled under the ferocious bombardment.

'Okay, let's go,' yelled Mac to Ginger, lined up behind him, supporting Bakker on one side with the militiaman supporting him on the other.

Mac led them across the open ground, firing indiscriminately at the building as they ran. He motioned to the militiaman with them to hold the gate to give the rescue party time to make a start up the hill. It was going to be bloody hard going – Ginger and the militiaman were practically dragging the Dutchman, who didn't seem to have control of his legs. But if they could get across to the small stable block unharmed, they could work out a better way of transporting him – with more men, they could use clothing to rig up a makeshift stretcher and run up the hill.

They were through the gate now, and the ZU was continuing to do its vicious job. There was no doubt the other side had taken casualties, and even as their fire picked up again, it was nothing like it had been half a minute ago.

But halfway across the fifty-metre stretch to the stable, trouble reared its ugly head once more.

Chapter 57

Bahram Chah

Mac heard it before he saw it, but whipping his head round in the direction of the sound, he couldn't miss it. Jamali's Mercedes was coming back up the track from the village, followed by a couple of technicals, each with a Dushka on the back. They were angled to fire in the direction of the ZU and they were almost within range.

Fuck, this was where it could all go horribly wrong.

The Dushkas let rip, trying to take out the cover that the rescue team were relying on to get them up the hill safely. Thankfully, Beroj and his men were on the ball. One of the technicals exploded in a crimson fireball that dissipated high above Mac's head. The other stopped firing and took fright, executing a hurried U-turn on the track. But Mac wasn't going to leave all the fun to the FSG. He raised his weapon and let rip an arc of fire across the front of the Mercedes, taking out the windscreen. He heard a scream from within the car, as it careered off the track and skidded a short way down the hillside. However, the other Dushka wasn't down and out yet – its operator swung the barrel of his weapon round in Mac's direction.

Where was the fucking FSG when you needed them?

Mac put on a desperate burst of speed to reach the shelter of the stable walls. Now he was able to return fire and provide cover for the rest of the team behind him. The militiaman at the compound gate made the run to the stables and in this way the

349

two groups started moving in tactical bounds up the hill – one group going firm and providing cover while the other group moved.

Mac was running up the hill on the eastern shoulder of the quarry.

'Come on,' he yelled to Ginger, bobbing and weaving as fast as he could to present an impossible-to-hit moving target.

There seemed to be machine-gun fire coming from every direction, all around him. The FSG were taking on the Dushka, but it was still operational, even though the technical had taken a few hits.

Mac dived for cover behind a large boulder. Every muscle was burning and it felt like his lungs were being ripped from his chest with every breath. But this wasn't recovery time – he needed to provide covering fire for Ginger and Bakker. Logan slumped down beside him, and the pair of them let rip from either side of the rock.

Just below them, Ginger and the militiaman were struggling to get Bakker up the slope. They moved as fast as they could, but it was slow compared to the pace Mac and Logan had managed, and with three of them linked together, they couldn't duck and weave effectively.

Mac took his eyes off them to return fire at one of the gangsters on the roof of the main building. When he looked back, the three of them were sprawled on the ground. The militiaman had been hit. With one hand on his throat, he coughed and choked, spraying red foam across the other two as he drowned in his own blood. Ginger was frantically trying to drag Bakker to his feet.

'Cover me,' shouted Logan, above the din.

He ran down the slope and swept the crouching Bakker into a fireman's lift. Ginger gave one last look at the militiaman, checking he was dead – but there was no real doubt about it – then followed Logan up the hill, now bobbing from side to side, until the three of them were able to throw themselves down behind the boulder.

Mac changed mags, yelling 'Magazine!' to alert the others that he wouldn't be firing for a few seconds. A moment's respite from the continuous thumping of the rifle butt against his broken collarbone.

'Right, straight for the top,' said Logan. 'We need outta here.'

As Mac gave him cover, he signalled to the remaining militiamen to carry on up. The FSG saw what was happening and doubled down on their efforts, effectively quelling the enemy response to give the rescue team time to get out. The noise was deafening. Mac ran as hard as he'd ever run in his life. He was drenched with sweat and every step seemed to take an hour. His chest might burst at any second, but he had to keep going, unless he wanted this breath to be his last.

Ginger caught up with him, and Logan was only a few steps behind, despite carrying Bakker.

As they crested the hill, Jamali's men made one last effort with a barrage of shots. Mac threw himself over the low ridge.

There was an agonised scream in his ear, then Ginger landed on top of him.

'Fuck! Fuck! I've taken one!'

Mac pushed Ginger to one side so he could sit up.

'Where?'

'Leg,' said Ginger through gritted teeth, curling onto his side and clutching at his calf.

Mac saw blood was soaking through Ginger's combat trousers. It would hurt like a bitch, but it wasn't life-threatening. He pulled Ginger round to sit up as Logan staggered past them with Bakker still across his shoulders. The remaining militiamen came over the brow, and one of them immediately squatted down and used a piece of webbing to give Ginger a tourniquet just below his knee.

Mac crawled back and peered down the hill. He could see the dead militiaman who'd been shot in the neck, but no others.

'Head count?' he yelled back at Logan.

Logan spun round, checking the men. 'One missing.'

351

'He's dead.'

'Let's go,' shouted Logan.

Not before time. The remaining technical had swung round again and was now heading up the hill to give chase.

'Fucking take him out!' He was addressing the FSG, even though there was no chance of them hearing him. But battle-field telepathy seemed to work just fine, because seconds later, the Dushka took a direct hit from the ZU, causing the technical to skid onto its side, slide down the hill and then over the lip of the quarry. It crashed down the rock face and exploded in a fireball at the bottom.

Silence.

Mac's ears were ringing. The air was full of smoke. Around him, men were moving. One of the militiamen pulled him to his feet. Then he fell into line with the rest of them as they jogged down the hill to where the Hiluxes were waiting.

Ahead of him, Logan was on the radio to Beroj, no doubt telling him to pull back.

Ginger was limping, an arm around the shoulder of the militiaman who'd helped him.

'You okay, mucker?' said Mac, as he caught up with them.

'I'll live,' said Ginger.

'Too bloody right,' said Mac. 'We did it – we got out alive. Now let's fucking get home.'

Chapter 58

Dasht-e Margo

Later, Mac would be the first to admit he'd spoken too soon, but in that moment he'd been overwhelmed with a huge sense of relief. They were out of the field of fire, one man down, one man injured, and most importantly they'd freed Bakker.

As they jogged down the hill to the waiting vehicles, Mac was able to get his wind back. In the distance, he could hear the approaching rumble of the GAZ-66 as it, and the Hilux carrying the machine-gun teams, came to join them. They'd effectively taken out the enemy in the form of the Dushkas. He'd riddled Jamali's car with rounds, so maybe the bastard was dead. Sure, his knee was killing him, and his collarbone felt freshly broken, but they'd done what they'd set out to do.

'Mac, Mac...' It was Baz, shouting at him from the open passenger window of the ancient Soviet truck.

The driver stopped for a moment, and he jumped up and squashed onto the seat beside her. She clambered onto his lap, so they could close the door.

'Jesus, thank God you're okay,' she breathed against his neck. 'I was terrified when things kicked off.'

'So was I,' said Mac, giving her a hug. It was no lie. This might have been just a normal day at the office for Logan, but Mac's previous job had been a detective inspector in the Met. He'd never been a soldier.

Mac watched as Ginger was hoisted onto the back of one of the SUVs by a militiaman. Logan lowered Bakker down next to Ginger and Mac heard his grunt of relief as the weight came off his shoulders.

They reached the spot where the Hiluxes and the Surf were parked a few moments later. They quickly rearranged themselves into the various vehicles, and within minutes they were heading out down the wadi.

With Tirich driving the Surf, Logan was able to confer with Beroj in the GAZ-66 over the best route back. Beroj favoured taking the most direct route through the desert to the Helmand Valley, where they would be able to pick up the road north. This was undoubtedly the quickest way back to Lash, but Logan suggested spending more time driving north through the desert, parallel to the river valley, and intersecting with the road at a later point. It wouldn't be a fast route but, he argued, they were less likely to be ambushed this way. But it was called the Dasht-e Margo, or Desert of Death, for a reason… As the two men hashed it out in Pashto, Mac turned his attention to Bakker, who was sitting between him and Baz on the back seat.

The Dutchman was in a bad way. Although they'd hurriedly given him some clean sweats to wear, he still smelt appalling. He was confused and frightened, and when they dressed him Mac had seen a multitude of welts across his back and bruises on his torso.

Baz gently touched Bakker's left hand. 'Look,' she said quietly to Mac.

He glanced down and saw that all four fingers were twisted. It was clear to him that Bakker had been severely tortured while captive.

Baz gave Bakker water and some painkillers. She offered him bread and fruit, but he didn't seem to have an appetite. He sat between them, staring straight ahead, with little interest in where they were going or in any conversation. He looked like he needed to sleep, but at the same time he appeared hyper – picking at the hem of his sweatshirt with his uninjured hand, his foot constantly kicking against the back of Tirich's seat.

This earned him a dirty look from the driver, to which he was entirely oblivious.

Baz caught Mac's eye. 'Didn't you find some meds in Bakker's room?' she said in a low voice. But it was all right, Bakker wasn't the least bit interested in what they were saying.

'Sure,' said Mac.

'What were they?'

Mac shrugged.

Logan turned back in his seat. 'I think they were antidepressants.'

Baz nodded, looking at Bakker. 'Makes sense.'

If he had been without his meds for a couple of weeks, as well as being tortured and constantly in fear of his life… Mac didn't like to think about what must be going on inside his skull right now.

It was daylight by the time they emerged from the wadi. Ahead of them lay an exposed plateau of sand and stone, stretching as far as the eye could see. Someone had once said to him that Helmand felt like the edge of the world, and the bloke hadn't been wrong. To Mac, right now, it seemed like they could be traversing the surface of Mars.

It was already ferociously hot, but Logan wouldn't allow the vehicle's air-conditioning to be switched on, as it used too much fuel. They had all the windows open, but it hardly helped – the blasts of hot air did nothing to cool them down. Out of the wadi, they were able to pick up speed, and once more drove in an arrowhead formation. There was plenty of space to swerve around rocks, so they didn't have to stop and move them, but the faster pace made for a bumpier ride, and Mac had to clamp his jaws shut to stop his teeth jarring against each other. It seemed like Logan had won the argument and they were heading far out into the desert to avoid trouble on the journey back.

Exhausted, ears still ringing, with the night's sweat dried on his body, he leaned against the window pillar, letting the hot air sandblast his face, too tired to move. It all seemed surreal – Bahram Chah with its crazy opium market, the firefight at the marble quarry, and Tomas Bakker, practically returned from the dead, sitting between them too zombied out to tell his story.

'You couldn't have dreamed it, could you?' he said, looking across at Baz. But she was asleep.

'Shhhhh,' hissed Logan, twisting in his seat to look behind them.

Mac did the same and picked up the sound of an engine – the high-pitched whine of a Hando. More than one. Far in the distance, like black specks shimmering in a desert mirage, vehicles were coming after them. Only it wasn't a mirage, because Mac could hear them. More now, the deeper, throatier roar of technicals, adding a bass line to the Hando's whine.

'Fuck!' said Logan. He grabbed the radio and started barking instructions to the other vehicles.

Mac continued staring out of the rear window. The desert armada seemed to be gaining ground on them, and he could see SUVs bristling with gun-toting bandits, motorbikes with armed pillion riders, and windblown men clutching onto Dushkas on the back of technicals as if they were surfing the sea of sand.

Baz, wide awake now, dug her camera out of the bag at her feet.

'Fuck's sake, get down,' said Mac.

'Must be Jamali's army,' said Logan. 'Coming for vengeance.'

On hearing Jamali's name, Bakker's head snapped up. He looked round. 'Don't let them come for me,' he said, his voice laced with panic. He abruptly unsnapped his seatbelt and started to clamber across Baz to open the car door.

'No!' screeched Baz, trying to push him back to the centre of the seat.

Mac grabbed hold of his arm and hauled him back. The man had taken leave of his senses. He struggled to pull Bakker's seatbelt back into place. 'Baz, can you reach behind for the trauma pack? Let's get him sedated.' Using his weight to keep Bakker under control, he addressed Logan.

'Plan?'

Logan was scanning the landscape ahead of them.

'We'll head for those rocks,' he said, pointing to an oxide-coloured outcrop about five hundred metres to the north-west. He gave Tirich instructions and the Surf swerved to the left. The other vehicles in the formation quickly discerned their destination and also changed direction. 'We'll take a stand. We should be able to wipe a lot of them out using the ZU before they get up close.'

It was then that the first RPG came in. It landed wide of the mark, exploding beyond their flank with a loud crack, sending a cascade of sand and stones into the air.

'Jeez,' said Baz, still rifling through the trauma pack for a sedative for Bakker.

Mac watched the militiamen on the back of the GAZ-66 and the PKM teams struggling to prepare their weapons to return fire as they were jolted up and down on the bumpy ground. There would be no chance of accuracy, but hopefully it would be enough of a deterrent to stop their pursuers coming too close. With the ability to fire four hundred rounds per minute, the ZU could sweep anyone coming up behind with a deadly arc.

More RPGs were crashing in around them, but they only needed to clear a short expanse of open ground before they'd be afforded cover by the looming rock formation ahead. Their PKMs were returning fire, and Mac could see that some of the motorbikes that had led the pursuit were now hanging back slightly, hoping to stay out of range. Not a bloody chance of that once the ZU let rip.

The air was rent with the sound of gunfire, and small stones thrown up by the grenades landing all around them were raining down on the Surf's roof like hail. Triumphant at last, Baz held up a syringe, then plunged the needle into Bakker's arm, straight through the sleeve of his sweatshirt. Bakker yelped with pain, his head turning towards Baz, but by then she'd whipped the syringe away and dropped it on the floor.

'It's okay, Tomas,' she said. 'We'll keep you safe.'

The Surf took a sharp turn to get behind the cover of the rocks, its back wheels skidding out, brakes screeching. Tirich managed to remain in control and as he straightened up, he revved the engine hard to take them out of danger. The GAZ-66 couldn't take the corner quite so sharply or so fast – it had to brake, causing the Hilux coming up behind it to slam its brakes on too. It was an ill-timed move. A grenade that wouldn't otherwise have made the mark smashed into the back of it, exploding its fuel tank along with several jerrycans of extra petrol. A huge fireball shot up into the air, turning into toxic black smoke before the sound had even died away.

'No!' shouted Mac. It was the car that Ginger was in.

The back of the vehicle was an inferno. At the front, both doors opened. Two militiamen, faces burned and hair singed black, scrabbled out of the driver's side, collapsing on the ground as they choked on the fumes. Mac craned his neck to see what was happening on the passenger side, but he couldn't tell. He couldn't wait either. He snapped off his seatbelt, grabbed his AK, jumped out and ran across the open ground, taking a dive to reach the cover of the burning vehicle.

It was an idiotic thing to do given the firepower raining down on them, he knew that, but he wasn't going to give up on Ginger. Not yet. Idiotic maybe, but he was right to have done it. Ginger was half slumped out of the passenger side of the Hilux. Black smoke was pouring out of the driving compartment above him and he was semi-conscious, struggling to breathe. Mac slung his AK round to the back and dragged Ginger onto the ground. His hair and eyebrows were completely burned off, and all his clothing was singed. His hands were badly burned and his face was mottled red and black – blood and soot. But he was very much alive.

'Ah, fuckin' hell,' he said, breaking into an uncontrollable coughing fit as Mac grabbed him under both arms.

'Come on, mate, I'm not leaving you here.'

Mac looked back at the rock formation. It was just fifteen metres away, but that fifteen metres was in full range of enemy fire.

Logan was standing at the edge of the rock, firing furiously, picking off one of the pillion riders. The GAZ was reversing to bring the ZU into a firing position. Logan stopped shooting and put up a hand to Mac, then pointed at the huge machine gun. Mac knew what he was saying: wait for cover. He waited, recovering his breath, hoping it wouldn't be too long. He looked down at Ginger. The coughing had subsided and he was unconscious.

Fuck.

Suddenly, the deafening roar of the ZU broke out. Mac peered around the side of the burning Hilux. Beroj Kaliq was raining down death, chaos and confusion on his uncle's enemies. Three Handos went down in quick succession. A technical veered from its path, its driver now just a red smear on the smashed-in windscreen. Two SUVs collided as they lost control.

Now was his chance to run. He took a deep breath, and with an unspoken apology to Ginger for what he was about to do, he dragged his friend roughly over the stony ground until they gained the cover of the rock formation. Baz ran over to them with the trauma pack, blanching as she took in the extent of Ginger's burns. Mac laid him down as gently as he could, then straightened up. He couldn't stick around to help – an image had burned itself onto his retina.

As one of the enemy SUVs had rolled and exploded, a dark figure had emerged with an AK47 raised against his shoulder.

Akhtar Jamali.

But he's dead, screamed Mac's mind. He was certain he'd killed him in the Mercedes at the marble quarry.

He ran back to the edge of the rocks and peered round. Akhtar Jamali wasn't dead. He was running from vehicle to vehicle, coming towards them, and some malevolent guardian angel seemed to be protecting him from harm.

'Today your luck runs out, buster!'

'What?' said Logan, coming up behind him.

'Just a small mopping up job,' said Mac, 'before we're done.'

He raised his AK and stepped out from behind the cover of the rock, firing the moment he got a line on Jamali's advancing figure. Bullets pinged off the rock face and whistled past Mac's head as the enraged narco baron got closer.

Like the fucking Terminator!

But Jamali was mere flesh and blood after all, and as Mac raked him with fire, his body danced like a puppet, then dropped.

'Job fucking done,' said Mac, lowering his weapon. 'Job fucking done.'

Day 13

Chapter 59

Lashkar Gah

'New name, mate. From now on, you're Ginger Tom – the cat with nine lives!'

Ginger opened one eye and raised a non-existent eyebrow at Mac. He was lying propped on a stack of pristine white pillows on a bed in a private room in the Italian Emergency Hospital in Lashkar Gah.

'Blown up, shot in the leg – gotta salute you. I would shake your hand, but…' Mac looked down with a grin. Both Ginger's hands were heavily bandaged, as was his head. His face was plastered with a noxious-looking ointment.

'Fuck off!' he said good-naturedly, before being overcome by a coughing fit.

'Nasty cough you got there.' After all, if you couldn't rib a mate when he was down, when could you rib him?

'Get out, Mac. It hurts too much when I laugh.'

Mac guessed they must have put him on some pretty powerful painkillers. The drive back to Lash the previous afternoon had been hell for Ginger. With the loss of another vehicle, space had been at a premium. Ginger and a wounded militiaman had been laid out flat on the back of the GAZ-66, on either side of the gun mounting, but the ancient Soviet vehicle hardly boasted the most luxurious suspension, and the men were bounced and jolted through the ferocious desert heat for over seven hours. Baz and Mac had done what they could with the scant resources of the trauma pack, but it was a gruelling experience Mac hoped he'd never have to witness again.

When Dr Marchesi had met them at the hospital entrance, Mac and Baz had practically melted with relief at being able to hand over their patients to a professional. The militiaman had gone straight to surgery for a gunshot wound, during which time Ginger's burns were dressed. He'd then gone to surgery to have the bullet removed from his leg. At the same time, Bakker was admitted and checked over. Marchesi told them later that the worst of his injuries were his broken fingers, which had quickly been reset. However, the abrupt cessation of his antidepressants had totally fucked with his head, and that was going to take longer to sort out.

'Can I talk to him now?' said Mac, bumping into Marchesi in the corridor after he'd visited Ginger the following morning. 'Need to debrief him on what happened.'

'You can talk to him for a short time,' said Marchesi warily. 'He will tire easily as he's been through a highly traumatic experience.'

Him and me both.

'What about you?' said Marchesi. 'How are you holding up?'

Mac's arm was back in the sling, and he was still walking with a slight limp. He decided it was probably wiser not to admit to the doctor that he'd spent part of the past forty-eight hours with the butt of an AK47 pressed up against his broken collarbone.

'Getting there,' he said.

Marchesi nodded. 'It'll take a while, but it would be quicker if you rested, you know.'

'Time and tide,' said Mac, leaving Marchesi with a puzzled expression as he went off in search of Baz.

—

They sat down, one on either side of Bakker's bed. It wasn't quite that they were going to play good cop, bad cop, but Mac knew that Baz would be a calming influence if some of the questions he asked cut too close to the bone.

Bakker still looked like a broken man, but he'd been cleaned up and his wounds tended to, and that was something of a transformation compared with how he'd been the day before. He was asleep when they went in, so they sat for a while, watching the rise and fall of his chest, happy to take a moment's respite. When he opened his eyes, he looked at them blankly, and it was several seconds before he recognised or remembered them.

'Hi Tomas,' said Baz.

He started to say something in Dutch, then switched to English. 'You... you were the people who rescued me, yes?'

Mac nodded. 'You were in a bad way, but you're safe now.'

Bakker glanced around nervously as if to confirm his words. Then he looked at his left hand, swathed in bandages, and winced.

'Did Jamali do that to you?' said Baz.

Bakker nodded.

'Jamali's dead,' said Mac. 'I killed him.'

Relief flooded Bakker's face. But there was something Mac didn't understand. Why had Jamali tortured Bakker, breaking his fingers, flaying his back to a pulp? Mac hadn't suffered in the same way when he was being held by Jamali.

'Did Jamali have you make a ransom demand video?' he asked.

'No, nothing like that. He didn't want me for a ransom.' Bakker rubbed his uninjured hand across his eyes, as if reliving some of the horror he'd been through.

Mac exchanged a glance with Baz. This didn't make sense.

'Tomas,' said Baz quietly. 'Let's just go back to the beginning, to the night you were taken. Tell us who killed Vinke and what happened next.'

The hand dropped away from Bakker's face abruptly, and he stared at Baz with wide, fearful eyes.

'But you know who killed Vinke, don't you?'

'No,' said Mac.

365

'Yes, you know,' he continued, nodding his head. 'It was me. I killed Lars.'

Mac could have fallen off his chair. Had Bakker completely taken leave of his senses? Was his memory playing tricks on him? 'No, Tomas, you didn't. There was someone else there. We found a shoe under Vinke's body that didn't belong to anyone who worked at the property.'

'*Ja, ja*, that was Khalo's shoe. It came off when Lars attacked him.'

'Sorry, who's Khalo?' said Baz.

Mac knew he'd heard the name before somewhere.

'My friend,' said Bakker. He looked down and his face coloured. 'I met him in a café in central Lash. We got talking, and he agreed to come back to the house.'

'So you'd just met him?' said Mac. 'But you said he was your friend?'

'I met him a couple of months ago. He came back to the house a few times.'

'Why did Lars attack him?' said Baz.

'Usually, I only brought Khalo home with me when Lars was away, and when Nazanina was at her own home. But on this occasion, Lars had returned unexpectedly. He thought what we were doing was wrong.'

'What were you doing?' said Mac. But then it dawned on him. A friend that Tomas only brought home when the house was empty. The condoms they'd found in his bedside table.

'Surely it was none of his business?' said Baz.

'Of course it was none of his business. But he threatened to report me to the country manager. He said he would get me sacked and sent home.'

'For seeing a man?' said Baz. She sounded outraged.

'For seeing a boy,' said Mac quietly. 'I saw Khalo at Jamali's stronghold. He can't be older than sixteen or seventeen.'

Bakker was immediately defensive. 'He told me he was eighteen. He looks younger, but...'

Baz's outrage had turned to revulsion. 'So he's just a kid? No wonder Vinke was angry.'

'Lars caught us… having sex. He lost his temper. He dragged Khalo outside and started hitting him. Khalo was small compared to Lars – he didn't stand a chance.'

'Then what happened?' prompted Baz.

'I went to defend Khalo. I was so angry with Lars for hurting him – he was my friend.' Bakker stopped talking and made a noise that sounded like he was trying not to cry. 'Khalo got away and he ran out of the gate. I was holding onto Lars to stop him going after Khalo. That's when Lars said he would make sure I lost my job. I grabbed him by the neck and then… and then… I realised I was strangling him. And I didn't stop. I didn't want to stop. He was such a bastard…' Bakker was crying openly now.

Baz got up and fetched a plastic cup of water. Mac studied his boots, giving Bakker time to compose himself.

'When I realised Lars was dead, I dropped him on the ground, and I ran after Khalo. I knew where he stayed – at a big compound on the edge of town. I went there, through the empty streets, and banged on the gate. By then it was nearly morning. No one answered, so I waited there until daybreak.'

At that moment all the pieces fell into place for Mac.

'It was Jamali's compound, wasn't it?' he said.

Bakker nodded, and Baz gave Mac a questioning look.

'Khalo was Jamali's *bacchá bazi*,' said Mac.

'Oh my God,' said Baz, putting a hand to her mouth.

'I tried to persuade him to leave Jamali so many times,' said Bakker. 'But Akhtar gave him money and clothes. He wouldn't leave.'

'What happened in the morning?'

'The gate opened and I pushed my way in, shouting Khalo's name.'

'Which is when Jamali took you hostage?'

Bakker nodded. 'He was jealous. He made me suffer and he made Khalo watch. He humiliated me in front of Khalo. I would rather have died. I deserved to die after killing Lars. You shouldn't have rescued me.'

Mac stared at Bakker's miserable face, at his red-rimmed eyes. He didn't know what to say. Baz was also lost for words.

Dr Marchesi came into the room and took one look at Bakker. 'That's enough,' he said. 'My patient needs to rest now.'

As soon as they were outside the room, Baz erupted with anger. 'That bastard!'

'Jamali?'

'No, Bakker. Actually both of them. Fighting over a teenage boy. They're as bad as each other and both deserve to rot in hell.'

'Jamali's already there,' said Mac. 'But there's not a lot we can do about Bakker.'

They went back to Ginger's room. Logan was there, hanging out of the window to smoke a cigarette.

'Jeez, Logan,' said Baz. 'Ginger's suffering smoke inhalation. Couldn't you give it a rest for just one moment?' She was still angry.

'That's why I'm leaning out the window, babe,' said Logan, turning back into the room as he exhaled a cloud of smoke.

'It's fine,' said Ginger, before succumbing to another monstrous coughing fit.

Baz gave Logan the sort of look that Mac hated being on the end of.

Over the next few minutes, Mac and Baz recounted what Bakker had told them.

'Man!' said Logan. 'You mean the whole thing was some sort of twisted love triangle? That's what we risked our lives for?'

'So it would seem,' said Mac.

'Hardly love,' said Baz. 'Exploitation is a better word for it. What will happen to him? He committed a murder.'

'I don't know,' said Ginger. 'I'll tell Anholts – it'll be up to him how to proceed.'

'But it had one good outcome,' said Mac. 'Jamali's reign of terror is no more.'

Logan shrugged. 'Sure, we've created a power vacuum. Now there'll be a turf war. Jamali's next in line will fight to keep his opium fields, while Khaliq and his brother will view it as an open invitation to move in. Not a great outcome for the local population.'

'I suppose not,' said Mac, feeling chastened.

'Don't sweat it,' said Logan. 'This is Afghanistan and you can't make a blind bit of difference to the way things go down here.'

'We can try,' said Baz. 'I want to make a difference.'

Logan snorted, but Mac thought Baz was right. If they were going to be here, they might as well try to be a force for good.

'Got a plane to catch,' he said. 'Can you give us a lift to the airport, Logan?'

'Sure.'

Baz's face lit up. 'A plane? Dubai, finally?'

'Uh, no,' said Mac, a little surprised that she thought that. 'I start my new contract in Kabul tomorrow. Had you forgotten?'

'So no holiday at all?' She looked crestfallen.

Mac gave her his most disarming smile. 'Come on, you've had two weeks of sun and sand, haven't you?'

She stepped forward and put her arms around his shoulders.

'Yup, and cocktails are overrated anyway,' she said. 'But you owe me, you bastard. You owe me a holiday big time.'

She wasn't wrong.

A note from the authors

Nick fell in love with Afghanistan approximately twenty years ago. Alison fell in love with the country over the course of writing this book.

Since we started working on this series, Afghanistan has been overtaken by the most horrifying humanitarian crisis in its history. It's heart-breaking to watch the events that are unfolding there.

There is little practical we can do to help, but we are pledging to donate ten per cent of the author royalties of *Death in Helmand* to Afghanaid.

Afghanaid is a British humanitarian and development organisation that has worked in Afghanistan for nearly forty years, building basic services, improving livelihoods, strengthening the rights of woman and children, helping communities and responding to humanitarian emergencies. With years of experience, their majority-Afghan team has a deep understanding of local, cultural and ethnic issues, and they have earned trust and respect among the communities they serve. Their work is now more critical than ever before.

A note on our dedication

The starting point for *Death in Helmand* is the ambush on the Well Diggers convoy in Marja District. Although what follows is entirely fiction, this attack is based on a real incident that took place in Babaji near Lashkar Gah in May 2005. Three engineers from the Alternative Incomes Programme (carrying out similar projects to Well Diggers in the book) were out on a field trip, accompanied by a driver and a single member of the Bolan police. They were attacked by a group of men on motorcycles and all five were murdered. The attack is thought to have been the work of a disgruntled narco lord who was angry that AIP wouldn't clear canals to irrigate his opium fields.

A note on night letters

Night letters have been used for hundreds of years to make threats and convey messages to people all over Asia. Many people think they are a thing of the past, a footnote in history, but the one that appears in *Death in Helmand* is the translation of a real night letter, scattered in the streets of Lashkar Gah by the Taliban in 2005. We've reproduced it verbatim, as Nick's translator at the time gave it to him.

A note on the Sikh community in Lashkar Gah

We chose to make one of our main Afghan characters, Nagpal, a Sikh because few people realise that there has always been a minority of Sikhs in Afghanistan. They are small in number, probably fewer than 50,000 now, and generally concentrated in Kabul, Ghazni and Nangarhar.

The Sikh community in Lashkar Gah was already shrinking in 2003, and now it has virtually gone – families have either relocated to other parts of the country or have emigrated to India after suffering continued harassment at the hands of both the Taliban and the local population. Although the Sikhs in Lashkar Gah are native Afghans, they have been effectively forced out in ways similar to those we detail in the story, and through economic ostracization. Life in India is no easier, where they are viewed as foreign refugees.

Acknowledgements

Creating *Death in Helmand* has been a great pleasure for both of us, not least for the opportunity it's given us to work with everyone else who's been involved in bringing the book to the page – we're exceedingly grateful for all the help and input we've received.

First, we would like to thank our brilliant agent, Jenny Brown of Jenny Brown Associates, for always steering us in the right direction, and also JBA rights director Andrea Joyce for taking our stories further afield.

Thanks go to everyone at Canelo, though first and foremost to our editor, Craig Lye, for his excellent guidance and thoughtful editing throughout. We are further indebted to Tom Sanderson for his superb cover design, to Kate Berens for stellar copy-editing and to the eagle-eyed Vicki Vrint for proofreading. Gratitude to Micaela Cavaletto for production, and to Thanhmai Bui-Van, Nicola Piggott, Elinor Fewster, Claudine Sagoe and Francesca Riccardi for Sales, Marketing and Publicity.

Thanks to our beta reader Jay Vansittart, who served on Herrick 11 and 14.